The DEATH of DULGATH

First Edition October 2015
978-1-943363-08-7 Print-on-demand paperback

Learn more about Michael's writing at **www.riyria.com**.
To contact Michael, email him at **michael.sullivan.dc@gmail.com**.

MICHAEL'S NOVELS INCLUDE:
The First Empire Series: Age of Myth • Age of Swords • Age of War • Age of Legends • Age of Empire
The Riyria Revelations: Theft of Swords • Rise of Empire • Heir of Novron
The Riyria Chronicles: The Crown Tower • The Rose and the Thorn • The Death of Dulgath
Standalone Titles: Hollow World

Published by:
RIYRIA
ENTERPRISES

The DEATH of DULGATH

By
MICHAEL J. SULLIVAN

RIYRIA
ENTERPRISES

Praise for Michael J. Sullivan

"This epic fantasy showcases the arrival of a master storyteller."
— *Library Journal* on *Theft of Swords*

"A delightful, entertaining and page-turning read that reminds us just how enjoyable, and how good The Riyria Revelations series is. A must-buy for all fantasy lovers."
— *The Founding Fields* on *Rise of Empire*

"Heir of Novron is the conclusion to the Riyria Revelations, cementing it in a position as a new classic of modern fantasy: traditional in setting, but extremely unconventional in, well, everything else."
— *Drying Ink* on *Heir of Novron*

"Snappy banter, desperate stakes, pulse pounding sword play, and good old fashioned heroics are all on full display here."
— *52 Book Reviews* on *The Crown Tower*

"With less gore and a smaller cast of characters than George R.R. Martin's "Song of Ice & Fire" but equally satisfying, Sullivan's epic fantasy will be gaining fans at exponential rates."
— *Library Journal* on *The Rose and the Thorn*

"This is social science fiction that H.G. Wells or Isaac Asimov could have written, with the cultural touchstones of today. A modernized classic, Hollow World is the perfect novel for both new and nostalgic science fiction readers."
— *Staffer's Book Reviews* on *Hollow World*

Works by Michael J. Sullivan

Novels

The First Empire

Age of Myth (June 2016) • *Age of Swords* • *Age of War*
Age of Legends • *Age of Empire*

The Riyria Revelations

Theft of Swords (The Crown Conspiracy and *Avempartha)*
Rise of Empire (Nyphron Rising and *The Emerald Storm)*
Heir of Novron (Wintertide and *Percepliquis)*

The Riyria Chronicles

The Crown Tower
The Rose and the Thorn
The Death of Dulgath

Standalone Novels

Hollow World

Anthologies

Unfettered: The Jester
Unbound: The Game
Unfettered II: Little Wren and the Big Forest
Blackguards: Professional Integrity
The End: Visions of the Apocalypse: Burning Alexandria
Triumph Over Tragedy: Traditions
The Fantasy Faction Anthology: Autumn Mists
Help Fund My Robot Army: Be Careful What You Wish For

Author's Note

I've been locked in a room for over two-and-a-half years, the only light—the soft glow of a computer screen. That's how I remember it, anyway. After finishing *Hollow World*, I began working on what was supposed to be a trilogy called The First Empire. Three books became five, and two-and-a-half years slipped away.

Readers of The Riyria Chronicles began requesting book three immediately after *The Rose and Thorn*'s release in September 2013. The Chronicles—previously expected to be a flop because prequels are the third rail of publishing—did surprisingly well. I apologize to everyone who has been anxiously awaiting this book, but at least the wait is over!

If you are new to the Riyria stories, you certainly can start with this book. The first two Riyria Chronicles told the origin story of how Royce and Hadrian met. With that tale told, this book was freed to tell a standalone adventure. If you do want to read other Riyria novels, then you should know there are two different ways you can approach the saga.

Publication Order: *Theft of Swords* • *Rise of Empire* • *Heir of Novron* • *The Crown Tower* • *The Rose and the Thorn* • *The Death of Dulgath*
Chronological Order: *The Crown Tower* • *The Rose and the Thorn* • *The Death of Dulgath* • *Theft of Swords* • *Rise of Empire* • *Heir of Novron*

Personally, I prefer order of publication, but I've heard from people who have read chronologically and they've been equally pleased with the experience.

If you are wondering if there will be a next Royce and Hadrian story, the answer is: I just don't know. As I've mentioned elsewhere,

I'm protective of the duo and would rather have them leave early than stay too long. Because of that, I never know if there will be more until after a Chronicle's release. If you want to advocate for more, by all means drop me an email. Even if you don't, you can still reach out. I always love hearing from people. My address is: **michael.sullivan.dc@gmail.com**.

One last thing I should mention. If you are interested in learning more about the novel creation process, I've created an e-book entitled: *The Making of the Death of Dulgath*. It's free, so just drop me an email at the address above. Some people might find the process interesting.

Now turn the page, tap the screen, or adjust the volume. Old friends are waiting to take you on a new adventure.

Thanks for all the amazing support.
Michael J. Sullivan
October 2015

To 1,876 generous backers
and one amazingly supportive woman.
I couldn't have done it without you.

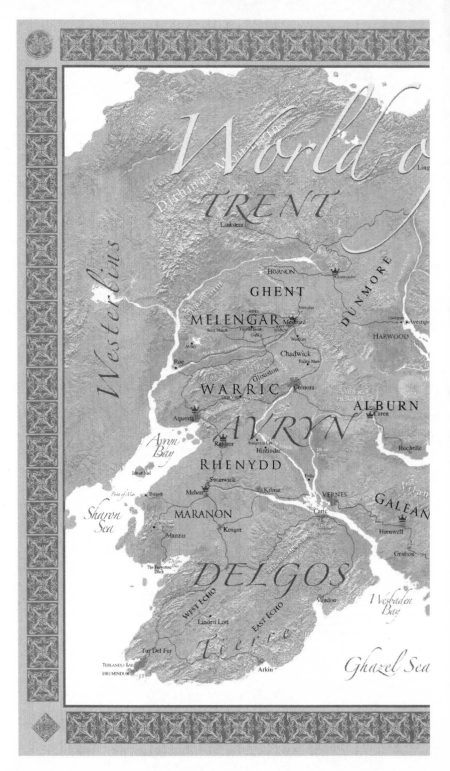

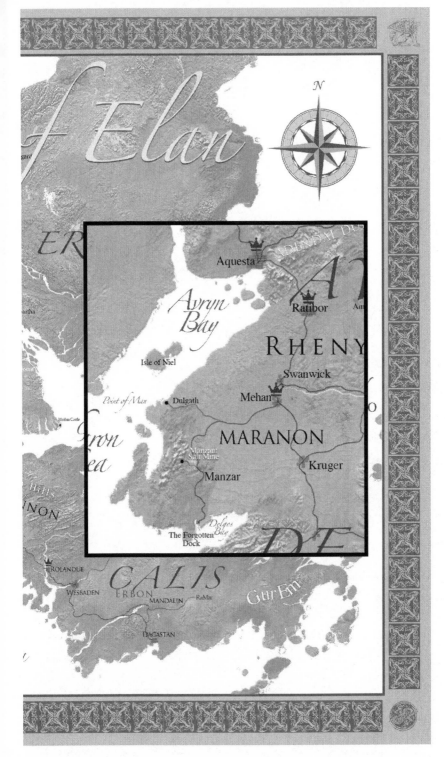

CONTENTS

CONTENTS

The DEATH of DULGATH

Chapter One
THE NEW SIGN

If anyone had asked Royce Melborn what he hated most at that moment, he would've said dogs. Dogs and dwarves topped his list, both equally despised for having so much in common—each was short, vicious, and inexcusably hairy. Royce's contempt for them had grown over the years for the same reason: They had caused him an incalculable amount of grief and pain.

That night it was a dog.

At first, he thought the furry creature on the mattress in the third-floor bedroom was a rodent. The dark thing with a curled tail and flat nose was small enough to be a good-sized sewer rat. Royce was pondering how a rat had gotten into a posh place like the Hemley Estate when it rose to its feet. The two stared at each other, Royce in his hooded cloak holding the diary and the mongrel on its four tiny legs. One second of held breath lasted long enough for Royce to realize his mistake. He cringed, knowing what would come next, what *always* came next, and the little beast didn't disappoint.

The mutt began barking. Not a respectable growl or deep-throated woof but an ear-piercing series of high-pitched yaps.

Definitely not a rat. Why couldn't you be a rat? I never have problems with rats.

Royce reached for his dagger, but the rodent-dog leapt away, its tiny nails skittering on the hardwood. He hoped it would flee. Even if the little monster woke its master, it wouldn't be able to explain that a hooded stranger had invaded Lady Martel's boudoir. Aroused from a blissful sleep, the owner might throw something at the mutt to shut it up. But this was a dog, after all, and like dwarves they never did what he wanted. Instead, the animal stayed a safe distance away, yipping its turnip-sized head off.

How can such a tiny thing make so much noise?

The sound echoed off marble and mahogany, amplifying into a wailing alarm.

Royce did the only thing he could: He leapt out the window. Not his planned exit, not even his third choice, but the poplar tree was within jumping distance. He caught a broad branch, pleased it didn't break under his weight. The tree, however, shook, rustling loudly in the quiet of the dark courtyard. By the time his feet hit the ground, Royce wasn't surprised to hear—

"Stop right there!" The husky voice was perfectly suited for the job.

Royce froze. The man coming at him held a crossbow: cocked, loaded, and aimed at his chest. The guard looked disappointingly competent; even his uniform was neat. Every button accounted for and glinting in the moonlight, each crease sharp as a blade. The guy had to be an overachiever, or worse—a professional soldier reduced to guard duty.

"Keep your hands where I can see them."

Not at all an idiot.

Behind the first guard came a second. He trotted over with heavy footfalls and a jangling of straps and metal chains. Taller than the first, he wasn't so well attired. The sleeves on his coat were too short, the lack of a button ruined the symmetry of the side-by-side brass rows, and a dark stain marred his collar. Unlike the first guard, this second one didn't have a crossbow. Instead, he carried three swords: a short one on his left hip, a slightly longer one on the right, and a huge spadone blade on his back. These weren't the weapons of Hemley guards, but the man holding Royce at bay didn't spare a glance when the second guard jogged up.

Drawing the shortest of his three swords, this second man didn't point it at Royce. Instead, he placed the sword tip against the back of the first guard's neck. "Put the bow down," Hadrian said.

The man hesitated only an instant before letting the crossbow fall. The impact jarred the trigger and sent the bolt whispering through the grass of the manicured lawn. Behind them, the rodent-dog still yapped, the sound muffled by the walls of the mansion. Now that his partner had things in hand, Royce tucked the book into his belt and glanced toward the manor. No lights. Nobles were sound sleepers.

Turning back, he found Hadrian still holding the fastidious guard at sword's point. "Kill him and let's get going."

The guard stiffened.

"No," Hadrian said with the indignation Royce would've expected if he'd asked his partner to throw out a good bottle of wine.

Royce sighed. "Not again. Why do we always have this argument?"

The ex-crossbowman had his shoulders hunched, hands in fists, still expecting the thrust that would end his life. "It's all right. I won't raise the alarm."

Royce had seen the look many times and thought the guy was doing well. No blubbering, no screams, no begging. He hated when his victims fell to their knees and whimpered, although he had to admit that made killing them easier. "Shut up," he ordered, then glared at Hadrian. "Kill him and let's go. We don't have time for a debate."

"He dropped the bow," Hadrian pointed out. "We don't need to kill him."

Royce shook his head. There was that word again—*need*. Hadrian used it often, as if justification were a requirement for killing. "He's seen me."

"So? You're a guy in a dark hood. There's hundreds of men in hoods."

"Can I say something?" the guard asked.

"No," Royce snapped.

"Yes," Hadrian replied.

"I have a wife." The man's voice shook.

"Man's got a wife." Hadrian nodded sympathetically while still holding the blade against the guard's neck.

"Kids, too—three of 'em."

"Maribor's beard, he's got *three* kids," Hadrian said with a decisive tone and drew back his sword.

The guard let out a breath. Somehow, he and Hadrian both assumed that the ability to reproduce had some relevance in this situation. It didn't.

"And I've got a horse," Royce declared with the same righteousness. "Which I'll ride away on just as soon as you kill this poor bastard. Stop dragging this out. *You're* being cruel, not me. Get it over with."

"I'm not going to kill him."

The guard's eyes widened in hopeful anticipation; a tiny smile of relief tugging at the corners of his mouth. He looked at Royce for confirmation, for a sign he would indeed see another sunrise.

Royce heard the sound of a door bursting open, and someone called out, "Ralph?" Lights were coming on in the house. Seven windows on four floors glowed with candles.

Maybe it just took that long to light them.

"Here!" Ralph shouted back. "Intruders! Get help!"

No, of course he wouldn't raise the alarm.

That did it. Royce reached for his dagger.

Before he touched the handle, Hadrian clubbed Ralph with the pommel of his sword. The guard dropped to the grass beside his spent bow. Whether Hadrian had hit the man as a result of his shout or because Royce went for his dagger was impossible to tell. Royce wanted to think the former, but suspected the latter.

"Let's get out of here," Hadrian said, stepping over Ralph and pulling Royce by the arm.

I wasn't the one delaying us, Royce thought, but he didn't bother arguing. Where one crossbow existed, there would be others. Crossbows were neither short nor hairy, but ought to be on his list. He and Hadrian ran along the shadow of the wall, skirting the blooming rosebushes, although Royce didn't know why they bothered. In his sentry getup, Hadrian sounded like a fully tacked carriage horse.

Melengar's Galilin Province was a tranquil, agrarian region not prone to the threat of thievery, and the estate of Lord Hemley suffered from woefully ineffective security. While Royce had spotted as many as six guards on various scouting missions, that night there had only been three: a sentry at the gate, Ralph, and the dog.

"Ralph!" someone shouted again. The voice was distant, but it carried across the open lawn.

Behind them in the darkness, five lanterns bobbed. They moved in the haphazard pattern of a bewildered search party or a host of drunken fireflies.

"Aaron, wake everyone up!"

"Let Mister Hipple loose," a woman's voice shouted in a vindictive tone. "He'll find them."

Above it all, the incessant yipping of the rodent-dog continued— Mister Hipple, no doubt.

The front gate was unmanned. The guard stationed there must have run for help after Ralph's shout. As they passed through unopposed, Royce marveled at Hadrian's luck; the man was a walking rabbit's foot. Three years in Royce's School of Pragmatism had barely scratched his partner's idealistic enamel. If Mister Hipple had been a larger, more aggressive animal, they might not have escaped so easily. And while Hadrian was more than capable of killing any dog, Royce wondered if he would have.

It has puppies, Royce! Three of 'em!

The two reached the safety of the dense thicket where they'd left their horses. Hadrian's was called Dancer, but Royce never saw any point in naming his. While stowing the diary in a saddlebag, Royce asked, "How many years were you a soldier?"

"In Avryn or Calis?"

"All of it."

"Five, but the last two years were…well, less formal."

"Five years? You fought in the military for *five years*? Saw battles, right?"

"Oh yeah—brutal ones."

"Uh-huh."

"You're mad I didn't kill Ralph, aren't you?"

Royce paused a moment to listen. No sound of pursuit, no lights in the trees, not even the yips of a manic rodent-dog chasing them.

He swung a leg over the saddle and slid his foot into the stirrup on the other side. "You think?"

"Look, I just wanted to do *one* lousy job where nobody got killed." Hadrian stripped off the uniform's waistcoat and replaced it with his wool shirt and leather tunic from his saddlebag.

"Why?"

Hadrian shook his head. "Never mind."

"You're being ridiculous. We've done plenty of jobs where we didn't kill anyone. Anyway, it's fine." Royce grabbed his reins, which he kept knotted together.

"It's what? What did you say?"

"Fine. It's fine."

"Fine?" Hadrian raised a brow.

Royce nodded. "Are you going deaf?"

"I just…" Hadrian stared up at him, puzzled. Then a scowl took over. "You're coming back later, aren't you?"

The thief didn't reply.

"Why?"

Royce turned his horse. "Just being thorough."

Hadrian climbed into his own saddle. "You're being an ass. There's no reason to. Ralph will never pose any threat."

Royce shrugged. "You can't know that. Do you understand the meaning of the word *thorough*?"

Hadrian frowned. "Do you understand the meaning of the word *ass*? You don't need to kill Ralph."

There it was again—need.

"Let's argue later. I'm not killing him tonight."

"Fine." Hadrian huffed, and together they trotted out of the brush and back onto the path that led to the road.

THE DEATH OF DULGATH

The two rode side by side on the open lane. Rain began falling before they reached the King's Road. The sun was up by then, although it was difficult to tell with the heavy clouds leaving the world a charcoal smear. Blissfully, Hadrian remained silent. In any given tavern, whether he knew someone or not, Royce's partner would strike up a conversation. The man would talk to strangers with the ease of reunited friends. He'd clap them on the back, buy a round of drinks, and listen to riveting tales such as the one about the goat who had repeatedly gotten into a neighbor's garden.

When just the two of them were out on the road, Hadrian commented on trees, cows, hillsides, clouds, how hot or cold the weather was, and the status of everything from his boots—which needed new soles—to his short sword—which could use a better wrap for the handle. Nothing was too insignificant to warrant remark. The abundance of bumblebees or the lack of the same would launch him into a twenty-minute discourse. Royce never spoke during any of it—didn't want to encourage his partner—but Hadrian carried on about his bees, the flowers, and the mud, another favorite topic of self-discussion.

Despite his indefatigable insistence on blabbering to himself, Hadrian was always silenced by rain. Perhaps it put him in a bad mood or the pattering made it difficult to hear himself. Whatever the reason, Hadrian Blackwater was quiet in the rain, so Royce loved stormy days. Luck remained with him nearly the whole way home. Melengar was experiencing one of its wettest springs in recent memory.

Royce looked over from time to time as they rode. Hadrian kept his head down, his hood crushed and sagging with the weight of water.

"Why don't you ever talk when it rains?" Royce finally asked.

Hadrian hooked a thumb under the front of his hood, lifting it to peer out. "What do you mean?"

"You talk all the time, but not when it rains—why?"

Hadrian shrugged. "Didn't know it bothered you."

"It doesn't. What bothers me is when you blather nonstop."

Hadrian peered over, and a little smile grew in the shadow of his sopping hood. "You like my talking, don't you?"

"I just got done saying—"

"Yeah, but you wouldn't have said anything if you really liked the silence."

"Trust me," Royce said. "I *really* like the silence."

"Uh-huh."

"What's *uh-huh* supposed to mean?"

Hadrian's smile widened into a grin. "For months we've ridden together while I've held whole conversations by myself. You've never joined in, and some of them were really good, too. You haven't said a word, but now that I've stopped—look at you…yapping away."

"A single question isn't *yapping away.*"

"But you expressed an interest. That's huge!"

Royce shook his head. "I just thought there might be something wrong with you—obviously I was right."

Hadrian continued to grin with an overly friendly look of self-satisfaction, as if he'd scored a point in some imaginary contest. Royce pulled his own hood down, shutting Hadrian out.

The horses plodded along through mud and occasionally gravel, shaking the water from their heads and jangling their bridles.

"Sure is coming down, isn't it?" Hadrian said.

"Oh, shut up."

"Farmer's wife back in Olmsted said it's the wettest spring in a decade."

"I'll slit your throat as you sleep. I really will."

"She served soup in cups because her husband and Jacob—that's her sleep-all-day-drink-all-night brother-in-law—broke her good ceramic bowls."

Royce kicked his horse and trotted away.

Royce and Hadrian were back on Wayward Street in the Lower Quarter of Medford. Spring was nearly over; in other parts of the world, flowering trees were busily trading pink petals for green leaves, and warm breezes blew earthy scents while farmers rushed to finish their planting. On Wayward, it meant four days of steady rain had once again made a murky pond in the low spot at the end of the street. And as usual, the water level reached the open sewer that ran behind the buildings. Euphemistically known as the Bridges, the sewer bled into the growing lake, spreading the reek of human and animal waste.

The rain was still coming down as Royce, Gwen, and Hadrian stood on the planked porch of Medford House, staring across the muddy pond at the new sign over the door of the tavern. A fine lacquered board hung from a wrought-iron elbow brace, displaying the crisp image of a vibrant scarlet bloom and a curling stem that sported a single sharp thorn. Surrounding the flower were the elegantly scripted words: THE ROSE AND THE THORN.

The sign looked oddly out of place in front of the dingy tavern with its saddle-backed roof of mismatched shingles and weathered timbers. For all its dilapidation, the alehouse and eatery had substantially improved. Only a year before, what had been known as The Hideous Head needed no illustration to explain itself to its illiterate patrons. Grime-covered windows and muck-splattered walls told everyone what they needed to know. Since gaining control of the tavern, Gwen had cleaned up the dirt and the muck, but the real improvements had been inside. The new sign was the first enhancement to the exterior.

"Beautiful," Hadrian said.

"It will look better in sunlight." Gwen folded her arms in judgment. "The blossom turned out perfect. Emma did the drawing and Dixon helped with the painting. Rose would have liked it, I think." Gwen looked up at the dark clouds. "I hope she somehow sees—sees her rose hanging above Grue's old door."

"I'm sure she can," Royce told her.

Hadrian stared at him.

"What?" Royce shot back.

"Since when do you believe in an afterlife?" Hadrian asked.

"I don't."

"Then why did you say—"

Royce slapped his hand on the porch rail, which had just enough rain on it to splatter. "You see?" he appealed to Gwen. "This is what I have to deal with. He admonishes me about my behavior. *Why can't you smile,* he says. *Why didn't you wave back to the kid? Would it have killed you to be polite to the old woman? Why can't you ever say a kind word?* And now, when I try to be a little considerate, what do I get?" Royce held out both of his palms, as if presenting Hadrian to her for the first time.

Hadrian continued to stare at him, but now with pursed lips, as if to say, *Really?* Instead, he replied, "You're only being nice because she's here."

"Me?" Gwen asked. Standing between them, she swiveled her head to look from one to the other, as innocent as a dewdrop. "What do I have to do with this?"

Hadrian rolled his eyes, threw his head back, and laughed. "You *are* a pair. Whenever the two of you are together, it's like I'm with strangers—no, not strangers—opposites. He becomes a gentleman and you feign ignorance of men."

Royce and Gwen maintained their defensively blank looks.

Hadrian chuckled. "Fine. Let today henceforth be known as Opposites Day. And as such I'm going across the Perfume Sea to have a drink at the Palace of Fine Food and Clean Linens."

"Hey!" Gwen snapped, bringing her hands to her hips in a huff of indignation.

"Yeah!" Royce said. "Who's the rude one now?"

"Stop it. You're scaring me." Hadrian walked off, leaving them alone.

"I missed you," Gwen told him after Hadrian had gone inside, her eyes on the rain as it boiled the giant puddle.

"Was only a few days," Royce replied.

"I know. Still missed you. I always do. I get scared sometimes—worried something bad will happen."

"Worried?"

She shrugged. "You might get killed, be captured, or maybe meet a beautiful woman and never come back."

"How can you worry? You know the future, right?" he joked. "Hadrian said you read his palm once."

Gwen didn't laugh. Instead, she said, "I've read many palms." She looked up at the sign with the single blooming rose, and sadness crossed her face.

Royce felt like stabbing himself. "Sorry, I…I didn't mean…"

"It's all right."

It didn't feel all right. Royce's muscles tightened. Both hands became fists, and he was glad she wasn't looking at him. Gwen had a way of seeing through his defenses. To everyone else he was a solid wall fifty feet high with razor-sharp spikes on top and a moat at its base; to Gwen he was a curtainless window with a broken latch.

"But I do worry," she said. "It's not like you're a cobbler or bricklayer."

"You shouldn't. These days I don't do anything worth worrying about. Hadrian won't let us. I'm stuck with fetching lost possessions, stopping feuds—did you know we helped a farmer plow his field?"

"Albert got you a job plowing?"

"No, Hadrian did. Farmer took sick, and his wife was desperate. They owe money."

"And *you* plowed a field?"

Royce smirked at her.

"So Hadrian plowed and you watched."

"I tell you, the things he does." Royce sighed. "Just doesn't make sense sometimes."

Gwen smiled at him. She was likely siding with Hadrian; most people did. Everyone thought good deeds were great—publicly at least—and her expression was one of patient understanding, as if she were too polite to say so. It didn't matter. She was smiling at him, and for that brief moment it wasn't raining. For that instant the sun shone, and he had never been an assassin and she had never been a prostitute.

He reached out, wanted desperately to touch her and hold that moment in his arms, to kiss that smile and make it more than a fleeting brilliance he would otherwise only recall as a dying spark. Then he stopped.

Gwen looked down at his faltering hands, then up at his face. "What is it?"

Is that disappointment in her voice?

"We're not alone," he said, nodding across the street to where three wretched figures moved in the shadows near the kitchen door.

"You need to talk to your bartender. Dixon is dumping scraps outside the door, and you're drawing flies."

Gwen looked over. "Flies?"

"Elves. They're pawing through your garbage."

Gwen squinted. "Oh, I didn't even see them." She waved a hand. "It's fine. I told Dixon to give them any leftover food. I hope he's not just throwing it in the mud. I'll need to get a barrel or set out a table."

Royce grimaced while watching the miserable creatures. The rags clinging to their bodies were little more than torn scraps pretending to be clothes. Soaked with the rain, the elves looked like skin-wrapped skeletons. Feeding them was an example of cruelty by kindness. Gwen gave them false hope. Better to let them die. Better for them, better for everyone.

He looked at her. "You realize they'll just come back. You'll never get rid of them."

Gwen nudged him and pointed up Wayward Street. "Albert's here."

On foot and veiled behind the hazy curtain of solid rain, Albert Winslow approached the dreaded pond with disgust. Soaked through and through, the viscount's new brimless hat lay flat against his head, sliding down one side of his face. His cloak was plastered to his body. He looked at the murky lake and then across at them with a frown. "If it's always going to be like this," he called across, "can't you put in a bridge for your moat, Gwen?"

"I don't have a charter governing the street," she called back. "Or the Bridges, for that matter. You'll need to take that up with the king, or at the very least the Lower Quarter Merchants' Guild."

Albert looked down at the churning pond and grimaced as he waded in. "I want a horse!" he shouted at the clouds as the water reached the middle of his calves. "I'm a viscount, for Maribor's sake! I shouldn't have to wade through a sewer just to report in."

"Can't afford three," Royce replied. "Can barely afford feed for the two."

"Can now." Albert pulled back his cloak to reveal a purse. He shook it. "We got paid."

Six shiny gold coins stamped with the Melengar Falcon and twenty silver bearing the same image lay on the table in the Dark Room. The only room without a single window, it once was used for all manner of kitchen storage. Gwen had transformed the space to serve as the headquarters for Riyria, his and Hadrian's rogues-for-hire operation. She'd added a fireplace for warmth and light, and the table where Albert had emptied his purse.

Royce brought over a candle. Every kingdom and city-state produced their own coins, but the tenent was international and supposed to be of consistent weight—equal to a typical robin's egg. A silver tenent weighed the same as a gold tenent, but it was larger and thicker to make up for the lighter metal. That was the intention, and, for the most part, it held true. These felt to be honest coins.

"You got away clean, by the way." Albert stood by the fire and pulled off his sodden hat. "Lady Martel either doesn't know her diary was taken or is too embarrassed to report it. I'm guessing the latter."

Albert began to wring his hat out onto the floor.

"No, no, no!" Gwen shouted at him. "Here—give me that. Oh, and just get out of the rest of your things. They have to be washed. Dixon, can you please get a blanket?"

Albert raised his brows at Gwen as she stood with hands out, waiting. He glanced at Royce and Hadrian with questions in his eyes. Neither said a word. Both responded with grins.

"Albert, do you really think you have anything I haven't seen before?" Gwen asked.

Albert frowned, wiped the wet hair from his face, and began to unhook his doublet. "Anyway, as I was saying, Lord Hemley hasn't called for so much as a search. According to our employer, Lady Constantine, Lady Martel only reported a nasty scare in the middle of the night that turned out to be nothing."

"Nothing?" Royce asked.

"I'm not sure Ralph and Mister Hipple would agree," Hadrian said.

"What kind of scare did she say they had?" Royce inquired.

Albert shrugged off the dripping brocade, which Gwen took. The big bartender returned with a blanket, and they traded material. "Can you please give this to Emma and ask her to do what she can?"

"Tell her to be careful," Albert said. "That's expensive."

"We know," Royce reminded him.

"Emma is experienced with brocade," Gwen assured him as Dixon left. "Now let's have those stockings and breeches."

"Can I have a chair?"

"After the breeches are off."

"What was the nasty scare Lady Martel mentioned?" Royce asked again.

"Oh—" Albert chuckled as he rolled off his long stockings. "She said a raccoon came in through a bedroom window and set her dog to barking. Hearing the noise, one of the grounds' guards came running, and, in the dark, he banged his head against a poplar branch. He called out, thinking he'd been attacked."

"*Thinking* he'd been attacked?" Royce asked.

"His story was that two guys broke in and threatened to kill him. Lady Martel called him delusional."

Royce took a seat opposite the fire and tapped his fingertips together. He wondered what was in that diary that made Lady Martel want to avoid an investigation.

Hadrian just laughed.

"What?" Albert asked, handing over his second stocking, which Gwen took with a look of disdain.

"Lady Martel just saved Ralph's life," Hadrian said.

"Oh really? Who's *Ralph?*"

"The delusional guard. Royce has been waiting for the rain to stop, and then he was going to pay ole Ralph a visit."

Albert clapped his hands together. "Then it's a day for everyone to celebrate, isn't it?"

"After the breeches are off." Gwen scowled.

"Are you this way with *all* your customers?" Albert asked.

"You're not a customer, Albert."

"No—I'm a viscount."

After a short pause, everyone burst out laughing. "All right, all right, here, take my trousers! Take them. What do I need trousers for? I've already lost all my dignity."

"Who needs dignity when you have coin?" Royce tossed him a stack of silver pieces topped with a gold.

Albert caught them as if he were a practiced juggler. Standing naked before the fire, he appraised the coins with a smile. "I'm noble once more!"

"Wrap this around you." Gwen handed him the blanket. "We've seen enough of your nobility for one day."

She gathered up the rest of his clothes and headed out.

Albert draped himself in the soft wool and sat in a chair as close to the hearth as he could get without setting himself on fire. Rubbing the coins between his fingers, he said, "Silver and gold are so pretty. It's a shame you have to trade them away."

"And these won't last." Royce sighed, then faced Albert. "At the rate we've been taking jobs, and the small purses, things are getting tight. We need something that pays more."

"Actually, I have another job ready to go. This one is worth—get this—twenty *gold* tenents *plus* expenses. Which is good because it's way down in southern Maranon."

Royce and Hadrian sat up.

"That was fast," Hadrian said. "You don't normally work that hard."

"True, but this one fell into our laps." A drop of water slipped down Albert's face, and he paused to scrub the wet from his hair with a corner of the blanket. "Sounds incredibly easy, too."

"You're not qualified to judge, Albert," Royce said.

"Ah, but this one is. They don't even want you to do anything."

Royce leaned forward and eyed the viscount. "Who pays twenty yellow for nothing? What's the job?"

"It seems that someone is trying to kill Lady Nysa Dulgath."

"We aren't guards for hire."

"Oh, she has guards. Lady Dulgath is a countess and will soon be the ruler of a tiny province in the southwest corner of Maranon once she pledges fealty to King Vincent. Apparently her father, the Earl Beadle Dulgath, recently passed, and she's his only child."

"Was he murdered?" Royce asked.

"No. Old age. The fellow was ancient, nearly sixty. But someone has it out for his daughter. From what I've been told, there've been three attempts on her life in the last month. After those failures, they want a professional. That's where you come in." Albert looked squarely at Royce.

"I wouldn't call assassinating a countess *nothing*. Besides, you know how he gets about those kinds of jobs." Royce gestured toward Hadrian.

Albert waved a hand. "No, you misunderstand. You're not being hired to kill her. Rumors say they've already hired someone."

Royce shook his head. "Unless they went cheap, the hired hand is a bucketman for the Black Diamond. The BD and I have an understanding not to interfere with each other."

"I remember," Albert said. "But they don't want you to catch the killer. Your job is to assess the situation and inform Sheriff Knox how *you* would go about killing Lady Dulgath so he can formulate plans to prevent it."

"Why me?"

Albert smiled. "I let it slip that you used to be an assassin for the Black Diamond."

Royce glared.

"No one in Maranon cares about what you've done elsewhere. These are nobles we're talking about. Morality works on a sliding scale for them. They're excited to have someone with experience."

"Sounds…" Hadrian began and searched for the word.

"Suspicious," Royce provided.

"I was thinking *odd*," Hadrian said. "But yeah. It's strange. Is it possible this sheriff is the one who wants her dead?"

"Unlikely. I'm not certain he even knows about this. He's not the one who hired us. And I don't think this client is in the habit of assassinating heads of state."

"And who has? Hired us that is."

Albert hesitated a moment, then said, "The Church of Nyphron."

Chapter Two
THE ARTIST

Sherwood Stow held his paintbrush with unconscious effort as he stared at Lady Nysa Dulgath. The woman stood ten feet away, one hand poised over her stomach and the other at her side, clasping a pair of riding gloves as if she were about to race off on a hunt. She stood divinely straight, chin high and level so the dangling pearl earrings hung in precise balance. Her hair was up, braided, coiled, and wreathed her head like a royal diadem. She wore an exquisite gold silk-brocade dress with billowing sleeves, and around her shoulders a grinning-faced fox stole curled, as if it, too, were delighted to be so near this magnificent woman. While the lady's gaze was regal in its elevated, distant focus, Sherwood's only regret was she wasn't looking at him. She was, in fact, staring over his head at the chandelier that hung at the center of her private study.

The room was small by Castle Dulgath standards. *Intimate* was how Sherwood thought of it, like a dressing room or a parlor used for courting. Even more so since parlors came staffed with chaperones, and they were the only two present in the study.

THE ARTIST

"Why don't you look at me?" Sherwood asked.

"Is that a requirement?" the lady replied, her eyes fixed on the chandelier. Her lips held fast to an indifferent near-smile, the obligatory face of state. Usually he appreciated subjects who could maintain a certain statuesque quality while he painted, but she took the request to an extreme. Nysa wasn't posing for him; she was hiding.

"Let's say it's a request."

"Request denied." The words were as sweetly neutral as her lips, neither warm enough to suggest familiarity nor cold enough to imply displeasure.

I can't even tell if she's breathing.

Nysa was altogether too stiff. This, of course, was the image she wished to portray, but Sherwood Stow wasn't interested in painting the soon-to-be Countess of Dulgath. He was after the woman. And while he never spoke the name publicly, in his mind he always thought of her as Nysa—never Lady Dulgath.

The Dulgath line was an edifice, a monument, a dust-covered dynasty of renown. Nysa was a woman in her early twenties—he didn't know how early, difficult to tell because her body possessed a youthful vigor, but her eyes were ancient. A beautiful and mysterious being of light, but her movements exposed the charade. Too graceful. Sherwood had known many women—ladies, princesses, even queens—but none possessed a fraction of her poise and elegance. Nysa was a spiraling leaf caught by a breeze, and if she landed on the surface of a placid lake she'd leave no ripple.

"Mister Stow, isn't it usually customary when painting to actually bring the brush to the canvas?" she said to the chandelier. "You've stood there for twenty minutes mixing paint and holding that bristled stick aloft, but never once have you employed it."

"How can you tell while looking at the chandelier?"

"Seeing and looking are unrelated. You, of all people, should know that."

Sherwood nodded and once more added walnut oil to the thickening umber. His old master, Yardley, was no doubt heaving in his grave. Yardley had always insisted on working with egg tempera, but Sherwood preferred oil. Not only did it enable him to give a translucent depth in his portraits, but its slow drying time granted him the luxury to do…well…everything.

"Yes, indeed, and since you know that as well, you understand the necessity for my delay and the importance of going slow."

"*Slow* doesn't properly define you, Mister Stow. A bead of honey in winter is slow. It pours, as if with great reluctance, but it does pour. You, Mister Stow, are not a drizzle of honey. You're a rock."

"Pity. I do so like honey. Perhaps you could reconsider your assessment?"

"A rock, I say. A vast block of granite, immobile and resolute in your refusal to budge."

"Am I, now?"

"How else do you account for two months of daily, hour-long sessions? That's sixty hours. I've heard good artists have been known to finish a portrait in a week's time."

"True. True." He tapped his chin with a finger, leaving a bit of paint. "I suppose the only explanation is I'm not a good artist."

Sherwood corked his bottle of oil and set it back on the easel's tray along with the stained rags and vials of pigments, some of which were deceptively expensive. Beyond the Sea—or Ultramarine—was the most prized because the stone used to make the dark blue paint had to cross the ocean from the same fabled land whence came the incomparable Montemorcey wine. The paint was worth twenty times its weight in gold. Luckily, few non-artists knew this or his brethren would be routinely beaten and robbed.

"You admit it then?"

"Absolutely, I'm not a *good* artist." He used the rag he'd made from his last decent shirt to wipe oil that had dripped from the stem of his brush to his hands. No matter how much care he employed, his hands were magnets for paint and oil. "I'm the *best* artist."

She let out an uncharacteristic puff, which was almost a laugh, while one delicate brow rose in skeptical declaration. "You are an arrogant man."

Finally, a reaction.

"No, I'm confident; there is a difference. Arrogance is an unjustified belief in oneself. Confidence is the simple understanding of one's abilities. I do not boast about being a great lover—although I very well may be. On that particular subject, I simply am not in a position to accurately judge. I leave that determination to the women I entertain."

This time both of her brows rose, creating the tiniest crease in her forehead.

"But we were discussing art, and when it comes to that, I *am* an expert. So you can trust me when I say there isn't a greater artist than I, and the reason I say that is because there is no finer judge of artistic merit than myself."

"Mister Stow, I don't believe I can trust you about art or anything else. How can I when you refuse to let me look at your work? You've denied everyone even a glimpse at your two-month masterpiece."

"Truth isn't created on schedules."

"Truth? Is it truth you are painting? I thought it was me."

"I am painting you—or at least trying to—but you are causing the delay by your refusal to cooperate."

"Whatever do you mean?"

"You hide from me."

"I—" Her eyes almost shifted. He saw the pupils quiver with the struggle. Biting her lower lip, she gathered herself, and the lock of her gaze redoubled. She lifted her chin, just a smidge, in defiance. "I'm right here."

"No…you're not. The Countess of Dulgath in all her refined nobility and grand regalia stands before me, but that's not you—not who you really are. I want to see the person inside. The person you keep hidden from everyone for fear they'll see—"

She looked at him. Not a glance, not a stare, but a fierce glare of fire. Only a flash, but he saw more in that instant than he'd seen in two months. Powerful. Violent. A tempest corked in a woman's body and glazed over with the sadness of loss and regret. He'd *seen* her. The vision rocked him, so much so that Sherwood took a step back.

"We're done here," Lady Dulgath declared, breaking the pose and throwing off the fox. "And I see no reason to continue with this foolishness. I only agreed to this portrait because my father wanted the painting. He's dead, so there's no need."

She pivoted on her left heel and strode toward the exit.

"I'll see you tomorrow, then," Sherwood called after her.

"No—you will not."

"I'll be here."

"I won't." She slammed the oak door on her way out, leaving Sherwood alone in the study, listening to the echo of her fading footfalls.

He stared at the door, which had bounced with her thrust, rebounding and hanging agape so that he caught a glimpse of her gold dress as she retreated down the corridor.

Fascinating.

A heartbeat later Sherwood picked up his brush and rag, both of which he'd dropped without realizing, and started to paint. The brush flew with unconscious ease, moving from palette to canvas in a blinding fury. So intense was his concentration that he didn't notice the young man enter the study until he heard him speak.

"Is there some kind of trouble?"

Sherwood recognized the blue satin doublet even before seeing the goatee and immediately pulled the drape over the front of the painting. He kept the cloth tacked to the top of the canvas's frame for quick deployment. Covering works in progress to keep gnats, dust, and hair out of the paint wasn't unusual, but now it served a more important purpose.

"Lord Fawkes. Sorry, I didn't see you. What did you say?"

"I was asking if there was a problem," Fawkes said, looking around the study with his trademark mix of bewildered innocence and sinister suspicion. "I heard a loud bang and saw the countess storm out. Is there some way I can be of assistance?"

"Not at all. This was a particularly good session, but it's over. I'll just gather my things. We made excellent progress today."

Fawkes circled around the easel and frowned at the covered portrait. "I hope that isn't one of the bed linens."

"My nightshirt, actually, or what's left of it."

"What do you wear to bed?"

"Now? Nothing at all. Can't afford it."

"Thank Novron it's nearly summer." Lord Fawkes picked up Sherwood's bottle of Ultramarine and tossed it from hand to hand. For him to choose to play with *that* particular bottle of pigment was too coincidental. Unlike the rest of his ilk, Lord Christopher Fawkes must have been familiar with the art trade. "Why are you still here, Sherwood?"

The artist pointed at the covered painting and smiled. Pointing was easy; the smile was more of a challenge as he watched Fawkes continue to toss the blue bottle.

The lord glanced over his shoulder with a dismissive sniff. "You painted my aunt Mobi's picture last summer at her villa in Swanwick."

"Yes, I remember. Beautiful place. Lady Swanwick was most gracious and generous."

Fawkes nodded. "Yardley painted her portrait as well, two years before, and yet she insisted on one by you, his apprentice."

"Actually, that happens quite often."

Fawkes paused in his game of toss to hook a thumb at the covered painting. "Everyone gasped when you unveiled her portrait."

"I get a lot of that, too."

"Aunt Mobi sobbed when she saw what you'd done. Ten minutes passed before she could say anything at all. Uncle Karl was certain you'd offended her."

Sherwood nodded. "The Earl of Swanwick called his guards."

"I heard they took you by the wrists and started dragging you away when Aunt Mobi found her voice and stopped them. *That's me!* she said. *That's how I really am—no one has ever seen me like that before.*"

"I get that, too."

"Did you sleep with her?" He tossed the bottle higher than he had before.

"Excuse me?"

"Is that how you impressed her so? How you got her to be so *generous?*"

"Did you see the painting?"

Fawkes chuckled. "No. I just heard the tale. Aunt Mobi keeps it locked in her bedchamber, where I'm certain she dreams of the young artist who *captured* her so exquisitely. I wonder why a woman married to an earl would be so impressed by a penniless artist."

"Does this story have a point?"

Fawkes smirked. "My point is, that painting—which captured Aunt Mobi so perfectly that she may have betrayed her husband—

took five days to create. So once more I ask, why are you still here, Sherwood?"

"Some portraits are more difficult than others."

"And some women are harder to seduce."

Sherwood snatched the bottle in mid-toss. "Pigments are not toys."

"Neither is Lady Dulgath." Fawkes stared at the bottle in Sherwood's hand for a moment, then turned away. "I assumed you were merely freeloading off your patron's goodwill. Possibly lingering because you had no other prospects. Now I believe I've been naïve."

He looked again at the linen-draped painting as if it were a veiled face watching them. "Life as an itinerant artist must be taxing and perilous. I suspect that living in a castle with your own bed and studio is a significant improvement. But you've forgotten one thing. She's noble; you're not. There are laws against such things."

"No, there aren't." Sherwood placed the bottle of blue pigment on the easel's tray and stepped between it and Lord Fawkes.

Fawkes glared. "There ought to be."

"If we are speaking of things that should be, you would have been born a dairy farmer in Kelsey instead of the cousin to King Vincent. Although that would have been a terrible injustice to cows, which I'm certain is what Maribor was thinking when he made you a landless lord."

Sherwood was exceedingly pleased that Lord Fawkes no longer held his precious bottle of Beyond the Sea. The Maranon lord of no-place-in-particular sucked in a snarl. His shoulders rose like the fur on the back of a dog. Before he could open his mouth to cast some vile insult, Sherwood cut him off. "Why are *you* still here? The funeral was more than a month ago."

This had the effect of pouring cold water on a flame. Fawkes blinked three times, then settled into a murderous glare. "In your single-minded efforts to enter Her Ladyship's bed, it may have escaped your attention that someone is trying to kill her."

"And what does that have to do with anything?"

"I'm staying to protect her."

"Really?" Sherwood said with more sarcasm than he intended, but he was more than nettled with the lord. "Perhaps it has escaped your attention that she has a contingent of well-trained guards for that. Or is it your belief that the only thing standing between Lady Dulgath and death is the assassin's fear of the king's second cousin?"

This comment did nothing to alleviate Fawkes's glare, but his gaze did shift to the easel again.

Sherwood knew what the lord was thinking and took another step forward. The painter had no grand illusion of beating Fawkes in a brawl. A law *did* exist making it illegal to strike a noble, even a despicable one. Sherwood's advance was a bluff, but the artist tried to sell it as best he could by rising to his full height, which was an inch taller than Fawkes, and returning that venomous glare with a firm jaw and ready hands.

Bluff or not, Fawkes chose to merely spit on Sherwood's shoe before walking out.

He, too, slammed the big door, but this time it stayed shut.

Chapter Three
MARANON

The weather remained horrible all the way to Mehan. If the clouds weren't following them, as Hadrian imagined, and all of northern Avryn was suffering the same deluge, then Wayward's pond was likely a lake after the three additional days of downpours that soaked Royce and Hadrian's travels south. On the morning of the fourth day, the skies woke clear and blue, a huge southern sun shining upon a land of gorgeous rolling hills.

Most of the jobs Riyria took occurred in and around Medford, with a few sending them only as far south as Warric. Although Hadrian had grown up less than fifty miles from the border, this was his first trip to Maranon. If the peninsula of Delgos were a mitten, Maranon would be the thumb, and a green one at that. A land that was deep, velvet-rich, and the color of a forest by moonlight stretched out in all directions, broken by small stands of leafy trees. Maranon was known for its horses—the best in the world. At first, Hadrian thought he saw deer grazing in the meadows, but deer didn't travel in herds of fifteen or more. Nor did they thunder when racing across the fields, shifting and circling like a flock of starlings.

"Are they owned? Or can you just grab one?" Hadrian asked Royce as they rode their mangy northern mounts, which were at least clean thanks to three days of rain.

Royce, who had thrown his hood off and was letting his cloak air-dry on his shoulders, glanced at the horses racing over a distant hill. "Yes and no. They're like deer up north—or anything anywhere, really. There's nothing that isn't claimed by someone. Those are wild, but everything here belongs to King Vincent."

Hadrian accepted Royce's expertise. Despite his partner's lack of idle conversation, he knew Royce had traveled extensively—at least in Avryn. He appeared most familiar with the congested areas around the big cities of Colnora and Ratibor, those places a thief and former assassin would find the most work. For Hadrian, the trip to Maranon felt like Riyria was taking a holiday. The change in weather only added to the sense that they were in for some relaxation.

Rising in his stirrups, Hadrian gazed across the open land. Aside from the road they followed and the mountains in the distance, Hadrian didn't see a soul, city, or village. "So what's to stop me from roping one and taking it home?"

"Aside from the horse itself, you mean?" Royce asked.

"Well, yes."

"Nothing really. Unless you're caught, in which case you'll be hanged."

Hadrian smirked, but Royce wasn't looking. "If caught, we'd be hanged for most of what we do."

"So?"

"So, this looks nicer. I mean…" He gazed at the few puffy, white clouds, which cast fleeting shadows over the hills. "This place is incredible. It's like we crawled out of a sewer and wandered into paradise. I've never seen so many shades of green before." He looked down. "It's like our Medford grass is sick or something. If we have to steal, why can't we take horses for a living? Got to be easier than climbing trellises and towers."

"Really? Ever try grabbing a wild horse?"

"No—you?"

"No, but explain to me how a man on a horse catches a riderless horse. And a *Maranon* one at that. In a land of endless rolling hills, there's no place to trap them. And even if you were to catch one, what then? There's a difference between a wild horse and an unbroken one. You know that, right?"

In one of the back corridors of his mind, Hadrian recalled having heard something like that, but he hadn't remembered until Royce brought it up. Horses born on farms were raised around people. They weren't trained and didn't take to having folk hop on their backs any more than a dog would, but they were still relatively tame.

"Got just as much chance with a wild horse as you would have saddling a stag."

"Just an idea," Hadrian said. "I mean, how long will we do this for?"

"Do what?"

"Steal."

Royce laughed. "Since I teamed with you, I hardly ever steal. Annoying really. There's a certain beauty in a well-done theft. I miss it."

"We stole that diary."

Royce turned to give Hadrian a pitying look and a sad shake of his head. "That's not theft; it's petty pilfering. And now this. The idea of preventing someone from assassination feels…"

"Dirty?" Hadrian asked.

Another look, this one baffled. "No. It feels *wrong*, like walking backward. Seems simple enough in theory, but it's awkward. I'm not even sure what they want me to do. Am I expected to talk to this woman, this walking target? Don't usually chat with the soon-to-be dead."

In three years, this was the most Royce had ever said while riding. The angry tone explained it. Royce hadn't been this far outside his comfort zone since the Crown Tower debacle. The master thief was rarely off balance, but when he was, Royce became chatty.

"She's noble," Royce went on. "I don't like nobles. Always so full of themselves."

"Brought up that way," Hadrian said as if he were worldly.

Hadrian had known a number of nobles, but they were all Calian, and that was like saying he knew rodents because he'd fed some squirrels. Calian nobles were nothing like those in Avryn. They were more casual, earthy, less pompous, and far more dangerous. Hadrian thought Royce would actually like most Calian nobles, at least until they hugged him. Hadrian had learned early on that Royce Melborn wasn't a hugger.

"Exactly." Royce nodded. "And this one is a woman—a Maranon woman at that."

"What's so different about Maranon women?"

"Remember that storm on the Uplands near Fallen Mire? The place where the breezes coming across Chadwick slam into the winds coming down off the ridge?"

"Oh yeah." Hadrian nodded, remembering a night when neither of them had slept.

"They're like that." Royce waved his hand dismissively at the lush, beautiful countryside that ran as far as Hadrian could see. "Look at this place. Do people here work hard? Do you think common folk's mattocks go dull on the rocks in this soil? Or that people go to sleep hungry three nights a week? The serfs on these manor farms live better than Gwen. Now imagine what their nobles are like. I expect this Dulgath woman will be the worst possible sort. Did you know the Province of Dulgath is the oldest fief in Avryn?"

"Exactly how would I know that?" Hadrian smiled at him, entertained by a talkative Royce.

"Well, it is," Royce said, irritated, as if Hadrian had disputed him. "If Albert can be trusted to know the history of the various noble houses, Dulgath was founded around the same time as the Novronian Empire, and the family that rules here is as old as the First Empire's origins. Most nobles adopt the name of the region they're given stewardship of, but here it's the other way around. The Province of Dulgath was named for the people who founded it. So, given that, how entrenched do you think Lady Dulgath's sense of privilege is? Her family goes back for hundreds of generations. And I have to save her?"

"Technically, I think they want to know how you would murder her."

Royce gave Hadrian a wicked smile. "The hard part, I expect, will be not carrying it out. Having you whispering in my ear not to kill may be of benefit for once." Royce looked up at the perfect sky stretching far and wide. "There's no way I'll get out of here without blue bloodstains."

The road forked; A left turn hooked south while their path continued into the distance where the green hills ended at a wrinkle of green mountains.

Royce paused for a long time, staring down the left branch, which made Hadrian look as well. The road was straight, level, and followed along the skirt of the green ridge toward larger stony mountains tinged blue in the late-morning sun. Minutes passed while Royce continued to stare, and Hadrian became certain his partner had lost his way, something which was more than odd. For three years, Hadrian had never known Royce to lose his inner compass through dense forests, amid fog as thick as a wool blanket, during starless nights, or even in a blinding blizzard. And yet, the thief continued to sit on his horse, staring down that long southern route.

"Is it that way?" Hadrian finally asked.

Royce looked up, as if he'd been asleep. "What?"

"Is that how we get to Dulgath?"

"Down there?" Royce shook his head. "No—no, that's not the way. That doesn't lead anywhere."

Hadrian looked at the broad well-worn track marred by the passage of wagon wheels and the half circles of horses' hooves. "Pretty well traveled for a dead end."

Royce smirked, as if Hadrian had made a vulgar joke. "Yes, it most certainly is."

Urging his horse to stay on their path, Royce continued to look back at the road more traveled, as if he didn't trust it. Whatever haunted him, he didn't say, nor did Hadrian ask.

When they'd first begun working together, marrying their unique skills for mutual gain, Hadrian had tried on numerous occasions without any luck to pry open the box of Royce's history. Only near-death brushes—or, as it would seem, the anticipation of meeting Maranon nobles—managed to loosen that lid. Wherever that southern road led, Hadrian wouldn't learn about it from Royce. The two things he was certain about were that Royce had been down that road and it went somewhere.

The road they were on went somewhere as well. Up.

After several hours of silent riding, it narrowed through a series of switchbacks until it snaked into a tight pass beyond which a vista opened onto another world. This one even more beautiful than the one they'd left behind. Wildflower meadows and leafy forests sat beside an ocean, a vast expanse of water that cut jagged coves and bays from massive cliffs. Hadrian guessed they had come to the western edge of Maranon and the start of the Sharon Sea. This was his first time seeing it, but at that distance it looked no different from the eastern oceans. On this *backside* of Maranon, where the roads were narrower and little more than grass-covered greenways, there were more trees, more streams, and many more waterfalls.

Tucked inside a space less than ten miles from mountains to sea was a shadow-valley, cozy and snug, dangling its toes in the vast blue that crashed white against a stony point. Castle Dulgath stood on a singular promontory that hooked south like a crooked finger. Built from cliff stone, it blended with the tortured rock except for the straight edges of its towers and its flags flying blue and white.

"Pretty," Hadrian said.

Royce huffed. He pointed to the red berries along the trail. "So are those, but I wouldn't suggest eating any."

The trip down was quick and silent. Royce drew up his hood as they neared the valley's floor and farms and travelers started to appear. The homes were built of fieldstone, covered with neat, thatched roofs. Often the buildings were multistoried, and always picturesque. The people were darker than those in Melengar: black-haired, olive-skinned, and brown-eyed. Well fed and healthy, they dressed in colorful clothing of greens, oranges, and yellows, a stark contrast with the people of Melengar. There, the poor wore a natural-wool uniform dyed with dirt to a dingy gray. Mud was the pigment of the north, but the south delighted in color.

Heads turned and friendly faces looked up at them as they passed. Royce never paused, never slowed. Once, he urged his horse to a trot when a man said "Hello," which sounded like *yellow* in the Maranon accent. Hadrian, on the other hand, smiled and returned waves, especially from pretty young women.

"We should move down here," Hadrian said.

"Our contacts are up north. I know my way around better, and we have resources and a reputation. Down here, we'd be starting from scratch and working blind. We don't even know the laws."

"But it's pretty."

Royce glanced back. "You said that already."

Hadrian spotted another young woman, this one with painted eyes. She smiled at him. "It's gotten prettier."

They traveled down the road through dappled shade and to the songs of peeping tree frogs. Before long, the sounds of wagon wheels and conversation replaced the frog calls as Royce and Hadrian reached a cluster of buildings. Rounding a bend, they entered into a proper village with candle shops and cobblers. Buildings here displayed tiled roofs, glass windows, shutters, and eaves. Moss covered old foundations, and thick ivy climbed chimneys and wreathed windows. The grassy trail became a stone-covered broadway where it passed through the village, although it was difficult to see the road, given the crowd gathered upon it.

Men and women clustered in the village square—an open market where merchants and vendors might set up displays to sell buttons, copper kettles, and the day's fresh catch of fish. Instead, a crowd surrounded a large smoking pot suspended over an open fire. At first, Hadrian thought the two of them had stumbled on a festival. He imagined being welcomed to a communal picnic, but he didn't smell any food. Instead, he smelled the gagging stench of boiling tar. In the middle of the throng of townsfolk, a dozen angry men held an elderly fellow with his wrists bound behind his back. They led him past four sacks of feathers toward the cauldron of bubbling tar.

"We should do something," Hadrian said.

Royce lifted enough of his hood to see him clearly. "Why?"

"Molten tar can kill an old man."

"So?"

"So, if we don't do something, they'll kill him."

"How is this our problem?"

"Because we're here."

"Really? That's your argument? *We're here?* Haven't won too many debates, have you?" Royce looked around. "You'll notice we aren't alone. The whole village is in on this. That poor bastard is probably a criminal—a poisoner of children, torturer of women— maybe a cannibal."

"Cannibal?" Hadrian shook his head. "Honestly, the way you think. It's—"

"Practical? Sensible?"

"Sadistic." Hadrian pointed. "Royce, look at his cassock. The man is a priest."

Royce scowled. "Worst sort of criminal."

Faces had turned their way. People were pointing at the pair of strangers watching them from horseback. Hadrian, and his three swords, received the most attention. The crowd quieted, and four of the bigger men from out front approached and stood boldly before them.

"Who are you?" the biggest one asked. Shoulder-length hair didn't quite hide the bull neck that was nearly as wide as his head. Broad jaw, wide nose, eyes sunk deep beneath an eave of brow, he narrowed his eyes into a quarrelsome glare and then cracked the knuckles on two massive hands.

Hadrian grinned and introduced himself by name.

Royce cringed.

"No reason not to be friendly." Hadrian said while dismounting. Then more quietly he said to Royce, "What difference does it make? We aren't doing anything illegal."

"Not yet," Royce whispered back.

Hadrian stepped forward and offered his hand to the four men. None took it.

"You a knight?" the bullnecked man asked.

"Me?" Hadrian chuckled. "No."

"Probably another vagabond lord here to freeload after the funeral." This was said by the slightly shorter gent to Bull Neck's right, the one whose friendly orange tunic undermined his efforts to appear menacing. Another of the four, who liked his hair short but didn't know much about cutting it, nodded his agreement.

"Maybe they're from the church? Seret and Sentinels consider anyone who doesn't bend a knee at Novron's altar a heretic," said a man standing in the back.

"Well, whoever you are," the bullnecked man said, "you shoulda brought more men with you if you plan to stop us from feathering Pastor Payne."

Hadrian let his shoulders droop. "Actually, we don't—"

"Need more men," Royce broke in.

Hadrian turned to look at him. "We don't?"

"No," Royce confirmed. "But they do." He rose up in his stirrups and waved for the other men who were holding Pastor Payne to come forward. "C'mon up here. Your friends are going to need your help."

"Ah—Royce?" Hadrian said as five additional men pushed their way through the crowd.

Not all of them were brutes, and none stood as big as the bullnecked man and his buddy in orange. Two were older fellows with graying hair. Three were young, long and lanky, with pretty, unmarked faces. On the positive side, none of them carried so much as a stick.

"So, do you want to know why Hadrian here carries three swords?" Royce asked the crowd. A few nodded, and he gestured toward his partner with a grin. "Tell them."

The two had done this before. It didn't always work.

Hadrian pasted a friendly smile on his lips and faced the crowd, paying particular attention to the wall of muscle in front of him. "In my travels, I've found most men are reluctant to fight someone wielding a sword unless they also have one. Most good-natured folk—like yourselves—don't have weapons. So I carry extras in case a situation like this arises. That way, I can hand out a couple so people aren't so disadvantaged in a fight."

Hadrian drew both his side blades in an elegant, single motion. The crowd stepped back and let out a communal gasp.

"So you can have your choice." He spun the smaller weapon against his palm. "This is a short sword, the workhorse of combat, an ancient, reliable design. Great for close quarters and frequently used with a shield. Or…" He spun the larger one in his other hand. "This is a hand-and-a-half sword, also called a bastard sword—I think because no one knows where it came from." He chuckled.

No one joined him.

Hadrian sighed. "Looking at the handle, you can see it has room for two hands, but it's also light enough to swing one-handed. A really nice, versatile blade." Hadrian slammed both weapons back into their scabbards with practiced ease. Then, reaching up, he slid the great sword off his back.

Once more, people gasped and gave way, backing up another step as the massive blade swung out.

"Now, *this* is a spadone." With one hand, Hadrian held the blade out level, pointing at the crowd. "As you can see—it's big. Sort of a three-and-a-half sword."

He grinned at them, but the crowd remained cold. Everyone's eyes followed the tip of the blade as if it were a snake's head.

"This is obviously a two-handed weapon and not for the faint of heart. You might be thinking it would be a good choice due to its long reach, but most would have trouble swinging it, much less holding it out as I'm doing now." Hadrian swung the big sword in large sweeping arcs, making it sing in the wind; then he let go and caught it with his other hand. "And while you're struggling to raise it, I'd stab you with the short sword."

"I've seen him do that," Royce lied. "Usually catches a poor sod in the stomach. One quick thrust. A wound like that can take days to kill you. And painful." He shook his head and frowned. "One sad case screamed and moaned for so long, his own mother wanted to smother him with a pillow."

Faces blanched. Royce was a good liar.

Bull Neck's mountain-ridge brow wrinkled, and his stalwart friend in orange retreated a bit more, stepping on the foot of a woman behind him. She cried out and shoved him with both hands.

"And if you're thinking of rushing him…" Royce chuckled. The sound wasn't at all jovial. Hadrian had never witnessed Royce laughing in good humor. When he laughed, babies cried. "I should mention that he can mow down scores of men with his big sword, and with less effort than you scythe wheat. Of course, doing so is louder and messier. Wheat doesn't bleed, and straw doesn't scream."

Eyes, still locked on the sword, widened. Hadrian knew they were picturing him swinging the blade into the crowd as if through ripened crops.

Royce leaned forward in his saddle, the leather creaking with the strain. The chuckling had stopped, and what smile he wore melted into a grim, straight line. "Now that you've met Hadrian, let me introduce myself. I'm the one you don't want to know." He paused, letting that sink in. "Let the priest go, or I'll be forced to demonstrate why Hadrian is the lesser of two evils."

The wall of muscle retreated, walking backward and forcing the gathered throng to fall back as well. Then everyone scattered, slipping through doorways or darting up side streets. The crowd dispersed so quickly they didn't bother untying Pastor Payne; they simply left him standing in the noxious smoke of the sizzling cauldron.

The priest shuffled toward them, coughing as he came.

"Thank you—thank you," he choked out, doubling over. He struggled to draw a clean breath. The old man wore a round felt cap. Two tufts of white hair jutted out from either side. Satchels of loose skin drooped below sad eyes. Around the frame of his jaw and chin flared a bristling white beard, but his upper lip and cheeks were clean-shaven. His cassock, a ruddy rusted color, was buttoned to the neck and skirted the ground so closely it hid his feet.

Hadrian cut the rope off the priest's wrists before putting the great sword away. "What was that all about?"

Pastor Payne made use of his free hands to cough into. Then he wiped his lips and eyes. He shook his head at the retreating villagers in disgust. "These are backward people, heathens and blasphemers. Time has forgotten this corner of the world, and those who dwell here are lost in barbarism."

"That doesn't answer the question." Royce dropped to the ground.

"They resent my presence. No, that's not exactly right. They resent the Nyphron Church, which has neglected bringing them into

Novron's fold for far too long. They are mired in the past, and it's my job to bring them into the future."

Hadrian turned to Royce. "I thought this wasn't our problem."

Royce shrugged. "Turns out it was."

Hadrian surveyed the deserted streets, which, he then noticed, were paved in a pleasant cobblestone. He could still hear the sound of slamming doors and whispered mutterings. "We made a lot of enemies just now. How come?"

Royce grabbed the lead to his horse and pointed at Payne. "Because a dead client doesn't pay. Pastor Payne is our employer."

"By the way, Payne is spelled with a *y* and an *e*—not with an *i*," he told them, coming to a stop before a rickety shack slapped together from warped boards and cracked stones, perhaps the only building in town not covered in ivy. The priest turned and eyed the two of them carefully, then sighed. "Doesn't matter, I suppose. Neither of you is literate, correct?"

"Wrong," Royce said.

"Really?" Pastor Payne pushed up his lower lip. "Down here, only those in the clergy know their letters. I would have assumed that—your sort—wouldn't."

"Our sort?" Royce asked.

"Paid killers," Payne explained. "That's what you are, correct? I was informed that at least one of you has worked in that capacity for the Black Diamond Thieves Guild. Isn't that right?"

"And for that reason you assumed we're ignorant?" Royce said.

The priest nodded with enthusiasm. "People who spill blood for a living are always ignorant." He looked them both over again. "Well, almost always, I suppose."

"Ignorance isn't prejudiced about who it afflicts," Royce replied.

Payne looked puzzled for a moment, then smiled and nodded, causing Royce to raise an eyebrow at Hadrian, who shrugged.

"Welcome to my church," the pastor said, indicating the tilting shack that leaned heavily on the twisted trunked of an olive tree beside it.

"This is a church?" Hadrian asked. "In Medford, the church is…bigger."

"Medford doesn't have a *church*," the old pastor said. "It enjoys a *cathedral*. We're just starting here. I can assure you things will be much different the next time you visit. Come in. I'll make you something to eat."

Lacking any windows, glass or not, the inside of the church was illuminated by stripes of sunlight shining through the gaps between wall planks. Thick dust clouds swirled as the priest moved around in the tiny space. Looking through large ceramic pots resting on the floor and peering into smaller ones shelved above, he finally found what he was after.

"Ah-hah!" He grinned, pulling out a cloth-wrapped wheel of cheese. "Now if I could find—I swear I had some blackberries somewhere. Gathered them myself. I'm sorry I don't have more to offer."

Hadrian searched for a seat and didn't find anything he was confident would hold his weight. Royce refused to venture more than a step inside the door, where he stood with his arms hidden beneath his cloak.

"Found you!" Payne pulled a basket of berries off a dark shelf, grinning at them as if he'd discovered gold in a stream. "Help yourself. I know where there are more." The pastor popped two into his mouth and chewed, humming in delight. "Food is wonderful, isn't it? Winter will be a challenge this year."

"Isn't it warmer down here?"

"Sure, sure, but the people are ice. At least in summer, I can fend for myself. In winter, I won't exactly be able to rely on the *generosity* of my congregation to get me through." He popped two more berries, then used a whittled stick stripped of its bark to cut away a piece of cheese.

"They certainly don't seem to like you," Royce said.

"The monks have turned them against the church."

"Monks?"

Payne nodded in reply as he chewed with a full mouth then swallowed. He pointed at the western wall. "Up there is the old monastery. Been here since imperial times and named after a ridiculous piece of cloth." He swallowed again. Seeing their blank faces, he waved a hand before them. "That doesn't matter. My woes with the monks aren't your concern. The church will take care of them. You're here to stop a murder."

"No," Royce replied. "Just giving a professional opinion."

"Right—right, of course. Well, no sense in going to the castle now. Be dark soon. You can stay here tonight, and in the morning I'll introduce you to Knox. Hugh is the high sheriff of this province. He'll be the one you'll be working with. I'll also introduce you to Lord Christopher Fawkes. He's been of great assistance to the church and Lady Dulgath recently. Wonderful young man—cousin to King Vincent. He's actually the one who suggested speaking to Viscount Alan Wind-something. The fellow who referred you."

"Albert Winslow."

"Yes, that's him." Pastor Payne took a seat on a rolled bundle of straw, making Hadrian wonder if he'd be better off sleeping outside. "He's close friends with Bishop Parnell from up north. The bishop dropped me off here when he came down to administer last rites to the late earl. Then he went on to the spring conclave in Ervanon. The bishop met with Viscount Winslow, who sent you our way."

"What can you tell us about Lady Dulgath?" Royce asked.

Payne paused and wiped his mouth. "Well, she's the only daughter—only child—of Lord Beadle Dulgath, formerly the Earl of Dulgath. She's young, twenty-two I believe. Very pretty. Got her looks from her mother, who died in childbirth. Beadle never remarried. He was a sentimental man. Emotional sort. Weak is what Bishop Parnell says. He has let this province run wild with lawlessness, as today's little demonstration can attest. Can you imagine what would happen if the peasants of Medford hauled a priest out in the main square to be tarred and feathered? King Amrath would post their heads on poles lining the King's Road."

"You know a lot about Medford," Hadrian said.

"I studied at Sheridan University. We used to spend our free days in Medford."

"Small world. We know a Professor Arcadius from Sheridan. He's the—"

"Can we get back to Lady Dulgath," Royce insisted.

"Oh yes. Let's see…" The priest tapped his chin. "She's well liked. Some might even say loved by…well, I guess everyone."

"Apparently not." Royce started to lean against the doorframe but must have thought better of it and straightened again. "When did the attacks start?"

"Maybe a few weeks after Beadle's funeral or so I've heard."

"Maybe?"

"It's hard to say exactly. We only know about the attempts that got noticed, but Knox will tell you more about that."

Royce had a sour look on his face. Usually Albert dealt with the client who wanted an item taken. Then Hadrian and Royce would watch the place for a few days, noting visitors and guards—if there were any—and determining when the lights went out and from what windows. Only on rare occasions did his partner check out interiors.

If they needed floor plans or inside details, Albert would be sent for a visit. Hadrian knew Royce didn't speak to many people, but he especially avoided priests, nobles, and most certainly high sheriffs. The last law enforcement officer he'd talked with had been found grotesquely butchered and decorating the fountain in Medford's Gentry Square. Hadrian doubted Pastor Payne was aware of Royce's involvement in that affair. If he were, he wouldn't be so casual about introducing the thief around.

Chapter Four
BEYOND THE SEA

The next morning, Sherwood let himself into the study as usual. The castle staff had stopped bothering with him after the third week. Not that they'd known what to do with him before. An artist was an oddity in a castle—even a large one. In Dulgath, he was an outright enigma.

While gossip wasn't something he intentionally provoked, Sherwood was delighted by the whispers his contradictions generated. He hobnobbed with the nobility, but dressed like the staff. Being friendly, he spoke kindly and easily to everyone without any hint of haughtiness, but he also told tales of intrigue in the courts of high kings.

On fine days, he kept to his room. On mornings after a night's rain he took long walks, mostly along the coast. The castle staff didn't know he was out searching for ocher, which stood out better from the cliff walls when wet, or that the snails he used to make Imperial Purple were more plentiful after a rain. The servants probably considered him daft. Oddly enough, his eccentricities gained him a queer sort of acceptance.

Before he'd left Mehan for Dulgath, everyone had warned Sherwood that the people he'd meet there would be *a bit off.* As a result, he fit right in and had become a part of the "castle family." And since he had no title before his name and required no special treatment, Sherwood had become little more than furniture to the people who worked there—all except one. She was Nysa's handmaiden, Rissa Lyn. He knew her name from the number of times the lady had called it during their sessions.

Rissa Lyn, make certain to lay out my blue gown for this afternoon.

Rissa Lyn, ready a hot bath for when I'm done here.

No, Rissa Lyn, don't close the drapes. He needs the light.

In two months, Sherwood hadn't heard Rissa Lyn say anything in reply other than *Yes, milady.* But she was all eyes. Rissa Lyn watched Her Ladyship, and she watched Sherwood. She was peering at him again that morning as he hauled his easel into the study. Standing just under the stairs, she blushed when he looked over and withdrew.

He placed the easel where he always did, the floor marked with charcoal to indicate where each of its tripod legs went. This maintained consistency of view from one day to the next. Consistency of light was a bigger problem, and the reason the sessions were held at the same time each day. He went to the windows and threw back the drapes, tying them up. He was lucky—no clouds. Still, the shift of seasons was devastating. He should have asked her to start their sessions earlier to compensate. Now she might not come at all.

He hadn't seen Nysa since the door had slammed the day before. That wasn't unusual. He rarely saw her outside their sessions, and he always arrived first.

Sherwood took off his jacket and hung it on the back of his easel. He rolled up his sleeves and pulled out the tray to oil his paints.

He kept his palette loaded so as not to waste pigments, but overnight the paint thickened. He liked his paint to be the consistency of buttercream. He wiped the stems of his brushes clean and lined them up in neat rows—largest to smallest. His favorite was in need of a re-bristling. It flared from fatigue, and too much paint lay trapped in the stem. Sherwood was a curse to a fine brush; Yardley had always said so.

Sherwood had begun his apprenticeship when he was ten years old, making Yardley more than merely an art instructor. The old perfectionist, with the irritating laugh and disgusting habit of spitting every few minutes, had been more like a parent to Sherwood than the tin miner and his wife who bore him. In addition to portraiture, finding and crushing pigments, and caring for his brushes, Yardley had taught him to fish, whistle, dance, navigate courtly life, and how to defend himself with fists and a blade. Where Yardley had learned sword fighting was anyone's guess, but he knew what he was doing and he'd taught Sherwood well. An artist wandering alone on the open road was a target too tempting for many, and Sherwood's prowess had been tested more than once.

His prep work done, Sherwood pulled up the stool and sat.

The room was quiet except for the sound of the sea drifting in through the open window, soft and muffled, a distant unending war fought between wave and rock. A seagull cried twice, then was silent. Wind buffeted the drapes and rocked parchments rolled up on the desk behind which Nysa usually stood.

Sunlight moved in an oblong rectangle across the floor, slicing over the desk and running up the paneled wall. Sherwood knew the time by the path the light took, tracking it with a painter's eye every morning. He'd worked on the background of the painting only when Lady Dulgath wasn't in the room, but he had finished everything that wasn't Nysa weeks ago.

As the light reached the edge of the stone fireplace, he knew she was late.

Sherwood touched the leg of the stool, patting it as if for a job well done. While not the stool's doing, it managed to still be there. She hadn't ordered its removal.

That's something—isn't it?

As the light moved across the first stone of the hearth—the one he'd struggled to match in color because he was low on hematite— Sherwood began to face the reality that Lady Dulgath was making good on her declaration. He hadn't believed her. They'd only had a small quarrel, a spat. People didn't—

He felt his heart skip and a pressure on his chest, a tightness that made it difficult to breathe.

I'm only a painter. I'm nothing to her.

He tried to swallow and nearly choked on his own saliva. *I've never lost a subject before,* he thought stupidly, as if that mattered, as if it ever had. *Never failed to complete a project.*

Sherwood stared at the empty space before the desk, at the marks he'd put on the floor to show Nysa where to place her feet.

It's like she's dead. The thought crashed in. *What if she is?*

He shook his head. *No, the castle would be thrown into chaos. She just isn't coming. She isn't coming because she doesn't—*

The familiar *swoosh-swoosh* of the brocade gown preceded her entrance. Lady Dulgath entered without acknowledging his presence. She whirled on her mark, spinning on her left heel. After looping the fox over her neck, she clasped the riding gloves in her hand. Her eyes focused on the chandelier.

"Chin up, just a tad more," he said softly.

She tilted her head without a word.

Outside the study's door that Nysa had left open, Chamberlain Wells could be heard saying, "She's indisposed at the moment. But… well, let me inquire. I suppose she might see you. Wait here."

That was Wells's way of saying *She's only wasting time with that infernal painter like she does every morning.* Sherwood didn't have a problem with Wells, which was good, since he ran the castle and could make the artist's life miserable if he wanted to. That said, he was of the same mind as many in his position, believing a painter's time to be worthless.

Lady Dulgath allowed herself a glance at Sherwood. He smiled. She smiled back. His heart vaulted a hurdle, forcing him to take a deep breath. He nearly lost the presence of mind to pull the cloth over the painting before Thorbert Wells entered.

"My lady," Wells said, pausing at the doorway to bow.

Thorbert Wells was a rotund man with a fondness for expensive belts that neither he, nor anyone facing him, ever saw. The chamberlain's girth also hid his shoes, which that morning were a fine pair with soft leather uppers. Wells rarely wore the same pair twice in a week. He owned so many shoes that Sherwood had once asked Wells's manservant if he ever placed a mixed pair on the chamberlain's feet to see if he noticed. This was the sort of joke that gained Sherwood access to the kitchens at night and a swig from the hidden jug of barley whiskey kept under the floorboards.

"Sheriff Knox has some gentlemen here to meet with you," Wells said.

"Gentlemen?" she asked.

"Ah…yes, concerning the recent unpleasantness." Wells had a problem saying the words *assassination, murder,* or *killing.* Even when it came to butchering quails to eat, he was apt to say, *The birds will be dressed for dinner,* as if the fowl shared his penchant for belts and shoes and would be seated at the table.

Again, the lady focused on Sherwood, and he was certain she was looking for—perhaps not permission, but understanding.

Sherwood's heart climbed up his throat, as if searching for a better view of this extraordinary moment.

"Very well, let them in," Lady Dulgath said with just enough irritation in her voice to suggest that interrupting their time together *was* a disappointment.

Wells bowed again, then waved three men in.

Sherwood recognized Sheriff Knox, although he hadn't had cause to speak with the man. Still, he had seen him around, especially of late, and Hugh Knox wasn't the kind of person one overlooked—he was the sort you crossed the street to avoid. Harsh, with a tendency to glare, he wore his blond hair tied back and had a red sash across his chest and wrapped around his waist. Edged in gold, the garment was the mark of his office. He wasn't from Dulgath. The color of his hair and stubble told that story. The habitual squint of his eyes and sneer on his lips told the rest. This wasn't a genteel man. He wore two sabers and steel shoulder guards over a thick three-quarter-length leather gambeson. That day he looked tired, understandable, given the *recent unpleasantness*. The man charged with enforcing the law and protecting the countess couldn't be sleeping well.

A pair of men accompanied him, neither a native of Maranon.

One was tall, with a friendly smile and a relaxed stride, acting as if he were meeting a familiar bartender instead of a countess. He was dressed in worn leather and had dull buckles on three separate belts—none of which Thorbert Wells would have been caught in if his trousers depended on them—and a long cloak tossed jauntily over one shoulder. He one-upped Knox by wearing three swords. The one on his back looked big enough to fell a tree. The other man, a few inches shorter, might have been a woman for all Sherwood could tell. He was tented inside a dark cloak, hood up and his hands lost in its folds. Only a sharp nose, thin lips, and a pale chin presented themselves.

"Your Ladyship." Knox went down to one knee. Rising, he gestured to the others. "This is Royce Melborn and Hadrian Blackwater of Melengar. They come highly recommended by Viscount Winslow of Colnora and Bishop Parnell."

"Highly recommended for what?" she asked, tilting her head from side to side, studying the two.

Knox hesitated and glanced awkwardly at Wells and Sherwood. "Perhaps we could speak privately?"

"Is it a secret?" she asked.

"In a way, milady."

"They are here to protect me, yes?"

"No," the one in the hood said without so much as a pleasant tone, much less a *milady*.

The countess raised her head to stare down her nose at him, no attempt to hide her irritation. "Then why *are* you here?"

"We've been hired to find the best ways to kill you."

Sherwood dropped his favorite brush, adding to the woes of its bristles. Wells clamped a meaty hand over his mouth, making his big cheeks swell as they flushed red. Knox closed his eyes, tilted his head up toward the ceiling, and opened his mouth but said nothing.

Lady Dulgath folded her arms under the head of the fox and raised an elegant brow. "Really? And how much are you being paid? Hadrian—is it?"

The hood shook. "Name's Royce, and that information is between me and my employer."

This time even Knox brought a hand to his face.

"Pardon me," the taller one with the swords butted in, "my lady, I'm Hadrian." He offered a gracious bow. "I hope you'll excuse my partner. He's not accustomed to speaking to...*people*...ah, people such as yourself. You see, we were asked to evaluate security measures to see if there are ways to improve them. Royce is an expert at finding flaws, particularly when it comes to threats of assassination."

The chamberlain cringed at the mention of the "a" word.

"So you believe my life is in danger. That's why you're here?"

"Don't you think your life is in danger?" Royce asked.

"Not particularly." She expelled a huff of air, pivoted on her left heel, and turned her back to them. She took three steps toward the window, stopped, then spun on the same heel back to face them once more. "If I did, would I allow a man with three swords and another shrouded in a hood to enter my private study?"

Royce shrugged. "I just thought you were stup—"

"Royce!" Hadrian snapped. In a milder tone, he continued, "My friend is very tired from our long trip. Now, if no one is trying to harm you, there's no reason for us to be here. But since we've traveled so far, and on the expectation of payment, I hope you won't begrudge us the opportunity to at least tour Dulgath. Neither of us has been to Maranon before. Your corner of it is most beautiful."

Lady Dulgath continued to stare at Royce. "Draw back your hood," she ordered.

Hadrian laid a hand on the other one's shoulder and whispered something to him.

"Is there a problem?" the lady asked.

"I'm here to do a job," Royce said. "Not entertain you."

"You've come to my castle unbidden and have failed to show any sign of decorum or decency. Would you rather entertain me from my dungeon?"

Royce sneered. "Would you rather I—"

Sherwood didn't know why he did it. If anything, it was because he couldn't abide the words that were likely to finish that sentence. He grabbed the nearest bottle of pigment and hurled it at the man. The artist was to the side and slightly behind the visitors when the bottle flew. With his hood up, Sherwood couldn't see the man's eyes, and he knew Melborn couldn't have seen him. The bottle was small but heavy due to its thick glass—as ideal for throwing as a polished river stone. His aim was perfect. The container should have cracked against the hooded man's head, but it didn't. Instead, a slender hand darted from the dark cloak and snatched the bottle from the air. Then the hood turned, and Sherwood felt like a mouse who'd caught the attention of a hawk.

The taller man stepped in again. "Perhaps we should attempt this meeting at another time?"

Wells's face was so red it neared purple. "I think you are right. I shouldn't have allowed this intrusion in the first place. Gentlemen, if you will?" He shooed at them, his large sleeves flapping with the effort.

Lady Dulgath said nothing, but she continued to stare at the hooded man as he and the others left.

Only then did Sherwood look down at his tray. He was sickened to realize he'd thrown the bottle of Beyond the Sea.

Chapter Five
CASTLE DULGATH

Castle Dulgath consisted of three unadorned square towers perched on a precipice of stone. A small rock wall bordered the front, while the backside was a sheer and mortal drop to the sea. Inaccessible except to seagulls, the promontory offered limited space for luxury. The castle's foundation took up most of the narrow point, leaving little room for the courtyard, which had been foolishly given over to uncontrolled azalea bushes. They grew to a surprising size along the stone wall. And there, among the pink and purple blooms, Royce, Hadrian, and Knox found Pastor Payne, waiting.

"How did it go?" he asked.

"Not well," Hadrian said.

"You should have expected as much," Royce added, shaking his fist that still held the bottle of pigment. He hadn't meant it as a rebuke, but he was irritated.

The pastor took a step back into the blossoms, his eyes big as goose eggs.

"Perhaps you should have come in with us," Sheriff Knox said. "Why didn't you?"

"Lady Dulgath isn't what I would call a supporter of the Church of Nyphron. Since my arrival, I've tried to keep a safe distance between us. Is there a problem?"

"It's all right," Sheriff Knox said. He was calm, but wore a sour look. Then he turned to Royce, and asked, "You don't need her cooperation to do this, right?"

Royce nearly laughed but wasn't in the mood, even in the face of such absurdity. "You might be surprised to learn, Sheriff, that I never obtain the cooperation of those I plot to murder."

Everyone stared at him in a palpable silence. Even Hadrian had his brows up.

Royce rolled his eyes. "I didn't mean—oh, never mind." He turned to Payne. "Look, are you planning to pay me extra to *actually* kill her?"

The pastor took another step into the bushes, the blossoms starting to swallow him. "No—of course not!"

Royce looked back at the others. "There—see?" Remembering the young woman's glare as she threatened to imprison him, he glanced back at Payne. "Are you sure?"

"You're here to *protect* Countess Dulgath!" Knox admonished, spraying Royce with saliva as he spat out the word *protect*.

"Might have told *her* that." Royce leaned toward Hadrian and said, "What did I tell you about spoiled nobles—spoiled noble *women*? Maybe we should forget this whole thing."

"If you do," Payne put in, "I'm sure the church will insist on withholding payment, including the funds for travel expenses. Since you don't need to interact with the lady, why not just follow my example and keep your distance? Speaking of which…" The pastor looked toward the castle entrance nervously. "I've done my part, and there's little else I can accomplish here. I should be going." Payne bowed curtly, and, with his usual stale smile, withdrew.

As the pastor exited the courtyard, Hadrian turned to Knox. "It couldn't hurt to look around a bit, right?" He was standing closer than usual to Royce, with that everything-is-going-to-be-all-right smile on his face. "Why not fill us in on some of the failed attempts. What *exactly* has happened? What made you think the countess is in danger?"

"I'll show you." Knox waved for them to follow.

The sheriff led them up a set of stone steps to one of the rear parapets. Royce scanned the length. No guards, no sentries posted. Down in the courtyard, not a single soul was visible. Tilting his head up, he noted the numerous windows, tiny dark holes in the face of the rising towers. *I could walk in on a cloudless day, dressed to kill, and no one would notice.*

"Here." Knox pointed to a missing merlon.

Royce spotted grooves and gouges where someone had used a pry bar. Peering over, he saw the road hugged the wall just below. The square, two-foot block of stone stood out pale against the green grass, lying where it had rolled after crashing down.

"Missed Her Ladyship by inches," Knox said.

After giving Royce some time to examine the area more closely, Knox led them back down to the grassy common.

"What time of day?" Royce asked.

"Pardon?" Knox replied.

Royce rolled his eyes. "When the great big rock nearly crushed the pretty lady, what time of day was it?"

"Oh, midday or thereabouts."

"And no one saw anything?" Hadrian asked.

Knox shook his head and spread out his arms. "As you can see, Castle Dulgath isn't a busy place."

"Nor very well protected," Royce added with an insinuating glare.

"You're just looking to make all kinds of new friends today, aren't you?" The sheriff licked his lips. "You know, I told the bishop we didn't need outsiders coming here to tell me how to do my job. Dulgath isn't Colnora. We don't have people like *you* around here. This is a peaceful province."

"Really? Then why am I here?"

"I honestly don't know."

"I imagine that's a list that's grown uncomfortably long by now, hasn't it?"

Knox reached to shove Royce, who took a step back and to the side, causing the sheriff to fall on his face. "You son of a bitch…" The sheriff came off the ground with a look in his eye that told a story.

Hadrian read it as well and moved in to block. He had a tendency to do that—get in the way—but this time Royce appreciated it. He hadn't traveled four days and ridden a hundred and twenty-five miles to kill a province sheriff. Royce wasn't sure Hadrian would be able to douse the sparked fire, so he shifted the bottle of pigment to his left hand then reached inside his cloak for the handle of Alverstone, his dagger.

"Sheriff Knox!" a man called from the front doors of the castle. He walked quickly toward them. "Why don't you introduce me to your new friends?"

Knox violently brushed bits of grass off himself while baring his teeth at Royce.

"Hugh, please!" the man shouted, breaking into a jog. "Don't be rude. It's not proper to introduce oneself."

The sheriff took a breath, then another. "This is Lord Christopher Fawkes, second cousin to King Vincent."

"Hello, gentlemen!" the lord exclaimed in a jubilant voice. He clapped his hands together and rubbed briskly, giving the appearance of a man about to embark on some great work. "You must be Royce Melborn." He extended a hand, then drew it back, exchanging it for a raised finger. "Ah—no, you're probably not the handshake sort, are you? That's fine. Artists need to be mindful of their tools."

He turned to Hadrian. "But you're a different sort altogether. Mister Hadrian Blackwater, isn't it?" The hand went out again and, once clasped, Lord Fawkes pumped it soundly two times, then clapped Hadrian on the shoulder. "Nice sword! Spadone, right? Quite the antique. Don't see many of those anymore. My friend Sir Gilbert—he's the senior knight of my cousin Vincent—never uses one. Says they went out of style centuries ago…back when knights actually fought in wars!"

Fawkes laughed loudly at his own joke.

No one else did, but the lord either didn't notice or didn't care. "Oh, Hugh, these two are a wedge of sharp cheese, aren't they? Please, allow me to give them the tour. I'm certain you have better things to do, *don't you?*" The last two words lacked the gaiety of the others, and were punctuated with authority.

"Certainly, Your Lordship." Knox gave Royce a parting scowl. He adjusted his sword belt and strode toward the front gate.

"Excitable fellow, that Hugh," Fawkes said, his tone quieter, calmer. "Hails from somewhere in Warric, if memory serves. I'm sure he has a bloodstained past. He's hiding down here, I imagine."

Royce's eyes followed Knox's back until he disappeared from sight.

"So, you are the men Bishop Parnell has picked to properly plan Lady Dulgath's murder." Fawkes grinned and winked at them.

Royce wasn't certain if the man was a fool or a genius. He displayed signs of both. Neither made him comfortable, but over the course of his life he'd been at ease with only four people. None of them was a well-dressed noble with a loud voice who winked. No one ever winked at Royce. The fact that this man, with his black goatee and expressive hands, did so was a curiosity worthy of further scrutiny.

"It's all right," Fawkes told them, spreading his hands out and fanning his fingers. "I'm privy to what's going on. Brilliant, really, like that adage about fighting fire with fire. And from what I've heard, you two know how to handle yourselves in heated situations." He moved in closer. Lowering his voice, he added, "Rumors say a rather high-profile noble was assassinated up north. I suspect you know a little about that."

"Rumors can't be trusted," Royce told him.

"No, of course not." Fawkes glanced toward the front gate. "Still, I doubt our good sheriff knows about that incident or realizes he may owe me his life. As I recall, that dead noble was a high constable. Knox should be more careful. One doesn't buy poison and handle it without gloves. A fine and dangerous instrument deserves respect. Wouldn't you agree?"

"Absolutely." Royce nodded. "And now that you mention it, I do seem to recall something about that rumor. Happened in Medford, didn't it?"

"Why, yes, I believe that was the place."

"I can see why you were concerned about the sheriff, but just so we understand each other...the man killed wasn't just a high constable; he was also the king's cousin."

Lord Fawkes escorted them inside Castle Dulgath's stables, which were situated beyond the cleft wall and down the road where the land flattened out enough to be safe for horses. Made to appear like a fancy cottage, the stables had twelve-paned windows and an interlocking-brick floor. The place was cleaner than Wayward Street—even cleaner than The Rose and the Thorn despite Gwen's hard work. The building didn't smell like a stable. There wasn't a trace of manure nor a glimpse of straw. Chandeliers hung from a high ceiling, and the doorways benefited from decorative molding. Horses lounged in stained oak stalls with black-painted metal gates. Each wore a tailored blanket, and in front of every bay sat a large, beautifully crafted trunk.

"Nice barn," Hadrian remarked, looking up at the tongue-and-groove ceiling.

"Adequate," Fawkes said with a bulging lower lip and a curt dip of his head. "Dulgath doesn't have the resources, talent, or inclination to indulge in serious equestrian endeavors. I realize you meant it as a jest, Hadrian, but in Maranon, *this* is hardly impressive."

Lord Fawkes strolled along the long row of gates and stopped outside the stall where a horse stood cloaked in a beige warming coat. Large, black eyes spotted Fawkes, and a white head poked out through the opening in the bars designed specifically for that purpose. The lord cooed, made kissing sounds, and scrubbed the horse's neck. "This is Immaculate—she's mine." Fawkes opened a small pouch on his belt and palmed out a sugar cube. The horse snatched up the treat, smacking her lips with a loud, hollow thumping clap of appreciation.

"Why are we here?" Royce asked.

Annoyance flashed across Fawkes's face but was instantly stripped and replaced by a warm smile. "Not a fan of horses?"

"I like riding more than walking, but I prefer women for the friendlier stuff."

"Ha! Well said. Still, a good horse can be a blessing from Novron." He patted Immaculate's neck fondly. "No one understands our love, do they?" he whispered loud enough for them to hear, then turned away with a grin.

Fawkes moved to the next stall, which housed an entirely black horse, this one with a snow-white velvet blanket. The horses were so perfect, so uniform in color; Royce wouldn't have put it past these pretentious people to dye the animals. Even the horse's hooves were pitch black. Fawkes reached down and flung open the chest. Inside, a saddle rested on a stand beside a folded blanket, a bridle, and a lead. The saddle was two-toned, tooled leather with an embroidered suede seat and shiny brass fittings. It had the fixed head and lower leaping head of a sidesaddle, which accounted for its plush luxury, although Royce imagined Lord Fawkes's saddle to be just as ostentatious.

"This is Derby, Lady Dulgath's mare. And this"—he lifted the sidesaddle—"is Her Ladyship's as well." He held it up to them.

"It's very nice," Hadrian said.

Fawkes chuckled. "Look at the cinch."

Royce tilted his head to peer at the fabric band that dangled down. Unlike the dual D-rings he and Hadrian tied leather straps to, this one had a set of buckles hidden under the saddle flap. Made of wool, this girth band was bright white.

"Again, very pretty," Hadrian said.

"It's new," Royce noted.

The lord grinned. "Good eye."

Fawkes dropped the saddle, closed the chest, then walked to the far wall, where an open barrel stood. Reaching inside, he withdrew a near-identical girth strap. This one was sweat-stained and lacked the fluff of the other.

Royce took it from Fawkes and examined the edges—crisp and clean up to a point and then ragged where the wool banding had torn. Hadrian looked at him expectantly. "Someone cut it a little more than halfway through. The rest tore while riding."

Fawkes nodded. "Lady Dulgath was shifting from a three-beat canter to a four-beat gallop when it happened. She took a nasty spill. Thankfully, she wasn't jumping at the time, although she was setting up to do so. The strap broke during her practice ride for the Dulgath Steeplechase of Roses."

Fawkes retrieved the strap from Royce and dropped it back in the barrel.

"So that's two," Hadrian said. "How did they try to kill her the third time?"

"Poison," Royce replied.

Hadrian and Fawkes looked at him in surprise.

"How did you know?" Fawkes asked.

"I didn't, until just now, but it seemed likely, given the azaleas in the courtyard."

"Those pink flowers are poisonous?" Fawkes said as if Royce had shattered a childhood trust. "They're so beautiful."

"And toxic. When I was with the Diamond, a common practice was to send a bouquet of azaleas in a black vase as a warning to other guilds that might be encroaching."

"We should have those torn out immediately!"

"Don't bother. They don't pose any *real* danger to anyone but dogs or maybe children. There are a lot of poisonous flowers— chrysanthemum, lily of the valley, hydrangea, foxglove, wisteria. Eat any of them and you'll get sick but probably won't die. To do someone in, you want hemlock—eight leaves will kill you. Monkshood is excellent because it absorbs through the skin and leaves no trace. Belladonna is also nice; just one leaf or ten little berries will do the job. Old Bell is a favorite of female murderers because they always have it on hand. Rubbing the leaves on their cheeks makes them rosy. Later, you can brew tea with the same leaves and rid yourself of a troublesome husband. The best choice, of course, is arsenic, but finding some is nearly impossible, and making the extract is difficult."

"Then why did you think she'd been poisoned?" Fawkes asked.

"Because you aren't dealing with a professional. Dropping a block of stone and cutting a saddle strap is pathetic, lazy work. I don't even think the killer is a novice. What you're dealing with is a first-time idiot. A lot of people have heard azaleas are poisonous. So if you're a moron, but looking for a means to bury someone, those pretty blossoms would be hard to resist. I'm guessing the countess was sick recently?"

Fawkes nodded. "We were enjoying breakfast, and she complained about a burning in her mouth. She was eating a pastry at the time, then she drooled a bit and vomited. Disgusting."

"She has a taster now?" Royce asked.

"Yes."

"And what makes you think that this feckless would-be killer has given up and hired a professional?"

"Rumors, mostly. Well, that and the fact that nothing has happened lately. I don't know anything about these sorts of things, but my guess is it would take time to find the right man, have him travel down here, and plan the deed. That's why I'm glad you arrived. So how would *you* go about killing Countess Dulgath?"

Royce shook his head. "I don't know—yet. You're right about proper planning. Things aren't to be rushed if they're to be done right."

"When *will* you know?"

"I need to get a feel for this place, observe Lady Dulgath's habits, find her weaknesses and vulnerabilities. A good assassin is like a good tailor—everything is fit to order."

"So this could take a while." Fawkes sounded disappointed.

"Well, like you said, if it didn't she'd be dead already, so I wouldn't complain. Given that I'm in a race here, I should get to work." He turned to Hadrian. "Can you get us a room or something in the village while I take a look around?"

"You can stay in the castle," Fawkes said. "There are extra rooms, and I'm sure I can convince Wells about the value of having you there."

Royce shook his head. "I'd rather retain my autonomy and perspective. But that does bring up a point. We need an alibi, an excuse for being here."

Hadrian looked around them. "What about horse traders or trainers—something like that?"

Fawkes shook his head. "In these parts, horses are our religion. And a layman can't fool the devout."

"Besides," Royce said, "it has to allow us to poke around and ask questions without drawing attention."

"Maybe Payne could say you're deacons of the church?"

"Most of the town saw me flash my swords," Hadrian said. "By now the other half has heard the story. One guy thought we might be Seret because we were helping Pastor Payne. Could we play off that?"

"Swords? Helping Payne? What are you talking about?" Fawkes asked.

"When we arrived, the townsfolk were going to tar-and-feather him. Seeing as he was our client, I thought it was best if they didn't," Royce said.

Fawkes nodded. "The people around here are not overjoyed with the church, though that will change now that Bishop Parnell is building a ministry. I wouldn't advise posing as a Seret. The military arm of the church are fanatics and its best not to get on the wrong side of their kind. But that does give me an idea. What about…"

"What?"

"Well, we could use the incident to our advantage. You saw a crime being committed and stepped in. We'll make you sheriffs."

"W-what?" Royce asked.

"Yes, of course. I'll talk to Knox."

"I won't work for him," Royce declared.

"In a way, you already do," Fawkes said. "But you're right, he didn't seem too taken with you. That's fine. I'll tell you what. I'll say that the two of you are special royal constables sent by the king himself to investigate attempts made on Lady Dulgath's life. It makes perfect sense. Vincent is scheduled to visit here in the next few days to review the fief, accept Lady Dulgath's pledge of fealty, and renew the homage. It's only sensible he would want to send his own men to ensure his security, if not hers. Yes…" Fawkes grinned. "Two royal constables—you'd have authority to go anywhere and question anyone."

"How do we prove it?"

"I'll vouch for you and talk to Wells and Knox—convince them it'll help protect Lady Dulgath, and they'll need to back me up if anyone asks. I can be quite persuasive when I need to. We'll draw up some official-looking papers with Vincent's signature. Almost everyone here is illiterate, but if it looks official, and if I, Wells, and Knox confirm your story, they'll believe."

"Constables?" Royce muttered more to himself than them. He'd played roles in the past: shopkeepers, tradesmen, soldiers, tax collectors. Once he'd even impersonated an executioner—he was good at that one. Never had he imagined acting as the chief law enforcement official of a realm. The notion left him unsettled, like being asked to eat human flesh.

"Appropriate, too," Fawkes said, and threw his arms out to remind them of their surroundings. When they didn't show a hint of understanding, he explained, "The word *constable* comes down from imperial times, when the officer responsible for keeping the horses was the *count of the stable*. It's like a sign from Novron."

Royce agreed. He just wasn't certain what was on that sign.

Chapter Six
THE HOUSE AND THE BEDCHAMBER

While riding by himself back to town, Hadrian concluded something wasn't right about the village of Brecken Dale. He felt it in that faint, absent way he noticed the first kiss of a cold— nothing specific, nothing he could point to, just a general sense of things being askew. Seeing the pretty berries along the trail reminded him of what Royce had said about them being poisonous. *Could he have been on to something or was that just another example of Royce being Royce?* Over the last couple of years, Hadrian had witnessed many Royce-being-Royce moments and developed a truism about his partner's unique brand of paranoia and cynicism. *Offered help* was either an insult or a ploy. *Needed help* was a con or a ploy. Pretty much *everything* was suspected of being a ploy of some sort, except perhaps *admitted exploitation*, which Royce oddly identified as honesty.

Believing the worst of people, of the world in general, was a trap too easy to fall into. Hadrian had fought beside soldiers who'd developed similar views. Such men saw evil and virtue as concepts of childhood naïveté. In their minds, there was no such thing as murder, and killing was just something you did when circumstances warranted.

A terrible way to live. What good is a world—what is the point of living—if generosity and kindness are myths?

Royce, like everyone, saw what he looked for, what he expected to see. Hadrian looked for goodness and believed he was better for doing so.

Who doesn't want to live in a brighter world?

He rode along a short wall that decorated rather than protected one of the many stacked-stone farmhouses. Farmers always built from what was at hand, and being tucked between the toes of old mountains, the fields had to be a veritable quarry of rocks. As a blacksmith's son, Hadrian had never suffered the trials of turning the soil in Hintindar, but he knew many who did. Most came to his father with mangled plows, battered mattocks, and anguished faces. Rocks were as much a curse to farmers as the weather.

Only two things can be reliably grown—rocks and weeds. He'd heard the saying repeated by the villeins in his childhood village of Hintindar whenever spring threw up another crop of each. And every year the walls surrounding the fields got higher and longer. There had been a time when he wondered if those walls would seal him in.

Noting the height of the wall he now rode beside, Hadrian couldn't help but wonder why it was so short. Once more that feeling of strangeness descended, underscoring the notion that everything about the town was off, askew.

No, not just askew, awry.

Approaching the twin oaks that marked the southern boundary of the town, he noted how they resembled a pair of porch pillars. These broad columns, however, were clad in dark bark and hid beneath a canopy that cast deep, wide shadows. The hollow—the *dale*—where the village clustered was a leafy pocket at the base of the ravine where that singular road from the outside entered the Valley of Dulgath.

Outside. Already Hadrian thought of things in such terms as *here* and *beyond here*, as if he were in a different place from everywhere else, from *normal.* On this, his second visit to Brecken Dale, he thought the gathered ivy wasn't simply decorative and pretty but a blanket that hid everything. The sound of Dancer's hooves on the stone road echoed in the hollow.

Everything echoes. Noises bounced back off the ravine. *Not even sound escapes.*

When he reached Pastor Payne's ramshackle hovel, the old man was outside, pulling loose boards. More than a few had come free and teetered in a stack next to him.

"Hey there," Hadrian called. "Could you recommend an inn? I'm going to get a room for myself and Royce."

"This town doesn't have one. At least none I could recommend. Your best bet would be Fassbinder's place."

"What's that?"

"Fassbinder is a soap maker, but his two boys died last year. It's where I stayed my first night, but now Bishop Parnell has arranged for this"—he gestured toward the shack—"*wonderful abode.* He's assured me the new church will be the envy of the region."

Hadrian tried to imagine Royce taking supper with Fassbinder and his wife. He didn't relish night after night of awkward silence.

"How about something a bit more *public.* A tavern with some lodging, perhaps?"

"There's Caldwell House, but as I said, I wouldn't recommend it."

"Why wouldn't I want to go there? Do they have bugs or something?"

"Worse. It's down by the river near the square where we first met." Payne's arm stretched out, one bony finger aimed downhill toward the center of the village, where the ivy and old oaks grew the thickest. "A house of sin and debauchery."

"They sell beer then?"

The pastor's response was an irritated *pfft*, which Hadrian took as yes.

"I stay away from the river. The far side is godless; that's the *bad side*."

"What's over there?" Hadrian lifted his head. A depression snaked through the far side of town, where he imagined a river ran. Beyond roofs and gables, he saw only trees and a hill.

"Nothing—nothing of any worth."

Hadrian had trouble reading clergy in general; they always managed to project a disconnected yet knowledgeable attitude—less than helpful when gauging reliability.

"Fassbinder is up that way," Payne told Hadrian, pointing toward the majority of the freshly planted fields to the south.

"Thanks." He dismounted, preferring to walk through the remainder of the village and guessing Dancer appreciated the gesture.

The sun was in the middle of the sky and warm—another beautiful day in Maranon—but few people were out. A pair of boys and a dog chased sheep in a high meadow up the ravine, and a woman drew water from the central well, but he didn't see anyone else. Two doors closed as he approached, and the shutters on nearly every house abutting the street were sealed.

He hoped the pastor wasn't watching him as he turned downhill toward the river.

The House and the Bedchamber

On that day the village market was open. The dale's version was small, airy, and lined with stalls and carts selling salt, spices, leather goods, candles, copper pots, and brass buttons. Caldwell House wasn't hard to find. The building sat on the corner of THIS WAY and THAT, which was a confusing sign, given that five separate lanes came together at the same intersection; two, however, were only small pathways. One of these led to a reclusive home surrounded by a stand of trees, while the other marked the entrance to what Hadrian thought must be Caldwell House, easily the largest building in the village.

The place was tall, a full four stories if you counted the three dormers and five gables built with all the planning of an afterthought. It, too, was made of fieldstone supported by thick timbers. Like everything else, it was covered with thick ivy. The place was a living plant with doors and two smoking chimneys.

No sign was posted at the entrance or from the eaves. But the door was open, and three men stood in a cluster on the porch, smoking long black pipes. They scrutinized him; not one smiled.

"Excuse me, is this an inn?" When no one replied, he added, "You know, a hostelry, an auberge, a lodge, a way house?"

Just stares.

"A place where people rent rooms for the night to sleep in?"

The group puffed and walked back inside, leaving a cloud behind.

Not to be deterred from the possibility of a good mug of beer—even a reasonable imitation thereof—Hadrian tied Dancer to one of the porch posts. He clapped the horse's neck. "Hang in there. I'll see if I can find something for you, too."

He walked around the railing and up the stairs onto the porch.

"Don't mind them," a voice said. A moment later a young woman stepped out of the gloomy interior of the house, emerging from the ivy-wreathed hole.

Red hair—lots of red hair.

Divided down the middle of her head, the woman's ginger tresses spilled to her waist after first cascading off bare shoulders. Small and dangerously pretty, she wore a gown elegant in design but not material. Black felt pulled together with leather laces formed the plunging front, while the sleeves were made of coarse wool. Side panels—hidden beneath her arms—were made of suede, and the cuffs and pleats were comprised of stitched together burlap scraps. Not remotely refined, the patchwork dress was a bold attempt to imitate the wardrobe of a lady using the means of a waif. Yet unlike any chaste noble garment, this concoction of wool and leather greedily gripped the woman's body, straining the imperfect stitching.

"No?" he asked, willing his eyes to remain on her face, not a poor alternative given her friendly smile.

"No." She reached up, gathering her hair with both hands and casting it behind her like a net. "You're the one who stopped the feathering last night, right?" She didn't wait for an answer, obviously didn't need one. "Some folk are holding a grudge."

"Not you, though?"

"Wasn't there. Heard about it. People talk in a small village. You thirsty?"

"Yes, but right now I'm looking for a room and a place for my horse. So, *is* this an inn?"

"Caldwell House is pretty much whatever you need her to be." She winked. Her age was difficult to guess. The dress said young, but her confident tone made him think she was a year or two older than himself.

"Do you…work here?"

"What? Like a whore or something?" There wasn't any tone of offense and no emphasis on the word *whore*. Just a question asked in a delightfully casual manner, as if they were discussing lemonade or the lack of rain.

He absolutely had been thinking prostitute, but given her reply, he felt it safer to retreat. "Barmaid, perhaps?" That, too, might have been an insult. She could be like Gwen and own the place.

"An entertainer." She made a little hop, threw her hands up, and spun around in an elegant twirl that made the hem of the gown flare. "My name's Dodge." She pulled at her hair. "*Scarlett* Dodge. My mother had all the creativity of an eight-year-old with a spotted puppy."

He chuckled. "Nice to meet you, Spot. I'm Hadrian."

"Pleasure is mine." She made an equally elegant curtsey. "You're from up north, then?"

"Most recently from Melengar."

Her eyes brightened, and the smile grew even more inviting. "Fancy that. I came down from Warric—Colnora, to be exact. But you probably guessed I wasn't a native, on account of how pretty I talk." She chuckled. "And my lovely complexion"—she held out a freckled arm and rubbed—"which I share with the bellies of dead fish on a hot day." She made another smart spin, turning her back on him but trailing a hand that beckoned with a curled finger. "C'mon in, Hadrian of Melengar. I'll let you buy me a drink, and we can regale each other with stories of our adventures in foreign lands."

Hadrian glanced back at Dancer. "It won't take long. I promise."

The inside of Caldwell House was about as pleasant a place as Hadrian could have hoped for. Overhead ran heavy beams of rough-cut wood from which a wagon-wheel chandelier hung. The place was brimming with pewter mugs, fishing rods, forgotten coats, burlap bags, garlic sprigs, and the occasional spider web. Someone had carved the initials W. A. in the center post. More initials, words, and other scars marred the six round tables and the elbowed bar, behind which rested a rack of three barrels, one marked BEER, another ALE, and the last WHISKEY. On a chalkboard was written the words: FISH ARE GOOD, BUT GILL'S THE BEST.

Nine patrons occupied the main room. The three men from the porch were now at the bar; four others sat at a table in the center, and two more stood to the rear, holding tankards. One waved at Scarlett, who smiled. "Hey, Brett, when'd you get back?"

"This morning," Brett replied. He was one of those standing, talking to a fellow across from him who was leaning with his back to the initialed post, one foot bent up and resting on it.

Scarlett trotted across the floor and gave the man a hug—a polite, friendly sort. No kiss preceded or followed. Brett had the typical black hair and dark eyes of Maranon men, so he wasn't her brother. But he didn't appear to be a husband or lover, either. That was good. Hadrian recognized the four men at the table as Bull Neck and company. That was bad. They sat hunched over drinks, elbows on the table, their heads close. Luckily none looked at him, and he tried not to stare at them, either. Like an abandoned boat, Hadrian continued to drift toward the bar, where a man with a short beard and rolled-up sleeves wiped his hands on a towel. He didn't seem to notice Hadrian, either, as he, and almost everyone else, was looking at Scarlett.

"Have a drink with us," she cooed to Brett.

The not-her-brother shook his head. "Got a wagon to unpack, honey."

A playful push and pout followed. "What about you, Larmand?" she asked the one holding up the post.

"Sorry, Dodge, Brett needs muscle." He held up a bent arm, flexing.

"What does that have to do with you?" Her comment brought a communal *oooh* from some of the others. "Suit yourself."

She swept back to Hadrian's side and faced the bartender. Putting a hand on Hadrian's shoulder, she said, "Wag, this man is buying two ryes and a pair with foam."

"That so?" the bartender asked.

"Sure," Hadrian replied. "Why not."

"Gill!" the man with the towel shouted, and a boy came out from an archway. "Fetch Scarlett a bottle from the cellar."

Hadrian pointed at the barrel marked WHISKEY, puzzled.

"I assumed you weren't a cheap bastard," Scarlett said as Gill went down the steps to their left and used a key hanging around his neck to enter a small door. "Wag knows what I like."

While Gill fetched the bottle, the bartender used one hand to hold two pewter mugs beneath the barrel spigot marked BEER. "Wagner Drayton," he said, extending his hand while still holding the beers in the other.

"Hadrian Blackwater." He shook and received the drinks as a reward.

Only a truly forgiving or desperate woman would consider Wagner a handsome man. His face suffered from numerous pockmarks and deep wrinkles. The latter cut across his brow and added unnecessary dimension to his cheeks. The beard was likely an effort to cover his face. He kept it short, but it, too, was unsightly, as it grew in patches. He was smiling.

Well, that's something.

Scarlett pulled over a pair of high-backed wooden stools. "Have pity on your paws." She clapped the face of a seat and hopped up on her own, kicking her heels up onto the footrest that ran around the base of the bar.

Hadrian pulled off his spadone, propping it next to him. He sat down and picked up the mug before him.

"To a fine meeting." Scarlett rammed his mug hard enough to send foam over the edge.

The beer was good—warm, rich, and far from flat.

"So what do you do here, Scarlett?" Hadrian asked, hoping to learn more about this woman who freely hugged men, dressed like a patchwork princess, and demanded only the best whiskey.

"I told you, I entertain."

"Give him a taste," Wagner said, picking up three shot glasses, which he tossed at her.

Scarlett caught each with practiced ease and began juggling, sending them higher and higher. She stood up, moved to an open space, and began catching them behind her back. Continuing their rotation, she rested each on her forehead momentarily, and then, without Hadrian seeing it happen, there were only two glasses—then just one. She walked back to her seat, the final glass vanishing into thin air.

"Impressive." He applauded.

"Thank you." She bowed before hopping back on her chair.

Gill returned with a dark, corked bottle, plucking straw off it as he came. The boy handed it to Wagner.

"Glasses, darling." The bartender smiled at Scarlett, who reached up toward Hadrian's head and pulled a shot glass from behind his ear. She placed it on the bar while reaching up for another. By the time she produced the third glass, Wagner had poured two shots of amber liquid.

"Some of the best rye whiskey in Maranon," Wagner said, re-corking the bottle.

Scarlett lifted hers and smelled it. Her eyes closed as a dreamy look took her and an alluring smile spread across her lips. "I love this stuff."

"That's why I have to keep it locked in the cellar." Wagner pointed at her and tapped his nose at the same time.

"What will we drink to this time?" she asked.

"To whiskey-loving women who juggle," Hadrian supplied.

She grinned, and they clicked glasses more gingerly this time. She took the whole shot in one swallow.

Hadrian did the same. "I have to admit, I wasn't expecting such a welcome reception after my friend and I interrupted things."

"Where's your friend?"

"He'll be along. Sent me ahead to get a room. Which reminds me. Wagner?"

"Yes, sir?" The bartender popped a bright smile on his ugly lips.

"Could I get a room with two beds and a stall for my horse?"

"Absolutely. Horse out front, is it?"

"Yep."

"Gill!" Wagner yelled. The boy was there in a flash, and Hadrian was starting to see why Gill was the best. "Take care of the man's horse."

"So tell me, are my partner and I the only new people in town? Anyone else visiting?" Hadrian asked Wagner.

"Been slow," Wagner replied. "Why? You expecting to meet up with someone?"

"Me? No. Just making conversation is all. And now that I think about it, what's the deal with Pastor Payne? What'd he do to deserve a tarring?"

Wagner shook his head. "Nothing. It's not *him;* it's what he's trying to sell. We don't need the Nyphron Church in these parts."

Scarlett switched to a polite smile as she crossed her legs. "Dulgath has an old tradition that dates back to imperial days. The church hasn't bothered with us until now. Brecken Moor is where the Monks of Maribor were founded."

"Wait." Hadrian stopped her, confused. The whiskey had hit harder than he expected. "I thought this was Brecken *Dale.*"

"It is," Wagner said, then pointed across the bar, as if Hadrian could tell what direction that was. He couldn't; the rush of the drinks on an empty stomach, combined with the twists and turns of the village roads, had left him baffled. "Brecken Moor is the old monastery up on the hill, just outside town."

"Oh yeah, Payne mentioned something about a monastery, didn't speak too highly of it."

"Up north, the two sects tolerate each other, but down here…" Scarlett shook her head. "Like Wag said, we aren't buying what they're selling."

"Which is?" Hadrian asked.

She waved a dismissive hand. "That crap about Novron and his heirs. If they had their way, we'd return to imperial rule, everyone bowing down to one man. We like things just as they are. Especially now that Lady Dulgath is going to be in charge. Don't get me wrong, the earl was fine, a good man, really. But Lady Dulgath is something else, something special."

Scarlett held out her glass, and Wagner poured another drink. She continued, "A lot of changes are going on outside our little corner of Elan. But you'll find that people around here like our traditions. I've heard rumors that the other provinces of Maranon have switched allegiances from Monarchist to Imperialist. Swanwick was the most recent."

Hadrian nodded, and the room swam. He checked his beer and found that most of it was still in his mug.

While it was true he hadn't eaten in hours, he wasn't such a lightweight that a single shot—

I'm sweating, too. Something isn't right.

He scanned the room and noticed that the four at the table had gotten up. The two who were in such a hurry to unload a wagon had moved to the door but forgot to leave. They were no longer looking at Scarlett. Everyone was looking at him.

"What'd you put in the drink?" he asked her softly.

"Don't worry," she said. "It won't kill you, but we are going to finish what you stopped. Only this time you'll be tarred and feathered right alongside that bastard Payne. When you see Bishop Parnell, tell him we don't need the Nyphron Church around here, and anyone he sends will get the same treatment."

Hadrian got to his feet and drew his swords, but the room was soup, his arms lazy, his hands going numb. *Probably fed me some azaleas.*

Bull Neck charged forward, and Hadrian made a wild swing at him.

"Leave him," Scarlett said. "He'll pass out soon enough."

Anger bloomed, but years of training helped Hadrian push it away. He had to think, but his mind was spinning like the room, and he was running out of time. He considered making a run for his horse, but Gill would have taken Dancer away. The kid was already back, and Brett and Larmand were guarding the door.

Out of options.

Hadrian's vision narrowed as the poison worked through him. He was weaving, struggling to keep standing.

What will Royce say when he finds out. What will he do?

Hadrian looked sympathetically at Scarlett. She hadn't meant him any serious harm; she just wanted him to leave. But Royce was another matter, and she had no idea what he was capable of. That single sobering thought provided him an instant of clarity, and in that moment, he saw the sign again.

FISH ARE GOOD, BUT GILL'S THE BEST.

The kid was back near the cellar steps, watching him, waiting like everyone else to see him fall. Hadrian dropped his swords. They couldn't help him now; only Gill could.

Gill's the best.

With a sloppy stagger, Hadrian grabbed the kid. Behind him, people shouted, but he wasn't listening to them anymore. All his focus was on one thing—the key that Gill had around his neck.

With a yank, which must have hurt, the chain broke. Gill probably screamed, but Hadrian couldn't spare the attention. His sight was already dimming as he nearly fell down the steps. Luckily the boy had neglected to lock the door. He rolled into the small room filled with hay-packed straw, slammed the door closed, and with shaking hands struggled to put the key into the lock. If he could just seal himself in, then...

Fish are good and Gill's the best, but now it's time to take a rest.

The words began to repeat stupidly in his head. Then they began to jumble.

Resting fish and Gill...how best is now to rest?

Hadrian, who by then was sweating a puddle, was happy to find the cool stone of the floor and lay his face on it.

Gill the fish...rest is best...time is now...it feels so good to...

Royce explored the grounds of Castle Dulgath. No one questioned his presence; no one even noticed as he studied gates, windows, and walls. The lack of security was appalling, and the castle wasn't much better. Roughly squared stones were stacked without mortar and covered with lichen, moss, and ivy. The place practically wheezed with old age. One tower at the southern corner had fallen, and no one had bothered to rebuild it. The pile of collapsed stones had lain forgotten for some time, judging by the thick roots of the trees growing over them.

A desolate place. The thought lingered in Royce's head as he circled the point. *Nice that way.*

He imagined few would share his opinion, Hadrian being among the least likely. But Royce found beauty in the windswept rock and the constant battle it waged against the sea. Stripped bare but standing strong, the promontory displayed an insolent resilience he appreciated. Why anyone would erect a castle there, he had no idea. Strategically, it made no sense. Dulgath was miles from anything notable and had nothing to defend or protect.

Traffic did pass along the coast, but Castle Dulgath was inland from the infamous Point of Mann, where ships went to die. The name came from Captain Silas Mann, who'd discovered the dangerous reef when his ship plowed into it and sank with all hands. A more common and colorful rumor declared the landmark's name had its origins in the prayers of drowning sailors who were asking Maribor for life's meaning. The treacherous, ship-sinking obstacle protected the coast, making the castle unnecessary. Yet another reason its location made no sense.

The pinnacle of stone the castle sat on, an upthrusting slab of nearly vertical basalt rock, was ideal for a defensive fortress, but Castle Dulgath made little use of it. The entrance through the front wall wasn't much more formidable than a garden's gate. Made of simple wood with iron braces, the gates stood less than ten feet in height. Any kid with a fruit crate could climb over them—a theory that wouldn't be tested, since the entryway was never closed, much less locked.

Just as well, Royce concluded, given that none of the towers were built for defense. Castle Dulgath possessed no arrow loops, barbican, or curtain wall, and not a single murder hole. Even the crenellated battlements appeared to have been built more for style than for use. Either the builders had no thought of defense—odd, considering the isolated perch they placed the castle on—or they didn't know the first thing about fortress defenses.

After the sun had sunk into the sea, Royce moved along the parapet in earnest, imagining himself as an assassin with a contract to eliminate the countess. In many ways, he wished he were. The job would be insanely easy. Aside from the lack of a gatehouse or closed gates, there were precious few guards. The tiny Hemley Estate with Ralph and Mister Hipple was more heavily, and competently, watched. The castle's courtyard went dark with the setting sun. No attempt was made to set a lantern or light a torch. *And the ivy!* Old and entrenched, the plant grew everywhere, the branch-thick vines making excellent ladders.

He didn't have the slightest trouble reaching the tower, where an open window gave him access to—he struggled not to laugh—Lady Dulgath's bedroom. The chamber was paneled in dark-stained oak, had a little hearth all its own, and a luxurious bed with a red velvet canopy and silk sheets. She had four freestanding wardrobes, a dressing table, a wash table, three wood-and-brass trunks, a full-length mirror that tilted on a swivel, a table littered with seashells, shelves filled with books, a painting of an elderly man dressed in black and green, two chairs—one with a cushioned stool before it—and a set of thick candles, three-quarters melted.

She wasn't in the room. He didn't expect her to be. If this had been a real job, he'd have waited until late and slipped in while she slept. Then, placing a hand over her mouth—to hold her still and keep her silent—he'd slit the lady's throat. The red covers would help hide the blood. There would be a dark stain, but it could just as easily be spilled water. He'd pull the covers up to her throat to cover the wound.

Royce preferred to be neat when he didn't have a point to make. He'd wash off any blood in the basin, assuming he got some on him, which was unusual but did happen. With everything in order, he would climb back down the unwatched ivy, walk along the unmanned parapet, and saunter out the unguarded, and always open, gates.

It's a wonder she's still alive.

Footsteps made Royce slip between a pair of wardrobes as the chamber door opened. Nysa Dulgath entered, guarding a candle flame with a cupped hand. She set the light down, closed the door behind her, and then stopped. Pressing down on her left heel, she spun upon it like a child's top.

"What are *you* doing here?" she asked, but her eyes weren't on him—they were searching.

Royce hesitated. He was good at hiding, always had been. In the dark, no one ever saw him. The only light in the room was the single candle, hardly enough to give him away. Her tone also threw him. Too relaxed, too calm. If she really saw him hiding in her private chambers, if she'd spotted him, the pampered girl would have begun caterwauling not unlike Mister Hipple's little fit. The inflection of her question wasn't without emotion, of course: She was decidedly annoyed.

A moment of silence followed. She huffed and folded her arms roughly, as if that might mean something. She then shifted her weight first to her left and then her right hip. "Are you going to answer me?"

She was staring directly at him then, an indignant frown on her lips.

How can she see me?

No point in pretending he wasn't there or that she hadn't caught him, he replied, "My job."

"Your job entails lurking in my bedroom?"

"I didn't expect you to be here."

"Where else would I be at night?"

"I—"

"And why are you here at all? Have you been going through my clothes?" Once again she pivoted on that left heel, moved to a wardrobe, and flung open the doors, sending Royce into retreat.

"Why would I go through your clothes?"

"I haven't the slightest idea. But it's really all that's here, so why else would you be in my room?"

"I was hired to determine how a professional assassin might go about murdering you."

"You think hiding in my wardrobe might be a good tactic, do you?"

"I wasn't in your wardrobe."

"I can only hope that's the truth." She slapped the doors shut.

Such an odd girl.

That was always true of those with noble blood. They failed to act as any normal person would. For a time, Royce had been convinced that nobles were another species and that the idea of *blue blood* made them different from others, just as they claimed. While they boasted about being superior, Royce always found the opposite to be true. Nobles were born without the survival instincts granted every other living thing. Believing themselves special, they were oblivious to dangers and surprised when catastrophe followed. Lady Dulgath was a shining example.

For a moment, he thought she was about to show a degree of intelligence when she picked up the candle. He expected her to flee. Instead, she held it up and came closer.

"Pull back the hood," she told him.

"Not that again. And let me explain in advance—a stay in your dungeon really isn't going to happen."

Her eyes narrowed, and a smile formed on her lips—not a friendly one, more of an amused, curious grin. "So sure of yourself. Your problem is that you lack the capacity to imagine a young woman could be a threat." She lowered the candle, accepting, he hoped, that the hood was staying up. "I know that particular arrogance all too well. Assumption of superiority is quite dangerous."

"When I was first hired, I wondered why anyone would want to kill you. I don't anymore. Honestly, I'm surprised there isn't a line."

Lady Dulgath laughed, nearly blowing out the candle. She crossed to one of the tables and set it down.

Royce continued, "I'm not kidding. The good news—for me anyway—is I'm not here to protect you, find the assassin, or even determine who hired him. That's Knox's job. Given this castle's security, and—as I mentioned—the fact that it could be literally *anyone,* I don't envy the sheriff. He's doomed to failure. If you don't already have one, make out a last will and testament as soon as possible. That way at least you won't leave a mess for others to clean up."

"I wonder who your parents are," she said, leaving Royce baffled.

"What?"

"Your parents—who are they?"

"Hatred and disillusionment, how about you?"

She smiled at him, the same unperturbed grin, as if he were great fun.

"You know," Royce said, "most young ladies would be terrified to find someone like me in their room."

"You know, most men would be terrified to be caught uninvited in the bedroom of a countess, but then…" She took a slow step forward. "You're not a man, are you?"

Royce took a step back. He wasn't sure why. The woman before him was small, thin, and delicate. And while the gown she wore, with its high collar and long sleeves, wasn't provocative, it did emphasize her feminine frailty.

"Does your partner know?" she asked.

"Know what?"

"What you are?"

"What am I?"

She smiled again.

"Is this a guessing game?" he asked, annoyed.

"I was only—" She stopped and her eyes widened. "You don't know." She clasped her hands before her, touching fingertips to her lips while grinning. "You have no idea, do you?" She looked him up and down and nodded. "You hide it well, and you're still young. In your first century?"

"You're a very odd girl."

"And what about you?" She let out a childlike giggle, which somehow managed to sound frightening. "No human could have caught the paint bottle Sherwood threw. You didn't even see it. You *heard* it. And the speed you displayed was beyond that of a mere man." She turned and blew out the candle. "I can hardly see you, but you have no trouble seeing me. The starlight entering the window is enough to reveal the color of my eyes."

That wasn't a question, and she spoke with complete confidence. "Heat and cold don't bother you nearly as much as they do your friend, but ice, snow, and boats—oh, ships! You never go sailing."

The House and the Bedchamber

Royce was pleased the candle was out, but not so certain she couldn't see him. She seemed to see him all too clearly, and he didn't know how.

"No, Mister Royce Melborn, your parents weren't hate and disillusionment," she said, her pale, white face lit by starlight that did, indeed, revealed the brown of her eyes. "At least one of your parents is what people call an elf. I think you sh—"

Chapter Seven
A GAME OF TEN FINGERS

Royce had never been one for etiquette. Appearing in the bedchamber of the countess had to rank high on anyone's list of faux pas; leaving while she was still mid-sentence was probably worse. He was halfway back to Brecken Dale before it even occurred to him to wonder why he'd done it.

She'd rattled him.

This was the only explanation he could come up with. A spoiled, noble girl had shaken him so badly he'd run away.

Run away.

He'd fled from a young woman who had a disturbing way of looking at things. On the way back to town, a loop of two words ran through his mind: *Not possible.* Every once in a while he'd toss in a colorful adjective or add: *The bitch is nuts.* Mostly, he gritted his teeth, breathed heavily through his nose, and strangled the reins between fists until the leather cried. The only consolation about Lady Dulgath's pronouncement was that Hadrian hadn't been with him, hadn't heard.

A Game of Ten Fingers

At least one of your parents is what people call an elf.

Elves were as respected as cockroaches, pond scum, and bread mold. Once, very long ago, they had been slaves of the First Empire. When it fell, they were freed but had nowhere to go. Since then, the slaves-turned-beggars clustered in the worst parts of every city. Dumb as bugs drawn to a campfire, they crowded in cesspools holding out hands and pleading for scraps. Every day they kissed the filthy feet of those who spit on them.

Royce had been wrong that night when he'd debated whether dogs or dwarves were the worst. His answer should have been, elves—no doubt about it. They were just so low on the list, he usually left them off it entirely.

I can hardly see you, but you have no trouble seeing me. The starlight entering the window is enough to reveal the color of my eyes.

She was right, even though she couldn't have known. Builders knew the best ways to destroy buildings, and Royce prided himself on breaking down falsehoods. He saw through deceit, flattery, and fake smiles. He followed logic, and when something didn't add up, he knew the sandy grains of a lie sat at the bottom of the foundation. But this time everything made sense; everything added up. He just didn't want to accept the truth.

Royce had never known his parents. He had been told he was abandoned in a muddy sewer in the city of Ratibor when just an infant. Other kids had taunted him, called him an *elf*. He was small, thin enough, and certainly looked every bit as destitute. Being young, he'd believed them. When he got older, he realized the children were wrong. *Elf* was simply the most despicable word they could come up with.

Over the decades he'd witnessed so much inhumanity that he'd come to accept his abandonment as typical, one more brace in a consistent framework. The question wasn't: *How could my mother leave me in a sewer,* but, rather: *Why aren't more children abandoned in the mud?* Just dumb luck. He'd built an existence on the belief of an unsympathetic world, but after fleeing Lady Dulgath's bedroom, he felt that underpinning crumble. If she was right, it would explain a great deal. Royce still believed in the callousness of life—but perhaps brutality wasn't handed out so capriciously. He hadn't been abandoned because the world was cruel; he'd been cast away because he was an elf.

When he arrived at Payne's door, the clergyman sensed the thief's mood and didn't bother inviting him in. Instead, the pastor directed Royce to Caldwell House, saying he'd tried to warn Hadrian away but had seen him go in that direction.

Royce arrived at the place Payne had indicated, but he didn't find a sign, just an ivy-covered porch. Three men stood together near the open door, watching him as he tied up his horse.

"This Caldwell House?"

They ignored him.

Royce leapt the guardrail onto the porch, and the men scattered.

"Don't mind them," a young woman said as she stepped out of the gloomy interior of the ivy-covered building.

Royce turned toward her, and the face beneath the tumble of red hair went ghostly white. Her eyes and mouth opened wide, and she waved her palms like little white flags. "Bugger me!" she exclaimed.

"No thanks," Royce said. "Not in the mood, and you're not my type."

She backed up, stumbling over her own feet while trying to get away. Her reaction was odd, but the absolute horror in her eyes tipped him off to trouble, and Royce slowed down. He remembered her from his days in the Black Diamond, though as little more than a face. Known as Feldspar, she'd been a low-level sweeper, a grunt in the Diamond's army who worked in a team on one of Colnora's less productive corners. He seemed to recall her working with a guy who went by the guild name of Glitter, who drew in a crowd with juggling and magic acts. The real sleight of hand went on behind the scenes.

Being scared of him was reasonable considering the miniature war he'd waged on the guild a few years back, but a more immediate fear radiated from her face. Surprise, even dread, would've been expected, but Feldspar exhibited an expression normally only seen in those *expecting* a visit from him. She radiated guilt, and Royce followed her retreat into the tavern.

Hadrian.

A quick look around revealed no sign of him. He might have gone to their rented room, but that seemed unlikely given the presence of the bar. His partner should be sitting, drinking, and chatting up a pretty—

"Where is he?" Royce asked.

Feldspar was still backing up, but slowly. *Smart.* Everyone knows you never run from a predator; it just invites an attack.

Royce counted eight others in the bar. The same herd of four who'd wanted to tar the pastor sat at a table, trying their best not to be noticed, and yet they kept casting concerned glances. Two more leaned on a post, watching. The bartender and a kid who likely worked there were equally interested.

"I didn't know it was you. I swear to Maribor, I had no idea. If I had known…"

"Go on," Royce said, following her into the room. "If you had known…what?"

She realized her mistake and closed her mouth.

"Dodge?" one of the men near the post called, and two more at the table pushed out chairs that scraped across the stone floor.

Wasn't supposed to go this way. They're just realizing the play has stopped following the script.

Royce darted forward and caught a fistful of red hair, jerking Feldspar back and kicking the feet out from under her.

The rest of the boys at the table hopped up, and the two near the post started across the room, coming at them.

"Stop!" he ordered, and placed Alverstone's blade to her neck. "Everyone take a seat. I'm guessing she's not the only one who can tell me what I want to know. When she's struggling to breathe through a new hole in her throat, the rest of you will be more cooperative."

"You little—" one started to say.

"Sit down!" Feldspar screamed. "He's not screwing around. He'll do it."

The room froze. Royce was the first to move. Hauling her by her hair, he dragged the woman across the floor to the open door and pulled it shut. He jerked the bolt across. "There," he said. "No one leaves until we have a little talk."

No one sat.

"Sit your asses down—he doesn't ask twice!" she shouted.

Everyone found a chair.

"Okay now." Royce pulled her head back to look into her eyes. "Seeing as how I know you pride yourself on sleight of hand, we're going to play a game of Ten Fingers."

She whimpered.

"Ah, you remember how it's played, good. I wasn't planning on explaining it." He dragged her to a table. "C'mon, I'm not the patient sort."

Feldspar placed a shaking hand palm down on the table.

"Spread your fingers. You wouldn't want to lose two at once by accident, would you?"

"What the bloody—" the fellow in the orange tunic started to ask.

"Shut up!" she screamed. "Just shut up! And don't you move. Please, for the love of Maribor, don't anyone move."

She had tears in her eyes, and the table, which wasn't quite level, quivered. The uneven legs made an unnerving, hollow *dud, dud, dud* sound.

Royce set the tip of Alverstone between her right pinky and ring finger. The mirrored blade reflected the room. "First question: Where is Hadrian?"

"In the cellar, over there." Knowing the rules, she indicated with her head.

Royce lifted and dropped the knife between her ring and middle finger. "Second: Is he alive?"

"Yes, just sleeping."

"Lucky, lucky lady." He placed the knife tip between her middle and index fingers, both of which were shaking so badly he thought she might cut herself. It'd be easy to do; Alverstone wasn't a forgiving blade. "Third: Why is he in the cellar?"

"He locked himself in after realizing I drugged him."

"Drugged him?"

Her breath stopped for a moment. When at last it resumed, it came in stutters.

"Fourth: Why is he still in there?"

"He took the only key, and I was a sweeper, not a pick. I've no skills. We figured you'd be coming soon, and we didn't want to be caught breaking the door down when you arrived. But I didn't know it was *you* who was coming."

"Five: When I let go of you, are you going to run?"

"No."

"Other hand," Royce told her and dragged the first clear. A stain of sweat remained on the table. She tentatively slid the other into its place. Royce placed the tip of Alverstone beside her left-hand pinky and let it twist into the wood. "Six: Why not?"

"No place I can go that'd be far enough."

"You're good at this game." Royce grinned, then startled her by moving the blade in rapid succession, darting it between her next four fingers so fast it made a tiny drumroll. Feldspar shuddered, her legs jumped, and she let out an anguished squeak. But she didn't move the hand on the table even the breadth of a hair. "Seven: Did Hadrian manage to get a room before you drugged him?"

"Y-yes."

He pulled the blade from the table. "Get up," he ordered, and let her find her own feet. "I'm going to open that door. While I do, you're going to explain to your friends why they're going to be very good boys."

Royce crossed the room, moving without a sound. The cellar had a primitive two-pin lock; it took him more time to get out his picks than it did to unlock the door. Inside, he found Hadrian slumped on the floor.

"Tell your stocky friends to carry him to the room."

Feldspar nodded and gestured to Bull Neck to get moving.

"C'mon, Dodge," he objected. "The guy is scrawny as a chicken."

Her voice was stern. "Do what he says, Brook."

"There's eight of us. I don't see why we should do anything he says."

Feldspar glanced at Royce. "Excuse me," she said, then walked over to the bar and grabbed a paring knife. She crossed back to Brook and, without warning or comment, buried the knife in the man's thigh. He screamed and bent over, clutching his leg. Then he fell backward onto the floor, sending one of the chairs skidding.

"Do. You. See. *That?*" She bent over him, shouting and pointing at the blade in his thigh.

"Why'd you do that?" the bartender asked.

"She obviously likes him," Royce explained.

Feldspar grabbed the knife, stood up, and wiped away tears with the back of her hand. "Get Hadrian upstairs. Right now!"

Chairs toppled as the men got up and headed for the cellar.

Royce kept a careful eye as they carried Hadrian. "Tuck him in nice, boys."

"Yes—for Maribor's sake, don't hurt him." Feldspar laid the knife on the table and held her hands up again. "Duster, I swear to you, I didn't know. I wasn't here when you two arrived. I heard that two guys broke up Payne's tarring, and I thought the church had sent down some muscle to watch over him. I also heard rumors of a hired assassin, but had I known you—"

"Congratulations for a well-played hand of Ten Fingers. You're good at it. No wonder you still have all of yours." Royce watched the procession carrying Hadrian up the stairs of the inn without incident. They looked like pallbearers at a funeral.

"Hadrian will be happy he saved your life by locking himself in the cellar," he told her. "He's odd that way."

Chapter Eight
EYE OF THE HURRICANE

Christopher Fawkes hung the lantern on the brass hook dangling from the stable's ceiling. Flies—woken by the light—competed with moths for the stupidest things in the world as they butted the lamp, frustrated with their inability to incinerate themselves. Knox had objected to using a lantern, but Christopher wasn't going to conduct business standing in a dark barn.

No one finding the chamberlain, high sheriff, Pastor Payne, and the king's cousin chatting in a lighted stable, even late at night, would hardly think it noteworthy. But if the same men were caught together in the dark—anywhere—that *would* be suspicious.

"Well? What do you think?" Christopher asked Chamberlain Wells.

Thorbert Wells stood with arms folded, his long face sagging more than usual. "I'm thinking that I'm still not comfortable."

"What more assurance do you need?" Payne asked. "The church is behind us, and you have the king's cousin before you."

"It all seems so...I don't know...wrong," Wells said.

"What the church does is always right. We are the arbiters of right and wrong," the pastor assured him.

Wells settled his sight on Payne with an appalled wrinkle in his brow. "You shouldn't assume just because I'm native to Dulgath, that I'm stupid."

"Yes, yes, of course, but—"

"No one thinks you're stupid," Christopher cut in before Payne could do any damage. "We wouldn't be trying to enlist you if we felt that way. What you *are* is ambitious. A modest, content man doesn't rise from fisherman's son to castle chamberlain. We appreciate your achievements, but you lack noble blood, so you've reached your full potential. You've topped out here in Dulgath. There's no place higher to rise to in this backwater. Nothing has changed here for centuries, and it won't if the Dulgath line continues."

The constant tap, buzz, and flutter of the flies diving at the lantern unnerved Christopher, reminding him of more nefarious insects. At the age of six, he had been traumatized by a pair of bumblebees. While not stung, he had, nevertheless, been trapped behind a rosebush, too scared to venture forth. Night came, and Christopher still refused to move for fear they were lurking in the dark. When his brother finally dragged Christopher home, his father had beaten him for being a coward. The humiliation and subsequent taunts drove Christopher to learn the sword and shield. But although he performed adequately in court contests with live blades, the buzzing of bees still sent chills down his spine.

He gave a nervous glance at the lantern. *They're flies!* he told himself, but still folded his arms to hide his shaking hands.

Not a good way to start a legacy.

He consoled himself with the knowledge that no one would remember it this way. Many important events in history occurred in less-than-ideal fashion but were *corrected* in recollection. Had

Novron really stood atop that famed hill challenging the might of flying beasts? And afterward, had he made that grand and eloquent speech about freedom and bravery? Had the Patriarch embraced Glenmorgan, and had the steward appreciatively knelt, allowing himself to take a lesser title? Christopher couldn't imagine power struggles being so amiable.

When people looked back on how the landless Christopher Fawkes became Earl Christopher Fawkes of Dulgath, no one will recall that it started in a stable. In the future, this night never happened.

"I was loyal to Beadle—to the *Earl* of Dulgath."

"I'm certain you were. But Beadle is dead. Do you really think Nysa Dulgath is capable of filling her father's shoes?"

Wells sighed. "She doesn't listen to me—doesn't listen to anyone. Thinks she knows everything."

"If you support me, Wells," Christopher told him, "together we'll transform Dulgath. Make it powerful. This place is rich but untapped. I'll levy taxes, conscript an army, and Knox here will train them. The Nyphron Church's influence will grow. They'll help me expand Dulgath's borders, and I'll need lords loyal to me. You'll have your *own* castle then."

"I won't kill her," Wells announced.

"No one is asking you to."

"You have no idea what those assassins will come up with." Wells pointed at him with a pudgy finger. "What if they suggest bribing the chamberlain to knife the girl? I'm telling you now, I won't do that."

"We wouldn't ask you to." Christopher suspected that the chamberlain's concern stemmed from the fear of getting caught rather than a distaste for spilling blood.

"I don't trust them," Knox said, jumping in. He had his arms folded, leaning back against the stall.

Christopher could have stabbed him. They were there to convince Wells to join, and this was no time for airing concerns. *I have to do everything myself.* "Well, that's natural. They're rogues, assassins, and thieves. If they were trustworthy, we'd have cause for concern."

"One of them—the big one—is familiar," the sheriff went on. "I've seen him before. Don't remember where."

"So?"

Knox scowled. "Look, how long is this going to take them?" His tone was disapproving; so was the frown on his face, but then Knox usually looked that way. The man was a thug, a northern soldier of some sort recruited by the earl, who'd wanted a tough, impartial hand. What he got was certainly impartial—to everything but coin. Knox was *very* partial to gold tenents.

"How should I know?" Christopher said. "Do you think I make a habit of this sort of thing?"

"Damned if I have a clue about what you do."

"Well, see, that's where we differ," Christopher said. "Because I know exactly what you do, Knox. Absolutely nothing. As a high sheriff, you'd make a great sundial."

Christopher didn't even know what that meant, but his mother used to say it all the time. *Is that all you did today, Chris? As a fetcher of wood, you'd make a great sundial. I asked you to box up my gowns; as a valet, you'd make a great sundial.*

He never understood what she had against sundials. They never bothered anyone, were quiet, kept to themselves, and did what was asked of them in all kinds of weather. His mother just couldn't see their value. As for his father, he had no problem with sundials—just with his son.

Christopher doubted Knox had any greater clue about the shortcomings of sundials than himself, but the point was made.

Knox's frown became a sneer. He muttered an insult under his breath, too quiet to catch, but the sentiment was unmistakable.

The man was a violent bully. No one became high sheriff without a little fury in them, and Knox was testing him. Either Christopher would force the sheriff to accept a bit in his teeth or the table would be turned. He needed to show Wells who was in charge. Besides, Knox was too comfortable in Christopher's presence. Dangerous thug or no, there were lines, boundaries that had to be maintained. For now, he'd have to work with the brute, but afterward Knox might prove to be an opportunist, and ambitious men were likely to try something stupid, like blackmail.

Give a crow a carcass and it'll just want another, he thought. *Knox is just like the bees, and he needs to know his place.*

Christopher summoned his courage. Laughing amicably, he started to turn away, then with a quick shove, he drove the sheriff back against the horse gate, making it clang and startling Derby. Christopher drew his sword.

Knox stared, his mouth open, as Christopher stuck the tip of his blade into the leather collar of the sheriff's gambeson. "Unless you plan on leaving Dulgath soon, I'd watch your mouth. I'm the king's cousin. While that might not earn me much back in Mehan, it does mean I can kill you without having to clean up the mess. Do we understand each other?"

Knox hesitated. He wouldn't be the man Christopher thought he was if he didn't show some backbone, but the sheriff wasn't stupid. After a run of heartbeats, he nodded.

"Good." Christopher withdrew his blade, noting with great relish the little nick left in Knox's leather collar. From then on it would serve as a reminder to them both.

Christopher slapped his sword back into its scabbard, trying to give the appearance he wasn't concerned and his heart wasn't racing.

He'd just taken a huge gamble and won. This wasn't a time to show concern.

"Can I ask a question?" Wells asked.

The uncertainty in the man's voice pleased Christopher. His point had been made, and the proper respect was being paid.

"Yes, of course, Chamberlain. What do you want to know?"

"What about the painter?"

"Sherwood Stow? What about him?"

"He and Lady Dulgath have been seeing each other every morning for months, and he has a—a reputation, doesn't he? What if this Sherwood were to, well, you know?"

Christopher was mystified by Wells. The man who had clawed his way to the position of chamberlain was squeamish about so many things. If Bishop Parnell hadn't insisted they acquire him, to have an inside man to help cover their tracks, he never would have given him a second thought.

"It still takes nine months to make a baby even if he was *you knowing* her. While I'm patient, I'm not *that* patient."

"But expectant mothers become more reclusive." Wells wrung his hands. "They don't go out. They stay in their chambers under constant observation from fussing midwives. That might make killing her impossible. If the rogues you hired feel they have a good thing here, they might drag their feet. You're paying their expenses, right?"

"I'm not *paying* them anything," Christopher said. "Once they tell us what we need to know, I'm shipping them off to Manzant."

"What?" Knox asked. "Why not just kill them?"

Christopher offered up a wry smile. "Killing is such a waste. Ambrose Moor pays good money for—"

"But living men tell tales," the sheriff said.

"Yes, precisely," Wells said, aghast. "What if the king should speak to them…"

"Do you honestly think Vincent will take a trip to a salt mine to chat with two assassins?" Christopher's patience was wearing thin and it was difficult not to show his frustration.

"No," Wells admitted, "but what if he sends constables there, or what if they escape?"

"No one ever escapes from Manzant," Christopher replied.

"And the constables? I'm not sure I want to take that risk," Wells muttered with a grimace.

"If they're dead, no one can talk to them," Knox said. "Ever."

"Look." Christopher sighed. He hated the slow and the frightened; they could never understand the bold steps one needed to stride to reach greatness. "I've already made the arrangements."

Knox stiffened. "Unmake them. We need corpses to blame for the murder, not walking, talking men."

"And how do we explain two corpses *before* Nysa is dead?" Christopher asked. "Kinda hard for dead men to do the deed. Or are you saying we should wait until after she's killed? That creates its own problems. First, they'll want to be paid as soon as their part is done—a payment I don't have, by the way. And second, they're not going to hang around afterward. You'll have to track them down, and pray they don't say anything before you find them. With my plan, we can scoop them up as soon as they give us the information. No one has to know *when* they were sent to Manzant. All that's important is that they were arrested and justice carried out before a formal investigation starts. But corpses decay quickly, especially in this climate, so you'll have to kill them *after* Nysa is dead."

"Let me worry about when, where, and how the two meet their end. I'll hold up my end," Knox snapped.

Wells was nodding. "I've watched Knox for years, and I trust him in such matters. I'm not saying anything against you, Lord Fawkes, but if my opinion means anything, I'd be more comfortable with the thieves dead rather than locked up."

Christopher ran a hand over his face, sighing again. "Okay, okay, fine. We'll do it your way."

"And Sherwood?" Wells asked.

Christopher raised his hand, patting the air between them. "Trust me. Stow isn't winning any points with Nysa."

"Other noble ladies have succumbed to—"

"It's not a matter of her being noble when he's not. It's that he's human and she's—Novron knows what—cold as frost in a frozen lake. Point is, he's not making headway and isn't likely to. But if it would make you more comfortable, I could make plans for Sherwood of the Endless Canvas and ensure that things are handled as expediently as possible."

The chamberlain didn't answer. He took a breath and ran a tongue along his lips as his eyes shifted from one face to the next.

Now was the time for Christopher to set the hook. "You see, you've already proven your value, and great things come to people who show such potential. So, Chamberlain, what do you say? Shall we consider you on board? Do you want to continue your rise and expand your horizons?"

He stared hard at Wells. They all did. The chamberlain's eyes darted around once more.

Christopher rested his hand on the hilt of his sword as a gentle reminder that Wells might already be in too deep. He wasn't, of course. The matter would still be word against word, but his little demonstration with Knox was bound to pay dividends.

"All right." Wells nodded. "What *do* you want me to do?"

"Nothing at the moment. We'll wait to see what the *consultants* have to say."

"And Sherwood?"

Christopher just smiled.

Sherwood put a breakfast biscuit in his mouth. Holding it with his teeth, he shifted the painting to his left hand and opened the study door with his right. Another lovely Maranon morning cast spears of sunlight across the floor, over the desk, and up the wall. There was something magical about early light—late evening, too. Sherwood had a fondness for both dawn and dusk. Fairy tales said that these *between-times*, the not-quite-day and not-quite-night periods, were when the doors between the world of men and the worlds of the fantastical opened. These were the enchanted minutes when wonderful and dreadful things occurred. Sherwood wasn't one for superstition, myths, or legends, but he admitted to the truth of the *between-times* being enchanting. The light was always more golden, its angle casting dramatic shadows, and everything came alive with color. That morning should have been wonderful, but instead, Sherwood was greeted by the dreadful.

At first, he didn't know what he saw. Something strange was in the center of the room, lying on the floor in a twisted, unnatural way.

As usual, Sherwood had arrived early. Lady Dulgath, always punctual, wouldn't be there for half an hour. He had intended to finish the last of his breakfast as he oiled his paints. He hadn't left much time to set up. He'd lingered in bed, suffering a mild attack of depression. The morose feelings came over him often. Most times they were fleeting and easy to weather. Yet occasionally a random hurricane hit, the world turned dark, and rain fell in unimaginable torrents.

During those times, death by drowning was all but certain—and quite often welcomed. What had been fine the day before became too much to bear when the depression hurricane descended, and any memory of happiness was dismissed as a delusion. He was worthless; his work was atrocious, his life a miserable failure, and obviously Elan would be a better place without him breathing the air. While the attacks came without warning or trigger, that didn't mean they couldn't be provoked. Given that he had begun that morning experiencing a sprinkle, what lay on the floor of the private study threatened to bring the thunder.

For a brief instant Sherwood thought he saw a person, a horribly broken and mutilated corpse. Then he realized he wasn't seeing flesh and bone, but splintered wood. He was looking at his easel, shattered in a dismembered sculpture of wanton destruction. Worse still were his paints. Bottles had been thrown, leaving brilliant bursts of colors on the walls and glass shards on the floor. A yellow ocher starburst had exploded near the window, looking like a second sun; a splatter of vermilion made the wall appear to bleed; a fan of umber had sprayed the wooden floorboards.

Sherwood always left his tools in the study. The room was never used and always closed. It made no sense to carry everything up to his room and then back down every morning. Early on, he left the canvas, too, but grew paranoid as the image of Lady Dulgath took form. He couldn't afford to let anyone see it until finished. Maybe not even then.

He had taken the painting with him the night before and slept with it beside his bed, breathing oil fumes all night—one of the things his despair latched onto and labeled as stupid. He no longer felt that way; his depression couldn't care less about such crumbs when a banquet lay before it.

The easel had belonged to Yardley, who inherited it from his master, who very likely got it from his. No telling how old the thing was—easily a hundred or more years. And every inch was covered in paint, with some places showing a buildup of layers, the sediment of decades. The screw that held the crossbar had long been cracked; so had the crossbar and the back leg. This had always caused the canvas frame to wobble, and the tray never was tight enough to suit Sherwood, especially not when it held a vial of Ultramarine. He'd cursed the thing countless times and considered having a new one made.

But seeing it on the floor, broken into a dozen pieces with bright jagged splinters, he felt he might vomit. This was the easel he'd learned on. This was the platform from which he discovered how to properly see the world. He'd taken it everywhere, sleeping with it on ships and in winter camps on high mountains. It had leaned against walls while he bedded ladies of varying ranks, and he'd whispered his fears to it more than once after coming home drunk.

Almost as tragic as the easel were the pigments. Seventy-five or maybe as much as a hundred gold tenents decorated the walls of the study. No blue burst, though—he'd thrown away the vial of Beyond the Sea all on his own. He still hoped to catch the man—Royce Melborn—and ask for it back. If Melborn had half a brain, he'd deny knowing anything about it, but laymen rarely understood the value of paint. That one vial was worth a dozen easels and everything presently on the walls.

Sherwood felt the hurricane build as he saw his brushes, also vandalized. Each one had been snapped in half, and some of them had the hairs pulled out or mashed with so much force that the ferrule had split. The painting was safe, but what good was it now that he had no hope of finishing it?

"What happened?"

Sherwood turned to see Lady Dulgath standing in the doorway.

How long have I been standing here?

He couldn't talk and only pointed at the disaster, shaking his head.

"Who did this?" Her voice rose in volume and anxiety. "Did you see, were you here?"

He continued to shake his head. He felt like crying, afraid he might. Already his face was hot, his eyesight misting. He blinked fast to hold everything back.

"You there! Stephen," she called out the door, "run and fetch the sheriff. Then tell everyone in this castle to assemble in the Great Hall. Do you understand? Everyone!" Her voice was angry, violent.

Sherwood picked up a brass candle tray and bent to sweep up as much of the pigment as he could. "I don't understand why anyone would do this." His voice was shaking, his words slurring. He didn't care. "Stealing is understandable, but—I mean—this is worth a lot of money. Why destroy it? What have I done?"

"I'll have it replaced," Lady Dulgath said.

"You can't. The time, the cost—it's…" He actually didn't know how much. Thinking about the totality of the loss was like asking how high was up.

"Doesn't matter. You are my guest. I consider it my failure. I'm responsible, and I'll make it right again." She took a step, and glass crunched under her shoe. She froze and looked around, frightened. "The painting, is it—" She saw the covered square of canvas resting beside the leg of the desk, and her shoulders relaxed. "They didn't touch it?"

"Wasn't here. I took it to my room last night."

She offered him an encouraging smile. "Well, that's something, isn't it?"

"Yes—that's something."

She continued to stare at the painting. He couldn't stop her from looking at it. All she had to do was take two steps and lift the cover. He was certain she would, but a moment later Sheriff Knox and Chamberlain Wells entered.

"I want to know who did this," Lady Dulgath demanded.

Knox took a moment to look around thoughtfully, finally focusing on the door. "That might be difficult."

"Why is that?"

"No lock. Anyone can get in here."

"Could be anyone in the castle then," Wells said.

"Not just the castle," Knox corrected. "Virtually anyone could have come in last night. I pulled Throm and Frewin from the gate to guard your bedroom door. We were shorthanded on the wall. You really need to let me recruit more guards. Burying your head in the sand must stop. Your life is in danger."

"Whoever did this wasn't trying to kill me."

"But someone is."

"Dulgath doesn't need a standing army. This is a close community, and I won't allow you—or anyone else—to destroy that."

"I'm just asking for a few more guards—to protect you!"

"I don't need protection. I need to know who did this. Find out. Go!" She turned and faced the chamberlain. "I've ordered the staff to be gathered. See to it that they are…everyone. I'll speak to them shortly. I want this solved, and I want it solved today."

"As you wish, milady."

She closed the door after they left and crossed the room to Sherwood, who was still struggling to gather as much pigment as he could. She found an empty cup, a decorative stein from a high shelf, and helped him. "I'm so very sorry this happened, Sherwood."

He paused and looked up. "You know my name."

"Of course I do."

"You've never said it before."

She shrugged. "Is that significant?"

"To me it is."

She looked at him, curious, forehead furrowed, those elegant brows creeping closer together. He could see it again, that vision through her eyes; an image beyond the window, a hazy shadow like someone peering out through frosted glass.

Sherwood had struggled his whole life to see beyond the veil that people hung over themselves. They wore clothes to hide their truths: the bravado of cowards, the humility of the courageous, the indifference of caretakers, and the sins of the pious. He scraped back veneers to find bone. These were the buried secrets that unlocked the sincerity of his work. Understanding—seeing—what others couldn't, or refused to, allowed Sherwood to put into paint the same underlying honesty that made his portraits so lifelike. Everyone kept secrets; most simple and easy to spot.

Wells was practically naked. The man was a glutton. Knox was a barely restrained animal at heart. Fawkes was a different matter. Something cold dwelled within his chest and throbbed rather than beat. Sherwood wouldn't trust Fawkes to piss every day.

Nysa Dulgath was nothing like them, or any woman he had ever seen. She had a secret, to be sure, but she'd buried it deeper than he thought possible, beneath the dirt, below gravel, under shale and heavy rock. All he ever saw were these fleeting glimpses of shadows peeking out the windows of her eyes, little cupped hands pressed against the glass, a lonely soul trapped in an empty house.

Seeing how she looked at him then, that concern in her face, made the clouds part. He stood in the eye of the hurricane. The world blew around him dark and terrible, but he was safe. He was with her under a single shaft of sunlight, and everything was perfect.

The religious spoke of divine moments of grace when whatever gods they worshiped paused from their daily routine to stretch out a finger and touch them. Lives were changed, prophets made, and nations shifted when that happened. Sherwood felt touched at that moment, rocked to his core and then some. For a time, he thought he might be falling in love with Nysa Dulgath, but *love* was no longer a word large enough to encompass everything he felt. Mothers loved their children. Husbands loved wives. What Sherwood felt was more akin to worship. A prophet was born among the broken glass and scattered pigment, and while nations didn't tremble, they should have.

Chapter Nine
THEFT OF SWORDS

Hadrian awoke to the song of birds and a cool breeze. A window was open, the only movement the thin curtains rippling with the wind. He lay on something soft, a pillow beneath his head. Somewhere distant, he heard muffled clinks of glasses, voices, laughter, and the drag of chairs on a wooden floor.

Sounds like a tavern.

The thought drifted in with the gentle breeze and whistling whoops and chortles of a thrush—then he remembered.

He sat up, expecting a nasty headache, something similar to the morning after a drunken pass out. He had figured his head would be throbbing, his eyes dry and reluctant to shift. Surprisingly, he felt okay, good even. His mouth might have been the last resting place for a deceased chipmunk, but other than that he was fine.

Hadrian had no idea where he was. Along with his morning-after apprehension, he had expected to open his eyes on a different scene—if he ever managed to open them again.

He was indeed on a bed, a nice bed: thick mattress, soft blanket, linen sheets, feather pillow, no stains. The rest of the room was just as charming. Big, dark-wood beams supported the ceiling. A rug stretched across the floor. Drapes framed a solitary window, where a bright light shone on a table and an upholstered chair. In the chair sat a familiar shadow.

"They drugged me," Hadrian said. "She—*she* drugged me."

"I know," Royce replied. He was staring out the window, looking down.

Hadrian began taking inventory with his hands, no pain, cuts, or bruises. No tar or feathers. He was in his clothes, shoes still on, cloak missing. No, not missing, it lay across the foot of the bed.

He looked at his hands and remembered fumbling with a key. "Did I—did I manage to lock the door?"

"Yes, you did." Royce threw his booted feet on the table. "I had to pick it to get you out." He pushed back his hood, revealing a confused expression.

"What?"

Royce shrugged.

"You're impressed I did that, aren't you? That I thought to lock myself in."

"Be more impressed if you hadn't allowed a pretty girl to drug you."

"A pretty girl…how'd you know? And how did you find me?" Hadrian stood up, continuing to test himself, but his balance was fine. Whatever she'd given him was friendlier than rye whiskey.

Royce didn't answer.

Do you understand the meaning of the word thorough? Hadrian's stomach sank.

"Oh, Royce, you didn't…"

Royce cocked an eyebrow. He didn't say anything for a moment, and his sight shifted to the floor in thought. Once more, he displayed a puzzled expression. He shook his head. "No. I didn't."

"Not even the woman?"

"I know her. She's from the Diamond, so she's not an idiot. Not stupid enough to seek retribution, and she was adequately cooperative."

"Really?" Hadrian wondered if he were dreaming, or perhaps dead. He should have been lying on a lonely road outside of town, his body burned with tar and covered in feathers, not waking up in a cozy private room.

Royce saved me but didn't kill anyone? Apparently the world has forgotten how life works.

Spotting a washbasin on a dresser, Hadrian went over and splashed water on his face, then dried himself with a folded towel. He turned around, and his hands went to his sides. "Where are my swords?"

"No idea. Where'd you leave them?"

"What d'you mean where'd I leave them? I—"

I dropped them. And I took off the spadone before that. They were all near the bar.

"Didn't you notice they were missing?" Hadrian asked.

Royce nodded.

"You didn't think to get them back?"

Royce scowled. "Don't see why I have to do everything. Need a hand when you piss, too?"

Hadrian threw the towel at him. Royce dipped his head, and the cloth flew out the window.

"How late is it?" Hadrian grabbed his cloak and hung it over his arm.

"Midmorning. You had a good rest. We missed breakfast."

"Excuse me while I get my things."

Royce stood up.

Hadrian stopped him. "No—stay here. My turn."

Heading down the stairs, Hadrian noticed that the barroom was different. Morning light flooded in through the windows as well as the door, all of which were open to admit the breeze to the otherwise stuffy room. Gill was the first person Hadrian saw. The kid wore a stained apron and was rushing to clear tables where recent breakfast patrons had left plates and cups. Fearful that the ones who had taken his weapons would be long gone, Hadrian was pleased to see Bull Neck and his orange-clad partner at the same table where they'd sat the night before.

Wagner was still there, too, behind the bar, the same towel hanging over his shoulder. With his attentive publican eyes, Wagner was the first to spot Hadrian. Concern flooded the barkeep's face as he glanced toward Bull Neck's table to check if they'd seen him. Hadrian recognized two other faces at a different table. Not the men that had held up the post—not Brett and Larmand—but these men had been there. Scarlett wasn't.

Getting up late had the benefit of a sparse crowd. Decent folk had come and gone. Aside from the ones he intended to speak with, Hadrian saw only one table of bystanders. A small family near the door was finishing up their porridge. The boy tilted a bowl to his lips, and his mother and father scolded him for bad manners. A girl in pigtails sat on a chair too big for her, swinging her legs.

Hadrian walked past Bull Neck and company to the bar, where Wagner pretended not to see him.

"I want my swords back."

"What swords are those, friend?" Wagner smiled and pulled the towel from his shoulder to wipe dry hands or perhaps wrap around knuckles.

Hadrian smiled back. He'd hoped it would go this way. While he didn't normally seek revenge, he didn't appreciate being taken for an idiot.

Besides, a fight ends when one person hits the floor. This fight hadn't ended. It hadn't even started, but it was about to.

"Seriously?" Hadrian turned from Wagner and walked over to the family. Fishing out a silver tenent, he clapped it on their table. "This breakfast, and the next one, is on me."

The man stared at him, looked at his wife and kids, and then asked, "Why's that?"

"Because I'm going to ask you to take your family and leave. Right now."

The man narrowed his eyes and glanced at his family once more. "Again, I have to ask *why*?"

"Because none of you were here last night when I was drugged and robbed."

The man didn't look as shocked as Hadrian expected. When the man leaned over and looked at Bull Neck, Hadrian realized the fellow wasn't as innocent as he'd first appeared. Hadrian had spoken loud enough for everyone in the room to hear, and Bull Neck and his orange-clad pal were grinning. The kids' mother was already up from her seat. She scooped up the coin, and without waiting for her husband, led her children out the door.

Hadrian waited.

"I think I'll stick around," the father told him, an amused, almost eager, glee in his eyes.

Hadrian nodded, then closed the front door to Caldwell House, sliding the bolt across. Turning back to the room, he saw that Bull Neck and his friend had risen to their feet.

"You, in the orange," Hadrian said. "What's your name?"

The man adjusted his belt and rolled his shoulders, making a show of loosening up. "Mostly, I'm called Bad-News-for-Bloody-Strangers." He laughed.

Bull Neck laughed with him. The rest smiled. "But you can call me Clem for short. I'm tellin' you so you'll know who laid ya low."

"Ah-huh." Hadrian nodded. "Well, Clem, you're gonna want to take that nice tunic off. Red and orange clash, and bloodstains are difficult to get out."

Clem laughed again. No mirth in it, but rather the sound of cruelty being fed. "Don't worry, I think I can avoid getting *your* blood on me."

"No blades," Bull Neck said, punching one fist into a palm. "And no creepy friend." He glanced toward the stairs to make sure that was true. "And no woman to protect you."

Woman to protect me? Isn't she the one who drugged me?

Hadrian couldn't figure out what had happened after he passed out. Bull Neck mentioned a *creepy friend,* but if Alverstone had come out to play, there would have been a lot of blood and more than a few bodies.

"You're in for some serious trouble, struth, yes—I can tell you that!" Bull Neck nodded his sincerity. "Weez gonna pound you to flour, boy. Weez surely are. Gonna mash you down to wort. You gonna be nothing but paste."

"You lads want to take this outside?" Wagner asked.

"I'd be happy not to do this at all," Hadrian replied. "Just return my swords, and we can all have breakfast."

"Breakfast is over, tosser," Bull Neck declared. He was cracking his knuckles and smiling so wide his gums were showing.

Hadrian ignored him and stared at Wagner for an answer.

"Don't know anything about no swords, mister."

"I think it'll come back to you after a few of these nice tables are broken." Hadrian moved to the middle of the room, the most indefensible place he could find. He hated starting fights and didn't think he'd have to this time. Presenting himself as an easy target was like laying out steak in front of hungry dogs. These men had wanted to beat him senseless since he'd arrived.

Bull Neck came at him first. He'd gone to the trouble of shoving Clem aside so he could have the first strike. Hadrian intended to indulge Bull, even though he had nothing against the man. There had been a lot of Bulls in Hadrian's life—big, loud, demanding men who expected respect based on size and volume alone. A few could fight, but most never bothered to learn because they assumed superior bulk was all that combat required.

Bull was the latter. Not the sort to use weapons, he probably had a fondness for fists and chokeholds. Hadrian wasn't going to make his point with Bull because he disliked his brand of fist-first thuggery, but because Bull looked like he could take a beating. The best way to change minds was to break the biggest bones first.

Bull took three lumbering steps, punching out with his big left fist in a wide roundhouse swing.

A lefty.

Hadrian had already guessed that from how he had stood with his right leg forward. Now he knew for certain because the swing wasn't a jab or a feint. The big boy had put everything into that punch, expecting to end the fight right there.

Hadrian turned sideways and guided the blow away from his face with his left hand. He caught Bull's wrist and twisted it slightly to roll the elbow up. Then, bracing with his right, Hadrian snapped his opponent's arm backward at the elbow.

Pop!

Hadrian heard, as well as felt, the joint give.

This was followed by a bellowing scream as Bull stumbled forward. Hadrian let momentum do the work, and Bull slammed into the table still laden with porridge. Bowls shot into the air, wooden legs severed, and the table collapsed as Bull crashed into it.

Clem took a step forward as Hadrian backed up. "Wait!" Hadrian held up his palms and then pointed at the debris. "You might want to pick up one of those table legs. Makes a good club, don't you think?"

This made Clem pause for a moment. Then he glanced at the floor where Bull was rolling in the spilled porridge, whimpering and clutching his twisted arm. Hadrian hoped that if Clem took a moment to reflect upon the torment of his friend it'd be enough to make Clem—and everyone else—think twice. It didn't. But Clem did take Hadrian's advice and picked up a broken table leg.

The first swing was wide. Hadrian took a step back anyway. The second, a backswing, was on target and Hadrian ducked, taking another step back. Then another. By the time they reached the oak post where Brett and his friend had been talking the night before, Clem was getting tired. Swinging that table leg as hard as he could was difficult, and sweat glistened on the orange-clad man's forehead.

Hadrian waited for the next swing, and this time he stepped inside and guided his opponent's hand. Easy to tell that the loud *thwack!* was Clem's hand rather than the table leg hitting the post. The man dropped the club with a cry and jerked his hand to his chest in agony. Regardless of what else it might have done, the post had skinned Clem's knuckles. Blood smeared the front of his nice tunic, leaving two faint streaks.

Hadrian thought this would end the fight, but the father who had remained behind had opened the door, and Brett, followed by two others, entered. Apparently, the wife was no more innocent than the husband.

All three charged Hadrian, arms spread for a waist-high tackle.

Hadrian stepped behind the pillar, ruining everything. He also picked up the table leg.

Brett went right, the family man went left. The third didn't know what to do, so he just stopped in front of the post. They hadn't seen Hadrian pick up the leg, and Brett still hadn't seen it when Hadrian clubbed him in the forehead. Brett's mouth made a wide O as his head snapped back and his legs crumpled under him. The father of two had intended to grab Hadrian's arms from behind, but Hadrian was standing too close to the post for him to easily get both arms around. Didn't matter. Hadrian brought the table leg back, punching into the man's stomach with the splintered end. The jagged teeth cut through his shirt. Porridge Dad let out a whoosh of air, folded, and collapsed.

By this time, Wagner had come around the bar to join the fray, and Clem had recovered enough to have a second go.

Hadrian dodged around the post and moved back to the center of the room, where Bull was howling on the floor, lying on his back, his knees up as he rocked from side to side. Hadrian snatched another loose table leg off the ground.

The remaining three men—Gill abstained from the fight, choosing instead to watch from the cellar stairs—came at Hadrian more slowly this time. They fanned out, trying to circle him. Wagner wrapped the towel around his knuckles, and the three shuffled forward, jabbing and swiping, some with open hands and outstretched fingers. Maybe they were trying to catch hold of him; Hadrian wasn't sure, but they looked ridiculous, like children. None had any training, much less experience.

They drugged me. Stole from me. Might have killed me.

The last one was unlikely, but he needed something. He was starting to feel like he was beating up on kids. When fighting skilled soldiers, Hadrian could anticipate moves. These people were erratic and foolish beyond prediction. They were so inept he might accidentally kill one. Not having his swords was a benefit; these imbeciles would probably impale themselves.

Hadrian cracked Brett on his reaching wrist. He howled and fell back. Thinking this provided an opening and not realizing Hadrian now had two clubs and was proficient with both hands, Clem lunged in. The second table leg caught him across the bridge of his nose. Blood erupted. Hadrian swung at Wagner then, who managed to jump out of the way but lost his balance in the effort and fell, slamming into another table, cracking it badly as he went down.

"Stop!" Scarlett Dodge stood in the doorway. She wore the same fetching patchwork gown, which looked out of place in the morning light. In her arms, she clutched three familiar swords. "Damn it, Brett! I told you to stall him, not fight him."

She threw the three blades on the floor, where they clattered on the stone.

"Hey!" Hadrian yelled.

"What? You threw my friends on the floor!"

"His swords are worth more," Royce said. He appeared from the shadows at the bottom of the stairs, hood up, arms folded. No one had seen him come down. Everyone still able to, shifted away.

"Royce, I thought I told you to wait upstairs," Hadrian said.

"You took too long. I got bored."

"What are you doing?" Wagner asked Scarlett as he got to his feet. "*Declawing the cat,* remember?"

"Yeah, that was last night and before I knew this cat doesn't need claws to kill you."

"We almost had him, Dodge," Porridge Dad said, still bent over and rubbing his stomach. "He was getting tired."

"He's had more sleep than any of you—trust me."

"I'd rather have gotten drunk and suffered a hangover. You want to explain what happened last night?" Hadrian asked.

"Not really."

"I'm afraid we're going to insist," Royce said, and began to slowly cross the debris-ridden room. "Miss *Dodge,* is it?"

"It sure as bloody Mar isn't *Missus.*"

"Watch your mouth, girl," Wagner snapped. "No need to blaspheme our Lord's name."

"Sorry, but he brings out the worst in me."

"I think Miss Dodge needs to take a walk with us," Royce said.

"She ain't going nowhere with you two." This was said by Bull Neck, who still lay on the floor, cradling his wounded arm.

"I'm afraid she is," Royce said. He drew out a folded parchment and held it up. "Can you read?"

She stared at the parchment. Shock spread across her face. "You're—you're…" Scarlett couldn't manage to say the word.

"Royal constables," Royce said. "Keepers of the peace."

"That's not possible. You were in the Diamond, for Maribor's sake."

"You think I whipped this up last night?"

"Sure, why not?"

"Ask Sheriff Knox or Chamberlain Wells. You can even talk to Lord Fawkes—he's the king's cousin. He ought to know if the king's signature is authentic."

Wagner growled. "I don't care who you say you are; she's not going anywhere with you two."

"It's okay, Wag," Scarlett said.

"It ain't."

"It is."

"These two ain't no royal constables."

Scarlett sighed. "If it's true, they could kill me in the name of the king, and Sheriff Knox would buy them drinks. And if it isn't, they can still murder me and disappear. If they wanted me dead, you'd already be picking out my box."

As she said this, Hadrian buckled on his two swords, then hefted the big one onto his back.

"Besides, how exactly do you plan to stop them?" She pointed toward Hadrian. "He pummeled all of you black-and-blue with two table legs. What do you think he'll do with those? And don't forget what I told you last night about *him*." This time Scarlett pointed at Royce.

"That's why I'm worried," the bartender said.

"I wouldn't worry about her," Royce told him. "From what I've seen of the people in this town, I'd vote Miss Dodge 'Most Likely to Survive.'"

Scarlett led them toward the door.

Hadrian paused and looked back at Clem, whose nose had bled like a spigot down the front of his tunic. "Cold water," he said. "Don't use hot. Believe me, hot water will set the stain and it'll be ruined." He shook his head. "What a shame. That was a nice tunic."

The three of them followed the cobbled street downhill toward the river. Morning light shone blindingly bright on a two-story whitewashed clapboard building with a stone foundation and a big waterwheel. The wheel creaked and trickled as it slowly turned.

"Royce, you hungry?" Hadrian asked.

"A little," Royce replied. He walked behind the other two, forcing Hadrian to peer back over his shoulder.

"I didn't get dinner last night."

He stared at Scarlett.

"What?"

"You know the town. Where can we go?" Hadrian asked.

"We?" She laughed, but there was nervousness in it. Scarlett glanced back at Royce before answering Hadrian. "I drugged you last night, and you want to eat with me today?"

"Sure, just don't do it again. If you do"—Hadrian jerked his head toward Royce—"he'll probably kill you."

"Probably?" Royce said.

"So where can we find food?" Hadrian asked again.

"Ah…" Scarlett hesitated.

"Someplace isolated," Royce said. "I don't like crowds."

"He's not kidding," Hadrian said. "And as far as Royce is concerned, two is a crowd."

"We can go back to my place. I have a slab of pork and some eggs I can cook up."

"Wonderful." Hadrian smiled at her.

"Is he always like this?" Scarlett asked Royce.

He nodded. "Annoying, isn't it?"

Scarlett Dodge lived in a small, ivy-bedecked stone cottage with a dirt floor, a yellow thatched roof, and a bright-red door. Chimneys stood at both ends, with the ubiquitous ivy hiding everything else. Inside were two rooms: a clean kitchen, and a disaster of a bedroom. Blankets, sheets, undertunics, kirtles, a bright-red cloak, and red gloves lay scattered across the rush-covered floor. There could have been a fight in her bedroom more violent than the one held at Caldwell House. A spinning wheel rested in the corner, tilted against the wall. A line of thread coming off the drive wheel was tangled around the bobbin in a massive wad. A nearby basket of unspun wool was tipped over, the contents looking like foam spilling out of a beer keg.

In contrast, the kitchen sparkled. Wood was stacked neatly near the fire, as were a series of six copper pots. Not a single one showed even a hint of soot. On three rows of shelves, ceramic and wooden bowls grouped by type descended in size from left to right. Plates and cups were proudly displayed, herbs hung in neat bundles from the rafters, and a series of sharp knives were stabbed into the support beam near a clutter-free table.

Scarlett paused, looking at her home with an embarrassed grimace, then shrugged. "I like to cook."

The fire was still smoldering in her hearth. She added wood, pumped it with a bellows until a flame caught, then went to a barrel. Popping the lid off, she hooked out a slab of pork. Scarlett clapped it onto the table, jerked a knife off the post, and began slicing a section free.

"Well?" Hadrian asked, taking a seat on one of only two stools in the house.

Royce remained standing. He walked around, studying the place.

"Well what?" Scarlett replied, expertly trimming fat. She handled a knife well, holding it lightly with a finger on the blade and using the whole edge. Hadrian had never been a butcher, but he knew when someone was at ease with sharp things. While Scarlett probably hadn't been a butcher, either, she certainly could have applied for the job.

"Why did you ruin a perfectly good glass of rye whiskey that might have led to a sleepless night for the both of us?"

Scarlett paused. She smiled then shook her head, clearing the expression. "You make it hard to hate you."

"Really?" Royce said. "Funny—I have the opposite problem."

"You mentioned something about us, the church, and Bishop Parnell?"

"Yeah, well, I may have been mistaken about that. It was before I saw…*Royce*, is it?"

"Pleased to meet you." He nodded. "*Dodge?*"

"*Scarlett.* Scarlett Dodge."

"Scarlett? Seriously? That's the best you could come up with?"

She scowled. "Hey, that's my real name. Thank you very much."

Royce shrugged.

Hadrian had one heel hooked on the crossbar of the stool and the other on the floor. He considered tapping his toe but figured they'd still ignore him. Instead, he said, "Can we get back to the subject at hand, please?"

"Which was?" Scarlett asked.

"Hello? We were talking about why you drugged me."

"Oh, that." She waved a hand dismissively. "Definitely a mistake. I thought you were hired muscle watching over Pastor-Pain-in-the-Ass. I had no idea that…" Focusing on Royce, her eyes became serious. "How much are they paying?"

"How much is who paying for what?" Royce asked.

"How much is the church paying you to kill Lady Dulgath? If I make you a better offer to leave, you'd be okay with that, right?"

"You're that wealthy?"

"No, but I'll take up a collection. If everyone pitches in, and they will—"

"We're not here to kill Nysa Dulgath," Hadrian said.

Scarlett rolled her eyes.

"We aren't."

She ignored him and continued to address Royce. "What do you say?"

"Let me get this straight—you'll pay us *not* to kill Lady Dulgath." Royce was nodding. "I think I might be able to do that. If you can—"

"Royce!" Hadrian slapped the table.

"What?"

"Stop it."

"She's going to pay us *not* to kill Lady Dulgath. That's easy money."

"It's dishonest."

Royce folded his arms and glared.

"Wait…" Scarlett looked from Royce to Hadrian. "You really aren't here to kill her?"

Royce scowled at Hadrian. "You ruin everything." He turned back to Scarlett. "Up to a minute ago, I thought you were part of it. Why else would a Black Diamond be hiding in Brecken Dale?"

She shook her head. "I'm not hiding—not really—and I'm not in the Black Diamond…not anymore."

"Freelancing?"

She shook her head. "Straight."

Royce looked skeptical.

Scarlett appeared confused. "If you're not here to kill her, then…I don't understand. Why *are* you here?"

"We were hired to help *protect* her," Hadrian explained.

"Ha!" Scarlett followed the outburst with mock laughter. She dumped strips of pork into a pan, then hooked it to a blackened rafter chain and let it dangle over the fire before adding another small log. "And exactly who hired you?"

"The Nyphron Church."

"Ah-hah!" Scarlett turned to Hadrian with a there-you-have-it look.

"Ah-hah what?" Hadrian said.

"The church is using you to help kill her."

"Churches don't kill people," Hadrian told her. "They burn incense, collect tithes, and mutter words in forgotten languages—they don't put out contracts on high-ranking nobles."

Scarlett and Royce exchanged glances, then both shook their heads.

Royce hooked a thumb in Hadrian's direction. "See what I have to put up with?"

"Adorable," Scarlett said.

"Look," Hadrian went on, certain they just didn't understand. "Lady Dulgath has had a number of attempts made on her life, and everyone insists a professional has been hired. But Lady Dulgath isn't acknowledging there's a problem. So the church is concerned for her welfare and hired us as consultants. Royce is an authority when it comes to assassinations."

"You don't say," Scarlett said with a bemused expression.

"That's why we were picked. He knows how such things are done."

"He's just *so* cute," Scarlett said to Royce, shaking her head in disbelief.

"Why is that hard to believe?" Hadrian asked.

"Is he serious? Is any of that even remotely true?" she asked Royce while cracking an egg into the same pan where the pork was starting to sizzle.

"Yes. And mostly."

"It's not that hard to understand." Hadrian unfolded his arms so he could use his hands to better explain. "Royce is going to review the situation, then report on how a professional might go about killing Lady Dulgath so they can—"

"Do exactly what he says," Scarlett said.

"What?" Hadrian paused a moment to rerun the idea. "No!"

"If you are really telling the truth—and I'm starting to think you might be—that's exactly what they're doing," Scarlett told him.

Hadrian shook his head, pushed up from the stool, and planted both feet square on the floor. "The two of you are *so* distrustful. You look at a black-and-white cow and see gray. No! You see a conspiracy to poison farmers with milk!"

"Or"—Scarlett smiled at him—"we look at a conspiracy and see a conspiracy."

"If the church wanted Lady Dulgath dead, why not just hire us to kill her?" Hadrian asked.

"Granted, that would seem easier, but this is the church we're talking about. They have a tendency to overbuild. Have you seen their cathedrals?" She cracked another egg. "Think for a second. Let's say they did that, and Lady Dulgath was killed. Do you suppose the king will just shrug and say, *Oh well*? No. He'll send *real* constables."

She sprinkled some pepper on the eggs. "They aren't going to risk getting caught up in this. They're trying to spread their tentacles here in Maranon—and doing a damn fine job of it. So what do they do? They find a couple of nonaffiliated cutthroats and get them down here. After they carry out the execution themselves, the cutthroats are arrested for it. Everyone knows they're the killers: The murder happened exactly the way they said it would. Now the conspirators have their scapegoats, who they'll execute before the king's constables arrive. There's no need for further investigation because justice has been done. The best part is you two aren't part of any guild, right?" She looked at Royce, who nodded. "So they don't have to worry about any retribution. Lady's dead. Killers executed. King is satisfied. Justice done. Everyone's happy."

Scarlett used a wooden spatula to flip the meat. The little cottage was filling with the wonderful scent of cooking pork. Hadrian wasn't certain if the smell of food had anything to do with it, but he was growing sympathetic to her points. He turned to Royce. "She could have something here."

Royce had wandered to the bedroom side of the cottage. He held a red glove in his hand, looking it over, and not saying anything.

"Royce?"

He dropped the glove on the bed. "What?"

Royce had the hearing of a bat. He could practically listen in on what was happening tomorrow. After dropping the glove, he found a basket of rushes interesting.

"You knew?" Hadrian asked.

Royce shrugged. "I suspected. Hiring a consulting assassin is a bit odd, don't you think?"

"Then why are we here?"

"Twenty gold tenents and expenses. The coffers were dry. We needed something. So we either took this or started thieving outright, and I knew how well that would go over with you."

"Twenty? Gold?" Scarlett's mouth hung open. "Damn. Glad I don't have to outbid them."

"Okay, sure, but we can't spend gold if we're dead."

"And I have no intention of being framed."

"So what do we do now?"

"Same as before. Nothing's changed."

"Really?"

"Sure. We still need the money, and Miss Dodge might be wrong—about them framing us, at least. Even if she isn't, they're paying to hear how *I* would do this job. And that's exactly what I'm going to tell them. They can try to follow my plan if they want, but even the best in the Diamond couldn't mimic my methods. The chances of them succeeding are as unlikely as someone stealing from the Crown Tower."

Scarlett was loading plates with meat and eggs when she turned with surprise. "That was you?"

"Figure of speech," Royce said.

"Oh—sure—of course." Scarlett continued to stare.

"Before I tell them anything, I want to know as much as I can about what's going on." He glared at Scarlett. "Like why an ex-Diamond would be willing to take up a collection, or why villagers would pay to save their ruler."

"Lady Dulgath is special." Scarlett set the plates on the table.

"Yeah, you mentioned that, but special how?" Hadrian asked.

"The Dulgaths have always treated their people well. They really care about us."

"No offense to your humble abode," Royce said, "but yesterday Hadrian and I were in the lady's stables. They're much nicer than this. Seems she cares more for her horses than she does her people."

Scarlett shook her head as she pulled a loaf of brown bread out of a box and set it on the table. "That's unreasonable. Dulgath is the home of several thousand people scattered in dozens of hamlets and fishing villages. The Dulgaths can't provide for all of us. No one could. She'll do what she can, just like her father had."

"Which is?"

"Let us buy, sell, and trade without crippling taxes. Protect us with fair laws, evenly executed." Scarlett grabbed a bucket and turned it over, making a seat for herself. "And…"

"And?"

"She heals people."

Scarlett sat down on her bucket before the table and bowed her head.

"What do you mean, she *heals* people?" Royce asked.

Scarlett kept her head down, whispering to herself.

Royce looked at Hadrian. "What's she doing?"

"I think she's praying."

"You're kidding." Royce rolled his eyes and slapped the table. "How does she heal people?"

Scarlett held up her index finger, asking him to wait.

Royce continued to glare at her, but Scarlett didn't see.

Hadrian took the break in conversation to pull close to the table. The plate before him was steaming. The inch-thick pork was crispy brown, nearly black on the edges, the eggs dripping with dark grease. He tore a chunk of bread, pulled his dagger, and—using the bread to hold the meat—cut a piece. After he took a bite, bliss came over his face. "Good," he told Royce, chewing.

"I think I'll wait to see if you pass out or vomit blood before I eat."

"Be cold by then."

"It's a trade-off I'm willing to make."

Scarlett's head came back up. Her eyes opened and she, too, tore a bit of bread free.

"Can we talk now?" Royce asked. He was still standing, but he put a foot up on the stool near him.

"Of course—as long as you don't mind me chewing at the same time."

"Then tell me how Lady Dulgath heals people."

"She goes around to the hamlets just like Maddie Oldcorn used to."

"Who's that?"

"Maddie was—I don't know, a legend really—an old woman who lived alone out in the forest near Brecken Moor. It's said she gave Nysa Dulgath her gift before she died."

"What *gift*?"

Scarlett took a bite of pork and chewed a moment, her lips glistening from the grease. "The gift of healing. Old Maddie was famous for it. Fever, pox, the Black Cough, blood sores, you name it, she healed it, and with little more than a wave of her hands. She was a divine servant of Maribor."

"Up north, they'd burn Old Maddie as a witch," Royce said.

Scarlett pointed at him with her bread. "Exactly. And the Nyphron Church would be the one building the pyre, proclaiming that evil comes from turning off Novron's path. Around here, we look to Maribor and are granted his blessings for our steadfast faith."

Hadrian tested the eggs with his fingers to see if they were too hot to pick up. They weren't, and he found them rich and silky, with a nice smoked flavor from the pork's fat. "What kind of blessings are we talking about?"

"Well, for one, it never rains here…not during the day at least. And the winters are mild. I've never seen anything like them."

Royce smirked. "You realize you're south, right? There's this thing called climate. Perhaps you've heard of it?"

She waved a hand in his direction. "And the blessing of Maddie? How do you explain her? Does the good weather make diseases flee from the body? Sure, people might not have as many colds in warm weather, but I'm talking about people who were stricken one day and fine the next."

"If that's true, I'd be more interested in the woman herself, not some god I've never seen lift his finger to help anyone. Where did Maddie come from and how did she get her so-called gift?"

"Don't know. Not sure anyone does—Augustine might know more. An odd bird, Maddie was. Saved the lives of hundreds of people, but she wasn't the least bit friendly." Scarlett thought a minute, then pointed at Royce with her crust. "Come to think of it, she was a lot like you, only she *saved* lives."

"Who is Augustine?" Hadrian licked his fingers. "In case we want to talk to him."

"Augustine Gilcrest is the abbot of Brecken Moor."

"Is he the one who ordered the tarring and feathering of Pastor Payne?"

Scarlett waved her bread this time, which Hadrian took a moment to realize meant no. "He's a Monk of Maribor. While the Nyphron Church takes issue with the monks, the monks don't feel the same way. Or maybe they do, but they would never act on it. The monks are a live-and-let-live sect."

"They might feel differently if the Nyphron Church really does have plans to move in," Royce said.

"No…no…it's not possible—they're…" Scarlett chewed for a while, swallowed, then stopped, still searching for words. "I don't know how to explain. You'd have to meet them, I suppose. But no, neither he nor anyone at the monastery would have had anything to do with that."

"Maybe we should talk to him." Hadrian was still cleaning pork fat from his fingers one by one.

"You talk to him." Royce took his foot off the stool and eyed his plate of food. "I'm not good with religious types. Besides, I need to get back and look around the castle some more."

"This is really good, by the way." Hadrian nodded at the plate.

"Thanks," Scarlett said.

"Feeling sick yet?" Royce asked.

"Nope."

Royce scratched his chin, then sighed and sat down, drawing his plate to him. He took a bite of pork and nodded. "*Very* good."

"Thank you," Scarlett said, but Hadrian couldn't tell whether she was being genuine or sarcastic.

"Where is this monastery?" Hadrian asked.

"She'll take you," Royce replied.

"Whoa, wait a second." Scarlett dropped the knife and bread and raised her hands. "Breakfast is one thing, but I do have a life."

"While we're here, you're working for us. Consider it payment for what you did to Hadrian last night."

"You can't do that."

Royce smiled at her and lifted the folded parchment from his pouch. "Amoral killer with a writ. I'm just about your worst nightmare. So what do you say you do it for your king? Oh, but just so we're clear"—Royce pointed the tip of Alverstone at Hadrian—"if he suffers so much as a stubbed toe, I'm coming after you first."

They finished breakfast, then Royce and Hadrian stepped outside while Scarlett cleaned. The sun was past midday, the shadows short, and the scent of magnolia hung in the air. Scarlett's cottage didn't have a yard. Her front steps led directly to the cobbles of the street.

"So you want to split up again?" Hadrian wasn't sure this was such a good idea, given how things had gone the night before.

"Here." Royce handed him his own piece of folded paper. "You have your steel, your credentials, and a guide. Even you should be okay given all that."

Hadrian shot him a smirk. "I'm not worried about myself. You're the one going into the lion's den. If the church is trying to frame us, then Payne, Knox, and Fawkes are all in on it, and who knows how many others. That means the odds are stacked against you."

"And how is that different from any other day of the week? Seriously, I'll be fine."

Hadrian had his doubts. Royce wasn't so much a closed book as one that was chained shut, locked in a box, and thrown into the sea. Still, he was starting to sense moods, subtle shifts like a change in the wind. Hadrian had no idea whether a storm was coming or if the skies were clearing. What he did know was that something was off about Royce.

"What happened to you last night while I was being stupid?" Hadrian asked.

Royce wiped a hand over his face. "I certainly wasn't being smart. I paid an uninvited visit to the lady's bedroom. She caught me."

"She *caught* you? How'd that happen?"

"I'm still trying to figure that out. Part of why I need to go back." His face hardened.

Royce didn't like privileged nobles as a general rule, but there was something about the look on his partner's face that Hadrian couldn't puzzle out. Royce seemed intent on hating Lady Dulgath for some reason, but Hadrian decided not to push.

"Okay, so while you're stalking Lady Dulgath, I'll investigate this monastery. What am I looking for exactly?"

"Don't know." Royce looked around. A two-wheeled wagon rested under the shade of an old oak across the street, flowers growing through its spokes. Scarlett Dodge lived on a lovely tree-lined lane that followed the curves of the little hills visible between the roofs of the houses. "Something strange about this place."

"You mean like how everything is covered in ivy?" Hadrian said. "Or how the spring doesn't uncover any new rocks?"

"Huh?" Royce asked.

"Rocks. You know, in the fields."

"I can honestly say I have no idea what you are talking about."

"Each spring, farmers need to clear their fields of rocks brought up over the winter. Frost heaves them to the surface, where they ruin plow blades. So the farmers dig the stones up and make walls with them because there's only so much material needed for building a house or well. Yesterday I rode by a dozen farms—you must have seen them, too. Had to have been here for centuries, but the rock walls are just little decorative things."

"Easy winters. Not much frost."

"Maybe. But what about it not raining here? And since when do the common people love their ruler so much?"

"So you *have* been paying attention."

"I'm not as stupid as you think I am."

"You have no idea how stupid I think you are, and honestly, we don't have time for *that* conversation."

Hadrian scowled.

"We'll meet back in the room at Caldwell House tonight," Royce said. "I might be late, so don't wait up. And don't turn your back on her again."

"Scarlett?"

Royce rolled his eyes, sighed, and grimaced. "She's not a pretty barmaid. She's not a *nice* girl."

"Seems like it to me."

"Of course she does. She was in the Diamond. Her working name was Feldspar, and the nice-girl thing is part of her act. Cute and disarming, she dances, sings—"

"She sings, too?" Hadrian smiled.

"Pretty sure, and she does magic tricks. One of her favorites is making people's coins disappear. She's not innocent. She's dangerous if you turn your back on her—so don't."

Hadrian recalled how deftly Scarlett had prepped the pork.

"And stay away from the pastor, too," Royce said. "It would appear he was lying."

"About what?"

"About there being no *i* in his name."

Chapter Ten
GHOST IN THE COURTYARD

The entirety of the castle staff had assembled in the Great Hall: two stewards, four chambermaids, two gardeners, two charwomen, the trio of cooks, the butterer, four scullery maids, the smith, herbalist, vintner, dyer, tailor, furrier, mercer, milliner, scribe, four grooms, a stable boy, woodcutter, food tester, sheriff, chamberlain, tax collector, treasurer, keeper of the wardrobe, her handmaiden, and the sergeant-at-arms with his six men. Lady Dulgath stood before them, demanding that the person or persons responsible for destroying Sherwood's easel and paints step forward.

No one did.

Sherwood wasn't surprised, but he was touched by the emotion in Lady Dulgath's voice as she made her demand. She was angry. Perhaps—most likely—certainly—she was upset that his property was damaged in her home. She had suffered the embarrassment of failing to protect her guest. Still, Sherwood entertained the whisper-thin notion that she reacted so harshly because she liked him. She had said his name, after all. Wasn't much to base a verdict on, but Sherwood was in a vulnerable state, and he clung to the idea like an ant riding a leaf in the middle of a flood.

The loss of his paints, palette, brushes, and easel was a mortal blow. They were irreplaceable. The set of tools had taken generations of master artists to build, amass, and perfect. Each painter loathed using up the better pigments, and was always saving to add more color to the collection. Some contributed a different brush or two; in Sherwood's case, it was walnut oil. When he died, the collection would have been left to an apprentice; he just didn't know who that would be. Now he had nothing to pass on.

Sherwood calculated that if he painted every noble's face for the rest of his life, he still couldn't hope to replace what had been lost. Deprived of the tools of his trade, he couldn't even feed himself. But worse than all that was the deep disappointment of not finishing Nysa's portrait. He had so wanted to. He needed to see all of what lay beyond the veil that could only be shown through the slow process of peeling back and layering up.

Feeling the winds of the hurricane blowing, Sherwood left the gathering and sat on the stone carving of a dragon that decorated the castle's reception hall. Castle Dulgath was famous for its sculptures.

Or ought to be, he thought.

Much of the castle was crafted from stone, and so beautifully done that rumors persisted about it once being a dwarven fortress. Sherwood didn't think that was true. He'd been to the ruins of Linden Lott and had seen the ancient dwarven capital. He'd witnessed the skillful precision on a scale no longer possible. The sort of creative artistry on display in Dulgath was wholly different.

Dwarven designs were massive, practical, and tended to use geometric shapes. Castle Dulgath's statues and reliefs were whimsical and breathtakingly lifelike. The dragon, whose paw he sat on, lay curled up, eyes closed as if it were a sleeping dog—only one of many such decorations. The west tower that stood on the very edge of the sea-battered cliff was adorned with clawed feet at its base—a beautification that few ever saw. The stone railings that led to the fifth floor—the private quarters off limits to all but a few—were adorned with delicately sculpted ivy that hung down like the real thing. A stone otter playing with a pinecone was hidden in a corner of the kitchen pantry, and the wall in the courtyard before the common well was decorated with a bas-relief of a school of fish swimming past. After two months, Sherwood was still discovering hidden treasures. Who had been responsible for the secret wealth of artistry, he couldn't discover. Apparently, no one remembered.

What am I going to do? The thought had been rattling inside his skull ever since its predecessors: *Why me?* and *This isn't real* tired themselves out. Two new thoughts muscled their way in: *I'm going to starve* and *My life is over.*

Sitting on the dragon's paw he felt tears welling in his eyes as the full weight of his loss descended. His mouth folded up, as if a purse string ran through his lips and a miser had pulled them taut. Just then, Lord Fawkes entered the castle. Sherwood hadn't thought his day could get worse, but his hurricane of bad luck wasn't done raining. Fawkes spotted him and changed course.

"Stow, I just heard," he said, shaking his head with sympathy so blatantly false that Sherwood could hear the laughter behind it. "Bad break. What are you going to do now? You don't have any extra supplies, do you?"

"I don't know."

"You don't know what you'll do now or whether you have extra supplies?"

"Leave me alone, please." Sherwood wiped his eyes, dragging the tears over his cheeks.

"Are you seriously crying over spilled paint?" Fawkes put a foot up on one of the dragon's massive claws and leaned in. "People are dying every day." He held out a hand about knee-high. "Children starving to death on crowded streets, women raped, men butchered in mindless campaigns for stupid rulers. The world is full of unjust misery, and here you are sobbing over paint? You're quite the sniveling little quim, aren't you?"

"Surely a lord of your stature has better things to do?"

"Of course, but I like to be generous to the downtrodden. I suspect you are low on funds—you artist types aren't known for budgeting your money. I thought I would offer my assistance. I've purchased a horse this morning and wish to have it taken back to Mehan. I'm in need of a courier, and you could use the money. I'll pay you to ride her home for me. I suspect Her Ladyship will be willing to provide you with adequate food and whatever supplies you'll need, seeing as how she's sort of at fault for your situation."

"She didn't do it."

"She didn't stop it, either, but that's a triviality. What is important is that this is your lucky day, Stow. On the heels of your disaster comes good fortune. The horse is in the stable, a chestnut named Eloise. She came with saddle and tack. You can pack your bags and be on your way to Mehan by midday. I'll pay you five silver for the trip because I'm feeling generous and because of your misadventure. So stop your blubbering and start packing." Fawkes clapped his hands and grinned, eyes bright with happiness, as if this news was equally good for him and Sherwood.

"Excuse me," Sherwood said. He got to his feet, turned his back on Lord Fawkes, and walked away.

GHOST IN THE COURTYARD

Sherwood had no idea where he was off to. Not thinking—not capable of sound thought—he'd taken the obvious path before him. He moved toward the light coming in the front doors of the castle instead of going back inside where he might have lost himself in the many corridors and rooms. All he wanted was to get away. Sherwood knew Lord Fawkes was watching; he felt eyes boring into his back.

He walked out through the big doors onto the stone porch. Castle Dulgath wasn't built correctly. Sherwood had been to most of the strongholds across Avryn and even a few in Trent and western Calis. None were like this. The differences went beyond the intricate decorations. The porch was a good example—castles didn't have porches. Fortresses were built for defense and were circled by a curtain wall with ramparts and turrets. The others all had a single massive entry composed of three formidable barriers—a drawbridge, a sturdy gate, and a portcullis. Such strongholds didn't always have moats, but those without had ditches.

In contrast, Dulgath sported a wide porch with columns that held up the extended roof to shade it from the summer sun. This was less a fortress and more a glorified country manor. That was one of the things Sherwood loved about the castle and, by extension, Nysa Dulgath.

Once on the porch, he made a quick turn to the right to break Fawkes's line of sight. Immediately his back felt better. Elevated as he was, Sherwood had a broad view of the courtyard. The shadow cast by the east tower divided the yard into dark and light, the contrast leaving those areas in the sun so brilliant they looked washed out. Having no place to go except away from Fawkes, Sherwood stopped three steps after making his escape and stood dumbly on the porch. He was acutely aware of how his arms hung pointlessly at his sides, how heavy his body felt, how dry his mouth was, and how none of it mattered. Depression was closing in; the dark clouds were circling, creeping up, preparing to smother. Just then, he saw movement, or thought he did.

Like his arms, his eyes had been left with no clear direction. Sherwood had been aimlessly staring because at that moment he found even the effort of shifting his gaze to be too much. If he had been walking or merely glancing around the way a person typically might, he never would have noticed the motion. Having seen the subtle shift of light and darkness near the well, he was slow to grasp the impossibility of what he saw. No one was there and nothing was moving in the breeze, because there wasn't one.

A cloud—maybe? Or a bird's shadow?

Sherwood stepped off the porch and looked up. The sky was clear.

Everyone—everyone is in the Great Hall. So who—or what—is near the well?

The *or what* surprised him. Sherwood wasn't usually a believer in the fantastical. He'd spent too many drunken nights with court entertainers. Minstrels, poets, and storytellers accepted him as part of their club and told him the real stories behind the tales of valor and wonder. At a young age, he discovered the truth about the world— mysteries were designed for a purpose, and if something seemed too fantastical to be true, it was. But he was the only audience in the courtyard, and he'd entered only a second before. What had moved in that corner of the yard didn't look *human*. Nothing more than a shadow, but the movement was strange, too fast, and—

Didn't it go up rather than across?

Such a thing wasn't possible. There hadn't been a sound. In the stillness of the empty, windless yard, Sherwood could've heard a leaf fall, but there was nothing.

GHOST IN THE COURTYARD

Who or what is near the well?

The question lingered, and Sherwood realized that the hurricane—with its dreadful, smothering clouds—was holding off. The storm had miraculously been brought to bay by this aberration. Keeping his eyes locked on the spot, he descended the steps and started across the courtyard.

Along with the odd sense that what he'd seen wasn't *normal* was the equally strong impression that it wasn't *good*. With each step, he became more certain of two things. The first was the wickedness of what he approached, and the second was that it was still there. Just a day before, he would have returned inside, but it wasn't the previous day and Sherwood found himself not so much brave as invincible. He was a soaked man caught in a summer rainstorm.

What harm can it do that hasn't already been done?

The inner ward's well was set in a niche surrounded on three sides by screening walls. Sherwood was certain something was hiding in that little space where his sight was blocked. Crossing the yard, he approached the well head-on, but saw nothing except the beautiful stone mural of fish and the side-cranking windlass that looked a bit like a sailing ship's wheel.

"Sir?"

Sherwood jumped at the sound.

"Mister Stow?" Rissa Lyn had followed him across the yard. In both her hands, she held empty buckets.

He must have looked strange, creeping up on the well and staring at it. The expression on her face said as much. She even gave a concerned glance at the well, and then another behind her.

"Is the…ah—has Lady Dulgath concluded her meeting then?" he asked, trying his best to sound sane.

"Yes, sir."

"No one admitted to it, did they?"

"No, sir."

"I didn't think they would."

"Me neither, sir."

Sherwood nodded and forced a smile that must have been miserable, judging by the way Rissa Lyn grimaced in return.

"I'm sorry. You're here to fetch water. Don't let me get in your way." He gave a curt nod and started back toward the castle.

"Sir?"

He paused, turning to look at Rissa Lyn standing in the sunlight. She was still grimacing, but not at him. She looked frightened.

"What is it?"

"I know who busted up your things," the maid said in a whisper, her sight darting toward the castle doors. Then she turned and walked to the well, setting the buckets down and reaching out for the windlass crank.

"Let me help you with that," Sherwood said, and rushed over to rotate the wheel.

"Thank you, sir. You're too kind, sir," Rissa Lyn said loudly. Then, as he began cranking, she whispered, "I was woken by the noise, an awful cracking. I often sleep in the linen storage. It saves me from crossing the yard in the dark."

She glanced around apprehensively at the old walls. "No one cares 'cause it's just me who goes in there. So I was just down the hall, you see, and I heard it. I don't know what I was thinking... going down there, I mean. It sounded like a monster was loose in the castle—crashes, shattering glass, cracks, grunts, and under all of that a muttering like someone was talking to themselves. I honestly don't know how I found the courage to peer through the crack in the doorway."

"What did you see?" Already Sherwood had convinced himself that the phantom shadow near the well was some ancient ghost or demon responsible for the destruction of his easel and paints. Rissa Lyn's answer was both disappointing and depressing.

"Was Lord Fawkes, sir." She emptied the water from the well's bucket into one of her own. "He was in the study working up a sweat after taking a real dislike to your painting stand. Hard work, I guess, difficult to break."

"Did he see you?"

"Oh—no, sir. I just took a peek, and when I saw who it was, I ran back to my cupboard. People think he's swell and all, but—he scares me."

Sherwood let the wheel spin, taking the haul back down to the bottom of the well. "Scares me, too."

This made her smile at him for the first time. "It just wasn't right for him to do that, not to someone as…well, as nice as you."

"Thank you, Rissa Lyn." He started cranking again. "Did you tell Lady Dulgath?"

The smile vanished and that look of fear rushed back. "No, sir."

"Why not? She was asking for—"

"She was asking for the guilty to step forward. His Lordship wasn't there. And if he were, he wouldn't bother."

"But you could've explained about seeing him."

She shook her head. Rissa Lyn had curly hair that jiggled like leaves on a bush well after she stopped. "He would find out, and who would believe me? He'd just deny it, and then I would be in trouble for lying, even though I wasn't." She bit her lip, and he understood.

Sherwood wasn't making idle conversation about Lord Fawkes being scary. The lord had the brutal aggression of ambitious men. He wouldn't think twice about crushing or intimidating those he saw as below him.

Sherwood grabbed the well's bucket this time and filled her other bucket. "You can still tell Lady Dulgath in private. Talk to her like you're doing with me now. No one but you and she would know what you said."

The curls shook again. "Me and Her *Ladyship*…we…I don't speak to her."

"You're her handmaiden, right?"

When Sherwood was interested in a noblewoman, he usually worked through her handmaiden. They were the front door to any lady's heart—or at least her bed. Noblewomen maintained a distinct delineation between servants and gentry, but exceptions were often granted for their personal maids, who were sometimes as close as sisters. This was one of the reasons why he'd always made it a point to say good morning to Rissa Lyn. He'd even brought her pretty shells from his walks on the shore and flowers from the roadside.

Rissa Lyn nodded, but behind her eyes was that same fear.

She's not afraid of Fawkes. She's afraid of Lady Dulgath.

"What's wrong?" He set the haul back on the edge of the well.

"Nothing, sir. Thank you for the help, sir. And please, don't tell nobody that I was the one who saw His Lordship, sir. I only told you because…I have to go, sir."

She grabbed up the two buckets and ran off, spilling much of the water as she went.

Sherwood stood in the well niche, watching Rissa Lyn disappear into the dark of the castle. She left an intermittent trail of damp spots.

"She's hiding something," a low voice said in his ear.

Sherwood jumped, pushed away, slipped, and fell on the decorative stone that fanned around the base of the well. Over him appeared a man in a long black cloak with the hood drawn up.

"I want to ask you some questions."

When Sherwood's heart stopped racing and his ability to breathe returned, he realized he knew who the man was—one of the two who had met Nysa the previous morning.

"Too bad. I don't want to answer any." Sherwood got his feet back under himself. "Go away."

"Your wants aren't my concern."

Royce Melborn—at least he thought that was the man's name—reached menacingly into his cloak.

Sherwood was already preparing his feet to run when the hand came out. He'd expected a dagger. What he saw instead stopped him. The man in the cloak was holding the glass bottle of Beyond the Sea. "I thought…I expected you would've destroyed that. Thrown it away or something." He held out his hand. "Give it back."

"No," Melborn said. "You gave it to me."

"I *threw* it at you."

"Gave, threw—same thing."

"No, it's not." He reached for the vial, but Melborn snatched it away.

"Better be the same thing because otherwise sending it my way could be interpreted as assaulting a constable. That's a serious offense."

"You're not a constable."

"I have a writ. Do you want to see it?"

"Have you forgotten I was there when you were presented to Lady Dulgath? I know you're not a constable. Any writ you have is a forgery."

"I don't need a writ to get answers. I have better ways to extract information. Let's go up to your room where we can speak in private."

"No!"

Royce smiled and tossed the bottle of pigment high into the air. It spun, glinting in the sun.

Sherwood gasped as it came hurtling back down. He expected a brilliant burst of blue on the stone at their feet, but Melborn snatched it out of the air.

"Are you sure you don't want to talk?" Melborn asked, and motioned as if he were about to throw it again.

"Don't! You don't know what you're doing!"

"Yes, I do."

"Do you even know what you're holding?"

"This?" Melborn looked at the bottle, turning it back and forth. "This is Ultramarine, commonly known as Beyond the Sea, a pigment made from pulverizing the semiprecious stone lapis lazuli into a powder. It's ideal for dyeing cloth or mixing with egg yolks to make tempera for painting."

Sherwood stared openmouthed for a moment. "I actually use oil."

"What kind?"

"Walnut."

"Try linseed sometime."

"How do you know all this?"

"Used to be in the business."

"*You* were a painter?"

Melborn shook his hood. "Illegal imports. Beyond the Sea is one of the exclusive trade items brought in through the Vandon Supply Company—a pretty way of saying it's pirated. This stuff goes for one hundred gold tenents an ounce. What is this?" Melborn held up the bottle to his ear and shook it. "Two, two-and-a-half ounces?"

"Three. Unless you've poured some out."

"Nope, all still here." Melborn began tossing the bottle back and forth between his hands. "Sure you don't want to invite me to your room for some tea and cookies?"

"I don't have either, but…" Sherwood's stomach lurched with each toss. "Are you saying you'll give that back if I cooperate?"

"That's exactly what I'm saying."

"Okay."

"And one more thing."

Sherwood cringed, knowing the offer was too good to be true. "What?"

"I want an apology for throwing it at me. That wasn't very nice."

"I'm sorry."

"There, doesn't that make you feel better?" Melborn stepped past him and led the way back across the yard.

Sherwood realized that the dark clouds had retreated a bit. That bottle—if he did get it back—would save his career and possibly his life. As much as he would loathe doing it, he could sell it in Mehan and use the coin to replace at least some of what was lost. There would be enough to get him painting again. Sherwood wouldn't be able to take any noble commissions, not without his precious blue pigment, but merchants liked portraits, too.

As he watched Melborn's cloak whip behind him, and the man slipped into the shadows of the porch, Sherwood was reminded of the thing in the shadows. The thing that wasn't quite human. He'd found his ghost.

Chapter Eleven
BRECKEN MOOR

Scarlett Dodge led Hadrian up the trail that corkscrewed around the balding hill. They were a few miles outside the village on the far side of the river—the *bad side*, as Pastor Payne called it. Didn't seem bad to Hadrian.

Down by the mill, where a big waterwheel turned, Scarlett had taken him across an arching stone bridge that was about as picturesque as they came. The rushing river churned below, its deep green waters frothing between sun-bleached boulders. A small mountain rose from the edge of the far bank. The river had cut a gash through it, revealing iron-rich layers of stone. There were no homes on the far side, no mills, no tilled fields, and everything was uphill. The little trail they followed had worn the roots of nearby trees, polishing them until the wood shone. Where the path passed over rocks—which was often—the surface of the stone was buffed as smooth as finished marble.

The path started in a thick canopy of cottonwood and hawthorn. As they ascended, it graduated to birch and juniper. Farther up, the trail widened when they reached a world of fir, aspen, and pine. The "bad side" of the river had an enchanting, mythic quality. Moss and lichen covered the rocks, some of which were the size of two-story houses. They looked to have been dropped and forgotten by neglectful giants.

"It's beautiful here," Hadrian said.

"It is," Scarlett agreed, striding up the trail with all the stamina of a mountain goat.

"Some of the rocks are shaped like faces," he observed. This was the sort of comment that made Royce cringe, and Hadrian expected the same reaction from Scarlett.

Instead, she nodded and smiled. "People used to believe stones like these were alive, you know? Trees, too—they believed everything had spirits. People worshiped river gods, the sun, the moon, and the four winds."

"Is that what the monks think, that there are spirits everywhere?"

"No, but that's what our ancestors thought. Ages and ages ago, long before the empire, people lived in scattered villages like—well, like Brecken Dale, and every one of them had its own personal god. They worshiped a statue of him *or her*, and even took it with them when they charged into battles. There were hundreds of spirits and demons back then. But all that changed, starting here."

"Starting here? What happened?" Hadrian asked, but Scarlett had scampered ahead and disappeared around a bend of cliff. Catching up, he discovered they had reached the top.

An open, rocky slope, covered in sedge, matt buckwheat, and forget-me-nots, spread out before him. He stood above the tree line, and below lay the world. Hadrian felt as though he could see into infinity. Green-blue ridges of forested hills ran south toward bluer, rocky mountains, and beyond those were white peaks. A cloud was caught between two ridges, a tuft of milkweed trapped in a cleft. Far below, the village was merely a smudge and the river only a shining ribbon wriggling through the green. To the east, and what looked to be just below their feet, the silver waves of the ocean shimmered. But what astounded him the most was the clear, blue sky threatening to engulf him. "Whoa."

Scarlett had stopped; she watched him, grinning. "Amazing, isn't it?" she asked. "It's like you've come to the end of the world and can see clearly for the first time."

On the still-rising slope that formed the bald head of the little mountain stood an ancient stone building. Massive, rough-hewn slabs were stacked without mortar. Corners had been worn and rounded, and while no ivy grew there, emerald-green moss and gold lichen decorated every block.

"Welcome to Brecken Moor," Scarlett said.

Augustine Gilcrest looked like a monk, old and weathered, with a face that had suffered from the merciless sun, the wind, and the cruel whims of gods. But in his eyes was the blue of an endless sky. A long white beard showed he hadn't shaved in decades, and the haphazard hair sticking out in all directions beneath a miserable flop of a hat told Hadrian the cleric likely hadn't seen a mirror in about as long.

Seeing Scarlett, the abbot of Brecken Moor howled with joy, then embraced her tightly, kissing her three times on the cheek. She returned the squeeze with the same comfortable closeness of a family accustomed to hugging.

"I'm so glad you've come to visit. Let's sit down in the shade. I know what a long stroll it is to get here."

They were out in the cloister, an enclosed garden surrounded by a pillared walkway. At the center, an artesian spring trickled down into a naturally formed pool. Around it, carefully cultivated plots of vegetables, herbs, and flowers grew. Around those, walkways and stone benches had been constructed.

The monk led them to one of those, in the shade of an old and twisted bristlecone pine. He gestured for them to sit. "It's so wonderful to see you again." He beamed at Scarlett. "You need to visit more often." His eyes darted over. "And who is this young man?" His tone was playful, mischievous, and his brows made an insinuating jump.

"This is Hadrian Blackwater, just a curious stranger from up north," Scarlett said. Her face looked a bit flushed, but it could have been from the mountain hike.

"The question is," Augustine said, continuing in his baiting tone, "what is he curious about?"

"Actually," said Hadrian, who was sticky with sweat and fixated on the trickling water, "I was wondering if you had anything to drink."

The abbot held out a hand to the bubbling spring. "That's what it's there for, the same as the air you're breathing. Maribor provides."

Scarlett walked over, bent down, and sucked water from the surface of the pool as if she were a deer in a glade. She stood up, wiping her mouth. "Best you'll ever have."

Hadrian followed her example. The water was cold, clear, and perfect. He drained almost half an inch before standing. Refreshed and revitalized, he took a deep breath of the fresh air and sighed.

"Nice, isn't it?" Scarlett asked.

"I could live here," Hadrian replied.

"If you wish, you can," Augustine told him. "We welcome anyone interested in a life of worship."

"Really?" Hadrian hadn't seen more than two other monks—or at least two other men in the same drab habits. "Not a lot of takers lately, I'm guessing?"

Augustine smiled. "We're a bit out of the way here."

"Certainly is beautiful," Hadrian said. "Everything here is. Even down in the village—across this whole valley, really."

"Yes, Dulgath is a little sliver of paradise perched at land's end." The abbot winked at Scarlett.

"So much natural beauty in one place, and yet…"

"Yes?" the abbot asked.

"I don't know, just doesn't feel natural. Something strange about this place."

The abbot and Scarlett exchanged looks. "Would you like to know? Would you *really*?"

Hadrian wasn't sure he did. He wasn't one for sermons. In the manor village where he'd grown up, they didn't have a church. A priest of Nyphron would visit a few times a year. He came to perform weddings, to bless the dead and the harvest, but mostly to break bread and drink with Lord Baldwin. No one in Hintindar could be considered devout, and Hadrian's father held an open contempt for the church.

The years Hadrian had spent in the military, not to mention his time in Calis, had done nothing to improve his indifferent view of religion. He supposed it served a purpose: calmed fears, eased suffering, gave hope, and occasionally helped those whom others ignored. Still, he'd never understood the blind worship of the faithful.

Deacons, priests, and bishops were ordinary men and just as prone to acts of good and evil as anyone else. From his perspective, there was only one difference: The religious loved to talk. Soldiers, merchants, even nobles were men of action. The devout were men of words—usually lots of them.

That afternoon, however, Hadrian was tired from a long uphill walk, and sitting down to listen to a story didn't sound so bad. It didn't matter that he was pretty sure it wasn't going to be a good one.

"Okay." Hadrian found his own slab of stone and got comfortable.

Augustine smiled at him, then stood up. He lifted his eyes to the sky and took a deep breath.

"Long, long ago," he began, fanning his fingers as if he were evoking the birth of existence, "our people came to this valley and thought to make a life here. But their dreams became a nightmare, for this place was ruled by an evil demon of the old world: a monster capable of leveling mountains, blotting out the light of the sun, and calling down bolts of lightning. Paths were guarded by cruel thorns, soil was made barren, and the water"—he pointed at the trickling well—"was poison. This was a cursed land, an awful, terrible place of darkness and death…until Bran came."

Scarlett grinned at the name like a child hearing a favorite tale and eager to share—to experience it again through the reactions of someone new.

Augustine's attention was distracted by a pair of monks who entered the cloister. "C'mon." He invited them with a wave.

One young, one middle-aged, they shuffled over silently and sat on the ground. They, too, had the eager, excited expression.

It must be really boring up here, Hadrian guessed.

"Now then," Augustine went on, "Bran was the protégé of Brin, the legendary hero of old. When Brin was a boy, no more than fourteen years old, his parents were killed by a marauding army of giants, who were so big they used trees as toothpicks. Brin slew every last one with his bare hands. But that wasn't his only exploit. He stole the secret of metal from the dwarven king, who back then ruled from the ancient city of Neith." The abbot pointed to the southwest, causing Hadrian to turn and look, but all he saw was a cloud-covered mountain range snaking down the back of Delgos like a jagged spine.

"The dwarven king's name was Gronbach, his heart so black it bled ink. He was worse than any fiend of Phyre."

"I've heard of that dwarf," Hadrian said. "He's in nursery rhymes. An ugly creature that promises girls treasure and then betrays them. He locks the poor child in a prison of stone, but the girl—usually a princess—manages to escape by some clever trick or magic."

Augustine nodded. "Which demonstrates how such tales take form. It's a less-than-accurate retelling of a real event between the mighty Brin and the evil Gronbach. But that's a tale for another day. I merely wanted to set the stage, and let you know that Brin's adventures ranged far and wide. It's because of Brin that we have blades like the ones you carry."

Everyone was staring at Hadrian's swords, heads nodding in unison.

Hadrian smiled politely and was thankful the abbot wasn't telling the whole story, or this would be a very long visit.

"There are many legendary tales of adventures featuring Brin. It is said he slew the last of the dragons, invented writing, and fought beside Novron at a crucial battle in the Great Elven War. He even saved the first emperor's life.

"But his greatest feat was leading a band of heroes into the underworld—into the land of death itself. That trip changed everything. Bran's tales of his teacher's adventures taught us about the *real* gods. Did you know that long ago men worshiped every tree and leaf?"

"I told him," Scarlett said.

"Oh good," he replied, but his face suggested otherwise. "Well..." Augustine stumbled, trying to find his place. "It's from Bran—the founder of the Brotherhood of Maribor—that we know of Phyre and the truth that there are only five gods. Erebus is the father of all; Ferrol, the father of the elves. Drome brought forth dwarves, and of course Maribor created mankind. As for the plants and animals, that was the work of Muriel."

"What about Novron? The Nyphron Church worships the son of Maribor as their god. Do the Monks of Maribor not?"

Scarlett cringed, but the abbot just smiled politely, as if placating a child who didn't know better.

"We are the keepers of the truth. We don't involve ourselves in what others believe."

Maybe monks were as adept as nobles at obfuscation, because Hadrian noticed Gilcrest hadn't answered the question. Still, he wasn't going to be rude and dig deeper.

The abbot once more stumbled to find his place. "While Brin's accomplishments are legion, his most important contribution is the knowledge that no one, no matter how vile their past, is beyond redemption."

"Sounds like a great guy," Hadrian said. "But what does this have to do with Dulgath?"

The abbot grinned, and a twinkle shone in his eye. "Several years after the Elven War, when the empire was still young and the capital city of Percepliquis was just being built, Bran heard of the hardships the people in this valley were up against. So Bran the Holy, student of Brin the Magnificent, came to help. He stood in this very place, the ground where this monastery now stands. On this hilltop, Bran faced the Demon of Dulgath. He wrestled with the monster and forced it to yield. Wise as he was, Bran didn't slay it, but rather made it repent for its cruelties. He charged it with making right every wrong it had perpetrated against the people of this land. Exhausted from his efforts, Bran took off his shawl and rested. Then he prayed for Maribor to bless this valley. Overnight everything changed. The waters became pure, the thorns were replaced with ivy, and the weather turned ideal."

Hadrian asked Scarlett, "You believe all this?"

"I've lived here for five years," she said. "I've never seen a drought, a storm, or a famine."

"That doesn't prove anything."

"The winters here are never very cold and always stunning. It's as if the only reason it snows is for the beauty it brings. You can see for yourself how lush everything is. Ivy is everywhere, and plants usually found much farther south thrive here. We have oranges, and there are palm trees along the coast. The growing season is incredibly long, and the land is never exhausted, no matter how often the farmers plant. They don't even rotate the crops. They plant whatever they want, wherever they want."

"Still doesn't—"

"Five years, Hadrian," she said with a smirk. "I've been here five years, and I've only seen it rain once in the daytime. You can see storms that devastate other parts of Maranon from up here. Hurricanes that wreck ships on the coast—or dark clouds filled with rain and hail—never reach us. They either turn aside or die altogether. If you travel, you'll find it blistering hot or deathly cold just outside this valley, but here, in this place, it's always sunny, always warm, always—perfect."

The monks nodded in agreement.

"Fruits grow heavy, there's never a blight, and crops are always plentiful. This land *is* blessed, Hadrian. Either we're benefiting from the efforts of a reformed demon or Maribor loves this valley— maybe both. The only problems we face are the occasional accident or sickness, and for those we had Maddie Oldcorn and now Lady Dulgath. Augustine can tell you about that. He was there when it happened."

The abbot turned thoughtful, a sadness leaching through his previous energy and making him appear old for the first time. "Her

Ladyship had been in the steeplechase and fell. Landed badly. Blood was in her eyes and leaking from her ears." He shook his head, grimacing. Having a few gruesome memories of his own, Hadrian knew the abbot was seeing it all over again. "She was close to death when they carried her into the castle and laid her on the bed. Maddie was called. She had always been the thorn on the rose, the sting of a bee, but she had the heart of a racehorse and would come when needed, no matter how late the hour. She would kill herself racing for the finish line. Most people think that night was what did her in. Maddie saved Nysa Dulgath and poured everything she had into the effort. The old woman saved that girl, but died doing so. We buried her on a hill in the village where folk lay flowers in her memory."

"And after that Lady Dulgath started healing people?" Hadrian asked.

Augustine nodded. "Apparently Maddie gave her more than just life. Maybe she knew she was dying and wanted to pass on her gift. In any case, it wasn't long before Lady Dulgath began healing the sick the same way Maddie had."

"No explanation for how she does it?"

Augustine raised his hands to the sky. "She has the grace of our Lord, and he listens to her."

"But you're the abbot. Shouldn't you be the one your Lord listens to?"

"Maribor chooses whom he works through. He has his reasons. That we might not understand them is a fault in us—not him."

That was more the sort of talk Hadrian was used to hearing from clerics. Experience had likely taught Augustine to expect skepticism. Hadrian figured the abbot had encountered it often—getting people to entrust their souls to something they couldn't validate had to be a hard sell. Doubt must have been readable on his face, as Hadrian hadn't learned Royce's art of the dispassionate stare.

Augustine stood up, clapping his hands together. Old and soft as they were, they made a muffled noise, but the old man's eyes were bright with excitement. "Come with me."

He led them through the nave of the church. The other two monks must have known where he was going, because they grabbed a pair of dead torches off the wall and lit them from a white-coal brazier near the entrance. The church was little more than a large hall with a raised altar and a podium. There were paintings on the walls and ceiling, but in the dim light Hadrian couldn't make them out. The middle-aged monk took Augustine's hand as they came to stairs that led down into the solid rock of the mountaintop. When they reached a door, the abbot pushed it open. Inside, a shaft of light cut through the ceiling on a slant that shone on a pedestal, which was actually a stunning sculpture of four kneeling people, their arms upraised. In their hands they held a golden chest. The brilliant box dazzled under the beam of sunlight.

The abbot lifted the lid and revealed the contents—a piece of cloth.

Green, black, and blue plaid, the material seemed to be a simple shawl or small blanket. Clearly old, it was faded, tattered, torn, and badly frayed around the edges. The fabric was lovingly laid out and tacked in place so its full width was visible, like a tapestry.

"After his battle with the demon," Augustine said, staring down into the golden box, his hands reverently clasped before him, "Bran the Beloved took off his shawl. In the morning, he left it behind. This is the One True Thing, the proof of my words. We believe this shawl—this very bit of cloth you see here—was handed down to Bran from Brin. If so, it would be older than the Novronian Empire, older by far than the Church of Nyphron, even older than Percepliquis. This is the Shawl of Brin."

In that dark grotto, next to the gold case held up by those eerie stone hands and bathed in that pure white shaft of sunlight, Hadrian did feel a sense of awe. A presence of the mystical crept over him, raising goose bumps. An old blanket in a box was what he saw, but what he felt was an intersection with eternity, a window on a world beyond, an impossible wrinkle in reality—a footprint of a god.

No one spoke for several minutes. They stood transfixed by the simple woolen cloth, as if they were holding their own internal conversations with it, with themselves, and with Maribor. Then, without another word, the abbot closed the box, breaking the spell. He led them back out into the daylight of the tranquil cloister.

The sun felt good, reassuring. Everything was normal again. Still, no one spoke, and Hadrian took another drink from the pool. This time he splashed water on his face, then looked around.

Is it possible that some ancient hero really did fight and defeat an old-world demon on this mountaintop? Is this valley really blessed in some way? Hadrian pictured telling Royce that story and once more felt the grass beneath his feet.

His doubt must have registered, because Abbott Gilcrest patted him on the arm reassuringly and said, "Don't worry, my son, if you don't believe in Maribor and the blessings he provides. Belief in him isn't a requirement. It doesn't stop him from believing in you."

Chapter Twelve
LADY DULGATH

The room they had lent Sherwood Stow was on the third floor of the south tower, and not as nice as Royce and Hadrian's at Caldwell House. The space was smaller and had but a sliver of a sea-facing window, which left it gloomy. With three of the walls made from stone, the place was as comfortable as a dungeon. In his explorations, Royce had discovered better rooms left vacant. Perhaps those rooms had been occupied when Sherwood arrived, or they were reserved for the coming of the king and his entourage. Or maybe whoever had assigned Sherwood's room wanted him to leave as soon as possible.

The artist had been provided with a bed, but even though evening drew near, no one had bothered to freshen the linens. Broken rocks of yellow ocher and ruddy iron littered a small table in the corner. A tiny hammer and a metal file lay among the debris. Hammer-sized impressions on the surface of the table suggested Sherwood held as much respect for his accommodation as those who had provided the room had shown to the artist. Chicken bones littered the floor near the chamber pot. Near misses, Royce guessed. From the rancid smell that greeted his nose upon entering, Sherwood's pisspot hadn't been dealt with any better than the bed.

"I don't get visitors," Sherwood said with a mix of irritation and embarrassment. He picked up the discarded bones, crossed the room, and dumped them and the chamber pot's contents out the window and into the sea. When he turned back, a look of shock flashed across the painter's face.

Royce didn't suffer from a lack of situational awareness. Some people—most people—walked around oblivious to nearly everything. How they survived more than a week was a curiosity to him akin to why turkeys had wings. In Royce's profession, being surprised was the same as being dead, so catching him unaware was a rare thing. Seeing the stunned look on Sherwood's face, however, Royce was certain someone had been hiding in the corner as they entered. Cursing himself for his stupidity and expecting the worst, Royce whirled while reaching for his dagger.

No one was there, just the artist's easel and paint tray propped in the corner.

Sherwood moved to the easel as if he'd forgotten Royce was in the room. He reached out and touched the tripod, running his hands over the surface of the paint-splattered wood. "Impossible."

"What is?"

Sherwood untied a rolled-up canvas pouch. It unfurled, one end dangling from the easel tray. The thing was a sort of carrying case for paintbrushes, with little pockets for each. There had to be two dozen brushes neatly stuffed into the compartments. "They're all here."

Sherwood opened the lid of the tray and gasped. He jerked back as if a snake had been hiding there. Reaching out, he timidly touched each of the pigment bottles. Then he picked up the paint-smeared palette and stared at it. "It's…it's…" he repeated, shaking his head. "This is the same palette. The paint it's…I just don't understand."

"Your easel, your paint, your room, what's not to understand?"

"These don't exist anymore, or I should say they didn't—none of them. Last night Lord Fawkes went into the study and destroyed it all. This easel was snapped into half a dozen pieces, and the paint vials were shattered against the walls and floor. And this…" Sherwood held up the palette. "This was broken in two. But it's all here now—not a mark, not a blemish."

"No blemishes? There are dents, scrapes, and paint splattered all over that thing."

"Yes!" Sherwood spun, holding up the palette like a tiny shield. "I know every mark, every drip of paint. This isn't a replacement or a replica. This *is* my old easel. These *are* my old paints."

Sherwood's eyes went wide with thought. He turned and scanned the pigments again. "Beyond the Sea…it isn't here."

"That's because I have it." Royce held out the bottle.

"Yes." Sherwood took the vial and put it in the gap where it belonged. "This doesn't make sense."

"Ponder it later. I have questions, remember?"

Sherwood faced him with a giddy smile. "Sure. Whatever. What do you want to know?"

"Tell me about Lady Dulgath. What's she like? What are her habits? Her interests? Her—"

"Her hair isn't black."

"I'm actually more interested in—"

"People don't know that," he went on, staring at Royce in earnest. "They would if they paid attention, if they looked close, but people don't. Everyone is so focused on themselves they never really take the time to look at others and rarely see them."

Royce sensed Sherwood was one of those quirky spigots that started by chugging and spitting out blasts of useless, dirty water. But after you pumped it a few times, it vomited the good stuff. He decided to continue to coax, to see what came out. "So what color *is* her hair?"

"Brown."

"Looks black to me."

"It's what I call *soft black,* but it's really a very dark brown. You can see it when she stands in front of a window on a sunny day. The light gives her a golden halo as it passes through the individual strands. Her eyes aren't really brown, either. There's a hint of gold and even a little green in them."

"I'm not interested in painting her."

"But that's how I know her. That's how I understand her. She doesn't have black hair and brown eyes like everyone else, because she isn't like everyone else. She isn't like *anyone* else. You can hear it in her voice. She drags her vowels, puts emphasis on the wrong syllables, as if she's from another country. But I've been to all of them, and I've never heard the like. Just looking at her you can see the differences. She's only twenty-two, but she has an old soul. Her not-young soul is visible through those not-brown eyes. She betrays it in the way she moves, the way she acts. Each step, each shift is poised and filled with total confidence. She's fearless in the command of her body. This confidence bleeds out in her voice and the directions she gives her staff. Firm, strong, but kind and compassionate, she has wisdom far beyond her apparent years. And courage!" Sherwood chuckled at the absurdity, as if Royce had just accused Lady Dulgath of being a coward.

"I once saw her stop a fight between two soldiers. One had a busted, bleeding nose, and he had just drawn his sword. The other man's face was red with rage, and he howled in anger. Everyone else—big men, some of them armed—backed away. She marched right up and slapped one and then the other. Just slapped them. I couldn't believe it. I don't think anyone could. She did the same sort of thing with an unruly horse."

"She slapped it?"

Sherwood chuckled again; the man was in a decidedly better mood than when they'd first met. "No, but…well, the animal was rearing and kicking, and Nysa—I mean, Lady Dulgath—showed no hesitation. She laid a hand on the animal's neck. The horse relaxed—calmed right down." Sherwood continued to stare at the easel, then blinked and laughed again. A self-conscious smile pulled at his lips.

Royce remained quiet, waiting to see if Sherwood would continue. Just as he thought the artist was finished, he spoke again.

"She's sad," Sherwood said at last. "Lonely, I think."

"Her father just died."

"It's not that. I arrived *before* he died. She was melancholy then, too. She actually took her father's death well, very stoically. Still, there's a regret that hovers around her. That's the thing I notice the most about her. She wears it like…like you wear that cloak—hides behind it. That's what makes her so hard to see."

Sherwood went on to speak of Nysa Dulgath with an awe that only infatuation—deep and fresh—produced. Sherwood was likely on the verge of declaring that the lady inhaled with more acumen than mere mortals, and yet…

Heat and cold don't bother you nearly as much as they do your friend, but ice, snow, and boats—oh, ships!

If she had added dogs and dwarves to the list of things he avoided, Royce would've concluded she knew him. And the comment about water…Royce could swim, he'd had to on a few occasions, but he avoided lakes, rivers, and the ocean. He hated having no solid ground to stand on. Boats and docks were somehow worse. They messed with his balance and made him sick. He'd never told anyone. Weaknesses were things only the stupid advertised. Nysa Dulgath knew his just by looking at him.

Royce spotted the cloth-covered painting behind the table. "Is that her portrait?"

"Yes."

"Can I see it?"

"No."

"Why not?"

"It's not done."

Royce considered looking anyway, but he'd seen plenty of portraits hanging in the halls of the wealthy, usually pudgy men and pasty women. He simply wasn't that interested. He'd learned what he came to find out. Sherwood wasn't a threat to Lady Dulgath—he was in love with her. Royce had suspected as much from the moment the painter threw a fortune in blue pigment at him in her defense. Now he was certain. With their deal concluded, Royce was content to leave the artist alone with his easel mystery. Still, he couldn't shake the feeling that he should have looked.

Climbing the ivy was even easier the second time.

Lady Dulgath was in her bedroom. He'd seen the light come on before he started his climb and made no effort to conceal his approach. Even so, the odds of anyone seeing or hearing him were slim. Practice and experience had made his stealth habitual. Cats— even when not hunting—were damn hard to hear.

She wasn't in bed.

Lifting his head above the sill, Royce saw Nysa Dulgath sitting at the little desk, her back to him. She was wearing a different gown.

This one was white and off the shoulder, drawing attention to the smooth dark-olive skin, and—he didn't care what Sherwood said—she had black hair.

He studied her.

The first time he'd met Lady Dulgath—he hadn't really noticed the woman herself. Instead, he'd seen the accumulated assumptions he'd built while riding to Maranon. This time he watched more honestly and found a beautiful woman. Slender, tall, relaxed in her body—Sherwood was right about the poise and confidence. She was just sitting at her desk, but she sat straight, ankles crossed. The movement of her hands and arms as she used a quill was—

"Are you here to kill me this time?" she asked without turning.

Royce slipped through the window and perched on the sill, his feet dangling inside the room but not touching the coiled rug that covered half the floor. "No. Why would you say that?"

Lady Dulgath set her quill down and turned halfway in her seat, throwing one arm over the back of the chair. Long hair covered the side of her face, obscuring one eye and blanketing one shoulder. The candle behind her gave it a pleasant shine. "Because no one hires an assassin merely to *plan* a murder. Was it Bishop Parnell or Lord Fawkes who hired you to kill me?"

She knows!

"Actually, they did hire me, but merely to provide them with a plan."

"Which they will execute?"

Royce shrugged. "Probably."

The degree to which Royce had misjudged this noble woman was earthshattering. He'd made bad guesses before, but he almost always overestimated his enemies. This time he'd pegged his target as a careless, negligent, oblivious child; he'd mistaken a fox for a hen.

"Since you obviously know people are plotting your death, why haven't you bothered to take precautions?"

"Mister Melborn, is it? Ruling a kingdom doesn't equal unfettered power. Take for example the Church of Nyphron—the chief sponsor of my elimination. I have no power to remove any of them. They don't work for me. Only the king can order such a ban, and he won't. This leaves me with an assassin on my windowsill—something that ought to be only a metaphor."

"And yet you don't seem the least bit frightened."

She rolled her shoulders, shrugging off the hair. "You just said you weren't here to kill me."

"And you believe the word of a killer?"

"Maybe I'm just not afraid of dying."

"Everyone is afraid of death."

"Says the deliveryman. And yet you make a business of it."

"I *used* to make a business of it," Royce clarified, then wondered why he bothered. She didn't care, and neither should he. "And people are not afraid of death *happening*, just of it happening to *them*."

"So you aren't a killer anymore?"

"Not an *assassin*."

"Ah." She nodded. "Now you merely advise others."

"This is an unusual job."

"No doubt." She brushed the hair away from her face, looking at him clearly with both eyes. "How *would* you kill me?"

She was being provocative, trying to push him off balance. She took great pleasure in that, enjoyed attacking and watching him retreat. "I'd slit your throat while you slept."

"You'd sneak up here while I'm in bed, catch me unaware, but… that didn't work so well last night…or this."

"I wasn't trying very hard."

"Right, of course, normally you succeed because—because of your special secret."

"Let's not go there again."

"Why not? Are you afraid to learn something about yourself?"

"I know myself quite well, thank you."

"No, you don't." Nysa stood up. The light of the desk's candle behind her left the lady's features in darkness, but the bright white of the gown practically glowed. "You think you're a man, but you're better than that."

"Better? Last night you called me an elf."

"You are."

"And you call that *better*? Where I come from, that's about as low an insult as there is."

"Where I come from, it's the highest form of praise."

Royce leaned in and peered at her with a disagreeable smirk. "I hadn't noticed Maranon holding any affection for elves. In fact, I don't think I've seen any since coming here."

Lady Dulgath bit her lip and turned away.

A point scored.

Royce could see what had so overwhelmed Sherwood. Lady Dulgath had an allure that even he couldn't deny. It didn't help that she looked a bit like Gwen DeLancy: same shapely figure, dark eyes, and dark hair. Some time ago Royce had realized that he judged the beauty of all women by how much they resembled Gwen, but there was more to Nysa Dulgath's appeal than that. She was younger and lighter-skinned than Gwen, but they shared the same intoxicating sense of mystery. In a world of mundane predictability, they were intriguing riddles—rain in sunshine creating rainbows.

"If you're not here to kill me, then why climb my ivy? Were you hoping to catch me dressing?"

Royce rolled his eyes.

"Sorry, I've never met an assassin. How would I know what you do? But if peeping wasn't your aim, what is?"

"Trying to figure out why someone wants you dead."

"No, that's not it." She showed him a smirk of her own. "You're deciding whether I deserve to live. You're trying to determine if it's worth the money to tell them how to kill me. You didn't have any problem doing so when we first met, but second thoughts have crept in since last night. And now—now you're undecided—on a windowsill, so to speak."

"You can certainly wring every drop out of a metaphor, can't you?"

She got up, spun halfway around on her left heel, and went to the bed. Sherwood was right about the way she moved. She didn't so much walk as glide, and that heel spin she did was as elegant as a dancer's pirouette.

The dress added to the drama of the movement, made of something shiny, satin, perhaps. It caught light from both the candle and the moon, rippling like waves on a still, night pond.

Ghostly. That was the word that came to mind. She sat on the bed and crossed her ankles again, this time folding her hands in her lap and pulling her shoulders back as if posing.

Maybe she is. Maybe she's trying to seduce me, flashing her big eyes in the false hope that it will save her life. Something told him he was wrong even before he'd finished the thought. *I've got to stop thinking she's like everyone else—she's a fox, not a hen.*

"Since you're on the sill about me," she said with a grin, "I'll offer a defense and see if I can persuade you to grant clemency."

"Knock yourself out."

She narrowed her eyes. "I'm sorry…what?"

"Go ahead, state your case," Royce said.

Nysa stared at him a moment longer, then used both hands to hook her hair behind her ears. Straightening up once more, she asked, "Did you know that the Dulgath family is the oldest continually ruling bloodline in Avryn?"

"That's not likely to sway me. I'm not big on tradition."

"It's my life on the line. Grant me a little leniency."

Royce shrugged and, expecting a long tale, curled up in the frame of the window. Putting his back against one side, he drew up his feet and placed them on the other.

"Let's see." Lady Dulgath tapped her chin and tilted her head toward the ceiling, as if she were trying to spot something very small or very far away. "About three thousand years ago—close to that—when the Great War ended and the Novronian Empire was born—"

Royce interrupted. "We really need to go back that far? Seriously?"

She ignored him. "Before the war, no one had ever come this far west. After the war, everyone did. A rush of people searched for fertile lands. Maranon was perfect. Mehan—the capital of Maranon—was originally the name of a prominent clan from that time. They were the first here and had taken the best fields. The latecomers went farther west. As you can see, we're up against the ocean in this valley, so those who settled here were the late and undesirable—outcasts. They were led by a man named Dul. He was so poor he nearly starved to death and was so horribly thin people called him the Ghast. This would've been right about the same time that the first stones of Percepliquis were being laid. Dul the Ghast led a miserable band of about a hundred members of Clan Mehan to this valley, which they found beautiful and rich."

"And they lived happily ever after," Royce finished for her.

"Not at all. There's a reason Dul the Ghast and his followers were undesirable—they were idiots."

This made Royce smile.

Nysa returned the grin.

"They had no idea how to take care of themselves on the frontier. When they exhausted the supplies they'd brought, they found themselves in desperate need. Back then—this was before Novron died, before his cult grew—people worshiped spirits believed to exist in nature: trees, rocks, bears, that sort of thing. In desperation, Dul and his dying people began begging the spirits of nature to save them. Dul probably never expected anything to come of it, but what he didn't know was that there really was a spirit dwelling in this valley, and the spirit heard him. Overnight everything changed, and that guardian spirit has watched over the House of Dulgath ever since."

"Are you saying that's why you're not concerned? Because you have a magical guardian protecting you?"

"I guess you could say that, yes."

Royce had no trouble believing her sincerity. Nobles and wealthy merchants were known to believe in ghosts and good luck charms. He once knew a silk merchant who had been convinced his dog of nineteen years was still alive. He would go down on one knee and pet thin air while making cooing noises at it. The odd thing was that his wife had died the same year as the dog—but she had never visited. A guardian spirit didn't surprise Royce at all, and normally he would've accepted her story as another example of wishful stupidity, except…

Fox, not a hen.

"Okay, so that answers why you're so relaxed. It doesn't explain why everyone wants to kill you."

"A few years ago, the Nyphron Church came for a visit. Five of their leading bishops were traveling from province to province, preaching to the noble families about the importance of restoring the faith of Novron. They came here and weren't pleased that the

Earl of Dulgath wasn't receptive to their belief in restoring the old empire."

The Earl of Dulgath? An odd way for her to refer to her father.

"They wanted his assurance that when the time came, he would cast his allegiance to an emperor of their choice. We've never worshiped Novron here. Even when we were part of the empire, we gave only lip service. This tiny valley has its own ways—old ways—and we're set in them. Old Beadle told them that he wouldn't cooperate."

Old Beadle?

"The earl was a problem, a rock in their road. A big, unmovable stone. Sadly, he didn't have the same life span as most rocks. When he died without a male heir—just a delicate, young, inexperienced girl—the church saw an opportunity." She shook her head and sighed. "But alas, the countess was no more pliable than the earl. So in the intervening years they found someone more amenable. Lord Fawkes will allow them to pull his strings, all while thinking he is the one in control." She shook her head again. "So foolish. Now the stage is set for the final act in their little drama, The Death of the Last Dulgath."

"And none of this frightens you because you're protected by the magical woodland spirit of the valley. Do I have that right?"

"You're the expert on killings. You tell me. They've tried three times now. How hard can it be to kill a delicate young girl?"

Something in the sound of her voice—not arrogance, but confidence—disturbed Royce, like hearing a deer howl or a rabbit roar.

"An interesting tale, but I'm not persuaded. I'm no fan of the church or nobility. It doesn't matter to me who rules. The lives of those at the lower rung remain unchanged. I've decided, and I'm going to tell them how I'd kill you. I want you to know that."

"How considerate of you."

"Of course, should that ivy be cut down and a sentry posted to patrol the yard, such a thing would be a lot harder. And if you locked your door and posted another guard outside it, anyone looking to end your life might be out of luck."

"You're not a very resourceful assassin, are you? I should think there would be cleverer ways than climbing in a window."

"Simple plans work. Every moving part is a potential failure point. Besides…" Royce shrugged. "Not a lot of incentive in this job. I'm just here to get paid. That's all that matters."

"Is it?" she asked, getting up.

She stood before him with her weight on one hip, arms limp at her sides. She had a predatory stare in her eyes. Royce found his muscles tensing. The look was threatening.

Is she thinking of pushing me out the window? No, that look isn't violent— it's inviting.

He'd seen that stare before, usually on prostitutes working a room. Gwen's girls donned that expression frequently, but none ever looked at him that way. They aimed their weapons at the loud and the drunk, the ones throwing money away like silver fountains. No one ever stared at Royce.

Nysa locked eyes with him and smiled, soft cheeks growing round.

"I think you're curious," she told him.

"About what?"

Not a shift, not a blink. "About me, certainly, but even more about you. I can see doubt in your eyes. You don't want to believe what I said, but the truth is impossible to ignore. Your problem is that you've lived with lies your entire life. What choice was there? Everyone agrees that elves are dirty, worthless, lazy, ignorant vermin. In a world without a dissenting opinion, how could anyone expect to judge fairly? The question before you isn't, *How could I be one of them?* but rather, *How could I have ever believed I was only a man?*"

"What does the daughter of an earl know about elves?"

"I read a lot," she said, then broke their contest and laughed.

She swirled, making the gown fan, and threw her head back. Gwen's girls did that, too. Maybe Nysa was bad at it, or Royce was wrong about her intent, for the act was uncharacteristically awkward and filled with frustration and annoyance. In that instant, her guard dipped, and for the first time he felt he saw Nysa Dulgath, the woman behind the mask. The lady hadn't planned it, but that slip succeeded where her previous efforts had failed. The truth was indeed hard to ignore. Royce decided he liked Nysa Dulgath, or at least he didn't dislike her. She certainly was interesting.

She took a step toward him.

"Time for me to go." Royce spun and threw his legs back out the window. "Don't forget about the ivy. You need to get rid of it."

"But I like ivy."

"It can grow back."

"And you? How will you visit me again if I tear it down?"

"I won't. Goodbye, Lady Dulgath."

Chapter Thirteen
FAWKES AND HOUNDS

The trip back down the mountain was faster, as downhill trips always are. Even so, it was night when Hadrian and Scarlett Dodge reached the section of the trail where the pitch flattened to a mere slope and broadened wide enough for side-by-side travel. The moon was three-quarters full and cast a spray of silver pools where it penetrated the leaves. The light ran up and over their bodies as they waded through moonbeam puddles, and Hadrian kept stealing glances at Scarlett. At first he thought he was getting away with it. Still acting as a guide, Scarlett was focused on the trail ahead, but when he spotted her smile, he knew she'd caught him. He also knew she didn't mind.

"So how did you end up in Dulgath—in Brecken Dale?" Hadrian asked.

"What do you care?" Her tone was both curt and cold.

Hadrian was surprised, then realized he shouldn't have been. Royce had all but placed a knife to her throat. "Look, we got started wrong. You poisoned me, and Royce threatened to kill you—fact is, we're not who you thought we were, and I have no idea who you are."

"Probably best that way, don't you think?"

"No—I don't think that at all."

She looked at him just as moonlight splashed her face. She had that puzzled squint he already recognized as one of her go-to expressions—at least the ones she used with him.

"But I'll tell you what I do think. I think it's easy to distrust someone you don't know. If you're ignorant of their past, you can't understand their motivations, so you jump to conclusions, which are usually wrong. For example, I'm a really nice guy, but you probably hold a different opinion of me."

"Yep—I think you're an idiot."

He smiled. "That's just because you don't know me. Once you do, you'll discover I'm really only an imbecile."

This made her laugh. He could tell she didn't want to, and her frustration made the sound even sweeter.

"See, you can't resist me. I'm like a dog that drops a ball at your feet."

"Hadrian," she said with a weary tone and a shake of her head. "I get it. You're attracted to me. You're trying to start something here—make me like you—but you're only going to be around for a few days, and Wagner and I—we're sort of a thing."

"Wagner? The bartender? That old guy?"

"He *owns* Caldwell House, and he's nice."

Hadrian nodded slowly with a pushed-out lower lip.

"What?"

"Just seems a little old, that's all."

"Yeah, well, most men worth something are. Boys tend to be lazy or have an overabundance of dreams; they're always looking but never finding because they haven't a clue what they really want."

She glared directly at him as she spoke. "Men like Wagner are past the stargazer stage. He understands the way the world is and makes the best of it."

"Ah-huh." Hadrian kept his eyes forward this time but felt her looking at him again.

"What's that supposed to mean?"

"Nothing."

"Wagner's been good to me."

"Didn't say he wasn't. Probably a great guy…when he's not poisoning people."

"I did that—and I didn't poison you. I drugged you. If I'd used poison, you'd be dead."

Hadrian nodded, giving in again. He shifted his short sword's belt just off the hip, where it rubbed him. The hand-and-a-half sword always hung low, but he wore the short sword higher when he rode to keep it clear of his thigh. "You know, I wasn't asking for your hand in marriage. I was just curious about how a woman from Colnora ended up here. Seemed a bit strange to me, that's all."

They continued on in silence. The two split, going separate ways around a hawthorn tree that Hadrian was surprised he remembered from the trip up. Same thing had happened with a boulder earlier. *Why is it I remember some things but not others? Why the tree and the boulder, but not that fallen log or that curve?*

This was the sort of internal conversation he often expressed verbally with Royce, the kind that drove his partner nuts. But it wasn't polite to travel with someone and not acknowledge them, so a little pointless conversation seemed reasonable. Rather than be irritated by the silence, Hadrian chose to—

"I ran into some trouble in Colnora," Scarlett said.

Hadrian didn't dare look over. He didn't show any sign that he knew she was there.

"Royce was telling the truth about me being in the Black Diamond." She paused.

Hadrian didn't respond, didn't want to sidetrack her into a discussion about Royce.

After a moment, she went on. "I grew up a farmer's daughter and ran away to the big city because I had talent and wanted to act in the theater there. I was only fourteen—didn't know women weren't allowed to be actors. They laughed at me, told me to go home. I couldn't do that. I'd watched my mother kill herself in silent misery. She'd cried herself to sleep at night. I wouldn't do that—wouldn't *be* that.

"I danced and sang on street corners for money. People liked me and dropped coppers in my hat. I thought I'd found a future, and I was so happy. Didn't know about the Minstrel Guild and how ruthless people could be. Like I said, I was only fourteen."

Hadrian risked a glance and discovered Scarlett wasn't looking at him. Her sight was fixed on the shadows, a hard, pained expression on her face. "I was just a stupid little girl," she said with a sneer of contempt, as if seeing herself and hating what she saw.

"The guild didn't care that I was young and naïve. All they cared about was me cutting into their profits. Beat me bloody and split my lip. My eyes were so swollen I couldn't see out of them for days. My left arm was broken, as well as the third finger on this hand." She held it up as if she were showing off a ring. "Still a little crooked." She grimaced and made a fist with that hand. "But that was all they did—could have been worse. If the Black Diamond found you cutting in on their territory, you'd be dead, not just broken, beaten, and left vomiting in a ditch. You see, the members of the Minstrel Guild pride themselves on being professional men, not predators and thugs. This was business, not pleasure. Nearly killing a stupid girl was just part of their job.

"Don't know what I would've done after that if it hadn't been for Chase. I wouldn't have gone home, so I probably woulda died, I guess."

"Who's Chase?"

"Chase *was* an entertainer—a magician and actor."

"Was he one of the men who—was he part of the guild?"

"No—which at the time surprised me, too, because Chase put on shows wherever he liked in the city. No one ever bothered him. Turned out they didn't dare. He was part of a different guild—the Black Diamond." She looked at him with a bitter smile Hadrian didn't understand. "His shows drew in crowds, big crowds. Everyone was fascinated and intent on watching his hands to see how he did the magic. Meanwhile sweepers—pickpockets—worked their own magic. *Misdirection is the key,* he'd always said. He pulled me out of that ditch and cleaned me up. Gave me food and a place to sleep. Had me sing and dance at his shows and taught me how to pick pockets and do magic. To him they were the same thing. He added me to his act and renamed me Dodge—Scarlett Dodge, the red-haired enchantress. He also sponsored my membership to the Diamond. Chase was a good man. Saved my life."

"Was?"

"They killed him—Malachite and Jasper. This was five years ago. Hoyte was running things in the Diamond and fortifying his position as First Officer—which is sort of like a duke, the second most powerful member short of the Jewel himself, who's essentially the king. And like any good duke, he was preoccupied with weeding out those not loyal to him. Most of us in the bottom ranks hated Hoyte. Chase was no different. He threw his loyalty to a new guy, a bucketman and rising star in the guild, who looked like he could replace Hoyte, but then everything changed.

"Hoyte cleaned house. The rising star went to Manzant, and Chase and a lot of others were found floating facedown in the Bernum River. I didn't want to be next, so I ran. Went south.

"In Ratibor, I joined, of all things, a traveling minstrel show. I performed magic, and we fleeced our audiences just like in Colnora. Kept moving to avoid problems. In Swanwick, trouble caught us. I was arrested. Kept my hands because they had decided to send me to Manzant Prison. The salt mine always needs workers, and workers need hands. On the road south, I pulled one more magic act and got my chains off. Chase taught me that, too. One more way in which he saved my life. I ran west into the mountains."

She slowed, then stopped. Scarlett stared at the shadowy path and then back at the black of the forest. "People here say a spirit haunts these woods and has protected the people in this valley for centuries."

"Augustine's reformed demon?"

"I guess." She seemed embarrassed. "I'm not saying I believe everything, but everyone believes something. They insist in the existence of the gods, or demons, or tree spirits, or they believe that such things don't exist. One person might profess that people are basically good, while another might think the opposite. But everyone believes in something, you know? And what we choose to believe in says a lot—not only about the kind of people we are, but about the kind of people we want to be, and the kind of world we want to live in."

"Augustine tell you that?"

She stopped and gave him an angry face. "What? You think a reformed thief can't conceive of such things? Or do you think a woman couldn't *possibly* ponder such ideas?"

She was opening up to him, saying things he imagined she didn't say to many people. Maybe she thought he would understand, that he might feel the same—and he did—but instead of agreeing, he'd accused her of being stupid. "Sorry," he said, and meant it.

"You should be."

"I am."

The scowl on her face lost its strength and slowly drained away as they walked.

Hadrian waited. He didn't dare say another word until she did.

"Anyway," she said, finally breaking the silence and erasing the slate of past awkwardness with a word, "I honestly feel that something guided me here."

"Here, here? Up this trail?"

She nodded. "I stumbled on this path and followed it to the monastery. It really was as if Maribor—or something—led me."

"And Abbot Augustine took you in."

"Like Chase before him, he saved me. Didn't rebuke, judge, or ask questions. He just told me I needed to change my life, as if he knew everything. He introduced me to the people of the dale, who, with his endorsement, welcomed me as one of their own."

She began walking again, moving faster and lighter, as if a weight had been lifted.

"And now?"

She gave a carefree roll of her shoulders. "I dance. I sing. I do magic tricks. Three times a week I entertain people at Caldwell House. The rest of the time, I try to master the spinning wheel or make clay pots. Haven't succeeded at a single pot, but I'm better at it than spinning wool. Spinning is a torment. I'm also trying to learn to bake."

Hadrian could hear the river and see the moon reflecting off its face when Scarlett asked, "What about you? How'd you learn to fight like that? How'd you end up with Royce? That has to be a tale."

"I grew up in the military, you could say, and then I became a mercenary for several years in Calis. How I ended up with Royce is indeed a tale—a long one." He pointed to the bridge that led to the dale and the end of their trip, then grinned.

"Not fair."

"I have an appointment with Royce tonight, but if you're really interested, you could invite me to dinner tomorrow."

She smirked. "You really are something, aren't you?"

"Just a dog with a ball."

Hadrian had said good night to Scarlett and was almost to the door of Caldwell House when he spotted a familiar hood near the stables. Even after three years, seeing Royce come at him was disturbing; he felt as perplexed as a bird might at the impossibly nimble flight of bats. Adding to that was how Royce remained visible in moonlight but disappeared in shadows. He appeared to fade out then materialize. Combined with the flutter and flow of his black cloak, the effect was creepy and—Hadrian imagined—absolutely terrifying to anyone on Royce's bad side.

"You're back earlier than I thought you'd be," Hadrian said.

"Got what I needed. You eat?"

"Not yet."

Royce glanced around. Unlike the Lower Quarter of Medford, where people wandered the night—or slept in alleys and on doorsteps—the streets around Caldwell House were empty. "We'll get something later," Royce said. "Let's talk in the room first."

"Something happen?"

"Spoke to *her* again. She has a way of…let's get inside and I'll tell you the rest."

Caldwell House was vacant; neither Wagner nor Gill were visible. A fire was burning low in the hearth. The crackle of wood and the groan of the door seemed loud in the stillness.

"Having a town meeting or something tonight?" Royce asked.

"Not that I know of, but I was on a mountain all day. They might just turn in early. This is mostly a farming community. People in the country don't stay up late."

They climbed the creaking stairs to their room on the second floor. Hadrian reached for the latch, but Royce grabbed his wrist. He pointed at the light flickering out from under the door. They exchanged looks of surprise, then Hadrian slowly pulled his side swords and backed up while Royce opened the door.

Three candles burned inside: one near the bed, one on the windowsill, and one on the little table where Lord Fawkes and Pastor Payne sat. The two were playing a game of cards and drinking from a pair of crystal glasses filled from a tall black wine bottle. They looked up as Royce and Hadrian entered the room.

"Ah! Finally," Fawkes said with a big grin. "Thought you'd never get here."

"Usually when I find unexpected guests in my room," Royce said, "they don't leave in the same condition they arrived in."

Royce's comment lacked any true menace, because he hadn't drawn Alverstone. Hadrian followed his partner's lead and sheathed his swords.

"Then I shall consider myself one of the lucky ones," Fawkes replied, stretching his grin even wider. He laid down his cards and winked at the pastor. "I had you anyway."

Pastor Payne frowned and slapped his set of cards on the table in frustration. He got up and walked to the window, where he stood with his arms folded, glaring at Fawkes and giving up the stage to His Lordship.

"I thought I'd save you the time of finding us," Fawkes said. "So you've seen the place, had a chance to evaluate the job. What say you? How would you go about killing Lady Dulgath?"

Hadrian glanced at Royce. He could tell his partner was irritated. Fawkes being in their room was unexpected, and Royce didn't like unexpected. Hadrian couldn't say he was overly fond of it, himself. The door had no lock, and they were only renting, but still. A noble lord might not consider it impolite. Courtesy and respect were required within the peerage, but they flowed in one direction. As far as Fawkes was concerned, Hadrian and Royce were most certainly inferior.

"You're not going to tell me you need more time," Fawkes said. He looked at Payne. "The pastor must be fiscally conscious when spending church funds. He's worried you two might be dragging this out to milk expenses. As for myself, I'm anxious, seeing that a noblewoman's life hangs in the balance."

"No, I don't need more time," Royce said.

"Well then"—Fawkes took a sip from his drink—"let's hear it."

"All right." Royce glanced at Hadrian, revealing he was still irritated about the intrusion, but holding it in check. "Personally, I'd scale the outside of the tower to her bedchamber late at night, slip through the window, and slit her throat while she slept."

Pastor Payne grimaced, and one of his hands stroked at his throat. "That's awfully brutal."

"Murder usually is."

"But how's *that* supposed to look like an accident?" Payne asked.

"It isn't." Royce moved to the table and, tilting the black wine bottle, looked for a label. There wasn't one. "The time for accidents has long passed. Everyone already knows she's a target. Pretending otherwise is foolish. If Lady Dulgath genuinely caught a cold and died weeks later from a fever, everyone would assume foul play."

"But her bedroom window is six stories up," Fawkes said.

"Seven," Royce corrected. "But the whole outside is covered in lush, strong ivy, with branches thicker than a man's thumb. Not much different than climbing a ladder. I know. I did it—slipped right into her bedroom."

"You didn't!" the pastor said, appalled.

Fawkes stood up. Pursing his lips, he began pacing around the table. He retained his glass, holding it with both hands, tapping the rim with an index finger. "What else? If we take precautions, if we clear the ivy, certainly the assassin will pick a new tactic. What else might he try?"

"Knox has been posting more guards, which is helping. He's got Lady Dulgath fairly well buttoned up. Poisoning will be difficult now that she's looking for that. The staff is too small and loyal to bribe."

Hadrian knew this to be a joke, a biting insult, and he struggled not to smile.

Fawkes didn't so much as blink. "Still, there must be a way."

"Of course," Royce replied. "Trickier, though."

"Let's hear it." Fawkes raised his little glass as if to toast the proposal.

"Well, if you can arrange it so you know where she'll be in advance, and if that place is outdoors, then I'd go with a long-distance bow shot."

"Long distance?" Payne asked. "What's that mean?"

"Means that you hide an archer close enough to ensure a lethal first shot, which if the lady's security is even one notch above a dead chipmunk will be very far indeed."

"So what are we talking about here?"

"A longbow—particularly if the archer is in an elevated position. The killer can pretend it's a walking stick until he gets into position. Then he can string it, make the shot, unstring, and walk away."

"What's the range on a longbow?"

"Three hundred, four hundred yards," Hadrian said.

"Yes, but accuracy is key," Royce said. "I wouldn't recommend more than a hundred yards. You'll only get one shot."

Fawkes was thinking, tapping his glass again.

"So if I had the job," Royce went on. "I'd contract this out, hire a professional marksman."

"Who?"

"Only three men I'd trust to make the shot with a longbow," Royce replied. "And one is dead."

"And the other two?"

"One is Tom the Feather." Royce glanced at Hadrian. "But he's way up in Ghent, and I don't think he'd do it regardless of the price paid. He's a man of scruples."

"And the other?"

"A man by the name of Roosevelt Hawkins. Now, he's actually local—real close—too close."

"How do you mean? Where is he?"

"Manzant Prison—but no one gets out of there."

Fawkes gave the pastor a long stare with the trace of a smile.

"What about a crossbow?" Fawkes asked. "I heard any idiot can shoot one of those."

"True, but for the same range it would have to be a big one," Royce replied. "And how are you going to get that past castle security? So as you can see, the tower climb is far easier and likely what your assassin will use. The other involves hiring someone. That not only complicates things, but also costs money and reduces the profit. And then there's the need to know Her Ladyship's schedule and hope she's going to be outside in a place ideal for the shot."

"What else?"

Royce shrugged. "If she were in a crowd, someone could just walk up and knife her. But that would likely result in the capture of the assassin."

"What if her staff wasn't totally loyal?" Pastor Payne asked. "What then?"

What are the odds of that? Hadrian couldn't avoid a smirk. The calculating, eager, nearly gleeful way the two of them reveled in the possibility of killing a young woman turned his stomach.

"Lots of possibilities there," Royce said. "Too many to guard against. If that's a real concern, my best advice would be replacing the entire staff."

"That's the best you have for us?" Fawkes asked.

Royce nodded.

He was lying. No one could tell by looking at his face, but three years had given Hadrian a special sense of the man under the hood. He was leaving things out. Hadrian had never been a professional assassin, but even he guessed there were other ways to kill Lady Dulgath. She was famous for going out into the villages to help sick and injured people. At the very least, she could be lured out and ambushed. The castle could even be set on fire, as had happened in Medford the year before. That blaze claimed the life of the queen. Could have killed the king as well, but he hadn't been there that night. Still, climbing the tower's ivy did seem viable and straightforward enough to work, which left Hadrian puzzled as to why Royce offered it up, rather than other choices.

If Fawkes were experiencing similar reservations, he kept them from his face. He smiled. "Excellent. That's wonderful news." He looked at Payne and nodded. "All we need to do is get rid of the ivy and make certain Lady Dulgath is well protected when outdoors. We'll also keep a lookout for men with crossbows or longbows. This is truly a relief."

Fawkes returned to the table, refilled his and Payne's glasses, and then retrieved two more from a small satchel hanging over one of the chairs. "I anticipated success tonight and brought the bottle of wine to celebrate. Sadly, you took so long, the pastor and I polished off most of it while waiting. Still, we have enough for a toast," Fawkes said.

"Did you also bring the money you owe us?"

"Absolutely." Fawkes grinned.

Payne walked back from the window and picked up his glass.

Royce sneered at the bottle in Fawkes's hand.

"That's no attitude to take. It's a Maranon tradition to conclude business with a toast."

"I'm not big on tradition," Royce replied.

Fawkes narrowed his eyes. "As with most traditions, there's also a point. Up north you shake hands. People do that to show they aren't holding a weapon and don't have one up their sleeve. Down here, we drink. Eating and drinking together establishes a personal connection. It proves a degree of trust."

"I don't trust you."

"I can't say I'm ready to leave my firstborn in your care, either, but we do need a certain degree of faith in each other. I need assurance you've done your due diligence and haven't, in fact, joined with your like-minded brethren and made it easier for the assassin by leading us astray. And you need to know we won't be wagging our tongues and exposing your identities to authorities who might be interested in your prior transgressions," Fawkes said.

"And drinking can do all that?"

"No, but refusing to join us does give me cause for concern."

"Be as concerned as you like. I'm not drinking anything you offer me," Royce said.

"I don't conduct business with men who doubt my integrity."

"Which means what?"

"It means you don't get paid," Fawkes said.

"You're right. I can't imagine why I should doubt your integrity."

"So you'll join us?"

"No, you'll pay me or you won't leave this room alive." Royce shifted his sight to Payne. "Either of you."

"You dare threaten me?" Fawkes exclaimed, taking a step back from the table while his hand reached for his sword.

"Hold on! Hold on!" Hadrian stopped him. "We'll have a drink."

"No, we won't," Royce said.

"Sure we will." He pointed at the bottle. "They've already been drinking the wine. It's fine."

"And the glasses?" Royce asked.

Hadrian pointed at a pair of cups on the shelf over their beds. "We'll use those instead." He retrieved the cups and held them out to Fawkes.

The lord frowned. "You aren't going to drink such fine wine out of wooden cups, are you?"

"Is there some rule against toasting with wooden cups?" Hadrian asked.

"No." Fawkes sighed and continued to frown as he poured a small amount in each. "You two are so untrusting."

"To peace between us and a long life to all." Hadrian lifted his cup and drank.

With a miserable expression, Fawkes did as well. Payne followed suit, but Royce never touched his cup.

The wine was rich but delicate—there one minute, gone the next.

"And the payment?" Hadrian asked.

"He hasn't drunk," Payne said, pointing at Royce.

"Doesn't matter," Fawkes told him. "Get the money."

Payne set his cup down and moved to the window, where he bent and blew out the candle. Downstairs the door to Caldwell House opened. Several booted feet ran across the wooden floor of the common room, heading for the stairs.

Concern flashed across Royce's face.

"Relax. They're just bringing it up," Fawkes said, but his words sounded odd.

Royce reached for his dagger, and Hadrian took a step to intercept him, then noticed the world was swimming. The room lurched strangely. Candlelight spread out, and the figures of Payne, Fawkes, and Royce moved in slow motion. The table between them was thrown aside as the door to the room burst open. The sound was strangely muffled, as if Hadrian were underwater.

Not again, Hadrian thought.

Six men in black uniforms, chain mail, and conical helms entered the room. They wielded swords, and violence gleamed in their eyes. These weren't villagers. They weren't even castle guards. They were something else, and it wasn't good.

The bottle of wine, which had toppled when the table was tossed, had struck the floor but didn't break. It rolled in a half circle, the blood-colored contents dripping from its neck. Hadrian reached for his swords. He was struck before he got either of them free of its scabbard. Another blow hit his back. One more made him cry out, and he crashed to the floor.

His swords fell from his hands.

"You'd better be right about this," Payne said.

"Coin equals options, my good pastor. Split only two ways, this will get you out of that hovel you call a church and save you from starving this winter."

"And you're certain there's no chance of them escaping?" Payne asked.

"You heard for yourself. No one has ever escaped from Manzant Prison—no one."

Hadrian's sight darkened as everything went black.

Chapter Fourteen
THE NOTE

The next morning, Sherwood waited in Lady Dulgath's private study, playing out a hunch. In many ways, he felt dishonest, even despicable given the circumstances, but he had to know. Sherwood went about his usual routine: adjusting the easel, setting the canvas, mixing his paints. He marveled at the exactness of his palette. He never cleaned the thing. The new oil kept the paint workable for days, and cleaning it would be a terrible waste—one of the other advantages of oil over egg, which dried up in minutes. Even with the oil, an inevitable buildup formed as paint dried beyond his ability to reclaim, but palettes were cheap and eventually he would replace the whole thing. He'd had this one for a while; none of the original wood was visible on the paint side. Even the backside was a mess of smudges and multicolored fingerprints—and every one was exactly the same as it had been. Sherwood didn't know how, but he was certain Lady Dulgath was responsible.

I consider it my failure. I'm responsible, and I'll make it right again.

The Note

Maybe it had been a coincidence that she'd said that, but deep down he was so certain. A feeling wasn't the same as the truth, though, so Sherwood waited while watching the sunrise, its light creeping across the ceiling and down the wall.

If she'd had nothing to do with it, Nysa wouldn't expect a session. No one else knew about the miracle except Melborn, and Sherwood was convinced he didn't care enough to say anything. So if Lady Dulgath came to the study, it would prove her involvement.

And what will that mean? He didn't know, didn't care. *One thing at a time.*

He finished mixing, then set the palette knife down. Hopping onto the stool, he wiped his hands on a rag, then returned to watching the sun creep while he waited.

He didn't hear her walking; he never did, at least not her feet. The dress was what he heard, that familiar *swish, swish.* Lady Dulgath entered, as she always did, without a word or glance. She wore the same gold silk-brocade dress, had the fox stole wrapped around her shoulders, and held the riding gloves. Moving to her mark on the floor, she turned, lifted her chin, and looked at the chandelier.

"Thank you," he said.

The two words just came out. Sherwood had run through a dozen different conversations in his head, everything from pointing an accusing paintbrush at her to kneeling at the lady's feet and weeping. He'd been undecided on what he would really do if she came. Now he knew and was pleased with the simplicity—so much better than weeping.

"For what?" Her words were aloof, her eyes still on the chandelier.

"I honestly don't know."

This made her look at him.

"You don't know why you're thanking me?"

"For restoring my property, certainly, but…I don't know *what* you did or—perhaps more to the point—*how* you did it. So, while I thank you for the gift, I'm not really sure what exactly I'm thanking you for. Does that make sense?"

"It does not."

"But you did repair my easel, brushes, and paints."

She looked down at his tools with squeezed lips and squinted eyes. "Oh, that's right. Are those new?"

"No, they aren't. They are the same ones that were destroyed. Somehow you managed to put them back together for me, down to the last sable hair in this brush."

"I don't know what you're talking about."

"If it wasn't you, how did you know to come here this morning?"

She resumed looking at the chandelier. "Habit."

"Habit?"

"Yes. To be honest, I'd forgotten about your mishap of yesterday. You've had me doing this for so long, I act by rote now, which, as I think on it, is most disturbing. You need to finish this foolish painting so I can have my mornings back. This has gone on far too long."

She lifted her chin and blanked her face.

"I know you," he said. Once more, the words came out without thought, as if a pipe ran directly from his mind to his mouth and someone had flipped open the spigot.

"No, you don't," she said.

"Oh, but I do. I can see who you really are. I can see what you're so desperately struggling to hide from everyone. I can see it clearly—and it's beautiful."

"If you knew the real me, you wouldn't think me beautiful."

"But I do, and you are—beautiful and wonderful and wise and…and I—" Sherwood caught himself. He looked at the restored easel, at the miracle before him, and threw caution to the wind. "I love you, Nysa."

There. Sherwood felt as if he'd expelled some kind of poison that had sickened him for weeks. Saying it filled him with relief and joy. The euphoric sensation lasted all of a second; then reality crashed down.

What have I done?

He expected either outrage or laughter. If the former, guards would be throwing him out of the castle. If the latter, his heart would break. Instead, Nysa Dulgath slowly shifted her gaze to him. Pity was in her eyes, a deep, mournful sadness so pained that Sherwood trembled.

A tiny almost-smile stole over her lips, a bitter, painful face. "You don't know me, Sherwood. No one does, and no one ever will. Just paint. Can you do that?"

He nodded, a terrible emptiness filling him.

Sherwood took his noon meal outside, sitting in the grass of the courtyard. The day was perfect, as every day in Dulgath had been since he'd arrived.

It never rains.

He only then realized this and found it odd he hadn't noticed before. The skies were perpetually blue. There was always a light, warm breeze, never hot. He sat in the shade along the south wall near an overgrown area where the scattered stones of the crumbled tower made scything the grass too much trouble to bother. He had his back to one of the great blocks and his legs outstretched toward the statue of a man and a woman kissing. Of the many wonderful pieces of artwork at Castle Dulgath, this was Sherwood's favorite.

The two figures intertwined and blended at the base, as if they were part of a tree trunk. Then, as the torso twisted up, a man and woman appeared like the frayed ends of a rope. The two embraced on the edge of a kiss, their lips a hairsbreadth apart, eyes closed, ecstasy on their faces.

The statue stood partially hidden in the tall grass, behind a wild bush and maverick tree. No one came there. No one visited that side of the castle, and at first he'd lamented the statue's isolation. He felt others should see its beauty and incredible artistry, which went beyond depicting the human form, lifting it above reality into the scope of what ought to be. Raw emotion formed from cold stone, the sculpture captured a moment of longing and triumph, passion and love.

What else is there to hope for with any art? To capture not just truth but a truth worthy of display, one that provides comfort, joy, or understanding, and moves the heart or makes it pause.

As the weeks had gone by, Sherwood came to see this neglected corner of the courtyard, this tranquil place of quiet solitude, as *his*. He appreciated its seclusion. The statue—those inspirational lovers lost in the forgotten weeds of a fallen past—gave him hope for the future. At times, when the shadows were just right, he thought the woman looked vaguely like Nysa. The cheeks were far too high and sharp, the face too long, but he obviously wasn't seeing with just his eyes.

He heard feet swishing through grass and was surprised to see Rissa Lyn coming toward him. No buckets this time. Instead, she carried a curled-up bit of parchment.

"Pardon me, sir." She halted the moment he turned her way and gave a curtsy. "I have a message for you."

"From whom?"

"Chamberlain Wells gave it to me, sir, but he says it's from Her Ladyship."

"Lady Dulgath?"

"Yes, sir."

Sherwood nearly toppled his plate in an effort to stand. "Let's have it then."

He reached out, but Rissa Lyn hesitated. She had a troubled look in her eyes.

"What is it?" he asked.

"Sir, I seen your easel. I seen your paints and brushes there in the study this morning, and…" Her face reddened. "I was outside the door and heard you speaking to Her Ladyship—about her knowing—about her having something to do with it and all."

"Yes?" he asked impatiently. Sherwood liked Rissa Lyn well enough. but if Lady Dulgath had sent him a message—for the first time ever—he wanted to know what it said.

"Well, I think you're right, sir. I think she does know—I think she was the one who did it."

"Thank you, Rissa Lyn, I appreciate you telling me, but—"

"Sir…" She bit her lip and looked at her feet. "I don't just *think* she did it. I *know* she did."

"What do you mean? Did you see her do something?"

Rissa Lyn shook her head.

"Then how do you know?"

"On account of how I've been Lady Dulgath's handmaiden for the last ten years. Served her since she was twelve years old, sir. I was there when she was carried in after falling off Derby's back. There was no saving her, sir. Poor Nysa. Her back was broken, neck too. She was dead before they got her to the castle."

"What?" Sherwood was so focused on the note in Rissa Lyn's hand he hadn't paid attention, but those last words were impossible to ignore. "What are you saying?"

"I'm saying the Countess Nysa Dulgath, daughter of Earl Beadle Dulgath, died two years ago. His Lordship was crying and wailing like I'd never seen him. She was his only child, the last link he had to his Lady Raychelle. He couldn't let her die. He had Abbot Augustine bring in that witch, Maddie Oldcorn. Was just His Lordship, the abbot, and me there when Maddie told him his daughter was dead and nothing could be done."

"Rissa Lyn, Lady Dulgath is alive. She's right up—You're holding a note she wrote to me!"

"That's not Her Ladyship. That's someone else—*something* else. I'm telling you because I know you'll believe me. You can see her for what she is. A mere lady couldn't have fixed your easel and paints, could she? A mere lady couldn't have survived being poisoned. And I was there that day when the stone fell. It didn't miss her, sir."

"What are you talking about? She would've been crushed. The stone was"—he pointed at one of the huge blocks half buried in the grass—"as big as these."

"And I watched her swat it away like a fly," the maid said.

Sherwood narrowed his eyes. "Rissa Lyn, have you been drinking?"

She scowled, then frowned. "I have not, sir! And I don't understand why you act as if you don't believe me."

"Because I don't!" He nearly shouted the words, but part of him was inwardly nodding and whispering, *Yes.*

"I thought…" Rissa Lyn folded her lips tight to her teeth. "I thought you were different." Her lower lip quivered. "I thought you'd understand."

She turned and started to walk away.

"The note!" he cried.

She spun. Tears were in her eyes as she threw the parchment at him. "You'd love a monster when…I'm…I'm right in front of you—damn you! Damn you, Sherwood Stow! Go on. Go to *it*. Let the demon drag you to Phyre. I don't care anymore."

With that, Rissa Lyn ran away in tears, leaving the note fluttering in the grass, blown by the perfect breeze.

Sherwood had memorized the note and replayed the words in his head as he dug his sword out of a pile in the corner of his room. No rust on the metal, but plenty on the man. Sherwood had taken better care of the blade than he had of himself. He couldn't remember the last time he'd used it, or when he'd done anything more strenuous than a long walk.

Like everything else, he'd inherited the blade from Yardley; where Yardley had gotten it, no living soul knew. Nothing too fancy, the sword had a straight guard and a hawk's-head pommel, but the work was of high quality and the blade professional, not merely decorative. Traveling artists didn't carry much, so whatever they kept long enough to hand down was worth the effort. In most kingdoms of Avryn, able-bodied men were required by their lords to own a weapon and use it if called upon. But only nobles and those so authorized, such as soldiers and sheriffs, openly carried. As a result, he, like his predecessors, kept the weapon in his bedroll—out of sight, but close at hand.

Sherwood had been accosted on several occasions. Mostly, one or two toughs came at him, usually armed with only a single knife between them. Pulling the sword from his bedroll nearly always ended the encounter. But there had been times when he'd faced thieves brandishing their own weapons—true highwaymen who weren't deterred by the show of a long blade—and Sherwood had been forced to fight for his life.

He'd done well. Sherwood was certain he'd killed at least one man but hadn't lingered to make certain. In another fight, he'd stabbed a young tough, no more than seventeen, through the stomach. He, too, probably died. In more than six fights, Sherwood had survived, suffering just three wounds, and only one of those could be considered serious. Luckily, Yardley had also taught him how to sew up a cut.

Sherwood harbored no illusions of his prowess. He only hoped that if Lady Dulgath required his blade, his skills would be equal to the task. He waited, watching the sun sink into the ocean. It was only three-quarters set, but he couldn't wait any longer. He wanted to arrive before she did.

Strapping the sword to his waist, he took the stairs two at a time and sprinted out of the castle.

Sherwood, the note had read. *Meet me at the cliffs on the west side of the castle at sunset. I need help, and you're the only one I can trust.*

His emotions were a volatile mix of jubilation and terror. The revelation that she both trusted and needed him was a blast of pure joy. That she was so desperate to meet outside the castle, in such a secluded place made him dread what she might say.

Perhaps she wants to come away with me?

No. That would be too much to hope for. He was letting his emotions override reason. Likely she needed him to pass a message to King Vincent, something she couldn't trust going through Wells or Rissa Lyn.

Sherwood ran across the courtyard and out the gate, making a quick left and hugging the wall before veering off into the grassy bluffs on the blind side of the castle. The wind was stronger there as it came off the ocean with a damp salty blast that permanently bent the hip-deep grass.

THE NOTE

She's scared of someone in the castle—maybe everyone… "You're the only one I can trust."

Clearly, she couldn't trust Rissa Lyn, but did she know her handmaiden believed she was a demon?

No, he realized then, saw it clearly. *You'd love a monster when… I'm…I'm right in front of you…*Rissa Lyn was jealous and either making things up or suffering from some form of delusion. Regardless of her feelings, she had to realize that wild accusations weren't going to keep him from Nysa. *I'll talk to her later…let her down easy.*

He ripped through the tall, wind-battered grass, which lashed at his feet and legs. The sounds of the surf grew louder; overhead, gulls cried. On the western side, the sunset tower of Castle Dulgath stood on the very edge of the promontory's sea-worn tip. The eight-story stone pillar, which appeared to be an extension of the cliffs, had no windows on that side. Some sixty feet below, relentless waves crashed against the stubborn stone.

Someone was near the base of the tower—a dark figure standing in the shadowed gap between two of the tower's massive carved feet. Sherwood slowed his run to a hesitant trot when he realized it wasn't Nysa, not even a woman. It was a man in a black cloak, the hood up.

"What are you doing here?" Sherwood asked, stopping short.

"Why, waiting for you, of course," Lord Fawkes replied. The wind on top of the cliffs was chaotic and violent, forcing Fawkes to grip the edges of his cloak to keep it from whipping like a flag. Despite his effort, the lower edges flapped behind him like a startled bird.

"*You* sent the message?" Sherwood kept his distance. He was out of breath, tired, and sweating from the run.

"Yes, I needed to speak with you privately, and I didn't think you'd come at my request." Fawkes stepped forward one stride. Maybe he was trying to get out of the wind or felt uncomfortable between the tower's claws. "You've actually succeeded in getting Nysa to fall for you."

"Fall?"

"Don't be modest, boy. I spoke to her this morning and explained how the king might be uncomfortable with her appointment, her being the last of the Dulgath line and all. I offered my hand in marriage but was rebuffed. Apparently she's found someone else. I know she has high standards—and I couldn't imagine you had inexplicably leapt that bar."

Sherwood wanted to believe. "She said there was someone else? Maybe she just wasn't interested in you."

"She was quite sincere and rather specific."

"What *exactly* did she say? Did she mention me by name?"

"No, but she spoke of a man who visits her regularly. Someone she's getting to know better each day, and the more she learns about him, the more she has come to believe that she has found someone she could be with."

"She…she said that?"

"Yes, but don't get your hopes up. You aren't going to live happily ever after. I invited you to leave, but you didn't take the hint. Now I must insist." He let go of his cloak, freeing it to fly behind him and fall to the grass, exposing his sword.

Sherwood fell back, drawing his own. "I won't leave. I'd rather die."

Fawkes looked at the blade, puzzled. "What's a painter doing with a sword? Was that a gift? Do you even know how to hold it?"

Sherwood grinned. "I've killed men with this—men who'd attacked me. How about you? Done a lot of exhibitions, I suspect. Performed pretty dances before courtly audiences with tipped blades, perhaps? I don't think many draw steel against the king's cousin and mean it."

THE NOTE

"Oh, they've meant it," Fawkes said, striding toward him and drawing his blade. "I'm not well liked by many in Mehan. People have lost limbs and some have died in exhibitions. Are you sure you want to do this? I'm giving you one last chance. You can simply leave."

"And I'll extend you the same courtesy. Leave now. Nysa has made her choice."

"I'll stay. This should be fun; don't you think?"

"For one of us," Sherwood retorted.

Lord Fawkes swung first. Sherwood danced back, letting the blade sing through the air.

He had most of his wind back, but he'd burned energy rushing to the cliff. Fawkes had the advantage of rest. On the other hand, the trip had warmed Sherwood, loosening his muscles. Fawkes could have been standing in the cool wind for who knew how long.

Sherwood let him swing again. The same move, right to left with a downward angle. A power stroke, attempting to take advantage of Sherwood's weak side. Or maybe the lord was just testing him, trying to get a feel for his ability.

A good fight is a short fight, Yardley always had said. *Show him nothing. Conserve your energy while burning his. Then, at the first opportunity, end it.*

Sherwood and Fawkes crashed blades, hard. Then, as fast as the artist could, he backstroked at an angle to catch Fawkes at the neck.

The lord ducked.

Damn!

Sherwood was afraid Fawkes might take that moment of exposed chest to stab upward. That's what he would've done, but Fawkes retreated three steps, bouncing on his feet.

That's the difference between an exhibition fighter and a survivalist, Sherwood thought.

Fawkes was going for points, trying to look good: engage, withdraw, reset, circle left, circle right, lunge again. It made for a pretty show, but on a lonely cliff with lives on the line, and only seagulls and grass for an audience, no one fought that way.

This might be Christopher Fawkes's first real battle. That was Sherwood's advantage.

He's never done this. I have him. But Sherwood had more than one voice in his head. The other one mused over how well Fawkes handled his blade. *He has a lot more experience, He has held that sword as often as I've held a paintbrush. And his teachers were skilled swordsmen, not aging portrait artists.*

But he's never killed. That reassuring rationalization was followed by a nagging thought. *First time for everything.*

Another attack. This time Fawkes employed more finesse. He began with the same swing—and Sherwood saw now that he'd done it twice to set expectations—then he spun left and brought the sword blade up, hoping either to slice across Sherwood's torso or—if he were really lucky—to catch the tip on his stomach and then thrust.

Sherwood foiled Fawkes's plan by spinning to his right. This wasn't skill. He had no idea Fawkes was trying something clever. Sherwood had merely decided that if he tried the same swing again, he'd catch it on the other side and try to get in behind the man. As it turned out, they outsmarted each other, and each bobbed away, trying to conceal the surprise and concern they felt.

"Impressive," Fawkes said, selling a sense of confidence that Sherwood wasn't buying.

Earlier he might have been intimidated, but he realized that Fawkes was mostly bluster and wasn't actually very good. In that instant, he realized he'd won.

Believing you will be victorious, Yardley used to say, *knowing it—not just in your head, but in your heart—is what will give you the ability to succeed.*

THE NOTE

You lose the fear, and it's the fear that kills you. Believe in yourself and you'll triumph.

Sherwood knew now that he was better than Fawkes. More importantly, he could see the fear in the lord's eyes.

Fawkes knew it, too.

To look at Lord Christopher Fawkes was to see a dead man.

Sherwood advanced this time. He held the sword more comfortably. He felt his muscles relax, his breathing slow. *In through the nose, out through the mouth.*

The two voices in his head went silent, and he found his balance. The wind was in his hair, gulls were crying, the surf crashed below, but Sherwood focused on Fawkes, who had his back to the cliff. He took a shuffled step forward and raised his swo—

Pain exploded across Sherwood's back.

Every muscle in his body seized. His breathing stopped. His eyes went wide.

In front of him, Fawkes's attention darted to something behind Sherwood, and His Lordship smiled. Not with sinister supremacy, but with relief.

The tension in Sherwood's muscles disappeared along with every ounce of his strength. He crumpled to the grass, limp, as if every bone in his body had dissolved. He needed air but couldn't breathe through the unbearable pain.

He wasn't sure how long he lay there before footsteps approached.

"Hope you don't mind," Sheriff Knox said. "I got the crossbow you asked for. It's huge, but it's the only one I could find. I just wanted to see how well it worked."

"Not at all," Fawkes said. "That thing is—it's amazing."

"Isn't it? Heavy as a boulder and not meant to be held while fired. Crossbows really aren't my thing. I was aiming for dead center, and it should have killed him instantly. Little bugger is still wheezing."

"Made an incredible hole," Fawkes said, his voice catching in his throat. "Help me throw what's left of him off the cliff."

Sherwood couldn't move, couldn't breathe, as they dragged him. He wondered what it would be like to fall from such a height.

Will the impact kill me or will I drown?

As it turned out, it was neither. Sherwood Stow died while still en route to the edge.

Chapter Fifteen
THE PAINTING

Christopher Fawkes was the empathetic sort. While he had a long list of enemies—an actual written list he kept in the lining of his doublet—he could generally find something about each person to respect or at least pity. This annoying predisposition toward understanding and compassion frequently robbed him of the unencumbered enjoyment of victory. A notable exception was the King of Maranon. Lord Fawkes was certain the only reason for King Vincent Pendergast's existence was to give Christopher something to hate without reservation.

Vince the Vile—as Christopher referred to him in the safe confines of his own head—embodied everything bad in the world sewn up in one awful package. He was short, which was unforgivable for a monarch, and also ugly, which was unforgivable for anyone. He took after the Pendergast line, with a huge, hooked nose hanging off his face. His deep-set eyes hid beneath a ledge of bone so wide that a stick of chalk could rest there. He had gaps in his teeth, not just between the center two like any normal monstrosity, but between all of them.

Why Vince the Vile didn't grow a beard over his pockmarked skin remained a mystery, unless growing hair proved just as unmanageable as running his kingdom. His Majesty's fingers were fat and stubby, little sausages complete with thin, stretched casings. The only difference? Christopher had never seen so much hair on sausages. The king's fingers weren't the only fat part of the man. Vince the Vile wouldn't be able to wear a barrel without a cooper letting it out a stave or two. Perhaps the king's worst aspect was his habit of spitting and his utter lack of skill at it. Vincent's face was usually wet with saliva, and a gob of phlegm often decorated his chin. His personality matched his appearance.

"Chrissy?" the king said when spotting him in the courtyard. "I'm surprised to see you in Dulgath."

"Your Majesty." Christopher bowed with a smile on his lips as he pictured unleashing a quarrel into the fat, spittle-dripping crown-stand. Christopher had the arbalest—what Knox called the huge crossbow—hidden as best he could behind the wardrobe in his bedroom. Being the size of a bass violin, the weapon wouldn't fit under the bed. Didn't fit behind his wardrobe, either. The wingspan of the prod—what Knox called the bow part—stuck out on either side. He had put a sheet over it, making it look like a midget ghost with outstretched arms.

The morning after he'd sent the two thieves to Manzant, Christopher noticed that the ivy on the west tower had been removed. The gardener had ripped it down, by order of the countess, the evening he and Payne were in Brecken Dale. Either she was a fortune teller or the thieves had warned her. Why they would care, the lord didn't know, but it didn't matter.

The Painting

Christopher had asked Knox to find a heavy crossbow and hoped the shooting-from-a-distance idea hadn't also been thwarted. Seeing the arbalest with its steel prod, its hand crank, and its three-quarter-inch-thick ash quarrels, he couldn't imagine anything stopping it. The giant bolt that killed Sherwood had entered his back, exited his chest, and flown out over the ocean without pause. The only challenge left was aiming the thing at Nysa Dulgath in such a way that neither she nor anyone else could see the assassin squeeze the trigger.

Christopher followed King Vincent and his retinue into the reception hall. The monarch left the bulk of his caravan—which if one included the men-at-arms might amount to more servants than in the whole of Lady Dulgath's castle—in a miniature tent city just down the lane from the stables. Christopher was sorry to see that his friend Sir Gilbert hadn't come. Instead, Sir Dathan and Sir Jacobus flanked His Majesty, along with Bishop Parnell and the usual set of hands for holding his cup, adjusting his collar, and kissing his ample arse.

Lady Dulgath waited with her entire staff lined up in their finest bleached whites and blues. Blue and white were the colors of House Dulgath, but the indigo dye was expensive. Still, each member of the household wore at least one article of blue. The scullery staff, dairymaids, charwomen, and stable boys all had light-blue neckerchiefs. The gardeners, woodcutters, and cooks donned blue belts, and the chambermaids and seamstresses draped sashes over their shoulders. The skilled servants, such as the scribe, tailor, and treasurer, sported blue vests. Chamberlain Wells, being in charge of the household, wore a tie and a long blue coat. The staff made a fine showing, backs and hair straight, eyes down, faces clean. The countess herself was stunning. Lady Dulgath was dressed completely in blue, a rich gown that matched the deep color of the sapphire around her neck.

Beautiful. Absolutely beautiful. A shame she turned down my marriage proposal. Such a terrible waste to put a three-quarter-inch-thick quarrel through that breast.

She curtsied with her usual unrivaled grace, bowing her head. The king took her hand and kissed its back. Christopher knew what was on the royal pimple's mind. Father dead. No suitors. The queen left at home in Mehan. And it got cold at night on the coast, even in summer.

He imagined exactly what Vince the Vile was thinking: *I'm the king, after all, and so handsome! How can she resist?*

The old wart is in for a frustrating night. If Nysa hadn't personally told Christopher about her growing interest in Sherwood, he'd have guessed she was frigid.

But she didn't actually name Sherwood, did she? And the painter looked so very surprised. Why? Should have been proud or at the very least guilty. Is it possible there's someone else?

"So very sorry to hear about your father, Nysa," the drooling magpie blathered without a dandelion tuft of sincerity. He was still holding her hand, mauling it with his own. "I would've come for the funeral, but the demands on a king's time often prohibit me from doing what I want."

How strange, Christopher thought, *given that you attended the Swanwick Spring Derby during that time. A race where your horse, once again, came in first.*

"I assure you that I have no intention of altering the fief. House Dulgath has always done a fine job of administrating its land. It would be a crime to change that after so many centuries," he said while glancing at the bishop. "Can we hold the ceremony tomorrow? That way I'll be out of your hair and you can resume your life."

And His Royal Majesty will go hunting. If a handful of drunks riding through a forest while an entourage of soldiers herds a host of animals to the slaughter can be considered hunting.

"Yes, Your Majesty," Nysa was saying. "We can arrange that. You might have noticed the decorations on your way in. I thought we would hold it outside in the courtyard."

"What if it rains?" Vincent asked.

This elicited several smiles from the line of servants.

"I don't expect it will, Sire."

"Why not?"

"Because…that would be unpleasant."

Christopher had stopped listening to the conversation, but his attention returned when the king asked, "And where is Sherwood Stow?"

"We don't know, Your Majesty. No one has seen him since yesterday," Lady Dulgath explained.

"He left?"

"No, Sire—at least I don't think so. His things are still here."

Vincent rubbed his glistening chin. "I've been thinking of having him paint my daughter, Evangeline—her portrait, I mean. I want it done while she's still young and pretty—before she starts looking like her mother. I spoke to Stow when he came through Mehan on his way here, but that was months ago."

"Two months and three days, Sire," Perkins Fallinwell, the king's body man, replied. Fallinwell had one of the most hilarious names Christopher had ever heard. There had to be a story behind it, but Perkins, being the pinched-nosed, prune-lipped tosser that he was, refused to divulge a word of it.

"Yes, that's right—*two* months. How long does it take to do a portrait? That's what he was here for, correct?"

"Yes, Sire," Nysa replied. "My father had commissioned him, but Mister Stow hasn't yet completed it."

"Slow bugger, but I've heard he's the best. And I want the best for my little E-line. You say you haven't seen him in days?"

"One day, Sire," Perkins Fallinwell corrected.

Vincent clapped Fallinwell on the back. "He carries the royal purse. Can you tell?" The king laughed—a sluggish, honking sound like an influenza-stricken goose. When the king gathered himself, he coughed and then spat on the floor, barely missing Fallinwell's shoe. A long elastic string snapped to his chin, where it stayed, a shimmering beacon to everyone watching, but the king was utterly oblivious. "Is the painting any good?"

"I, ah…" Nysa bit her lip. "I haven't actually seen it."

"You haven't? Not at all?" The king looked at Wells and then the handmaiden. Each in turn shook their head.

"Sherwood is very protective about works in progress." Nysa tried to make up for her ignorance with a smile.

"But two months?"

Nysa clasped her hands together. "I think he wants it to be a surprise unveiling. I'm inclined to grant him that pleasure."

"All fine and good, but I want to see if the man is worth waiting for or whether I should hire someone else. After two months, it must be nearly finished. And I don't think a painter of portraits will mind if the King of Maranon takes a peek. Where is it?"

"In his room. I'll have it brought down to the study." She nodded toward Rissa Lyn, who scurried off. "This way. Let me show you."

When Bishop Parnell started to follow, the king held up a hand. "Your Grace, your presence won't be necessary. I'm sure you have better things to do. Perhaps you could have some tea with Pastor Payne. I'm sure this won't take long, and I will join you shortly."

Lady Dulgath escorted Vincent down the corridor to the little room across from the stairs. Christopher watched them go, then followed. He wasn't interested in Sherwood's painting but was suspicious about Vincent wanting to speak to the lady in private.

THE PAINTING

Christopher waited outside the door while Rissa Lyn scurried past, carrying the large, covered canvas. He knelt down and fussed with the buckle on his shoe, and she curtsied in his direction after reemerging from the study, then scampered down the hall.

"How long has Christopher Fawkes been here?" the king asked in a tone far softer than he'd employed earlier.

"Since the funeral."

His Majesty spat. Christopher knew the sound. His memory conjured a vivid, disgusting image, and he grimaced.

"I would be remiss if I didn't warn you that he wishes to become the next Earl of Dulgath. If he has expressed interest toward you, I suspect it has more to do with winning your land rather than your heart."

"I appreciate your concern, Your Majesty."

Vincent went on. "As I said, I have no intention of changing what is working so well. Maranon has always been a lush, rich kingdom, but Dulgath is the icing on the cake. On the way in, I saw how every field was planted, every plant vibrant and strong. Your roads are without holes and the houses are in good repair. Your people are well fed, smiling and laughing. It's good to see, so I have no doubt about renewing Dulgath's tenure. You should know that I never had any, although many advised otherwise. Now, let's take a look at that painting."

"Oh, I assumed you merely wanted to speak in private. We really shouldn't—"

"Nonsense, I'm sure it'll be fine. Even if it's not finished, it'll give me an idea of the man's skill. I really am thinking of having him paint my Evangeline."

"I'll just stand over here," Lady Dulgath said.

"Don't you want to see?"

"No, thank you, Sire. It would be…rude."

"Suit yourself. Okay, so—ah, here we are…By Mar! That's…
that's—no, that's not right at all. I can certainly see why he wouldn't
let you see it, Nysa. This is most disturbing. Insulting is what it is.
Utterly—I can't believe…damn! This must be some kind of joke,
and it's not a funny one. No, I don't believe he'll be painting my
daughter after all. Absolutely not! And if I were you, I wouldn't pay
the man for this—this…excuse me."

The king hurried out of the study, his expression a twisted
frown. Vincent the Vile strode past Christopher as if he weren't
there. Nysa Dulgath didn't follow.

"Where's the Great Hall?" the king asked Wells as the chamberlain
came through the main entrance.

"This way, Your Majesty," the chamberlain said.

"And get me a drink!" Vincent bellowed.

"Of course, Your Majesty. Right away, Sire."

Christopher lingered in the hall, watching the open door to
the study. After several minutes, when Lady Dulgath still hadn't
emerged, he peeked in. Nysa was at the easel, gazing at the painting
and crying. In all the time he'd spent in Dulgath, he'd never seen her
display any emotion.

"Are you all right?" he asked.

She didn't reply. With one hand over her mouth, she ran out of
the study.

Stunned, Christopher watched her go. Nysa had more in
common with the many statues in the castle than with its people.
But she had been reduced to tears by a painting.

How bad could it possibly be?

Christopher listened to Lady Dulgath's receding footsteps, then
crept forward to the easel and lifted the cloth.

At first, he wasn't certain what he saw. A face certainly—a pair
of eyes looked back at him with stunning, even disturbing, clarity.

THE PAINTING

But it wasn't Nysa's face. This person was bald, cheekbones high and sharp. The eyes themselves were mesmerizing, but even they failed to be the most striking feature.

The ears! The ears are pointed!

The face in the portrait wasn't human—it was elven. But unlike any elf Christopher had ever seen.

Every elf he'd ever encountered was covered in filth and wore the most wretched, downtrodden expression. Driven from respectable society, they were forbidden in many towns. When tolerated, they could only be found in the worst sections. The males were notoriously lazy, while the females were known to neglect their children. The one thing the genders shared was incessant begging. Dirty hands were constantly outstretched while they mumbled something indistinguishable, and yet their intent was obvious.

Sherwood had portrayed one of those vile creatures dressed in Lady Dulgath's clothes. However, the most disturbing detail wasn't the subject's race but the expression on its face. The eyes bored straight into him, wide and clear. She wasn't begging, and her expression displayed no hint of shame. What was truly troubling was how the elven female in the portrait appeared to consider herself superior. Christopher could see it in her haughty stare, the square of her shoulders, and that hint of a smirk that declared she knew something he didn't. This elf was laughing at him, looking out from that canvas with painted eyes and judging *him* as unworthy.

Christopher snatched up the canvas without thinking. He couldn't concentrate with those eyes upon him—glaring with disdain, belittling him, insulting his existence, questioning his very right to exist. He smashed the canvas against the wall, splintering the frame. He pulled and wrenched at the thing, trying to tear it in half, but the canvas was stronger than it appeared. He hurled it to the floor and reached for his dagger.

I'll cut those miserable eyes from your—

"Lord Fawkes?"

Christopher turned and saw Lady Dulgath's handmaiden.

Her name was Rissa Lyn, and she stood in the doorway in her simple white dress with the faded-blue sash. Her eyes were huge, her mouth a large O.

Christopher froze with dagger drawn, then quickly put it away. When he saw she was alone he asked, "What do you want?"

The woman hesitated. She gave a nervous glance out the open door, then walked quickly toward him. Her eyes were on the broken painting as she said, "It killed Sherwood Stow."

Christopher's heart was still racing, his air coming in short, fast breaths. "What are you blathering about, girl?"

"I read the note Lady Dulgath sent to Mister Stow right before he vanished."

This got his full attention.

"Her Ladyship begged him to meet her on the cliffs above the sea. I told him what she was. Tried to stop him from going. Mister Stow is dead." She pointed at the painting. "That thing killed him. Killed him because he knew what she really was."

"And what is she?"

"A demon. Same one that possessed Maddie Oldcorn. Poor Lady Nysa died but was never buried proper. Now a monster walks around in her corpse. Mister Stow saw that. It's all in the painting, isn't it, milord? I went to his room last night, to try to convince him about the demon. He wasn't there, but the painting was, so I looked. Mister Stow saw the monster inside Lady Dulgath, and it killed him. He never returned from that meeting."

The woman was insane, and desperation filled her eyes as she clasped her hands against her chest, squeezing them so hard the fingertips went white.

The Painting

"You have to do something, my lord. The king is here. He can stop it. If you tell him what I—"

"Christopher!" the voice of the bishop called. "Fawkes!"

"Excuse me." He walked out.

Keep it together, Christopher. Just one more day—not even a whole day. Just a few more hours. Just a few more.

Chapter Sixteen
THE ROAD SOUTH

The world rocked again, accompanied by a loud, painful thump. Hadrian opened his eyes. His cheek—pressed against rough, vibrating wood—throbbed along with the rest of his head. Sunlight, bright and harsh, entered a barred window and stung his eyes. His wrists hurt and were tied—no, manacled behind his back. He tried to swallow. Yes, his tongue, throat, and mouth were dry, but the real problem was the wide iron collar. Metal links connecting his wrists to the neckband dug into his back.

He lay inside an enclosed wagon. Three barred windows—small ones on either side and a large one in the door at the back—showed they traveled a two-track road across flat, open ground. Another hard jolt and pain bloomed in Hadrian's right side. Having his arms wrenched up toward the middle of his back wasn't helping. After one more painful bump, a hard hammering blow that made him clench his teeth, Hadrian sat up—not an easy thing to do, trussed up as he was.

The sun between the bars indicated either the lateness of the day or a dawn newly born. Hadrian wasn't alone. Royce sat across from him, knees up, head down, chained in the same way as Hadrian.

"Thought you'd never wake up," Royce said.

"How long have I been out?"

Royce shrugged. "Day and a half, maybe."

Hadrian's mouth hung open. "Are you serious? That can't be right. Last time it was only a few hours. And I drank less this time."

Again Royce shrugged.

Hadrian dragged his pasty tongue across his teeth. "That would explain the taste in my mouth. I'm never drinking anything again."

Outside, three men rode escort—one on each side, another at the rear. They wore the same black uniforms as the men who had broken into their room at Caldwell House. The sun was on the right side of the wagon. If it was evening, they were traveling south; if morning, north.

"What happened?" Hadrian asked.

"They put the drug in the cups on the shelf before we arrived."

"Yeah, I gathered that much. I meant after."

"You passed out, and we had uninvited company. They were very rude. I can't believe you drank."

"I didn't expect everyone in Dulgath to be alchemists."

"Not everyone, just her."

"Her?"

"Feldspar," Royce said bitterly.

"You think Scarlett was involved?"

"Same place. Same drug. Everyone conveniently absent. Doesn't take a genius." Royce nodded. "She's working for Fawkes and Payne."

"You're not serious?"

Royce rolled not only his eyes but his head as well. "Let me guess. You're in love with her."

"No!" he said loud enough to anger the throbbing in his head. The wagon and the rough road were torturing him just fine; he didn't need to help. "I like her, that's all. She seems nice, sweet, and protective of her friends." He looked out at the soldier trailing behind them. "Are you sure? I mean…I can't believe I could misjudge a person so badly."

"You're not exactly known for your judgment of character, but don't feel too bad. The woman is a professional. Most Diamond girls are trained at manipulation, and seduction—two of their best tools."

Hadrian did feel bad. Not because he had been taken in by Scarlett, but at the thought that she could do such a thing. He really had liked her. Worse—he had believed her. Hadrian had bought that whole story about her escaping Colnora and finding a better life in the dale. Such a thing was easy to believe. He wanted it to be true, still did. "Any idea where we are?"

"The Old Mine Road."

"The Old—?" Hadrian lifted his chin. His side screamed again. Once more, he clamped his teeth in pain. For his effort, he saw mountains, the little green range separating Dulgath from Greater Maranon. "We're not in Dulgath anymore. This is that road—the one you paused at on the way in—the one that went south."

Which makes it late afternoon, coming on evening.

He looked again at the soldier behind them. He had his helm off and his chain coif thrown back. "Where are we going?"

"Manzant."

The name was vaguely familiar, and not in a good way.

Royce assumed he didn't know and added, "A salt mine on the rocky thumb of Maranon. It's also a prison—sort of. You're not going to like it."

A salt mine prison? "Can you unlock these?" He jingled the chain holding his wrists.

"No."

Royce let his head hang forward as if it weighed more that day. His hood was off, thrown back. So was his cloak, disheveled and torn, but his hair did a good job of hiding his face.

"Seriously?" Hadrian asked.

Royce took the effort to tilt his head and glare at him. "Hands are locked just like yours. I can't reach my tools."

"Well, maybe I can reach them." Hadrian shoved to his knees, making a rattling sound as chains clattered on wood, then gasped as the sharp pain stabbed his side again.

"Won't help," Royce told him, lowering his face once more.

"Why not?"

"My right hand is broken. So is the middle finger of my left. Besides, I doubt they missed them when searching us."

"Oh." Hadrian sighed, then let himself slide back down. He moved slowly, bracing for more pain.

"What about you?" Royce asked.

"Cracked rib, I think."

"That all?"

Hadrian nodded. "Pretty sure."

Royce had his head up again and studied Hadrian's face. "You look terrible."

"Really?" Hadrian shifted his jaw and moved his cheek muscles, searching for bruises. "My face doesn't even hurt."

Royce shook his head. "Just in general, I mean. I don't think I've ever just sat and stared at you before."

Hadrian frowned. Getting back to a sitting position, he let his head rest on the wall behind him. "Why is it you always find your sense of humor when we're about to die?"

Royce shrugged. "I suppose because that's when life is at its most absurd."

"We are going to die, right? I don't want to get my hopes up unnecessarily."

"If we're lucky," Royce replied without any hint of humor this time. "Manzant is a place where people go to disappear. A long, deep, narrow shaft. Dwarves built the mine centuries ago, a hideous achievement of incarceration. Inmates mine salt in the dark in return for food and fresh water. No tools, no protection, you either find a way to get salt or you die trying. In time, the salt leaches the very soul out of a man, or so I've heard."

"Well, you're in luck. Can't squeeze wine from a stone, right?" Hadrian pulled on the manacles again. Now he remembered the name Manzant, the place Scarlett had told him about. She'd gotten away by escaping her chains, but that was probably a lie like everything else. "If we're going to prison, what do you suppose the charges are? We haven't done anything wrong."

"You don't have to do anything wrong to end up in Manzant. Like I said, it's a mine as well as a prison. Ambrose Moor—he's the administrator—doesn't care where he gets workers. Criminals are fine, but he'll pay decent money for slaves, too."

"But we aren't slaves."

"We are now."

Hadrian scanned the wagon and found it empty except for some rotting straw and extra chains that had turned a dark-rust color. They added to the loud jangle accompanying each hard bump. "You still have Alverstone?"

Royce shook his head. "Manzant slavers are excellent at their job. Not done yet. They'll strip us naked when we get to the prison. Shave our heads, too."

"Quit talking it up. You're ruining all the surprises."

The wagon hit another bump, a big one. They both groaned as the fixed axle hammered the road. Then the movement stopped. "What now? Are we there?"

Royce shook his head. He peered out the side window, head cocked, listening. "Water." Royce paused. "Must be at Mercator Creek." He nodded. "They're watering the horses. We're farther south than I thought."

Hadrian heard a laugh. Two men talked, but their voices were too distant and muffled to understand.

"How far to Manzant?" Hadrian asked.

"Mercator Creek is less than ten miles from the prison, but in a wagon traveling up that twisting mountain road…" He looked out the window at the sky. "Be there tomorrow, I guess."

"So we have a whole night to figure a way out."

Royce gave him a pitiful smirk. "I really love the way you think things will all turn out fine. How did Feldspar put it? It's so—*cute*."

Hadrian frowned and tried to feel for the lock on his wrists, but his fingers were numb from being pinched.

Royce said, "Arcadius was right about you. It's like you're color-blind. Except it's not colors you can't see, it's reality. Your problem is you expect too much from people."

"I'm not the blind one here," Hadrian replied. "I've seen the lows people can reach, believe me. But I've also witnessed heroic, even ridiculous levels of kindness. You have, too, but you ignore them. *That's* blindness, my friend."

Royce shook his head slowly and made a hissing sound— condescending laughter—a Royce Melborn trademark. "Water flows downhill," he explained. "Cats eat mice. And sure, there's the odd cold day in summer, or the freak warm spell in winter, but as a rule that doesn't happen. In fact, it's so not the rule it's not worth mentioning. What you don't understand, or choose to ignore, is that people care only about themselves. They wouldn't risk money, much less their lives, for someone else. The only reason anyone would gamble their own neck for another person is if that other person's life is important to their own welfare, and even then…" He shook his head and let out the same wispy laugh. "Fear drives most people. Acts of bravery are most often the result of ignorance or impulse. Given even a moment to think, to realize and reflect on the possible dangers, your would-be hero always gets cold feet."

"I didn't," Hadrian said. "And you're alive because of it."

Royce smiled as if he'd expected this comment. "You're right, and you know what? That's bothered me for three years, but I've finally figured it out."

Something banged hard against the side of the wagon. "You two still alive in there?" a harsh voice called. A face grinned in the window over Royce's head.

"They're fine. Both of 'em sittin' up like this is their lucky day. You two just relax. We'll be moving again soon enough, and by tomorrow, you'll be home. Enjoy the sun, boys; it's the last you'll ever see of her." The man laughed and then moved away, chuckling as he went.

"Nice fella," Royce said. "Maybe *he'll* help us."

"Funny. So, what's this thing you've figured out?" Hadrian asked.

"Oh, right. I determined the only reason you came back around the tower instead of climbing down and getting away was because you wanted to die."

Hadrian's eyes widened.

"Still do, in a way, I think. When you came back from Calis all disillusioned and lacking direction, you felt life had no point or purpose. You can't stand to live in a world where people feed off others. You'd rather die in protest then accept the truth that life is misery and your fellow men are vicious animals who'll jump at any opportunity to get ahead by stepping on their neighbor's neck."

"Okay." Hadrian nodded. "Sounds like you've got me nailed down, but what about—"

"Gwen? She might just be that strange warm spell in winter. I don't know."

"No, not her. I was going to say, what about *you?*"

"Me?"

"The first time we entered Medford, you risked your life for me. More than that, you actually begged in the street for my sake. Why'd you do that?"

"Okay." Royce nodded. "You can add one more condition to the list. Acts which run contrary to one's own self interest are due to ignorance, impulse, *and delirium.*"

Hadrian laughed. "That's a fine fortress you've built there, although none too comfortable, I suspect."

"And that cloud you live on is going to disappear in Manzant. People don't help others unless there's something in it for them, and since we're of no use to anyone, no one is going to help us."

Out the rear window, between the vertical bars of iron, Hadrian spotted another traveler on the road. A wagon was coming their way.

Hadrian couldn't believe his eyes.

He glanced at Royce for validation and found his partner staring out the back of the wagon, his mouth open, brows twisted in confused knots. "What's she doing here?"

Scarlett Dodge was driving a buckboard pulled by a pair of mismatched horses. She'd traded her patchwork gown for a loose shirt and men's trousers. She'd tucked her vibrant hair under a wide-brimmed straw hat. Hadrian hoped she wasn't trying to pass for a man; she still looked every bit a woman despite the attire. As she neared, Scarlett steered her wagon to the left of the road, bringing it up alongside them. The bed of the buckboard was filled with six barrels: four marked BEER, the other two ALE.

"Hello there!" one of the black-uniformed men called to her.

"Hello," she replied, her voice soft, meek, wary.

Hadrian and Royce both shifted to peer out the left-side window.

"What's your name?" someone asked, too far past the corner of the window for them to see.

"I'm just stopping to water my horses. I'll be on my way in a—"

"Didn't ask you about your horses. I asked your name, sweetie. What is it?"

"Ruby." Scarlett was too far to one side for Hadrian to see her face. His view consisted entirely of the wagon, barrels, and the hind ends of the horses.

"See, she knows better than to give her real name," Royce said.

"She's here to help us," Hadrian told him.

"All by herself? Against six Manzant slavers?"

Hadrian looked out the rear window, searching for others. The road, flat and straight, was empty for miles.

Royce shook his head. "She's the one who put us here."

"What's with the boy's clothes, Ruby?" one of the slavers asked.

"Brother's clothes. Easier to work in."

"Where you taking all that beer and ale?"

One of them came to the wagon and jostled a barrel, then another. "They're full."

"They're, ah—old. Going bad. Has a real rank taste. I'm taking them to Manzant to sell. Guards are grateful for whatever they can get."

Hadrian leaned against the wall of the wagon.

She's lying—but why?

Fawkes could have sent her to ensure they were locked away.

Do you understand the meaning of the word thorough?

His brain knew it was possible, even probable, but his heart didn't want to believe.

She's here to help, he reasoned. *Maybe she tried to get others, too, but they refused. She's stubborn and foolish and chased after us alone.*

"You're in luck, little lady. We're from Manzant. You can give it to us."

"Wasn't planning on *giving* it to no one. I'm selling it, but sure, I can sell it to you. Let's see, for all six kegs it'll cost you…five yellow tenents or twelve with King Vincent's profile."

"Naw, I'm thinking these are donations."

"Then you'd be thinking wrong."

Two of the men lifted a barrel from the wagon and hauled it out of sight.

"Leave that alone!"

"Just taking a taste, honeysweet."

"Stop it!"

"Looks like we've got ourselves a party, boys."

"By Mar! We got beer, ale, and a pretty little thing to entertain us."

"And you didn't want to come."

"I know, right? I would've been kicking myself."

"We're spending the night here, aren't we? I mean, no sense in going any farther today, am I right?"

"Absolutely. Hey, Owen, why don't you make a fire?"

"And just leave the whoring and drinking to you? Screw that."

"I said stop it!" Scarlett's voice cut a note higher. She was scared. The horses didn't like it. The two on Scarlett's wagon shuffled, making their tack jingle, and the lorry shifted forward and back.

Hadrian jerked on his chains; they rewarded him by cutting into his abused flesh. He pressed his face to the bars of the window, but he couldn't see anything beyond Scarlett's barrel-laden wagon.

"Why don't you sit down?" a voice growled.

Startled by something, both sets of horses jerked. The wagon Royce and Hadrian were in lurched, slamming Hadrian's face against the window. At the same time, Scarlett gasped. Not quite a scream, but close.

Hadrian jerked on the manacles again, and blood dripped around his wrists.

"Ain't nothing wrong with this, is there?"

"Tastes fine to me."

"It's even a little cold."

"I think she's lying to us, don't you?"

"Lying to us about more than the beer, I'll bet. Those clothes are lying, too. They say you're frumpy, but I'll wager you've got quite a figure underneath."

"No!" Scarlett shouted.

Running feet slapped dirt, and a moment later Scarlett appeared back in Hadrian's vision. She stared through the little window, eyes wide with fear. "Help!" she screamed.

One of the men caught her by the arm. Scarlett jerked back and slammed against the side of their wagon. She screamed again. Another man grabbed her around the waist and lifted her up. Her hat came off, and that long red hair cascaded out. The men exclaimed in pleasure at the sight.

"Told you them clothes were hiding something special!"

Hadrian threw himself at the wooden wall. The boards, thick and solid, didn't even shudder. The impact only served to jar his ribs, and a fresh bolt of pain stole his breath.

"Settle down in there!" one of the slavers shouted, banging on the wall of the wagon.

"They're jealous of our good fortune," another said.

With arms and feet thrashing, Scarlett was carried out of sight. Hadrian continued to press his face hard to the corner of the little opening in the wall, struggling to see what they were doing. All he saw were Scarlett's horses standing, hoofing the ground and lifting their heads to watch what Hadrian couldn't see. On the ground just outside, Scarlett's hat lay in a rut, long red hairs caught in the brim.

Scarlett screamed. The sound was different this time, and Hadrian was surprised to discover that screams had their own language. Before she'd cried out in fear; now she shrieked in panic. Fear of the possible had become the terror of reality. She wailed until her cries were muffled. Things went quiet for a few seconds, and then she screeched again. After a minute or so, the screams stopped, and Scarlett settled into a whimpering ongoing sob.

Hadrian couldn't help himself. He began to thrash, trying to find a way out of the chains, out of the iron manacles that had him helpless—a way that didn't exist.

"Hold her!"

"Get her ankles! Get her goddamn ankles!"

Hadrian pulled on the iron, feeling the brackets cutting deeper, neither giving at all.

"Easy," Royce whispered.

"I have to do something! I can't just sit here and listen to this."

"Nothing you can do. Relax."

"I can't relax!" he yelled. "She wasn't involved, Royce. She's here to help and now…" Hadrian put his face back to the window but still couldn't see.

"You can't do anything else," Royce said in his all-too-cold, all-too-complacent, all-too-callous way. Times like this Hadrian hated his partner, hated his ruthless indifference. This side of Royce was devoid of compassion, of empathy. He could sit content while just outside—

Scarlett shrieked again, this time louder. The slavers replied with laughter.

Once more, Hadrian put his face against the bars of the window. The cool metal pressed against his cheek. "You sons of bitches!" Hadrian shouted. "Leave her alone!"

More laughter.

Royce did nothing. He sat on the floor of the wagon, his back against the wall. No struggling, no effort to squirm out of the manacles—he just sat there, head back, looking at his boots. At least he wasn't smiling. That was something.

Scarlett wailed louder, and then fell back once more to sobs. After that came a good deal of grunting and some sounds of gagging and spitting. Then slowly, bit by bit, the noises faded. The horses still jangled their tack and stomped their hooves, but he couldn't hear Scarlett anymore.

Did they kill her? The idea grew in his head.

At first, he didn't want to believe it, but as the silence continued, he grew steadily more certain of the possibility. They'd killed her and were sitting around her body, drinking and recovering.

Hadrian stayed by the window, straining to hear. Wind brushed grass, making a sound as light as rain. A single cricket trilled a lonely note. Somewhere, a swallow chirped. So quiet.

Why is it so very quiet?

Footsteps.

Hadrian heard them shuffle on dirt. They paused, then grew louder as they approached Royce's side of the wagon.

Feeling sick, furious, and drained, Hadrian turned toward the rear door, hoping someone would be stupid enough to open it. With his wrists bound up, there wasn't much he could do, but he was pretty sure he could kill at least one.

Hadrian was good at killing—that was his skill, his one true talent. Once upon a time, he had actually been proud of that ability. He'd since outgrown his pride and sobered up from an addiction to blood, but at twenty-two he'd come too late to the simple wisdom that killing wasn't something to take pride in. And yet there were times, moments like this, when he realized that even terrible talents had a use.

To his amazement, he heard a key enter the door's lock.

They're opening it!

Hadrian glanced at Royce with wide-eyed anticipation. His partner shifted to a crouch. His nimble, cat-smooth movement announced his agreement to an unspoken plan.

If the man opening the wagon door also has the key to our chains…

The door swung open. Both Royce and Hadrian started, then stopped short, confounded by the sight of red hair.

"Hang on, I have to find the right one," Scarlett Dodge said, holding up a large metal hoop filled with a dozen keys. A bit of dirt smeared her shirt, and she had a grass stain on one knee of her trousers. Other than that, she looked fine. "Here, turn around," she told Hadrian.

"You're…you're all right?"

"Yeah," she said with a little puff of air—an almost-laugh that said, *Why wouldn't I be?* "Turn around."

He did as she instructed, sending Royce a baffled look. Royce didn't look surprised, but his face was covered with suspicion.

Hadrian felt a tug on the manacles at his wrist.

"What did you do? Your skin is all torn up and bloody." She loosened one; then both popped open, and his arms were free. The relief in his shoulders was immediate. A surge of blood reached his fingertips, igniting a burst of pins and needles. The ache in his side—while not gone—eased a bit.

"Hold steady," she complained, starting to work on his collar.

"Are you sure you're all right?" he asked.

"Me? Of course I'm sure."

The heavy metal collar made a loud hollow *clunk!* as it hit the wagon's bed. Hadrian rubbed at his raw neck and swallowed several times, enjoying the simple pleasure.

Scarlett paused before Royce, holding up the key. "If I unlock you, are you going to be nice?"

Royce said nothing. He stared at her with an unfathomable expression: anger, suspicion, but also something else.

Scarlett let out a frustrated sigh and went to work on Royce's locks. As she did, Hadrian climbed out. A cool breeze chilled the sweat on his skin as he cautiously moved around between the two wagons. He headed toward the river, which proved to be no more than a pathetic trickle running over the road. High banks told tales of spring floods, but at that moment Mercator Creek wasn't impressive. There was no bridge; the two-track road just plowed through a shallow section where rocks refused to wash away. The team of horses that had pulled the prison wagon drank from the rippling water. Scarlett's pair were held by a hand brake, too far back to join the other horses. The two animals were slick with sweat, their hair soaked flat and dark beneath the leather straps and collar. She'd driven them hard—too hard to let them drink until they cooled down.

Around the front, a keg marked BEER sat upright in the road. It looked exactly like a miniature rain barrel; its lid had been broken into two parts. The dirt around the base was dark and wet. A few inches away, he spotted a tin cup in the dirt. Next to it lay a slaver. He wasn't alone. Hadrian counted the men and came up with all six. They were lying on the road or in the grass—although one was partially in the creek, the fingers of his left hand shifting in the current.

Royce came out of the wagon and pushed past. He descended on the nearest guard, his torn cloak spreading out like the wings of a vulture with the movement.

"You don't have to—"

Before Scarlett could finish, Royce had pulled a dagger from the soldier's belt and stabbed the man in the throat.

Royce moved to the next one.

"He doesn't have to do that," Scarlett said, moving to stand beside Hadrian.

"Don't bother trying to stop him. There's no way he'll let them live."

"No, it's not that," Scarlett said. "I didn't drug them."

Royce paused, looking first at her, then down at the man he straddled. He placed a hand to the slaver's throat. He nodded in a sort of grim approval and rose. Still holding the dagger, he returned to Scarlett, who took three quick steps backward.

"Royce!" Hadrian shouted, but the thief ignored him.

He caught her by the throat with his left hand. His middle finger being broken, he used his thumb to hook under her chin, forcing her head back against the side of the prison wagon. The dagger was clutched awkwardly, painfully, in his other hand, which still bore the boot mark where someone had stepped on it. "Why'd you do it?"

"Royce—let her go!"

"I want to know why."

"Because unlike you, she cares about people. We got to be friends the other day. She did it for me."

"No," Scarlett said. "I did it for him." She managed a shallow nod at Royce.

The thief stared. "Explain why you'd risk your life for me. Explain fast."

"Royce!" Hadrian yanked a sword from the belt of a black-uniformed man.

"I did it because you were drugged with my herbs. Someone took them from my place while I was out with Hadrian, but I knew you wouldn't believe that. I knew you'd blame me, and that Manzant can't hold you. And I heard what happened the last time you got out—what happened to those who helped put you there."

"Royce!" Hadrian shouted, coming at him with the naked sword.

Royce let go of her and gingerly shifted the knife to his other hand, wincing as he did. He moved away from her.

Hadrian slowed down as he stepped through the grisly scene, ignoring the gathering flies. "This was stupid. What if they didn't drink right away? What if they'd waited to celebrate their good fortune?"

"Riding in the hot sun all day?" Scarlett replied. "Pretty much a sure thing."

"So they didn't…" Hadrian looked at her but not directly in her eyes. It felt like too much of an intrusion. "They didn't—you know?"

"No." Scarlett gave her head a curt shake. She wore a little smile while narrowing her eyes, as if he both amused and bewildered her. Then she shrugged. "They were a little grabby near the end." She pulled out the side of her shirt and peered beneath it with a scowl. "I'll have a nasty bruise."

"What if they had drunk from another barrel?" Hadrian asked.

"They're all poisoned," Royce answered for her. "But what if not all of them drank? What if the first one dropped dead before the others got around to it?"

Scarlett exposed a knife beneath the long tails of her shirt and shrugged.

"Might have killed one—maybe. These were Manzant slavers. They don't go down easy." Royce shook his head. "That was way too dangerous."

"Glad you noticed," she said. "And you should also note that this is Wagner's entire supply of beer and ale—ruined to save you.

The Road South

So the two of you can go on back to wherever you came from, right? Hadrian's swords are in the box up where the driver rests his feet. Wag says he saw them load up. That pretty white dagger and your coin, you'll find on the bodies. Just take the horses, leave, and forget about Dulgath. Okay? Just leave."

Hadrian saw the way Royce was clutching his broken hand.

Royce looked back at him with a familiar expression that was easy to read.

"Sorry," Hadrian said. "We aren't leaving."

Chapter Seventeen
SHERVIN GERAMI

Covered mostly in salt and birdlime, the coastal village of Rye was worse than repugnant. Christopher honestly couldn't think of a word awful enough to describe it. An hour's ride south and west of Castle Dulgath, its shacks sat on a beach and looked like wreckage washed up in a storm. Their front yards were tiny slivers of seaweed-strewn sand covered by upturned hulls of little battered boats. Buoys, ratty nets, and snapped branches were heaped in piles. Leather-skinned villagers squatted over smoking campfires, dressed in little more than loincloths. Christopher had asked Knox to find someone unassociated with Castle Dulgath to do the deed but hadn't expected the necessity to visit another world in the process.

Christopher Fawkes couldn't claim to be well traveled. While he'd been to the major cities of Maranon, that wouldn't be considered worldly for a baron. Then again, Christopher Fawkes wasn't a baron. His father held that title. Christopher was instead the worthless fourth son, but like any contemptible child of a middling noble, he used his father's title to open doors. Most people never questioned him. This never pleased his father, but then nothing did—at least nothing Christopher ever did. His mother agreed with her husband, as a smart wife of a despot should. Christopher's brothers and sisters—of which he had six—followed suit in their opinions of him. This didn't surprise Christopher; siblings in a noble household were, by nature, mortal enemies.

The only surprising hostility Christopher faced had come from his previous horse. The mare had tried to bite him every chance she got. He'd named the horse Melanie de Burke after a woman at court; she was a gorgeous and expensive purebred Renallian. He'd once loved Melanie de Burke—the woman—but he was certain she still didn't know he existed. Melanie de Burke—the horse and biter—had been dead three years. He'd killed her—the horse, that is—and that singular act had ruined his life. As he thought about it, had he killed Melanie de Burke—the woman—he might have fared better. Such was the insanity of life in Maranon, and the reason he so appreciated Immaculate.

How far have my standards fallen when my love and loyalty are won by an animal that simply doesn't bite me?

"Are you certain you found someone suitable *here*?" Christopher asked, getting down from the wagon and scanning the desolate encampment.

This is how the natives in the dark recesses of Calis live. At least he imagined so. He hadn't been there, either.

"You'll see," Knox said with a grin.

Christopher didn't like the man's smile, something sinister in it. It had that I-know-something-you-don't-know look about it. Noting the nick still in the leather collar of Knox's gambeson, Christopher had to wonder if the sheriff might be plotting a little payback.

Lord Fawkes helped Rissa Lyn down from the wagon and shook his head, pretending that she could understand the million-and-one things that the shake was meant to convey. She didn't, of course.

THE DEATH OF DULGATH

How can she?

Her home was likely someplace quite like this, a backwater assortment of listing hovels whose inhabitants shared their beds with their goats and pigs to save their livestock from wolf packs and big cats. She did look adequately apprehensive of the strange world Knox had brought them to, but then she'd looked like that from the start. Handmaidens didn't normally go off on adventures with lords and provincial sheriffs, and that expression of wide-eyed shock, held in check by a surprisingly resolute determination, was still on her face.

Christopher followed Knox to the beach, and his feet sank into the hot sand just inches from where the surf smoothed everything out with its constant pawing. A wave rushed in, reached out, then receded before him, leaving a residue of white bubbles and green tubular plants. He looked at the waves and at the gray line of the horizon.

This is the end of the world.

Well, not quite. The Isle of Neil could be seen as a line of darkness on the water, as well as the Point of Mann, the strait known to eat ships. Beyond them was the Westerlins, but no civilization. Not a single city, town, hamlet, or village lay to the west of where he stood. This was the end of the *known* world.

So what is out there?

He'd heard the same stories everyone had about the Westerlins, rumored to be populated by an odd assortment of deformed people. One race supposedly had one large foot—so big that if it rained they could lie on their backs and shelter in the shadow of it. There were also monstrous single-breasted women, and men with the heads of dogs, and others with no heads at all, their faces in their chests. These things, along with dragons, giants, trolls, and ogres, were said to roam that distant shore, where the sun went to sleep each night.

In that darkness, no other light would be seen; there was no sound of music or lilt of laughter.

Staring across those waves, Christopher felt a terrible unease, a sense of impending doom, a desire to retreat from the edge of a cliff or the rim of a fire.

What kind of people could live here so close to oblivion?

"That's him; that's Shervin Gerami," Knox said, pointing at a man on the far side of the boats. The man sat cross-legged, fussing with the strands of a net before a particularly strange hut fashioned out of pale twigs. He was bald, and the afternoon sun glinted off his head with a brilliant shine.

Knox lumbered over, leaving Rissa Lyn and Christopher to follow. Sand got into the ankles of Christopher's shoes, making him grimace. He could feel it grind painfully against his feet.

My shoes will be ruined before this is done…and it's not like I have another pair. Being not-a-baron pays not-a-lot.

Passing through the cluster of shanties, Christopher was greeted by the powerful smell of fish and wood smoke. A pair of women with bare shoulders, wearing what looked to be just a wrapping of homespun cloth chopped stalks of grass with cleavers against a split log. Their faces held hopeless eyes born from a life of endless drudgery. Another man, dried up and dark as a raisin, sat listlessly against a shack, his bare feet outstretched. He smoked a clay pipe and watched them. There were others, but Christopher chose not to look. He felt uncomfortable here in this place of sunbaked people who slept in skeleton homes built on the edge of eternity. Knox showed no sign of concern, no hesitancy as he trudged through the sand toward the man with the shining head.

"Shervin!" Knox called over the roar of the surf.

The bald man looked up. He had keen eyes, clear and focused, and he fixed them on each member of the Dulgath party. He appeared to make a judgment, and then resumed work on the net.

"How do you know this man?" Christopher asked quietly as they approached.

"I'm sheriff," Knox replied. "I make rounds. Shervin was accused of murder. I judged him innocent."

"You don't have that authority."

Knox laughed.

For a man such as Knox to laugh at him was more than disrespectful. According to Payne, who got his information from Bishop Parnell, Knox had spent years in the military. He'd served Duke Ethelred of Warric and had seen combat in many conflicts, including the famed Battle of Vilan Hills. Payne had expressed a suspicion that Knox was wanted for murder, which was the real reason he was in Maranon. Once more, Christopher thought about the nick he'd made in the sheriff's collar and wondered if that had been such a good idea after all.

"Out here, I act with the authority of the earl—excuse me—*countess*. The Dulgaths can't be everywhere, and most of these people can't afford to make a pilgrimage to the castle to plead petty grievances or ask for restitution. That's my job. I act in their stead. I do the real work, the unpleasant tasks."

Knox stopped before the bald man, looking down at him.

"Who-low Meestah Knock-Knock," Shervin greeted him. "You still want me ta keel sum'tin fur you? I tell you a'fore, da Blade of ant-trickery do not slay any but da Old Ones."

"I remember," Knox said. "That's why I brought this woman… to convince you."

Shervin lifted a hand to shield his eyes from the bright sun and examined Rissa Lyn. No fingernails were on that hand. Christopher searched out the man's other fist, still clutching a wad of net, and found it also lacked nails. In their place were smooth divots.

Rissa Lyn shrank from Gerami's studious glare but didn't retreat. Her breaths were short and shallow, and she looked as if she might be sick. Still, the woman was proving to be quite brave.

"Con-fence da Blade? How you gonna do dat?"

"Is that our language he's speaking?" Christopher asked Knox.

Knox frowned as the fingernail-less man tilted his head to look at Christopher. "Who dis fancy man?"

"This is—"

"Royce Melborn," Christopher said, jumping in. "A famous thief."

Shervin chuckled.

"What's so funny?" Christopher asked hotly.

"Meestah Fancy Shoes couldn't steal nothin'. And any good thief can't be famous."

Knox snapped, "Well he is, and if I were you I'd watch my tongue."

"Can't see me own tongue." Shervin laughed—a deep, wicked sound—then demonstrated by sticking it out and looking down. "Not as long as *some people's*, I s'pose."

"This can't be the *best* you can find," Christopher said.

"Trust me on this," Knox replied.

But Christopher didn't trust him. He'd learned not to trust anyone, least of all men like Knox.

"Meestah Melborn think da Blade cannot keel? Me show Meestah Fancy Shoes." Shervin stood up and threw open the curtain that served as a door to his hut. "You look."

Christopher didn't want to. He didn't want to take one step toward, much less enter, that hut with walls woven from branches of bleached driftwood like a bony nest of some giant bird. An easy impression to reach, as several large gulls circled and many actual bones surrounded the shack. The skull of a great horned beast hung from a nearby post along with smaller skulls of squirrels or perhaps rats.

"Here," Shervin said, entering and waving for Christopher to follow. "Come see."

Knox shooed him forward, and Christopher felt compelled to follow or be seen as weak or frightened. He was scared—a little. Christopher didn't think anyone could be at ease in the presence of such a strange fellow as Shervin, who when standing was bigger than expected. Tall and lean, the man had muscles that stood out too much and looked the way Christopher imagined a shaved cat might. Only then did he realize...*the man has no hair.*

Shervin wasn't just bald, but hairless. No beard, no mustache, not a strand on his arms or legs. Not even his armpit showed a single thread of hair. There were, however, tattoos. Shervin had plenty of them. They weren't depictions of anything recognizable, just designs and symbols wrapping his arms and thighs.

Christopher gave in, and, with a hand on his sword, followed Shervin inside. He'd skewer the shaved cat if he tried anything.

The place didn't smell, which surprised Christopher; he expected it to reek with the stench of dead things. Instead, the interior was clean. Oddly, it smelled pleasantly of sandalwood. An extinct fire pit in its center was bordered by a neat bed of rocks. The rest of the space was filled with baskets of varying heights and widths, but none of this was what Shervin wanted him to see. The bald, hairless man with the tattoos directed Christopher's attention to the walls, where a variety of tools hung: an ax, a massive scythe, two primitive spears, and a wooden club with a big knob on the end.

"Dees are what I do me keeling wit."

"What killing?"

"I hunt and slay da Old Ones." He pushed out the curtain again, stepped outside, grabbed one of the rat or chipmunk skulls, and held it up. "Dees what's left after I chopping 'em." He made a cutting motion across his neck. Then he turned and glared again at Rissa Lyn. "But da Blade only keel da Old Ones—not men, not weemeen."

"What's an Old One?" Christopher asked, escaping the hut and feeling better for it.

"Day be da leftovers of da ancient world, driven to da corners and da edges where to hide in shadows from da light of men."

Christopher gave up trying to gain sense from Shervin and turned to Knox. "What are we talking about here?"

The sheriff shrugged absently. "Ghosts and ghouls."

Shervin was nodding. "And leshies, goulgans, and manes." He pointed to the surf. "And selkies. Lots of bulbane selkies. But not weemeen. Da Blade is not a murderer."

"She's not a woman." Rissa Lyn spoke up then. Her voice shook a bit but was loud and forceful.

"What den?"

"Lady Dulgath is a demon."

Shervin put the little skull back on the post, then puckered up his lips and began to shift them from side to side as he focused on Rissa Lyn. The only thing Christopher could think was that *da Blade* was contemplating how she might taste slow-roasted with a pinch of salt.

Rissa Lyn appeared to be thinking along the same lines as she wrapped her arms around herself, sending worrisome glances at Knox and Christopher.

Still sucking on his lips, Shervin began to nod. "Yes," he muttered.

"Yes, what?" Rissa Lyn asked, both defiant and concerned.

"Dis man here"—Shervin pointed at Christopher—"Meestah Fancy Shoes is a dry well. Meestah Knock-Knock." He pointed at the sheriff. "He a bucket ah blood. But you…" He shook his head again. "You are clear water from da mountain stream."

"What's that supposed to mean?" Rissa Lyn asked, her face perplexed as she struggled to determine if she should be flattered or insulted.

"Means I will come and see dis demon. If an Old One, I will keel it."

"How can you tell?" Christopher asked. He looked pointedly at Knox. "He's not going to try to speak to Lady Dulgath, is he?"

Shervin grinned, showing clean white teeth. "Are you an Old One?"

"What?" Christopher scowled at him.

"Are you an Old One?"

"No."

"How you know you not?"

"Because I'm not."

"Yes." He nodded. "Same way—see?"

"See what? No, I don't see anything."

"Dis is because you a dry well. Empty buckets cannot see nothing outside demselves." Shervin went into his stick house and returned with an oversized scythe.

"Won't need that," Knox said. "I have a better weapon."

"Is no better weapon," Shervin declared.

"Let me show you."

Together the four tramped back through the village, past the two women and the pipe-smoking man. The women didn't look up this time, but the pipe man watched with interest. They returned to the wagon, where Knox threw off the tarp and revealed the arbalest. With the bright coastal sun shining off the steel fixtures, the big crossbow appeared to be from another world.

Shervin's eyes widened at the sight. "A bow!"

"You've seen one before?" Knox asked.

Shervin shook his head. "But you are right, dis is a better weapon. Bows are sacred tings."

"This one is downright divine," Knox said. "Let's get a target up and you'll see."

Along with the arbalest, they had loaded a stuffed dummy and a pine post on a stand to hang it from. A long length of thin rope was cut to the required distance. Knox asked Christopher to carry the post while he grabbed the dummy and rope—giving one end to Rissa Lyn, who stayed by the wagon. Together they walked one hundred yards.

"You brought us all this way for a lunatic?" Christopher asked as they marched across rock and through tufts of grass, the seaside wind slapping their backs.

"Absolutely," Knox replied. "He's perfect."

"I don't see how. The man is ignorant *and* insane."

"Exactly. Who else do you think we can get to murder the countess? Any sensible person would know it's suicide. Besides, what do you think will happen after she's dead? If Shervin Gerami tries pointing at us, who will believe a man who says he killed Lady Dulgath because she's a demon?"

"And a man who calls me Royce Melborn," Christopher said, nodding. "All right, I can see the logic, but he's so *odd*. Do you think he can do it?"

"A woodchuck can use one of these. It's accurate to three hundred yards. He's shooting less than half that."

"Where'd you get it?"

"Wells dug it out of the castle's attic."

"Castle Dulgath has an attic?"

"Just what Wells called it. He knows every inch of that place. Once upon a time, Dulgath was a *real* castle and the walls were lined with arbalests. He picked out the best one for us. Although we're thin on quarrels, so I hope Shervin doesn't miss, or you and I will be searching these rocks for hours. It shoots a *long* way."

They reached the end of the rope and set up the dummy, a servant's tunic stuffed with fistfuls of straw. They tied a rope under the arms and hung the mannequin from the pine post, then started back.

When they returned to the wagon, Knox took down the arbalest and set it up. The weapon could be held in a man's arms but was too unwieldy to use that way. Instead, it came equipped with front legs that held the nose up. The rear had a block that supported the butt as well. Using wooden shims, the archer could adjust the vertical angle in advance, aim it, and then let go. So long as the target wasn't moving—and Lady Dulgath ought to be sitting—all Shervin had to do was squeeze the trigger lever. The arbalest also had a built-in hand crank lying across its top that drew the string back. Given that the bow's prod was made of steel and had a wingspan of five feet, no one was going to pull it back with bare fingers and a foot in a nose stirrup.

Peering across at the target, Christopher felt a stab of worry. The dummy that was nearly the height of a man looked to be the size of a wineglass.

After a quick demonstration and a few dry launches, during which Shervin didn't say a word, Knox loaded a quarrel. The things couldn't be called arrows. They were heavy missiles thicker than a man's thumb, with massive iron tips. Shervin crouched, then lay flat on his stomach, looking down the length of the stock. He lifted the butt and moved it.

"No!" Knox shouted over the wind. "I've already aimed it."

"Aimed wrong." Shervin held his hand up, pointing at the sky. "Wind."

Knox looked angry, then hesitated as he considered the word. "If you miss, you'll have to go fetch."

Shervin didn't miss. The quarrel traveled faster than the eye could see, and it seemed the moment Christopher heard the snap of the string a magnificent burst of straw flew up. A loud crack cut against the blow of the wind. A moment later he couldn't see anything—not the dummy, not even the post it hung on.

Together with Knox, Christopher ran out to the target. The pine post had been split in half and fallen over. The dummy didn't exist. They found the tunic a few feet away with a rip through the front and back. Straw was everywhere.

"What do you think?" Knox asked.

Christopher nodded. "Good choice."

They left Shervin in his village. The man had rituals to perform—he pronounced it *writ-tools*—that would take all night. Knox balked about having to come back for him in the morning, but Christopher sided with da Blade of ant-trickery, which he finally realized was supposed to be *antiquity*. Christopher had his own ritual to perform, and he guessed it would be easier without Shervin Gerami along.

Christopher had dreams of the future but usually restrained himself from indulging too much in anticipation. Such things could jinx his plans. He'd seen it before: Schedule an early trip and the next morning it would rain. Novron didn't abide prediction. The moment anyone made plans, the world changed, apparently out of spite.

Christopher also believed that it wasn't wise to spend too much time in his head. Thinking too much was a mistake. Plotting was the antithesis of doing. The man who sits and schemes continues to sit while others achieve. Christopher fancied himself a man of action, but as his defining day approached, he found thinking ahead hard to resist. Such was the case with the village of Rye. He found he hated that pile of twigs on the sand. When he became earl, one of his first orders would be to raze it. Not *the* first order, not even the second. Christopher—who didn't believe in making plans in advance for Novron to thwart—had at least a small list.

First he'd get rid of Knox and Wells. They were both too intelligent and too ambitious to keep around. Payne he'd have to live with, as an earl had no power over members of the church, and he wouldn't dare provoke Bishop Parnell. After that would come the rebuilding of Castle Dulgath. The place was nearly a ruin. He'd have to raise taxes. From what he understood, they were nearly nonexistent, and the farmers could well afford to pay more. Once he had his house in order—and in the process of being restored—he would turn his thoughts inland.

Dulgath was the smallest of the Maranon provinces and largely ignored as a result. He intended to change that. Christopher saw no reason for there to be four provinces. Swanwick and Kruger were both vast holdings, while Manzar and Dulgath were insignificant in comparison. If Dulgath swallowed up Manzar, there would be three equal-sized neighbors. Having control over a prison where any detractors could disappear was an added benefit, but the real attraction came from the expectation of tax revenue the salt mine would produce.

He'd need an army to bring Manzar into line. At present, Dulgath lacked even enough full-time guards to properly staff the front gate. He'd change that, too. Every family would be required to contribute one son to his military, along with their increased taxes. With a land as lush as Dulgath, he'd easily subdue the rocky highland of Manzar, which lacked any real towns. Then he wouldn't be just an earl—two full rungs above his father on the peerage ladder—but an important player in Maranon affairs. He'd have the ear of the king, even if he had to cut it off to get it.

As the wagon rolled and bounced along the twisting coastal road, climbing higher and higher toward the plateau of the Dulgath Plain, Christopher surveyed his new realm and nodded silently.

This will do for a start, he thought.

When they reached the top of the ridge, Knox rested the horses, and the three got down to stretch their legs. This was the southwestern desolation of Dulgath, nothing but lichen rock, wind-tortured grass, and a grand view. At that height, they could clearly see the Point of Mann, the Isle of Neil, and Manzant Bay.

"Stunning, isn't it?" Christopher said with deep-breathed pride.

Of course it is: it's mine. A mother always sees her children as beautiful.

He walked alongside Rissa Lyn. As they strolled aimlessly through the tall grass, he took hold of her hand. She stopped, stiffening at his touch, then stared at him as if he'd pulled a knife.

"Relax." He smiled, and, bringing her hand up slowly, kissed the back. "I just wanted to thank you."

The fear in her eyes was replaced by confusion.

"You did very well," he told her, and meant it.

Shervin Gerami had scared him, so he would've expected Rissa Lyn to be reduced to a sobbing mess. "You were very brave—courageous even."

He saw a smile fighting onto her face. "I want to thank you, Your Lordship. I've been so afraid of that *thing,* and being the only one who knew…well, it was difficult."

"Call me Christopher."

Her eyes went large. "Oh no, sir—I couldn't!"

Okay, so perhaps that was asking too much.

Rissa Lyn wasn't a child; she'd spent years as a servant. Christopher might as well have asked her to fly. Letting go of her hand, he held up his own and spread his palms. "That's fine. I just wanted to show my appreciation for all you've done."

"It's you that's doing it, sir." She shook her head as a look of dismay descended. "You are the only one to believe me. The only one—and I didn't even think you did, not at first. To be honest, I was frightened of you."

"I'm sorry about that." Christopher resumed walking, causing her to follow. "I was just so disturbed by that painting."

"Oh, I can understand that—shoot and sugar I can. That painting scared me, too. Seeing what awful thing was truly behind that pretty face was horrible. So no, sir, I won't be holding that against you at all, sir."

"Thank you, Rissa Lyn." He took hold of her hand again. This time she didn't flinch, didn't stiffen. She blushed. "Who were these others who didn't believe you?"

"Julia, the head maid. I went to her right after the lady *recovered*. I was so terribly frightened, hysterical and not making much sense. She said I was just imagining things. That seeing Lady Dulgath mangled and bloody was making me imagine all kinds of old wives' tales about ghost, ghouls, and demons. For a long time, I believed her. But as the years passed, I knew it was me who had been right all along. I could tell because Lady Dulgath changed. Folk said she became sober from nearly dying, but I knew the truth. Nysa Dulgath had died, and something else had taken over her body, walking and talking through it."

She squeezed his hand.

"I don't like to look into her eyes, but when I do, I can see *it* looking back. It scares me near to fainting sometimes, honest it does."

"Who else have you told?"

"Just Mister Sherwood. After seeing his painting, I thought he would understand. He was such a good man, and I was afraid she'd do something awful to him. And of course she did, didn't she? I feel so guilty about cursing him just before he went to—and then he disappeared. But he didn't believe me, either. No one believed me."

"I believed you," Christopher said, looking in her eyes and offering a sympathetic smile.

She smiled back, no fighting it this time. Her lips trembled, and tears spilled down, the wind streaking them at angles. "Oh, sir!" she whimpered. "You don't know how much I've wanted someone to tell me that, to let me know I'm not crazy."

He reached out and wrapped his arms around the woman, pulling her to his chest, letting her cry. Knox was back at the wagon, checking the front hooves of the offside horse. The sheriff glanced over once then resumed hunting for stones.

When Rissa Lyn slowed her sobs, Christopher said, "Look out there, Rissa Lyn."

She pulled back and wiped her eyes clear, then she followed his line of sight and faced the cliff and the sea below.

"Beautiful, isn't it?" he said. "Makes everything else seem small and insignificant, because looking out there you can see eternity, can't you, Rissa Lyn?"

"Yes, I suppose I—"

Christopher gave her a good solid shove. Rissa Lyn was light and not possessed of any great sense of balance. She went right off the edge of the cliff with no trouble at all. The entire moment was over so quickly. She just disappeared, although her wails did trail behind her for a few seconds, fading in pitch and volume. One minute she was there, and the next Rissa Lyn was gone, as if she'd never existed. All it took was a little shove.

If only all my troubles could be dealt with so easily.

Christopher inched up and peered over the edge. He spotted her body. She must have missed the rocks and hit the shallow surf. A wave came in and threw her corpse against the rocks then sucked it out again. Christopher watched as this happened three more times. Then any trace of Rissa Lyn disappeared just as Sherwood had.

I do so love the sea.

Christopher strongly suspected Rissa Lyn had been in love with Sherwood Stow.

Now at least they can be together. Of course, he's up the coast a bit. He imagined that Sherwood's ghost and Rissa Lyn's might wander those craggy shores for eternity and never meet. "How tragic would that be?" he asked the wind, and then walked back to the wagon.

"Horse all right?" he inquired of Knox.

"Thought she was favoring the left, but it looks fine."

Knox climbed back on the wagon, and Christopher joined him. Throwing the brake off and jiggling the reins, they continued on their way.

Chapter Eighteen
BROKEN BONES

Hadrian, Royce, and Scarlett rode back in Wagner's buckboard after pouring out the poisoned beer to lighten the load. On Royce's suggestion, they kept one full, *just in case.* What he'd meant by that Hadrian didn't know—didn't think he wanted to find out.

They'd cleaned up everything down to the splinters left by the broken keg lid and stuffed it all—bodies included—into the prison wagon, which they drove into the trees well off the road. The slaver's horses were unhitched and tied to the back of the beer wagon. With luck, no one would come looking for the men or their animals. According to Royce, slavers working for Manzant were independent freelance abductors. If anyone did come looking for them, odds were against it being anytime soon.

Royce's knowledge about slavers and Manzant reminded Hadrian of something Scarlett had said while Royce had her pinned against the side of the wagon. At the time, Hadrian was concerned he might kill her. Later, as they bounced their way back toward Dulgath, Hadrian had the time to remember.

"What did you mean when you said Manzant couldn't hold Royce?" he asked Scarlett, who sat beside him on the bench, driving the team. The horses had been driven hard to catch up with the slavers, and she was giving them an easy plod back for succeeding.

Hadrian looked over his shoulder to where Royce reclined on the bed of the cart, his hands resting carefully in his lap. "Were you in Manzant?"

Scarlett raised her eyebrows in surprise but didn't say a word.

"You already know that," Royce said.

"I do?"

Hadrian thought a moment and realized he did remember something. He'd been introduced to Royce by a professor at Sheridan University, and at the time Arcadius had mentioned a prison where he had found Royce. He couldn't recall the name of the place. "That was three years ago. You expected me to remember?"

Royce reached up with his better hand and tugged his hood over his head. "Taking a nap."

"Did you ever tell me why you were there?"

"Sleeping now."

"Did you mention what you did after you got out?"

"Hand hurts. Leave me alone."

Hadrian frowned, then glared at Scarlett.

"Don't look at me," she said. "I'm not getting in the middle of this."

They traveled until well after dark, then pulled clear of the road. Royce continued to sleep in the wagon while Scarlett and Hadrian bedded down beneath it, using blankets taken from the slavers. Six men—six blankets. This left them extras to place underneath and to use as pillows.

"You didn't happen to bring anything to eat, did you?" Hadrian asked, wadding up a blanket behind his head. The two lay side by side beneath the axle with the wheels flanking them. "I'm starving."

"Was in sort of a hurry," she said, pulling the blanket up to her neck even though it wasn't cold. "When I came to work, Wag said you guys had been grabbed up."

She wiggled a bit, then pulled a rock out from underneath. "Then I had to make the poison. Don't have that stuff lying about, you know? And I had to get it in the barrels and roll them on the wagon."

"You did all that yourself?"

"No, Gill and Brett got the wagon hitched. Tasha helped with brewing the poison, and Wag rolled out his beer—was real sad about that—you would've thought I asked him to kill his dog. Brook and Clem helped get the barrels up on the buckboard."

"Bull Neck and Orange Tunic?"

"That's them. Nice guys when you get to know them, all of them, really. 'Course Brook's still mad at me, but he'll get over it about the same time as his leg heals."

"*You* stabbed him? I thought Royce did that."

She shrugged. "Seemed like the thing to do at the time. Anyway, given my late start, you'll forgive me if I forgot to pack up supplies for a cookout." She dropped her head onto her blanket pillow with an exhausted huff.

The horses, which were tied up to a stand of birch trees a few yards away, loudly ripped up grass, shifting their feet and whipping their tails. Crickets and katydids trilled, and a soft breeze made that comforting rain sound again as it brushed the fields.

"Thank you," Hadrian said.

"I didn't do it for you." Scarlett stretched and yawned at the same time. "I did it for me. So I wouldn't have to worry about Royce. I told you that."

"I know."

"I mean it."

Hadrian looked up at the underside of the wagon, where bits of mud and old grass had gotten stuck.

"It had nothing to do with you," Scarlett said with more force, more volume.

"We should get some sleep," he told her. "Royce will be waking us before dawn. He does that—like he can hear the sun or something."

They lay together, listening to the night. He heard her breathing, soft and steady—a nice sound. He was tempted to touch her, reach out blindly with his fingers searching for hers. He didn't. She might get spooked and take her blankets and leave. Be a pretty poor way of thanking her for saving his life.

When he turned to sleep on his side, the pain stabbed him. He let out a grunt and set his shoulders on the grass again. He hated sleeping on his back.

"Need to have that wrapped up," she whispered.

"What I need is a stiff drink that isn't laced with something for a change."

"And sleep," she said. "You need that, too."

Hadrian took a deep breath and sighed. "Good night, Scarlett Dodge."

"Good night, Dog-with-a-Ball."

Hadrian chuckled, which caused his side to ache. "Don't do that."

"You deserve it." Scarlett turned over on her side, her back to him. "And I didn't do it for you."

Yes, you did, he repeated to himself, but let it go with that.

Brecken Dale hadn't changed. Not that Hadrian expected it would in the few days they'd been gone. The thought was larger than that; Hadrian didn't think the dale ever changed. Leaves might turn color and fall, snow might blanket fields, and the names of people and some of their faces might be different, but the dale remained as it always had been. He saw all this as they came down the road, as he got a clear bird's-eye view of the village from the trail above.

Timeless was the first word that popped into his mind. *Eternal* was another.

Why he thought that was harder to nail down. Then he realized that he saw no forgotten foundations of abandoned buildings, no blackened husk of a burned-out mill or barn, no grass-overgrown cart or wagon orphaned in a pasture. No fallow fields, either.

Hadrian wasn't a farmer, but he'd grown up with them and knew that a third of the land had to rest for a season or face exhaustion. Not so in Dulgath. Pastures looked to be permanent, and while every inch of cultivated land was sown, it all thrived. Rules that governed the rest of the world didn't seem to apply here. Hadrian hadn't seen any construction, either. In Medford, scaffolds were everywhere as buildings went up or came down. Bridges were in constant need of repair—and the roofs! No day passed that Hadrian hadn't heard the pounding of hammers on roofs. But in Brecken Dale the decay of time took a holiday.

Maybe it really is blessed.

Just a few days ago he'd felt uneasy in the little village. All the ivy and the talk of it never raining had put him on edge. Dulgath was different, even odd, but he no longer felt out of sorts. If anything, it seemed *proper*. His initial impression of tranquility had been the right one. Either that or the stretch of road coming into Dulgath, just before reaching the dale, was enchanted.

The sun insisted it was still morning when they entered the dale. The last time he and Royce had come that way, they'd arrived in the middle of a tarring. This morning, the village was empty. They rumbled past the peach orchard, which Scarlett said was owned by the Beecham family. With thirty head of dairy cows, they were also the largest producers of milk in the area. Clem was their third son and had once courted her with a basket of peaches and cream.

"He thought he was being clever," Scarlett said. "But I'd only been living in the village a few months, and it just reminded me about how much I stood out."

They passed through the market, where the stalls were shuttered and not even a single cart was parked. Hadrian didn't bother asking, since the confusion on Scarlett's face told him it wasn't expected.

Wagner burst out the door to Caldwell House when they were still heading for the stable. "You did it!" he called to Scarlett, shaking that same dirty rag at her. Clem and Gill spilled out after him, along with a woman with short brown hair, a friendly smile, and a fetching hat. Brook brought up the rear, favoring his right leg.

"You doubted me?" Scarlett smirked.

"Worried, darling, that's all. Guess I shoulda known better. All went well, then?"

"The one in the back has a broken hand and finger, and Hadrian has cracked ribs, but other than that everything's fine."

"I'll tell Asher he's got patients," the woman with the hat said and hurried off through the deserted market.

"Thanks, Tasha." Scarlett climbed off the wagon. "What's going on? Where is everyone?"

"King arrived yesterday. They're down at the ceremony."

Scarlett nodded as if understanding this.

"What ceremony?" Hadrian asked as she helped him down. He didn't really need the help, the pain in his side wasn't that bad, but he accepted her hand just the same. He liked the way her little fingers fit inside his.

Peaches and cream, he thought, and realized he would've made the same mistake as Clem, if he'd been smart enough to think of it at all.

"Lady Dulgath is paying homage," Scarlett said. "She's pledging her loyalty to King Vincent, and in turn he gives her a kiss and officially declares her to be Countess Dulgath."

Royce climbed off the wagon by himself, clutching his right hand to his chest. "People from Brecken Dale went to see this?"

"Sure," Wagner said, patting the necks of the horses and looking them over. "Folk from all the villages and countryside, I'd imagine. Not every day you get a new ruler. 'Course lots of folk just want a look at the king or have an excuse to get out of the fields."

"Gill, take care of Myrtle and Marjorie. I ran them ragged," Scarlett said. "Oh, and Wag, here's a few new horses for you. That ought to pay for the beer and your trouble."

"Where'd they come from?" Wagner asked.

"You don't want to know. As far as you're concerned, they were lost and you took them in." She winked.

As Gill worked on the buckles, Wagner turned back to Scarlett and slipped an arm around her waist. "You sure everything is good?" His voice had an added tone of concern. Maybe it meant something, maybe it didn't, but he pulled her close while looking at Hadrian.

"Everything's fine," she replied with enough of a sidelong glance to convince Hadrian she noticed the behavior, too.

Is that annoyance in her eyes?

"With so many people coming to watch, I'm guessing they're not holding this ceremony *inside* the castle?" Royce asked.

"Out in the courtyard is what I've heard." With his arm still around Scarlett's waist, he looked at Hadrian again. "You owe my Scarlett a huge debt of gratitude. You know that, right?"

"We do indeed," Hadrian replied.

Wagner looked to Royce, as if expecting to hear a thank-you.

Instead, Royce asked, "When does this ceremony take place?"

"Little after midday," Wagner replied with a frown.

"Why you so interested?" Hadrian asked.

"Because there's a bigger debt we need to repay, and I know just how to do it."

Asher, the dale's physician, had arrived with Tasha. By then, they were all inside the main room of Caldwell House, which was devoid of customers. Everyone had already left for the ceremony at Castle Dulgath.

After a sneer from Royce, Asher had decided to treat Hadrian first, which didn't take long. Not much could be done for cracked ribs other than wrap them tightly and frown a lot. Afterward, he sat across from Royce and looked at the thief's hands. That was all he was able to do, as Royce refused to let him touch either one.

"I need to examine your hands," Asher said. "And to do that I need to touch them."

"Touch my hand and I'll take yours as payment."

Asher, a friendly-looking man with a big bushy-bear beard and a sunburned nose, threw up his hands and looked to Scarlett. "Nothing I can do if he won't let me."

"You're right," Royce said. "Go have a drink. There's a barrel of ale in the wagon."

"Do *not* have a drink," Wagner told him. "I need to dump that thing."

"We need to get going," Royce said.

"Why?" Hadrian asked. "What's going on in that head of yours?"

"Lady Dulgath is still alive."

"So?"

"So, I told the countess to cut down her ivy," Royce explained to Hadrian as Asher remained sitting across from him. "Since she's still alive, I'm guessing she listened. That means Fawkes has switched to plan B."

"What's plan B?" Scarlett asked.

"You said plan B isn't possible." Hadrian put his shirt back on over the stiff cloth strips Asher had wrapped him in. "You said he'd need Tom the Feather or that other guy, but he was in Manzant. Wait—you don't think they got him out for this, do you?"

"What's plan B?" Scarlett asked again.

Royce shook his head. "Couldn't have. They didn't know the man existed until I told them. Wouldn't have had time to get there and back. Besides, Hawkins has been in Manzant for years. After so long, if he's still alive, he'd be in no condition to do more than drool. But Fawkes might have dug up a crossbow."

"Crossbow?" Scarlett looked at both of them, concerned. "What are you two talking about?"

"I told Fawkes and Payne that if they could get Lady Dulgath outside at a prearranged place, a place where they could hide an archer with a bow, then—"

"They're going to kill her at the homage ceremony?" Scarlett's eyes went wide.

"Be my guess, but with a little luck I think we can catch Fawkes, Payne, and their beloved church with fingers on the trigger—right in front of the king."

"We have to go. Now!" Fear filled Scarlett's face.

"He can't go anywhere with two mangled hands," Asher declared. "At the very least, I have to set the bones. If I don't, that hand will be a worthless claw the rest of your life."

"He's right, Royce," Hadrian said.

"You do it," Royce told him.

For a moment Hadrian thought he was joking—another way of saying, *You think so? Go ahead and try!* But Royce's expression was wrong. Hadrian wasn't foolish enough to think he could read the man's mind through his expressions. If so, he'd have concluded long ago that Royce wanted to kill every man, woman, child, and dog he encountered. For a time, Hadrian believed that might be true, but Royce had surprised Hadrian enough times that he came to realize this tree had roots no one could see.

Clues were there, but difficult to spot and harder to decode. The man didn't like being read. Every truth that slipped out was cursed. It was why their rides together were so one-sided. People always gave parts of themselves away when they talked. If Royce was going to sacrifice a clue about himself, it wouldn't be over idle prattle. Still, Hadrian had discovered some signs—he'd had to. Living with a man-killing tiger, you quickly learned the difference between a growl and a purr—or else.

Royce wasn't growling.

"The doctor here is—"

"I don't trust him." Royce didn't look at the doctor—hadn't done so since he'd arrived. Maybe if he had he might have reconsidered. Asher, doctor of the dale, was a big fluffy man with a concerned brow and helpful eyes. But then Royce didn't trust anyone. That he admitted—if only by assumption—that he trusted Hadrian didn't go unnoticed. Needing help was an admission of defeat. Doing so in front of an audience was unprecedented.

Hadrian sat down beside Asher. "I've set bones before, but not in a hand. What do I do?"

"First, just have him hold his hand palm-down and extend his fingers all the way out."

Everyone in Caldwell House was looking at Royce. His jaw was clenched, and he was breathing with irritation through his nose.

"Scarlett, Tasha, can you go ask Gill and Wagner to saddle our horses?" Hadrian asked.

"The two of you can't ride busted up the way you are," Scarlett said. "I'll hitch Midnight and Mack to a wagon. They're not as friendly as Myrtle and Marjorie, but they're fresh and are used to pulling as a team. C'mon, Tasha, the boys want to be alone for a while."

It took a second after they left, but Royce put out his hand and, with a wince, opened it as best he could. Two fingers and his thumb straightened out; the other two hung limp.

"Okay," Asher said with his warm, reassuring tone. "I can see from here it's not the fingers, but the bones in the back of the hand that need setting. So, Hadrian, what you need to do is gently lift the fingers—one at a time. Pull them out straight. Stretch them—don't yank or anything, just a gentle pull. As you do that, press down with your other thumb on the bone that's out of place. You'll need to feel around for the break. You'll find it. Just apply pressure until it lines up again. And Royce, try to leave your hand limp. You know, Scarlett can brew up something for the pain. She—"

"No!" both Royce and Hadrian snapped.

Hadrian shook his head. "We've had our fill of her recipes." He looked at Royce with a grim smile and took his hand. "You ready for this?"

"Just shut up and do it."

Hadrian guessed Royce was silently debating which was worse, the pain or the humiliation; he settled on the latter. Royce didn't ask anyone for anything. Hadrian found the protrusion he was looking for and wanted to be as quick as he could. Asher offered encouragement as Hadrian squeezed and pulled.

Royce made no sound at all. His eyes squeezed shut; he breathed harder, more forcefully.

The bone slid down, and Hadrian moved to the second one. When he had both in place, Asher asked Royce to extend his fingers again. This time all four came up.

"Great!" Asher grinned, that big beard bristling. "Now take these splints and put one on the back and one on the front. Wrap them tightly. Secure the fingers, too; the less movement the better."

The other hand was easier, just a matter of aligning the finger and splinting. Hadrian was wrapping it when Scarlett came back.

"All done here? Wagon's ready to roll," she said, moving behind the bar. "Looks like we have two, maybe three hours before the ceremony, but there's no sense cutting things close. I'll pack a meal for us; we can eat on the way."

"You're not going," Hadrian told her.

"If you're going to save Lady Dulgath, I want to help."

"I don't see what you can do."

She looked nettled by the comment but forced a smile. "For one thing, I can vouch for you. Might need someone to speak on your behalf to Lady Dulgath."

"Why would she listen to you?" Royce asked. "You're not even a native."

"I know her." Scarlett tore a loaf of bread in half and wrapped it in a cloth.

"You do?" Hadrian asked.

"Yes. Don't look so surprised. The countess visits the monastery a lot, and so do I. We've talked a few times. She's very…different. If given the choice among Fawkes, Payne, you two, and me—she'd listen to me."

"Okay, you can come," Royce said.

"What?" Hadrian glared at him. "This is going to be dangerous."

Royce tested the movement of his wrapped hands. "She's a Diamond, not a debutante."

"Great." Scarlett grinned. "What do you want me to do?"

"Watch the horses and wagon for us while we go in," Royce said.

"You got it." Scarlett continued to fill the basket.

"You got it?" Hadrian asked, dumbfounded. "He tells you to wait outside and watch the pretty horses and you're fine with that? If I'd said that—"

"I would've called you an ass." She dropped in some cheese.

"Why?"

"Because you'd be trying to protect me. Royce doesn't give a damn if I live or die. Besides, the first thing you learn in the Diamond is to never disagree with a mission lead, and *never, ever* question a guild officer."

Hadrian finished wrapping Royce's finger and looked at him, puzzled. "You were a guild officer?"

Scarlett picked up the basket and made a *pfft* sound as she swung her hair out of her face. "Seriously? Have you two even met?" Her face was incredulous. "You didn't know he was in Manzant. You obviously didn't know he's the only person to have escaped, and you didn't know he was an officer of the Diamond. What do you two talk about on all those long hours riding together?"

Hadrian started to laugh.

Royce shot him a glare. "Shut up."

Chapter Nineteen
PAGEANTRY

A fair breeze came softly across the breakwaters and up the grassy slope to the walls of Castle Dulgath. Christopher Fawkes stood on the cliffs above the sea and took a deep breath. He was wearing his best doublet, which was to say his only doublet. It was missing a button and had a small bloodstain on the cuff.

Sherwood Stow's blood.

He stood only a few feet from where Sherwood was killed—or at least where he had been hit by the quarrel. Christopher didn't know if the artist had died there, as his body fell, or whether he'd survived both the blow and the drop to drown in the sea. He didn't much care. Luckily, Christopher didn't believe in the vengeance of ghosts. If he did, returning to the scene of his—or mostly Knox's—crime might have been worrisome. Standing on a high bluff overlooking a crashing sea could provide a perfect opportunity for an angry spirit to dispense justice. As unconcerned as Christopher was, the thought had at least crossed his mind, which said something about his confidence.

He had only a few hours left before his life would be forever changed. He'd come to the bluff early to clear his head. It hadn't worked. The words were still there. Christopher had fallen asleep to an annoying mantra that continued to echo.

Don't kick the milk pail!

The phrase had manifested itself as he lay awake most of the night. Christopher's father had used it often, and so had his mother, as if the two of them were lifelong dairy farmers prone to losing their livelihood through awkward feet.

Standing on the bluff and looking at the clear sky above the sea, Christopher struggled to banish thoughts of his family—especially his father. They were the residue of a former and clearly insignificant life. He visualized tossing memories off the edge and watching them fall to the waves below.

If only it were that easy.

While the stable was fine for the likes of Wells, Knox, and Payne, he couldn't have asked Bishop Parnell to meet him there, and he couldn't risk meeting in any place more public. It wasn't long before Parnell came striding through the high grass, his great cape and the ends of his stole whipping in the wind. He had one hand on his high hat and the other swinging his staff, a vexed glare on his face. Christopher expected a reproach for the location of the meeting, but instead the bishop planted the butt of his staff in the ground, looked around—most notably at the windowless walls above them—and nodded.

"This is your last opportunity, Christopher," he said. "I'm growing tired of your inability to get this job done. Do you understand? The church can't afford to back failures."

If this was his way to welcome Christopher to the fold, it lacked faith, and for a clergyman that wasn't an encouraging sign.

"I took you in, paid your debts, fed, clothed, and protected you. Now is the time of your reckoning. Your chance to repay my kindness. Fail, and I won't know you. Do you understand?"

Guess the bishop is all out of carrots.

The bishop raised a hand as if to bless him, but instead declared, "You were a disgrace to your father and the king—to all of humanity. Worthless."

Christopher gritted his teeth. *My father? Sure. The king? Perhaps. But all of humanity? Really?*

Now he understood the point of the meeting—control. On the eve of Christopher's ascension, Bishop Parnell was making certain the soon-to-be earl knew his place.

Melanie de Burke was to blame. He'd purchased the animal, which had cost a small fortune, from Hildebrand Estates with money he didn't yet have. His plan had been to pay the debt with the proceeds from the Summersrule Chase. The beast was willful, ill mannered, and stubborn. No matter how much he used the whip, the horse just wouldn't run as fast as it could and eventually stopped altogether. Back in the stable, she bit him once more, and Christopher lost his temper.

He hadn't meant to kill her. Just wanted to teach the nag a lesson. The lesson went too far, and Christopher found himself with a bloody sword, a huge debt, and no chance of returning the animal. His father had refused to help, using the incident to wash his hands of his son. The king proved even less helpful, cousin or not. Christopher was on his way to Manzant, and genuinely frightened for the first time since being ambushed by the bees. Then the church entered his life. They removed one debt but added another.

"Hopefully, this is behind you now, and new opportunities await. But the church has a policy," the bishop told him. "No man can be given a position unless he can obtain it through his own abilities. You must achieve this for yourself. I have redeemed you for our Lord Novron. Win this contest—kill Nysa Dulgath without implicating yourself—and the church will throw its support to you and insist that Vincent make you Earl of Dulgath. Fail, and I won't know you."

"My plan will work."

"Your last three didn't," the bishop said. There was an incensed tone to his words, that airy, disappointed exasperation that came with age. And while Parnell was indeed old, somewhere in his fifties, he was young for a bishop. Most high-ranking clerics lived disturbingly long lives, adding credence to their claim of being favored by Novron.

"The church is not in the habit of failing. I've spent years—decades—shaping opinions and maneuvering individuals, here and in other provinces of Maranon. I have patiently redirected the course of this kingdom so it will be fertile for the return of the Heir of Novron. Succeed, and you'll be part of that future. Now tell me, who will loose the quarrel?"

"Knox has a man picked out. Shervin Gerami. He's a net-maker from Rye, a village down the coast a few miles. Not a smart man, but he has a keen eye and steady hands."

"Do you trust he can accomplish the task?"

"We've practiced," Christopher said. "Nine out of ten shots were lethal, and he's fast. He was able to fire an aimed quarrel every thirty seconds. If he misses, he should be able to try again before trying to escape. He won't get far. Knox will kill him during the apprehension."

"And if Knox fails, and the assassin is captured? What will he say?"

"That he was hired by Royce Melborn, the very man who came up with the plan in the first place. He might also claim he killed Lady Dulgath because she's a demon."

"Why would he say that?"

"He's local stock, and an avid believer in ghosts, ghouls, faeries, and witches. Spouting such nonsense will make it even less likely anyone will listen to a word he says."

"Very well." Parnell nodded, reaching up to prevent the wind from stealing his hat. "We shall see if our Lord Novron deems you worthy of power, Christopher. For his judgment is the true test. You will be either an earl, a vagabond, arrested, or dead." He turned and sailed back through the sea of grass.

Christopher remained a moment longer, looking out over the edge of the cliff, thinking, if only for a moment, that Novron didn't give a damn about him.

The courtyard of Castle Dulgath—which was usually little more than a lawn, yard, and garden surrounded by the shaky arms of stone walls—had been transformed. Everything that could be moved out had been; this included the smokehouse, the henhouse, the gardener's shed, the smith's anvil and workbench, and most of the azalea bushes. Where it all went to, Christopher had no idea. Carpenters had raised a stage of bright fresh-cut wood, which was now covered in bunting and streamers of white and blue.

Chairs had been placed on the stage, seeming out of place on the unfinished blond decking. The big chair from the Great Hall, where the late earl had sat during meals, was center stage. Today the king would sit there. A smaller, more delicate chair sat to the right of the larger one. This seat was for the lady of honor, Nysa Dulgath. On the king's left, another chair was reserved for Bishop Parnell. Not even King Vincent would want to snub the church in such a public display.

More chairs faced the stage, with an aisle between them. Who sat where indicated their significance and marked their place in the nobility's hierarchy. Christopher would be sitting on the aisle in the last row, which was better than no seat at all.

He had been briefed by Wells, who, as chamberlain, was responsible for every aspect of the ceremony. Of course, his wasn't the final voice. Even Lady Dulgath didn't have authority in the presence of the king.

Now that the time was at hand, Christopher worried about Bishop Parnell's ability to pressure the king into making him earl.

Why wouldn't Vincent give the fief to Sir Gilbert? The man is the best knight in Maranon. Or the king could choose one of his hunting buddies, like Baron Linder. Heck, why not award the title to my father, for that matter.

Christopher had no idea what leverage Parnell would use to influence the king's decision, but that wasn't his concern, at least not yet. And with that thought, he allowed himself a good long stare across the length of the yard, up toward the wall that was elaborately—and strategically—decorated. A large pair of heraldic banners were displayed over the parapet. Between the king's own colors and those of Dulgath, a massive arbalest was hidden, along with an insane, hairless man without a single fingernail. Christopher couldn't see him or the weapon but knew both were there—his gift for the newly pledged countess.

The people of Dulgath had been arriving all morning. He'd seen them from his window on the third floor. They had come in farm wagons, buckboards, and on horseback, but most had arrived by foot. Huge masses of people dressed in their finest colorful cloth brought a roar that drowned out the sea. They had formed small camps outside the castle walls, laughing, shouting, singing, and dancing.

Christopher was on the porch when Wells gave the signal and the gates were finally opened.

The sweaty-faced crowd tumbled into the courtyard where, in the absence of any real constabulary, the king's own men were acting as guards. With outstretched arms and loud voices, they funneled the surging crowd toward the far wall and directed the onlookers to form orderly rows until the whole courtyard was full. Those who hadn't arrived early enough found themselves outside the walls, but they were still excited to be present. This was a holiday for them, as good as an annual fair—no, better, as this happened but once in a lifetime. Or so they expected.

There had to be thousands. Men in variously colored cowl hoods to protect them from the sun; women holding babies in their arms, jostling and swinging in an effort to keep them quiet; wide-eyed children constantly tapping and pointing; everyone with smiles of excitement and anticipation. They wanted a show, and they would get one.

A trumpet sounded.

"That's us, My Lord," a mostly bald but otherwise white-haired man said. He was the king's scribe, and Christopher thought his name might be Robank or Robant.

They walked out together. Wells had orchestrated the event like a wedding, and in a way that's exactly what it was. Nysa was about to pledge her loyalty to her liege lord, and he in turn would grant her stewardship of Dulgath. The two would be bound to each other—and just as in marriage, she would be far more bound to him than he to her.

As Christopher and the scribe made their way through the crowd to their seats, he caught a fleeting glimpse of a black hood, so out of place in all the oranges, yellows, blues, reds, and browns. Like the fin of a shark, it cut through the assembly, slicing away from the stage, where everyone else was pushing to be, and heading toward the far wall—the distant one where the large set of heraldic banners hung.

Christopher froze, trying to follow the path of the dark hood that reminded him of—but that was impossible. Royce Melborn would be in Manzant by now locked away in that terrible hole of no return.

"Lord Fawkes?" the scribe said while tugging on Christopher's arm. "We're supposed to proceed together. Is anything wrong?"

Christopher scanned the throng of jostling, cheering townsfolk but had lost track of the phantom.

I'm just nervous.

He shook his head and replied, "No, no. Everything is fine. I was just overwhelmed with the pageantry and the splendor. Let us proceed, my good man."

The two continued to their seats but remained standing. No one would be allowed to sit until the king did. Next came the king's valet, and then the only other woman to be granted a chair. The king called her Iona, but Christopher had heard her real name was Bessie. She was His Majesty's mistress. Christopher was surprised she'd been granted a place at all, but then old Bessie had lasted longer than any previous courtesan. By his reckoning she was going on her seventh month in the royal bed.

Next came the esquires and the knights, Sir Dathan and Sir Jacobus, their crests emblazoned on formal tabards. Another trumpet blast and Bishop Parnell took his place on the stage, looking rather dignified.

The horn sounded again, and Lady Dulgath left her castle. She exited alone, and at the sight of her the crowd went so silent that Christopher could hear the swish of her long blue gown across the steps as she climbed onto the stage. She reached her chair and pivoted on her left heel to face the crowd. As she did, three more trumpeters joined the first, and together all four proclaimed the coming of the king.

The crowd before the stage, including the people granted chairs, went down to their knees at the brassy sound. Heads bowed, the trumpeters knelt as well, and nothing but birdsong, the wind in the banners, and the distant rush of waves accompanied King Vincent to the center of the stage.

"People of Dulgath," he said, "His Lordship, Earl Beadle Dulgath, is dead. I mourn his loss and pray to Maribor and Novron that his spirit is at peace. Today I'm here to appoint his successor— his daughter—Lady Nysa Dulgath."

The king took his seat, and like springs set free, the crowd popped up and cheered.

Christopher, along with the others who'd been granted a chair, took his seat amid the roar of the crowd. He leaned out and caught the eye of Lady Dulgath. He smiled at her, and she smiled back.

Everything's going to be fine, he tried to convince himself, but he didn't really believe it.

The hood didn't bother him nearly as much as the smile on Lady Dulgath's face. She'd never smiled at him before, and he didn't know what that meant.

Chapter Twenty
ASSASSIN

R oyce was good at navigating crowds. Small and agile, he could also anticipate currents and knots, working them to his advantage. Hadrian followed in his wake, swimming through the gap before it closed again. On the few occasions when Royce hit a dam, it took only a menacing stare to get people out of his way. Men with big fists and calluses avoided him for the same reason some pretty women never attracted suitors: People silently communicated with body language, eye contact, and open or closed stances. Some said, *I'm friendly, talk to me;* Royce's message was the same as a pointed blade. His glare could be relied upon to intimidate a roomful of hardened criminals, and the effect was magnified on simple farmers, mothers, and their children. To them, he must look like death moving their way. Most couldn't get out of his path fast enough.

Royce made for the far wall. That was the obvious spot. The raised parapet on that side of the courtyard was entirely draped in banners, perfect for concealment; was a reasonable distance to the target—less than a hundred yards—and held a direct and

THE DEATH OF DULGATH

unobstructed line of sight to the stage. Even an idiot like Fawkes could be counted on to solve that riddle. He clearly had. The far parapet was the only one without a ladder. The killer was up there neatly isolated. He could take his shot, then drop down outside the wall to a waiting horse. The assassin would be gone before anyone even knew what happened. Once the crowd noticed, the ensuing chaos would choke the courtyard, severely inhibiting any pursuit.

When Lady Dulgath entered and took her seat, Royce considered dashing to the stage to warn her but decided against it. The assassin was already up in his nest, probably looking down the stock of a crossbow and waiting for a signal to shoot. Royce's attempt to warn Nysa might become that signal, and he was hoping there was still time to stop the assassination. Royce's one advantage was that the killer didn't know he was coming any more than Lady Dulgath knew she was about to be murdered. As long as the plan remained unaltered, there would be no reason for the assassin to rush the shot. If Royce and Hadrian could gain access to the parapet, and if the bowman was intent on his target, they might be able to get close. If so, Royce would assassinate the assassin.

Then he would face a decision.

They could just disappear—*should* just disappear. He and Hadrian could follow the same exit plan the bowman had prepared. Every reasonable thought in his mind demanded that they leave. Then, he could come back later and pay Fawkes and Payne a visit on a dark, quiet night of his choosing, in a place no one would hear their screams. He could kill Fawkes whenever he wanted. It didn't— wouldn't—have to be in front of an audience.

The other less sensible option whispered teasingly in his ear to take care of everything right then. He could fill in for the crossbowman, but instead of putting a bolt through Lady Dulgath, he'd punch a hole in Fawkes—or Hadrian would. He was better at such things and had the benefit of two working hands. The only question was whether his partner would have the stomach for it. Hadrian still suffered from the handicap of his imagined morals.

If the quarrel pinned Fawkes upright in his chair—as they sometimes did—the ceremony might conclude with his death undiscovered until they came for His Lordship's chair. With all the noise of the crowd, and everyone's attention on the king and the lady, perhaps no one would notice. The powers that be could easily blame the dead assassin lying next to the bow, and he and Hadrian could leave for home that very afternoon without any worry of being hunted.

The more he thought about it, the more Royce liked that option. Killing Fawkes with the same weapon he planned to murder Nysa with had a poetic irony that appealed to him. And it would be nice to turn Fawkes's moment of triumph into his downfall, but Royce knew he was also being stupid. Emotions did that; passion made idiots out of everyone.

Royce hated Fawkes and wanted him dead more than anyone since Lord Exeter, the High Constable of Medford who had beaten Gwen a year before. He tried to convince himself it was because Fawkes had attempted to put Royce back in Manzant, the abyss where he'd spent the worst years of his life. That was more than reason enough for a death sentence. The last time Royce had been sent to Manzant, he'd rewarded those responsible with what was still referred to in the city of Colnora as the Year of Fear, even though it only took place over one summer.

Royce also tried to rationalize that Fawkes's other transgressions contributed to his desire to end the miscreant's life then and there: his mangled hands, drugging Hadrian, selling them like slaves. All told Fawkes had four capital crimes to pay for, but even all of them wouldn't have put Royce in that crowded courtyard on that afternoon.

As much as he hated to admit it, he was there because of *her.* He was trying to save Nysa, but justifying his actions by pretending he only cared about revenge. He reasoned that ruining Fawkes's plan was an additional victory. Suffering fools wasn't something Royce was good at, even when *he* was the fool. His rationalizations were crap, just excuses for his reckless behavior, and that truth was a problem for him.

She looks so much like Gwen. The thought bobbed up, but he dismissed the notion as he had his previous justifications—just one more excuse.

Sure, she had dark hair and olive-colored skin, but she wasn't as dark-skinned as Gwen; plus, she lacked the distinctive Calian features. Still, they both had a similar, and uncanny, ability to read him and shared an eerily haunting wisdom. The real reason was something else, something more, something he couldn't understand, and that lack of understanding scared him.

She feels familiar. When she speaks, it's as if she knows me.

Beyond all that, the fact that Hadrian hadn't balked about rescuing the countess, or hesitated at the idea of preventing the assassination, was evidence he was making a huge mistake. Yet despite all this, Royce was pushing through the crowd and making his way to a ladder laying in the grass, close enough for emergencies, but too far away to invite anyone to use it.

He's rubbing off on me.

Royce scowled at the thought, and his expression sent a little girl falling over herself to dart out of his way. She continued watching him long after he'd moved past. The day was warm, and the sun shone clear and bright, but when Royce glanced back at that girl, she shivered.

ASSASSIN

And I'm not even after you, he thought, feeling the stiff boards wrapped tightly to his hand and left middle finger.

The three good fingers and thumb of his left hand were more than enough to hold Alverstone, and that dagger could cut anything. He'd recovered the white blade from the belt of one of the Manzant slavers, where it had been casually stuffed like a pair of old gloves. If the slaver had succeeded in stealing it, Royce would've spent the rest of his days hunting him down, even if he had to excavate Manzant in the process. The blade was all he had to remember the man who had made the weapon—the first person to challenge Royce's worldview, the closest thing he'd ever had to a father, to a savior.

Usually to make something truly great, you need to start from scratch, Royce remembered him saying. *You need to break everything down, strip away the impurities, and it takes great heat to do that, but once you do, then the building can start. The result can seem miraculous, but the process—the process is always a bitch.*

Royce tried to squeeze his right hand and winced.

The process is always a bitch.

No one was looking as he and Hadrian reached the ladder. "You want it over there?" Hadrian asked, nodding toward the banners, but it was more of a statement than a question. When you knew what to look for it was easy to see.

Once Hadrian set the ladder, Royce led the way up. Using only the two outside fingers of his left hand, he climbed with no more difficulty than if it had been steps. Partway up, he disappeared beneath the blue-and-white standard of House Dulgath.

If I were doing this, I'd set up the crossbow down and to the left. Better angle and more reaction time if anyone comes up. But then if I were doing this, I would've pulled up the ladder.

Not for the first time, Royce wondered who he'd find holding the bow. Not Tom the Feather or Roosevelt Hawkins, and probably not a bucketman from the Diamond.

Creeping up the last few rungs, Royce poked his head above the level of the catwalk. Beneath the banners was a dim world, a long tunnel formed by the parapet, roofed and walled on one side by the huge linen pennants. On the outer side, merlons left squared open spaces, giving views outside the castle. Muted sunlight lent the space a tentlike feel. The underside of the banners acted as the backside of stained glass along the corridor. Less than twenty feet to his left, a man lay on his stomach with his hips turned, one leg bent and the other straight to fit within the narrow passage. He was bald, heavily tanned and tattooed. His arms were wrapped around a massive crossbow, his cheek resting on its stock; the weapon's nose barely protruded through the gap between the standard of Dulgath and the banner of Maranon. The prow of the bow was mounted on a stand, the other end pressed against the bald man's shoulder. As Royce had expected, a rope was tied around a merlon behind the assassin—his escape route.

Hasn't seen me.

A bell began ringing. Royce reached into his cloak and gingerly drew Alverstone with his left hand before creeping onto the parapet. The bowman was so intent on his target he never noticed.

Too intent.

The killer's eyes narrowed, and he was holding his breath.

The bell! It's a signal.

A busted right hand made it impossible to accurately throw his dagger. Instead, he raced toward the assassin, but a diving hawk couldn't cut that distance faster than the bald man could squeeze a trigger. Only two strides separated them when…

Thwack!

ASSASSIN

The sound was loud. Somewhere in the courtyard below, came a faint, muffled *thrump!* Followed by screams.

Royce wondered if the shooter had even seen where his shot landed before his throat was cut. The assassin was dead, but a price was paid. A jolt of pain exploded from Royce's broken finger as he killed the bowman. Soaked in blood, the slick blade slipped from his hand. Alverstone hit the parapet and fell through to the courtyard below. "Damn it!"

Hadrian, who had caught up to Royce, was pulling back the edge of the pennant.

"Did he hit her?" Royce whispered.

Hadrian drew the banner aside further so both of them could peer out. Lady Dulgath sat slumped in her beautiful blue gown, a massive quarrel protruding from the center of her chest.

She's dead.

Two knights were on their feet. One drew his sword, looking through the crowd for the enemy. Everyone else stared at the chair to the right of King Vincent. Hadrian released the cloth and it slid back into place.

"Can you climb down the rope with your hands like that?" Hadrian asked.

Before Royce could answer, a communal gasp rose from the courtyard. Several people screamed. "She's alive!" someone shouted. That one voice managed to cut through the murmur of the crowd.

Royce peeled back the canvas and saw the impossible. Nysa Dulgath's eyes were open. With both hands she pulled the quarrel from her body, looking at it, stunned.

How could she…how could anyone survive being impaled with a bolt that size.

Nysa dropped the quarrel. It hit the stage with a hollow *clunk.* Blood soaked the front of her once beautiful gown, turning the blue to black. She coughed, and blood bubbled out of her mouth, spilling in a gruesome display down her chin and neck. Her eyes looked up, looked across the length of the courtyard, looked directly at Royce. *Help me,* she mouthed.

They were separated by almost three hundred feet but she knew he was up there, once more hiding, once more watching. She always knew when he was near, and that he could see her lips because he was elven.

The sound of someone climbing the ladder caught Royce's attention, and he let go of the canvas, blocking his view of the lady and her pleading eyes.

Knox's voice arrived before he did. "Shervin! Damn you. Load another bolt or I'll have to smother the bitch in the infirmary!" When his head cleared the parapet he froze. "Melborn! Blackwater?"

Hadrian drew his swords and charged toward Knox, but the sheriff wasn't a fool. Grabbing an end of the banner, he leapt; his weight did the rest. Sheriff Knox fell to the courtyard, bringing the blue-and-white standard of Dulgath with him. He pointed at Royce and the arbalest shouting, "Assassin! Assassin!" His men headed his way, pushing through the crowd.

Hadrian dragged the ladder up. He jerked his head toward the rope. "I can buy you some time, but make it fast. Get moving."

The knights, along with other guards, continued their way toward the wall, hampered by the crowd. People were crying, as they backed away from the stage. King Vincent stood beside Nysa, shocked. Lady Dulgath continued looking at Royce with desperate eyes.

Help me.

I'll have to smother the bitch in the infirmary!

"I'm not leaving," Royce said.

"What?" Hadrian shot back.

"We need to get her out. Here, help me load another quarrel." Royce fumbled, trying to work the arbalest.

"Get her out? Royce, there's a thousand people between us and her. Maybe two thousand. How do you expect—" He shook his head. "Royce, get on the rope!"

"We can't leave her here. You heard what Knox said."

"Royce, you're being stupid! Get down the rope. It's not going to take them long to get another ladder."

"No."

"Since when are you a hero? Look, I'm all for saving people, but there is no way to *get her out*!"

"Yeah, there is. But I need your help." Royce said, continuing to work the weapon with his mangled hands. "Get over here."

Hadrian looked skeptical but joined Royce at the arbalest. He rotated the crank, spinning it as quickly as he could, pulling back the wire. "Okay, so what's the plan?"

"You're going down to the courtyard and carry Nysa Dulgath out the gate. Then, put her in the wagon and I'll use the rope to meet you outside the wall."

"If I go down there, they'll kill me," Hadrian said as the wire reached its firing position.

"I won't let them."

"You won't *let* them. How you going to—?"

"Just trust me!"

Hadrian stared at Royce for a moment, only a second, then nodded. Seeing him do it, seeing Hadrian accept *trust me* as an argument worth risking his life for, disgusted Royce. Had the situation been reversed, he never would've agreed. Royce would've already left.

Would I? Would I leave him behind to die?

He wanted to believe he would, but…

"What are you going to do?" Hadrian asked as he placed the bolt.

"Play chess."

❧

The bell rang.

Payne had been tasked with pulling the rope. The idea being that the noise would cover the sound of the shot. Christopher was preparing to look surprised, but he needn't have bothered—it came as a genuine shock when the quarrel struck Nysa.

He'd heard the crack, as if someone had split wood. In point of fact, Gerami had done exactly that. The quarrel had punched through Lady Dulgath's chest and shattered the wooden back of her seat. Christopher had to fight off a smile now that the deed was done.

It's over! I'm going to be earl!

The next shock came when Knox called out the thieves' names and pulled down the banner.

Why aren't they in Manzant? The thought fought with the sight before his eyes.

Then the third shock hit.

Nysa Dulgath sat up, and opened her eyes. The delicate woman reached up and with both hands pulled the quarrel from her body. The bolt was dark with blood. She pressed her left hand to the wound and dropped the quarrel with her right. Then, both hands pressed, blood leaked through her fingers.

How is she still alive?

He couldn't have been the only one thinking this. The knights jumped out of their chairs, and the king's men retreated, but no one moved to help Nysa. Not even the king, who stood an arm's length away.

ASSASSIN

She's going to die. No one can take a hit like that and live. This is just some freakish thing. She's going to collapse at any minute.

But she didn't. Nysa continued to hold her palms to the wound and stare at the distant parapet, where the knights had directed guards. While they were searching for a way to assail the wall, a voice rose above the murmuring of the crowd.

"No one move—or the king dies!"

Everything stopped.

Royce shouted his command again to make certain everyone heard. Vincent started to retreat. "That especially includes you, *Your Majesty!*" he added.

Vincent froze.

Royce continued, "I won't hesitate to punch a hole in the king, so don't test me. Everyone is going to do exactly what I say. If you don't, the king will die. Even if I'm killed afterward, imagine the treatment you'll receive for acting so rashly."

"What do you want?" Vincent shouted back.

"First, tell everyone to do as I say."

The king hesitated.

"Do as he says, Vinny," Bessie pleaded while sobbing. She had rushed from her bunting-covered chair to be at the king's side when Lady Dulgath was hit.

"Quiet, woman!"

"Look at Lady Dulgath. Look at that quarrel. I've got another aimed at your chest," Royce said.

"Do what he says!" the king shouted.

"Wise man. Second, I want you, and everyone else, to be silent. I'm the only one allowed to talk. Wouldn't want the king to die because someone couldn't hear me. Third, I want Your Majesty to sit back down. You're not going anywhere for a while."

The king didn't hesitate this time. He took his seat, putting both hands on the arms of the chair. He looked decidedly terrified.

"Now my friend is going to lower a ladder. Those of you at the bottom will want to move away. If anyone gets anywhere close to him, if anyone so much as gives him a dirty look…well, by now you ought to know what will happen. So for the sake of your king—and the wrath that'll rain down on you and yours if you do anything to cause his death—give my friend a wide berth."

The silence in the courtyard was so complete that Christopher heard the creak of the ladder as Hadrian Blackwater climbed down.

What are they doing?

Watching the crowd part, seeing Hadrian move toward him, Christopher felt his grand scheme collapsing.

What if they tell what they know? Will the king believe them? No. He won't, not now. They're threatening his life. This might work out after all.

Hadrian walked straight up to the center of the stage and was the only one to touch Lady Dulgath. As he stooped down to lift Nysa, Vincent whisper to Blackwater, "You'll hang for this."

"No, we won't," Royce shouted, making the king start. "And I said no talking."

With a pained grunt, Hadrian lifted Nysa in his arms. Her head wobbled; her eyes wandered blindly. One arm fell limp. Blackwater carried the countess off the stage and headed toward the front gate beneath the stare of thousands of eyes.

As Hadrian passed Christopher, he heard Nysa whisper, "Going to pass out. Get—get me to the monastery. Tell Royce…have to get me to the Abbey of Brecken Moor. You have to tell…you have to…"

"I heard. Calm down," Hadrian replied. "Save your strength."

"My strength is gone."

The whole of the courtyard watched as he carried their lady out the gate, leaving a trail of blood that dripped from the end of that long blue gown.

⁂

"What did you do?" Scarlett gasped, her eyes threatening to fall out of her head as Hadrian laid Nysa Dulgath in the bed of the wagon.

He did it as gently and carefully as he could, but the woman was a wilted rag covered in blood. Her dress was a sponge from which dripped a thick drizzle. Her skin felt slick and slippery.

While Nysa Dulgath couldn't have weighed much more than a hundred pounds, his ribs told him that carrying her had been too much. The stress had sent jolts not only to his side, but up to his shoulder and down his back. Taking deep breaths didn't help, but he needed one—more than one. Hadrian's arms were shaking with pain by the time he set her on the buckboard.

Scarlett had leapt up and scrambled to make a bed from the blankets they'd left in the wagon. She helped ease Nysa down and rolled up another blanket for a pillow, plucking blades of grass off it, as if Lady Dulgath would care.

"Drive the wagon to the wall over there." Hadrian pointed. "Around the back you'll see a rope dangling from the parapet. Royce will be down in a minute. I hope."

"What did you do?" Scarlett repeated in an accusatory tone, continuing to fuss over Lady Dulgath.

Does she think I did this? Fine, I'll drive.

Hadrian stepped on the spoke of a wheel and pulled himself up to the driver's seat. More pains, sharp as needles—very long needles—stabbed him in the side, stealing what little breath he had, and making him clench his teeth.

Hurt myself carrying her.

Hadrian took the reins off the stock, disengaged the wheel's brake, and urged the team forward with a kissing sound he'd heard Scarlett make, along with a jiggle and slap of the long leather straps.

Feeling the wagon move, Scarlett looked up at him. "What's going on? What did you do?"

Hadrian wheeled them toward the wall. The bounce and rattle of the wagon that made him twist in his seat did nothing to comfort him as he sucked in two more careful breaths.

"When Royce gets here, we're going to go really fast," Hadrian said, realizing how poor the suspension was on the wagon and how much the trip would hurt. He glanced back at Nysa, her pale face rocking from side to side with the motion of the wagon. She was either dead or unconscious; either way, she wasn't going to suffer.

"Where are we going?"

Hadrian looked down at Nysa. "The Abbey of Brecken Moor."

"The abbey? But—" They both looked up to see a dark figure slip over the wall.

Legs wrapped around the rope, Royce slid down like a raindrop on a string. Then he sprinted toward the wagon, shouting, "Go! Go!"

Hadrian slapped the reins, sending the wagon forward in a lurch as Royce jumped up. He caught the arm of the front seat with his three good fingers and plopped down beside Hadrian. The wagon bucked and banged over ruts, throwing Hadrian into the air and slamming him down again so hard he squeezed his eyes shut and saw little dancing lights.

When he reached the road, the earthquake stopped. There was plenty of shaking and still a little rocking, but they were no longer being tossed in the air like children on a tarp at a spring fair.

Royce climbed into the back.

"What did you do?" Scarlett asked him, shouting over the rumble of the wagon and the hiss of the wind.

"How is she?" Royce replied.

"She's drooling blood! That's how she is!"

"What's that mean? Hadrian, you're sort of a doctor, can you—"

"I'm *not* a doctor—but even I know she should have died five minutes ago. Should have checked out the moment she was hit." Hadrian braced himself as they rolled through a dip that turned out not to be as bad as he thought. "That bow was an arbalest. In the army, we used them to pierce armor, kill horses, and shatter the wheels of assault towers. A single quarrel will stop a charging water buffalo. Royce, there's no way she's going to live. She's spitting red because at least one lung is punctured, or more likely shredded. She's drowning in her own blood—what little she has left."

Royce looked at Scarlett. "You know anyone who can help her?"

"Hadrian said we're taking her to the abbey. I think that is the best place."

"The abbey? Why there?"

"Don't ask me," Scarlett said.

"It's where she asked to be taken," Hadrian supplied.

"Then that settles it," Royce declared.

Scarlett shook her head. "Wagon won't go up that trail."

Hadrian's attention was on the road, but the few glances he gave back to the three passengers revealed a sorry scene. Not trusting the makeshift pillow, Scarlett was cradling Nysa's head in her lap, her legs to either side of the lady. She looked close to tears as the wind whipped her fiery hair. Royce held on to the wagon's rail with his relatively good hand, rocking side to side and frowning at Nysa.

"She's right," Hadrian said. "We'll get partway maybe, but it narrows, gets too steep and rocky."

"We can switch horses in Brecken Dale," Scarlett shouted. "Get fresh mounts, saddle them, and leave the wagon, but someone will need to carry her on horseback—ride tandem."

"I'll take her," Royce said.

They hit another bump, and Hadrian grunted. If it weren't for Scarlett, Lady Dulgath's head would've been clapping on the wood. She wouldn't feel it. The lady couldn't feel anything, and he was certain she never would again.

"Is anyone going to tell me what happened in there?" Scarlett shouted. She was angry, frustrated, scared, and still holding Lady Dulgath's head, brushing the woman's hair away from her face.

"Got there too late," Hadrian said. "Then Royce threatened to kill the King of Maranon."

"You're not serious?" Scarlett looked at Royce. "That's got to be a step up, even for you."

"You want to tell me why we're doing this, Royce?" Hadrian asked. "Normally this is the sort of thing you'd be yelling at me for."

Royce didn't answer. He had his head cocked back, looking up at the sky. "Anyone else notice that it's starting to rain?"

Chapter Twenty-One
THE STORM

Clouds.

As a daydreaming boy, Hadrian had done his fair share of lying in fields and imagining some as dragons or trolls to slay. He'd seen castles in the sky and towers where damsels waited to be rescued. In their puffy white and billowing grays, Hadrian had peered into the glories of his future and witnessed wonders—wonders that never came to pass. To Hadrian, the man, clouds only meant rain.

These clouds were different. Not that they appeared unusual, and they did mean rain—plenty was falling by the time they reached Brecken Dale—but they also meant something else. Only no one knew what.

It never rains during the day. Scarlett must have said it at least a dozen times before they finally reached Caldwell House. From the moment Royce drew their attention to the rain, she'd had her head craned back with a look of surprise and fear.

What does it mean? Hadrian had also asked more times than he could remember.

Scarlett never answered him.

They made enough racket racing through the dale that those who hadn't gone to witness the homage came out to see them rattle by. Or maybe they were already out, standing on their porches and stoops looking up at the sky and, like Scarlett, wondering what was happening.

Wagner, Gill, Asher, and Clem were certainly out. Tasha was there, too, standing behind Asher and peering over the doctor's shoulder.

"Lady Dulgath is hurt!" Scarlett shouted as Hadrian brought the wagon to a stop.

Asher climbed up as Royce and Hadrian got off. Royce hesitated a moment, looking back at the wagon and the motionless woman. Then he and Hadrian ran to the stables.

Caldwell House's stables lacked the luxury of the castle's, but they were still grander than any stable in Medford. The long single corridor with stalls to either side was clean and just as livable as any of the homes along the street. With the double doors open wide, gusting storm winds and the sound of distant thunder agitated the horses and threw bits of straw dust into the air.

"How long we got?" Hadrian asked, searching the stalls for Dancer.

"They have to get out of that courtyard," Royce replied, searching for his own animal. "Get down to their stables, saddle their horses—and wait for others to do the same. The more coming after us, the longer it will take. Fifteen or twenty minutes? Maybe more. But that wagon was pretty slow."

Hadrian spotted the white diamond and two rear socks of Dancer. He grabbed the bit and bridle hanging on a peg just outside the stall and flung the gate open. "Did you kill him?"

"The king? No, that would've only made matters worse. Someone used our real names, remember?"

Hadrian was having trouble seeing how things could've been worse, but he felt a sense of relief at the news. When faced with the question of whether to kill or not, Royce had a nasty habit of choosing the former. For him, doing so was the same as checking the grass before squatting in a forest or looking in a boot before pulling it on in the morning. Common sense, he called it—dead people didn't seek revenge.

"Well, that's one point in our favor." Hadrian finished Dancer's bit, then dashed over to help Royce, who was having trouble with his own mount because of his injured hands. "Would you have killed him? If he'd refused—if they had grabbed me?"

"In a heartbeat."

"Not sure if I should feel touched or terrified."

"That's your problem."

"But what did you mean about playing chess?"

Royce appeared puzzled for a moment then smirked. "Oh, that—I literally put the king in check."

"Funny." Hadrian tugged the bridle over the horse's ears, and Royce quickly slipped the bit into her mouth. "And so now what's the plan?"

"I don't know. I'm making this up as I go."

Hadrian buckled the neck strap. "Don't tell me we're still playing Opposites Day. Seriously, why are we doing this?"

Royce didn't say anything. He simply grabbed the quilted horse blanket and tossed it over the back of his mount.

Royce often ignored questions he didn't want to answer. There had been times when—

"I honestly don't know," Royce said, smoothing out the wrinkles, not looking at Hadrian.

"You're joking." Hadrian paused in disbelief. "Are you...you aren't in *love* with Nysa Dulgath—are you?"

"It's not like that," Royce said.

"What *is* it like?"

Hadrian helped Royce set his saddle onto his horse. "I—I don't know...but there's something—"

"Something worth dying for?"

Royce sighed. "Certainly looks that way, doesn't it?"

When they rushed out of the stable, leading their mounts, Hadrian noticed that Scarlett was missing and Asher was still on the back of the wagon, kneeling over Lady Dulgath. A crowd had formed around them, mostly the old folk who'd stayed behind while the rest of the village headed to the castle.

"This woman is dead," Asher told them when they were near enough so he didn't have to yell.

Royce stopped as if he'd been hit.

The crowd had been generally quiet to start with, but with that pronouncement everyone fell silent. Rain pattered on rooftops, on grass, on the wagon, and on the people gathered in a circle. The sky cried at her passing. A silly thought, but at that moment Hadrian didn't find it so foolish. Dulgath wasn't like other places. Its differences lay somewhere below the mind's ability to reason. Ever since he'd arrived, Hadrian had sensed something odd, something different, somehow out of place. As Asher draped a blanket, pulling the wool toward Lady Dulgath's face, Hadrian felt a deep upwelling of sorrow, as if something profound was ending, something greater than a single life.

Thunder rolled nearer, and lightning flickered behind the thick clouds.

"I'm not dead."

Asher jerked back, his face going white.

Royce dropped the reins of his horse and lunged forward, shoving his way to the wagon.

"Get me to the abbey, Royce," Nysa told him. "I'm running out of time."

"Royce," Hadrian shouted, "mount up. I'll hand her to you."

Royce nodded, grabbed his horse, and leapt up. The crowd scattered as Hadrian lifted Nysa. The pain in his side screamed.

"Clem, Wagner…" Hadrian looked around and spotted the tavern boy.

Fish are good, but Gill's the best.

"Gill! Help me lift her."

With the boy's help, they got Nysa in front of Royce, who cradled her before him.

Scarlett appeared, coming down from the direction of her house on a saddled black horse. "Everyone ready?"

"Scarlett, no," Hadrian said. "You stay here. They don't know about you. No one knows you had anything to do with this."

"I don't give a damn. She's…I care for her far more than either of you do, and I won't stay here—"

"Don't have time to argue!" Royce snapped.

"Go," Hadrian told him. "Down to the river. Cross the stone bridge, then just follow the trail uphill to the left. The monastery is at the top of the mountain. I'll be right behind you."

Royce nodded, kicked his horse, and trotted down the cobblestone streets, as overhead lightning warned that the storm was coming closer.

THE DEATH OF DULGATH

చి

Christopher hesitated at the stall of Immaculate, then looked down five gates at Derby, Lady Dulgath's sleek courser. Immaculate's, while not an awful horse or a biter, was a durable linen shirt compared with the fine damask doublet that was Derby. Nysa certainly wasn't going to be using her that evening. Throwing open the chest before Immaculate's stall, Christopher took his saddle to Lady Dulgath's horse.

"Where did they go?" Vincent was shouting outside the stable, where a light rain was falling. "Did anyone see?"

A dozen men were in saddles and a dozen more were still working on it. The king himself was mounted after having a breastplate and helm slapped on him. Sir Jacobus had tried to dissuade His Majesty from coming, assuring the king they could take care of things, but Vincent was still fuming, and the rain did nothing to dampen his anger.

"They're rogues—assassins—hired to kill Lady Dulgath," Christopher said. "There've been rumors for weeks that two men— professionals from the north—were coming to kill her. It's likely they're headed for Gath Pass. From there they'll try to escape by racing north to Rhenydd."

"Chrissy," the king snarled. His face was furious red. His horse sensed his mood and spun, tossing his head...ready for the run. "Do be quiet. I need a chance to think."

"Actually, Sire," Sir Jacobus said, "I think he may be right. Several witnesses saw the lady placed in a wagon that went that way."

"If they're in a wagon, they'll have to stick to the road," Sir Dathan pointed out.

Vincent nodded. "If they're in a wagon, we should catch them before they reach the pass."

THE STORM

Christopher found his stirrup and swung up on Derby, who jerked sideways and turned around, bending her neck, trying to bite him.

Why do the good horses always try to bite me?

"Best watch out—the last one to do that died," he told the horse.

He gave Derby a sharp tug on the bit and pulled her head back hard. This caused the horse to back up, which was fine because Knox was behind him. The sheriff had a less-than-triumphant look on his face.

"This is a mess," he hissed.

"Relax, everything's fine," Christopher whispered back. "Just stay close."

"Everyone"—the king rose in his stirrups—"to me!" With that, he spurred his horse forward and the race began.

With Nysa Dulgath propped between his arms, Royce found the path. Like navigating crowds, he was also good at finding his way. He'd never been lost, not outside at least.

Because I'm elvish.

He looked down at Nysa as if she'd said the words, but her eyes were closed.

Royce had no idea if elves had a better compass than anyone else. Fact was, he didn't know much about elves. Common knowledge held that they were less intelligent and physically smaller and weaker than men. They were lazy, avoiding work like an intelligent man avoids a bare hilltop in a lightning storm. They were filthy all the time, too. Everyone knew elves hated water. They had ugly pointed ears and sinister slanted eyes. But some generous folk also said they had better hearing and sight than men. Others—shopkeepers, mostly—maintained they were strangely quick and agile, and could steal merchandise right out from under watching eyes. Their agility led to rumors that elves were somehow related to cats. That their god had cursed a family of felines, turning them into abominations. The one thing everybody agreed on was that back in the days of the First Empire, they had been slaves, and freeing them had been as foolish as turning milk cows loose or expecting chickens to fend for themselves.

Royce did have high cheekbones and was fast, agile, and could move quietly. He could see farther than others seemed to be able to, even in near-total darkness. His hearing was also better than that of anyone he knew, but his ears weren't pointed, and his eyes were like everyone else's. *I'm not completely elvish,* Royce qualified, arguing with the voice in his head. *A mix maybe, a half-breed of some sort.* And he never got lost. *Maybe that's a thing.*

Rain battered the leaves. It came down harder, sounding like a fast river or nearby waterfall. The volume of the shower helped muffle the sound of his horse's hooves as she plodded up the narrow trail. Royce didn't dare push. The path was uneven, steep, rocky, and growing slick. If she stumbled—if they fell—Royce would never get Nysa back up on the horse, not with his hands the way they were.

Nysa's head hung limply. He cradled it to his chest, sheltering her face from the raindrops with his hood. Her chin, lips, and the lower half of her cheeks were stained red. As he held her, as he looked into her face, Royce realized she wasn't breathing.

He touched her neck, feeling for that little pulsing thump that—

"I'm still here," Nysa said. Her eyes opened slowly and with effort, like jammed wooden windows swollen with humidity.

"Didn't look like you were breathing."

She offered him an effort-filled smile. "Thank you for this." Her voice was sluggish, cracking.

"Don't talk. Conserve your strength."

"Strength is fine." She coughed and spit more blood.

"Doesn't sound like it."

"Just hard to talk. Blood is in my throat." She coughed again. A dark, almost black line drooled down her chin.

Royce looked behind. No sign of Hadrian.

He should have caught up by now.

"Royce," Nysa said, her voice clearer. "Do you like me?"

Royce looked at her, surprised at the absurdity of the question, and decided to respond in kind. "Of course not. I always risk my life for people I hate."

She smiled. "I mean, are you attracted to me?"

In another place and time, and with someone else, Royce would have smirked.

She's delirious, he reminded himself. *Humor her.*

"Honestly? At this moment? You've looked better."

She jerked and coughed again. "Don't make me laugh."

"Most people don't find me funny."

"I'm sure most people don't share our sense of humor." She cleared her throat.

For a woman with a hole in her chest the size of a crown tenent, she was oddly lucid and unconcerned. Most people, even seasoned fighters, would be crying, begging not to die, screaming, or complaining about the pain.

"We're short on time, so I'll skip the formalities. Nysa Dulgath is the last of her bloodline. If she dies, the king will appoint a new earl, someone from the outside, someone like Christopher Fawkes."

If she dies? If Nysa dies? She's really delusional.

"I wouldn't count on Fawkes. I have it on good authority he'll be unavailable for...well, everything," Royce told her.

"But if Nysa has a child," she went on, "we can raise her to be a good ruler."

Royce's brows rose. "We? Are you asking me to *marry you?*"

Nysa looked up at him, her lower lip lifting, eyes drooping into an embarrassed, practically apologetic flinch. "I realize I have problems."

"No kidding."

"Oh—believe me, you don't know the half of it."

"What? You chew with your mouth open?"

She smiled again.

So odd. So very odd. How is she even talking? I'm missing something.

"Thing is—I never thought I could find anyone that I could... well, *be with*. But you're different."

"Because I'm part elven."

"Yes. I know you think that's an insult, but it's not—it's an incredible compliment. Look, I'm giving you the chance to become the next Earl of Dulgath. The offer comes with your own castle and an ocean view."

And a wife with a hole in her chest. "Tempting."

"But? There's a *but*, isn't there?"

"There is."

Nysa glanced down at herself. "Is it the blood? I could wash."

He couldn't help smiling. She did share his morbid sense of humor—even while facing her own death. That won her points in his book—a book with few pages. He did like her, and his admiration grew by the minute. If not for Gwen—and the fact that Nysa's life expectancy was akin to a soap bubble's—he might have considered it.

I could lie. She won't live. What would be the harm?

"I'm with someone," he said, his tone serious, regretful. "I know what it's like to be betrayed. I won't do that."

"Hadrian?" she asked.

"No." He chuckled. "A woman."

"Oh. She must be very special. You're turning down a title and an estate that would make you wealthy and respected for the rest of your life."

"She is special."

Royce glanced behind them again. Still no sign of Hadrian.

What's taking him so long?

"Oh!" Nysa looked up, hopeful. "You *could* bring her along. I won't mind."

Royce's brows rose in surprise.

Nysa frowned again. "Different cultures, I suppose. Where I'm from, we don't have marriage. People don't mate for life."

"People don't get married in Dulgath?"

She offered that same apologetic smile. "Look, I want to thank you for being honest—for telling me the truth. Now…I have something I need to tell you. Something I never thought I'd ever tell anyone. You see, I'm not Nysa Dulgath. That poor girl died two years ago. Fell off her horse in a steeplechase accident and snapped her neck. I arrived too late. Managed to fix her body, but by then she was long gone."

"You're not Nysa Dulgath?"

"No."

"And you expect me to believe that?"

"Of course."

"Why?"

"Because you're right—I'm not breathing. You're carrying a dead body."

❧

Lightning flashed. Thunder cracked. The storm was almost on them.

"You can't go!" Hadrian shouted at Scarlett.

She's being so stupid!

She wasn't. She was being brave, and he admired her for it. But that didn't take away the pain of knowing she'd die alongside him.

Going to the monastery was suicide. Lady Dulgath was certain to die, and they'd be trapped on top of the mountain. After what Royce did, after threatening the king, there would be no mercy. He and Royce would hang, or burn, or kneel before the block, or whatever they did down there. But no one knew about Scarlett. She could continue living her life, entertaining guests at Caldwell House and sleeping in Wagner's bed. Given enough time, she might even learn to spin and weave.

If she came with them, she'd be arrested as part of a conspiracy to murder the countess and threaten the king.

"You can't stop me!" Scarlett turned her horse, but Hadrian caught her mount by the bit and pulled her back. "Let go!"

Hadrian grabbed her wrist and pulled Scarlett down. He let her fall, hoping it would take some of the fight out of her. It didn't. She came up swinging.

He caught her again one wrist and then the other. She struggled, trying to kick him. He spun her as if they were dancing, making her face away and pulling her arms across her body, hugging her to him.

"You have to stay here," he said.

"Let me go!" She tried kicking backward with her heels.

Wagner, Asher, and the rest watched. No one moved or said a word.

"If you come with us, the king will execute you."

THE STORM

"Nysa is ours, not yours!" Scarlett shrieked as she struggled. "She doesn't mean anything to you! You don't understand!"

This was taking too long. He hoped Royce didn't need him, but he wasn't letting Scarlett throw her life away.

If only I could tie her up or—

The idea of locking Scarlett in Caldwell House's cellar came to him at exactly the same time that he heard the shouts.

"The king! The king!" Someone Hadrian didn't know was running up the street. He was pointing backward and yelling like a wild man. "Coming up the road!"

Hadrian was out of time.

He let go of Scarlett, who took the opportunity to kick him hard in the shin before leaping back on her horse. Hadrian grabbed Dancer and together they raced for the river and the bridge.

Lightning flashed. Thunder cracked. The storm had arrived.

While everyone else fought for a place nearest the king, Christopher lagged at the rear of the pack, Knox at his side. By the time they entered the dale, the rain was pouring, a heavy summer shower that, along with the growing darkness made it hard to see. Sunset was still hours away, but the clouds continued to roll in, thick and heavy. By the time the king's party reached the village market, the sky was as dark as dusk. Wind whipped the rain that fell in sheets, making puddles on the brick. Lightning revealed the world in colorless flashes, and the following thunder rolled with a deep, long voice, making it hard not to imagine this wasn't an ordinary storm.

Novron is with me, Christopher realized. *The son of Maribor is advocating on my behalf, marking this day with portent of my victory.*

Christopher saw the darkness as his personal cloak, the lightning as bursts of his mental acuity, and the thunder as the drumroll announcing his impending achievement. He was the storm, and his god was with him.

As they approached the market, Christopher reined in Derby and raised a hand, telling Knox to do the same.

"What are you doing?" the sheriff demanded. He pointed toward the king's company, who had taken the split to the right and were riding toward the mountain pass.

"The king is on a goose chase," Christopher told Knox as he fought with Derby, who wanted to follow after the other horses.

"What are you talking about?"

"They didn't go that way. Nysa Dulgath is headed for the Abbey of Brecken Moor."

"How do you know?"

"Because I heard her. It's where she asked to be taken." Fawkes watched the last of the king's retinue disappear around the houses. "If anyone else heard, they didn't listen. They think Melborn was there to kill her. We know better. He and Blackwater are trying to save her. She thinks she'll be safe at the abbey—that she can hide up there and recover. Then she'll return. Melborn probably expects a reward. Thinks the countess will be so indebted to him that she'll pay a fortune, grant him a title, or give him an estate or some other prize."

"So what are we doing?" Knox asked. Lightning flashed and in one instant revealed every strand of hair plastered to his head; rivulets of water streamed off his stubble. His eyes were angry, harsh and violent. That was the nature of the man. The truth of him shown to Christopher by the light of Novron. This, too, was a sign for Christopher, who needed such a man now. He needed an animal to help him kill, but Knox was merely a beast, something to be ridden then discarded when no longer of any use.

"We go after them," Christopher said. "We finish that bitch. Then we'll claim we arrived too late. Explain that they took her for ransom but she died during the trip. We'll be seen as heroes for killing them. If we don't catch up before they reach the abbey, if the monks witness anything, we'll have to take care of them, too. I trust you don't have a problem slaughtering monks?"

"Not for a worthy cause."

Spoken like a true monster—but at least he's my monster.

"Oh—you can trust it will be, my friend. I'll take very good care of you," Fawkes said even while he thought, *I'll slit your throat when you're not expecting it and tell King Vincent you were the one who hired the rogues—that you split off from the rest at the market and, being suspicious, I followed you.*

"You'd better," Knox said.

"I wouldn't be able to sleep at night if I didn't."

Chapter Twenty-Two
LONG STORY SHORT

Nysa Dulgath was indeed dead. Royce checked: no pulse, no breath, her skin cold. Not chilled, not clammy, but milk-jug-left-out-in-the-rain-over-night cold. He didn't panic or have an overwhelming need to put space between himself and the unexpected corpse he was pressed against. This wasn't the first dead body he had held. Corpses didn't upset him—still, talking ones were a new experience.

Royce leaned backward, holding her out to the full extent of his arms and glared into eyes that were staring back at him. He no longer supported her—its—head. He didn't need to. She—it—was holding her—its—own head up.

"Hmm. I'm not on the ground, and you're not galloping away," Nysa's corpse said. "Does that mean you're willing to hear the rest of the story?"

"First, tell me who or *what* you are."

"My name doesn't matter. Won't mean anything to you. I was a Fhrey; that's what our kind was called in the days before Nyphron. Before the First Empire. *Elf* is a human word, not ours."

"You *were* an elf?"

"Best if you let me start at the beginning or this will get very confusing."

Nysa's corpse waited, watching him as the horse continued to plod.

"Okay," was all Royce could think to say.

"Who I really am is too long a tale to tell just now. I wouldn't mind explaining everything, but we don't have the time."

You're already dead so, what's the hurry? Royce thought.

"The first thing you need to know is that Fhrey are nothing like you think. We are an ancient and noble—and granted, also an arrogant—race. We once ruled the world. Even this place was under our dominion.

Royce smirked. He wasn't about to be intimidated or hoodwinked, even by a talking corpse.

"It's true. There's evidence everywhere. Those smooth bluish stone ruins on Amber Heights above the Gula River near Colnora… that was once a Fhrey fortress called Alon Rhist. And words like Avryn, Ervanon, and Galewyr are Fhrey words. Rhenydd, too—at least the *ydd* part. The oldest of my kind can live for more than three thousand years."

"So is that what's going on here? You're practically immortal. You can't die?"

"Oh, no—I already died. My body turned to dust thousands of years ago. But I broke Ferrol's Law, and you need to be careful not to do the same. Ignorance of the law won't protect you, and having a little human blood won't either. You are part Fhrey, and as such you are forbidden from killing another Fhrey. Ever."

"Unlawful killing of anyone is called murder, and universally frowned upon. Unless you're at a higher social level than your victim, in which case it's called justice."

"Not the same thing. Humans have laws against killing one another, laws made by men. The law forbidding one Fhrey from killing another is made by Ferrol, our god, and it is *he*—not other Fhrey—who dispenses punishment for that crime. Ferrol's will is the cornerstone of our society, and since the dawn of time only a few have violated his sacred law."

Royce couldn't hide the sarcasm in his voice. "The punishment for murder in any society is death. What more could Ferrol do?"

"If a Fhrey kills another Fhrey, they are forever denied entrance to Alysin, the Sacred Grove, the afterlife. You might know it as Phyre, Rel, Nifrel, or even Eberdeen. For us, there is no greater loss. It means we are outcasts and will never again see the ones we love, and those who love us."

Royce, who'd never had much use for religion, didn't know any of those terms beyond how to curse with them, as in *Go to Rel* or *I hope you burn in Phyre*, which until that moment he'd assumed referred to a funeral fire.

"So you're a ghost?"

"Sort of." Nysa's shoulders shrugged.

Realizing this wasn't Nysa, Royce imagined a marionette and grimaced.

"What you think of as ghosts are actually humans who through stubbornness or ignorance *refuse* to go to their reward. But it's true we are both disembodied spirits unable to interact with this world in any meaningful way."

"You seem to be interacting just fine."

"In a body I can, as any spirit does. With a body I'm as capable as everyone else—more so, in fact."

More so? Like her comment, *We don't have much time*, this jumped out at Royce, but he kept quiet.

"The problem is, bodies don't last, and it's rare to find one unoccupied. I was lucky with Maddie Oldcorn, sort of like a squirrel moving into a bird's vacant nest. Caught in a blizzard, Maddie died, but her body was mostly intact. Toes were never right, but I was able to live with that."

"So Nysa isn't in there with you?"

"No, she was gone before I arrived. If she had been alive, even lingering between worlds, I could have saved her. Same with Maddie. I can't enter a body unless it's vacant. A body with a spirit is like a candle with a flame—the original spirit must be extinguished before the body can be relit."

Royce had heard many bizarre tales over the years. Most he didn't believe, but he'd actually seen a few things that made him wonder. He'd watched a four-day-old corpse sit partway up, burp, and then lie back down. And he'd watched a dead man shaking his head, although that turned out to be a rat rolling around inside an emptied skull. He had personally witnessed the fight on top of the Crown Tower and couldn't understand why there hadn't been any bodies at the bottom afterward. That last one still haunted him. But, if he were really talking with a three-thousand-year-old dead elf, this bizarre conversation took first place.

"Who'd you kill?"

"It doesn't matter. I was young and foolish and oh, so arrogant. When I died, I was alone—a face pressed up against a window looking in at the world I used to know but couldn't touch. I didn't know about entering bodies then and could only watch helplessly as the people I used to know made terrible decisions. The person I cared the most about was another Fhrey, who, like me, also broke our sacred law. I wanted to be with him when he died, but once separated, I couldn't find him. I looked everywhere. Then...well...I just kept heading west until I came to the land's end, to this place, and here I stopped."

"Nice place."

"Yes, until the humans came. I tried to keep them out. Can't do much without a body, but if I try really hard, I can make things move. I even possessed a few dead animals. Got a raccoon once. They have fingers, you know? Hands make all the difference and soon these will be too stiff to be of use. With hands I'm able to—" She stopped, refusing to look at him.

Said more than she wanted to. More than it wanted to, he corrected. *This isn't Nysa.*

He was having trouble remembering that and had to remind himself that if he touched her skin it would be like ice.

"So you were Dul the Ghast's nature spirit," Royce said.

"Ugly, ugly man. Sunken eyes, looked just like a skeleton. I don't know why I did it. I was lonely, I guess. He was up on top of this mountain crying and begging for help. They were starving to death, you see. Dul's son and daughter had died, and his wife was sick. The whole lot of them wouldn't have survived another month, so he climbed up and begged for help. I like it up here, nice view. I sat on top of the mountain often and was watching the sunset when Dul came up bawling and wailing. I'd started to leave when I heard him say, *I know you're there. I know you can hear me. Please help us.* At that time, no one had spoken to me for centuries, but here this creepy little man was talking right to me. I don't think I can explain how that felt—to be acknowledged after so long—to have someone recognize that you exist when even you had started to doubt.

"I didn't know what I could do. I followed him home. Together we watched his wife die, and I performed my first miracle."

"I take it she made an unexpected recovery."

"Yes, as far as everyone else knew. There really wasn't anything wrong with her, except the discomfort of acute hunger, the pain of losing her children, and a fever that was gone by the time I stepped in. Mostly, she'd just given up. People do that, more often than you'd think."

"So the squirrel settled into the bird's nest."

"Yes, and with human hands, hands nearly like my own, I was able to—" She stopped herself again. "I was able to help them."

"Did he know?"

"Oh yes. I set him straight right away. Did I mention how ugly Dul was? Didn't want him touching me. I've never liked humans. Dirty, awful things. It's why I never thought I'd find anyone to be with. Their kind can be so repulsive."

You're a talking corpse spitting up blood, and you think we're repulsive?

"And yet you helped them."

"Was nice being alive again, to be able to do things. I thought I had found a way to survive, but then *he* came."

"He?"

"The rumors of my miracles had traveled all the way to Percepliquis. When he heard, he came looking for answers."

"Who is *he*?"

"Perhaps the most remarkable human—no, *person*—I've ever met, and I've been around a *long* time. His name was Bran and he was looking for someone. Not me, as it turned out, but I think something led him here and brought us together. Bran recognized me the moment we met. Not specifically, not my name, but he said he knew what I was. What I'd done. He'd been taught about *my sort* and knew what to look for. He told me the most amazing story, about a woman named Brin. At first, I thought he was making it up, but he spoke of places where I had lived—oh, so long ago—and told stories that were handed down from this Brin. Then, just like

Dul the Ghast, I started crying. I didn't think I could anymore, but that story—*Brin's* story—gave me hope."

"What was this story?"

"That eternity isn't nearly as long as I thought; that there will come a day when I'll have a chance to redeem myself. That this time, these moments right now, are my chance to learn, to practice, and to improve. But most of all, that both Bran and Brin will be watching and rooting for me."

"Are these people still alive? Are they Fhrey like you were?"

"No, they were human and both died thousands of years ago. So long ago that the monks who practically worship Brin as a demigod have most of her story wrong—so wrong they actually think she was a man. I'd set them straight, but they wouldn't believe me."

"If these two are dead, how can they be watching?"

Nysa's lips smiled. "That's a completely different story, and we don't have time for it, either."

"You said that before. What's the rush? Why don't we have much time?"

"Because this body is dead. The muscles are stiffening. I'll have to leave it soon. You need to get me to the monastery."

"Why? What's at the abbey?"

"Nothing right now—but something will be."

The trail was quickly turning into a mountain stream as the rain flash-flooded over rocks. Overhead, thunder boomed, rattling the trees. Scarlett had slowed down as the trail became a darkened tunnel, shrinking in on the sides, becoming the narrow footpath Hadrian remembered. They were halfway, possibly as much as three-quarters. He searched for landmarks, things he could remember, but in the storm everything looked different. Surely they were close to the top; the trees were getting shorter.

The crash of rain made it hard to hear anything, and Hadrian might have died if it hadn't been for Scarlett. Despite her professed desire to escape him in her chase after Nysa Dulgath, she continued to look back—never more than a glance—but enough to see he was still there.

As they climbed into the shorter trees and low brush, lightning flashed while she looked back. She reined her horse and pointed. She wasn't looking at Hadrian; her sight went past, focusing behind him. Wide eyes completed the story. Before she even yelled her warning, Hadrian had drawn his bastard sword and wheeled Dancer around.

Lord Fawkes and Sheriff Knox came rattling up the trail. They were both soaked, slick, and shiny. They had drawn their swords, bright silver in the lightning flash. Both showed white teeth in vicious grins.

"Deal with him, Sheriff," Fawkes barked, letting Knox squeeze past.

"Keep going!" Hadrian shouted to Scarlett.

"There's two of them," she yelled back.

"I can handle two."

"Maybe on a good day, but this isn't a good day for you."

She knew not to mention his ribs, not to even say he was hurt, but that's what she meant. She refused to abandon him in the face of uneven odds.

"Trust me. I can handle this," Hadrian told her.

"I remember you now," Knox said, tucking the loose end of his sodden cloak into his belt after the fashion of some mercenaries. In the military, only officers wore them. Those that transitioned out brought their cloaks as status symbols but maintained the axiom that *only fools fight with a flag on their back.*

Seeing the cloak, Hadrian remembered Knox, too. They had both been at the Battle of Gravin River Ford. Hadrian had been an arrogant kid of fifteen who'd just joined Warric's Third Battalion, his first enlistment. Knox was a veteran in the same unit. Hadrian hadn't kept his fighting ability a secret, and when he rallied the troops and almost single-handedly held the line against Earl Francis Stanley of Harborn's forces, Ethelred had appointed him captain.

Showing up his elders and getting promoted hadn't won him many friends. Hadrian didn't remember Knox in particular but wouldn't be surprised if he still held a grudge.

"You know what I think?" Knox said. "I think you were lucky that day. Never heard of any great acts of heroism after Gravin Ford."

That was because Hadrian had resigned his newly awarded commission within a month of receiving it. As an officer he had the right to abdicate, and he did, leaving Warric altogether to join the ranks of King Armand's forces in Alburn, where he kept a lower profile and managed to serve for a whole year.

"And like the tart said"—Knox grinned his white teeth at Scarlett—"this isn't a good day for you."

The trail was narrow, forcing Scarlett to stay behind him. She was out of immediate danger, but that was Hadrian's only blessing.

Dancer wasn't a warhorse; she wasn't trained for combat. With one hand needed for the reins, Hadrian was limited to a single sword against two enemies. And his ribs hurt. Carrying Nysa had at best aggravated the wound, and possibly done real damage. Riding hadn't helped, either. Stiff and sore, he suffered constant pain that cycled with an annoying randomness between an ache and a stabbing jolt. Scarlett and Knox were right: This wasn't a good day for him.

The sheriff spurred his horse and charged forward, swinging as he came. Knox was a seasoned soldier and used an economical stroke that demonstrated more respect than the sheriff's words. He didn't expect to kill on first clash, which itself was proof of Knox's own martial acumen.

Hadrian caught the blade easily, but the impact sent a screaming thunderbolt down his side, making him cramp and preventing a proper counter. Trapped on the horse, he was limited to a twisting effort from his torso—and that part of him was broken. Instead, he took advantage of the part of him that wasn't. Rising, he slipped out of his right stirrup, gave a hard kick, and caught Knox in the stomach, sending the man over his horse's side and onto the ground.

Hadrian shot a look to his left, expecting Fawkes to be on top of him. With Knox down, Hadrian readied his blade to block whatever attack Fawkes would give him—only he wasn't there. Intent on catching Royce and Lady Dulgath, the lord had taken the opportunity to force his horse through the brush that bordered the trail, riding right past Hadrian.

He would have had a clear path, except that Scarlett was waiting.

As Fawkes attempted to race by, Scarlett, lacking a sword and holding only a small knife, did the only thing she could—she leapt at him. Flinging herself off her horse, she tried to grapple Fawkes to the ground. Hadrian expected Fawkes to cleave her in half, and if he'd been left-handed he might have. But his sword was on the wrong side. Instead, he backhanded Scarlett in the face, sending her to the ground.

Fawkes wasted no more effort on either of them and rode up the trail.

By the time Hadrian looked back, Knox had gotten to his feet and moved uphill, around to Hadrian's off side.

Trying to fight on horseback with broken ribs on a narrow trail had all the makings of a disaster. Using her as a shield, he jumped down on the far side of Dancer.

Hitting the ground was excruciating. The jolt brought more flashing lights, and he sucked air through clenched teeth for a second before he could think again. Then, slapping Dancer out of the way, he drew his short sword.

Knox had his second sword drawn now as well, but he was in a precarious position, with Hadrian in front and Scarlett behind. The woman was getting to her knees, bleeding from her nose and lip, but she still had her dagger.

Knox was an experienced fighter and not at all a fool. He knew the path of least resistance. Hadrian saw it in his eyes. He witnessed the subtle shift on the grip of the sheriff's sword, the tilt in his hips toward the downhill side of the trail.

Scarlett wasn't a fool, either, but she also wasn't an experienced swordfighter. Fights she'd known were likely limited to fists and thrown bottles. Because Knox was looking at him instead of her, she had no idea what was about to happen. She pushed up, rising to her feet, moving toward Knox. She probably thought to distract him, maybe even stab him in the back. She never saw the threat, didn't realize her own mistake, until he twisted and thrust half the steel of his blade into her stomach. Her eyes went big, her mouth opened, but she made no sound.

If there had been any lingering doubt about the sheriff's intelligence, or his sense of self-preservation, he erased it by jerking out his sword and racing up the trail past Scarlett. Knox caught her horse and, in a running mount, leapt up and sped away following Fawkes.

Scarlett collapsed face-first in the rushing stream of muddy water coming down the mountain trail.

"Scarlett!" Hadrian fell to his knees beside her. He took hold of Scarlett's shoulders and gently lifted, turning her over.

"No!" Scarlett screamed. "Don't touch me! Don't move me!" Her face contorted in pain as she struggled to inhale, swallowing air instead of breathing it.

She had mud on her face, her beautiful hair pasted to her skin with the wet. Her eyes were squeezed tight, her mouth wrenched in pain.

"Scarlett, I…" He didn't know what to say.

Hadrian had seen it happen on the battlefield. Thrusts to the abdomen were never good. Deep ones—this sort—were almost always fatal. The blood coming from her stomach, beneath her pressing hands, was dark and thick.

"Go," Scarlett was able to say, her voice weak.

"I can't."

"Go—go save Nysa."

"I can't leave y—"

"If you save her"—Scarlett gasped—"she'll save me. It's my only chance. Now go."

"But Nysa is—" Hadrian started.

"Trust me. Just do it!"

"Okay, okay, but you have to hang on, you hear me?" He pushed up out of the mud, picked up his swords, and grabbed Dancer. "I'll be right back. You wait for me!"

Hadrian hauled himself into the saddle, as below him Scarlett lay doubled over in the sodden path, clutching her stomach. With each gasp of air, she whimpered. A dark tail of blood snaked downhill with the trickling rain.

"Hadrian," Scarlett said. She managed to look into his eyes. "The Manzant slavers…you were right." She sucked in another breath. "I didn't do it because of Royce."

Hadrian stared at her, feeling the rain run down his face. "Don't you give up. You hear me? You wait! I'll be right back!"

Chapter Twenty-Three
MONASTERY BY NIGHT

The storm was letting up when Royce guided his horse into the courtyard of the monastery. Old stone, wet from the storm, shimmered and flashed bright with the last few flickers of lightning. Three monks were waiting at the front gate with mournful faces and soaked habits. None looked surprised to see them.

"In here. In here!" The oldest of the three waved Royce toward the warm glow of interior light. "How is she? When the storm arrived we knew something was wrong."

By the time they reached the abbey, Nysa's eyes had closed and she had gone limp. "Take her," Royce said, not trusting himself to get down without dropping her.

One of the younger monks reached up and took her from his arms. Royce felt relief followed by loss. He didn't understand half of what Nysa's corpse had told him, and believed less than that.

He didn't think she lied. She wasn't the sort, and the lack of breathing and cold skin backed up her story better than an eyewitness, but such things were hard for Royce to accept. He'd met his share of preachers, priests, and hermits, each selling their version of life and death, trying to convince new recruits. Royce never saw a reason to invest in their opinion when he had his own, especially when his worked and theirs didn't. But Nysa—or whoever it was—wasn't asking for his faith, his support, or his money. Still, that didn't mean she wasn't after something. No reason for her to spin such a yarn without a point. As he handed her down and watched them take her inside, he knew he was missing that point.

What does she want from me?

"You're the other one?" the oldest monk asked.

Took a moment for Royce to realize what he meant. "Yes. You must have met Hadrian."

He nodded. "I'm Abbot Augustine. Thank you for bringing her. We'll handle things from here."

If by that he meant for Royce to leave, he was mistaken. Risking his life for someone wasn't normal for him, and he wanted to know why he'd done it. Royce had heard a fairy tale, but not his place in it. She had a reason behind asking him to bring her.

Because I'm elvish? Maybe. But there's something more.

Royce was a man of few beliefs. He relied on the bedrock constant of man's propensity for greed and hate. No one did anything except to help themselves. This axiom had proved a sure bet so often, it ranked right alongside water running downhill.

She wants something, but what?

Royce dropped down and followed the rest of them into the big ivy-covered building. The monks made no move to stop him. One even held the door.

"Have you ever seen such weather?" the young man asked.

Royce nodded. The storm was bad, but not unusual for summer.

The monk continued to linger at the door, looking up at the sky. "I've only ever seen a storm once before. When old Maddie Oldcorn died, we had one of these."

"That was the last bad storm?"

The monk shook his head. "The last *storm*. The last time I saw it rain in daylight."

They carried Nysa through a large open room—the nave of the church—toward the altar. Royce had poked his head into Mares Cathedral in Medford; this abbey wouldn't be suitable as its privy. There were no seats, kneelers, statues, nor any marble or carved mahogany. And no hint of gold, just a stone floor and high wooden roof. Open-fire braziers and racks of candles gave the interior light, and the altar was nothing but a raised platform with a podium where a book might rest.

Royce saw no books. The place could have been a Medford stable, with two exceptions: the walls and ceiling. These were covered in painted frescoes. Mares Cathedral had paintings on its walls, too, pictures of a white-bearded man placing a crown on a young, handsome man's head while streams of light shone down— Maribor anointing Novron.

The pictures here were different. They had cracks, tiny spidery lines where the paint had turned brittle, and the wall itself had also cracked in places, leaving great fissures running through the images. The colors were muted and dull; in some places the lines were completely lost. These paintings were created by artists with less talent than those at the cathedral. As a result, the images were crude—flat, with no sense of depth or perspective.

The handsome man was nowhere to be seen; neither was the old bearded guy. Instead, a raven-haired woman sat on a big chair. Behind her, lost partially to shadows, stood a crudely dressed man with a violent black beard. To her right was a beautiful woman holding a longbow and wearing a wry smile. On the other side stood a crippled man leaning on a mousy woman who had her hands stuffed into the pockets of a smock. In the foreground, two more figures were seated on pillows—both young girls. One wore a silly-looking hat, held a staff, and had a wolf curled at her feet. The other clutched a book on her lap and held a quill between her fingers. There were no shafts of light shining on their faces and no glowing radiance. On their far right was painted a flat landscape of lush fields that led to a shining city. Royce had never seen such a place. Tall, elegant towers and grand avenues faded into the distance, where a massive gold-domed building stood. At the city's entrance, two great statues of lions loomed. Scaffolding held workers building additional structures.

Royce couldn't make sense of the image. This was more of a family portrait, like those he saw in merchants' homes. Moreover, in the dim light of the nave, few without his keen sight would be able to see the frescoes. He guessed they must have been painted by torchlight or before the roof was constructed.

The monks, who didn't pause to look at the paintings, took Nysa's body down a set of stairs. Royce was about to follow when he spotted something else in the painting—a small and seemingly insignificant village stood on the far left. Primitive beyond anything Royce had ever seen, the community was a collection of huts surrounded by an earthwork-and-wood wall. At the center was a big house; the entire place nestled in a niche of a great and seemingly endless forest. The contrast between the great shining city and the little village was what stopped Royce.

Who were these people? Why would anyone make a painting of them? They don't look like kings or nobility. Did she want me to see this? She knew I would be able to because I'm elvish. Is this important somehow?

The ivy that covered the monastery was densest around the nave. Some had even slipped in through the windows, the door, and cracks in the walls.

He tilted his head up to see the other painting. It was farther away, harder to see than the one on the wall. Even Royce had to squint. This long image depicted three realms with doorways leading from one to the next. Before the first was a long river with a hut beside it. The river flowed to a pair of great gates. The first realm was filled with people and ruled by a man on a mountain throne. The next was a dark place of shadow and flame ruled by a sinister-looking queen. Across a narrow bridge was another door that led to a beautiful place of flowering trees and green, rolling hills. This last place had no throne or castle, just a modest cottage. One more door led out of the realm to another place, a dark, walled area impossible to see into.

Royce stared up for several minutes, trying to make sense of this image, of this place. He felt the eyes of those on the wall watching him, the woman with the dark hair most of all. There was something about her that he couldn't quite put his finger on.

The pounding of horses' hooves entering the courtyard caught his attention.

Finally! What took you so long?

Royce waited.

Good thing I didn't need help, he planned to say. Then Lord Fawkes opened the door.

Soaked and windblown, His Lordship ducked inside, throwing his hood back and wiping the wet from his face. "There you are!" he said, spotting Royce. "And where is she?" His eyes shifted to the stairs. "Down there?"

Fawkes made no immediate move to cross the room. He took his time, shaking the rain out of his hair and squeezing it from his shirt, stomping his feet. "I hate water in my shoes. Gurgles when you step, and your feet blister in them."

"Where's Hadrian?"

Fawkes looked up as if unfamiliar with the name. "Oh, your partner in crime, yes—he's dead. Killed him on the way up. Him and his girlfriend."

"You killed *Hadrian*? *You* killed him?"

"He's a big man, I know, but also wounded. I was there when the slavers beat him, remember. Bruised, maybe busted ribs, I'm guessing. You, on the other hand…" Fawkes peered across at Royce. "How are they? Your hands, that is. They stomped them pretty good. That must hurt."

Royce reached for Alverstone, only to remember he'd lost it somewhere in Castle Dulgath's courtyard.

Fawkes grinned at him as he threw off his sodden cloak. He drew his sword and made two wide practice swings that sprayed the floor with rainwater. "Not even a knife?"

Royce imagined throwing Alverstone at Fawkes's throat, saw him clawing at his neck in fear and agony, and he hated the dead man with the crossbow for the loss of his blade. Fawkes had risen from a mere target to an enemy and then to an adversary worth taking Royce's time with. He wanted so badly to kill the man that he might drool at the sight of him—so close, so alone. The world was rarely this accommodating—but, of course, it wasn't. His hands were busted and his dagger miles away. Life was filled with cruel ironies.

Royce didn't buy the story of Hadrian's death. But if it was true, dagger or no dagger, hands or no hands, Fawkes would never leave this room alive.

I'll tear his throat out with my teeth if I have to.

Two things bothered Royce—besides his hands and the missing dagger. First, he still didn't know what Nysa wanted from him. Why she'd told that crazy story. Second, if Hadrian wasn't dead, then why hadn't Fawkes attacked? He'd taken off his cloak, shaken out his hair, wiped his face, and seemed content to take practice swings.

If Hadrian could come up the trail, why wait? What is he waiting for?

The answer came through the door a moment later.

"Have you killed her?" Knox asked. The sheriff looked across the hall at Royce and pulled his two blades. One had blood on it.

Hadrian's?

Royce felt rage ignite. As it did, his eyes narrowed, fixing on the two of them.

"Not yet. Was waiting for you. Kill this one. He's unarmed and his hands are broken. Should be easy."

"Then why didn't you kill him?"

"Can't afford to make mistakes this time," Fawkes said. "I think you can appreciate that. You're better with a blade, and he can't be allowed to get away."

The two moved forward. They spread out, forcing Royce toward the corner. Both Fawkes and the sheriff swung at him. Royce leapt back, giving them control of the room.

"See," Fawkes said. "He's harmless, and this is a butcher's work. You deal with it. I'm going after Nysa."

Royce could do nothing as Fawkes went down the steps, his sword still out.

Knox came at Royce with eager eyes. He swung again, and once more Royce dodged.

"You're quick," the sheriff said.

From the stairway came the sound of a door slamming shut.

"He's killing her, you know," Knox said. "Bitch has a nasty habit of living. He's going to cut off her head this time to make sure. We'll blame you for it." Knox moved closer, creeping in on bent legs, his eyes fixed on Royce. "I know your kind. Stabbing folk in the back is your style. Not very sporting."

Knox took another swing, first with his left saber and then with his right.

Royce wasn't there either time.

"You really *are* fast. I'll give you that."

Knox drove him back. Forced him into the corner to limit his ability to move. Royce tried to dodge, to pivot away from the walls, but Knox had been waiting. Two experienced swords were more than Royce could safely dodge, and he retreated again until his back was against the wall with the mural. He found himself standing between the girl with the book and the one with the wolf.

I bet neither of you ever had a day like this.

"Knox! Put the sword down!" Racing out of the rain, Hadrian crashed through the door with both swords drawn.

"About time!" Royce snapped. "Kill him and let's go."

Hadrian advanced without comment, his jaw set, his eyes locked on the sheriff, who shuffled back, raising his swords. Hadrian struck with his bastard blade. Metal met metal with a dull ring as the swords locked at the guards. Knox brought his second blade around, but a saber was slower than a short sword, and before the ring of the first clash faded, Hadrian had thrust two feet of dull metal under the sheriff's rib cage. He drew it out with an uncharacteristically cruel slicing motion. Knox let out a grunt that might have been a word, then folded over. He dropped his sword and grabbed at his torn stomach, trying to hold his bowels in. He fell with a wet slap.

Royce stared at the dead man, surprised. "What? No argument?"

Hadrian shook his head. "Not this time. Where's Nysa?"

Royce led the way down the steps. At the bottom was a closed door. He hit it with his shoulder and bounced off. "Locked."

"So? Pick it!" Hadrian shouted.

"Can't." Royce stepped aside to show him. The door had a handle, but lacked a latch and keyhole. "Bolted from the inside."

Hadrian pulled his big sword from his back and hammered the wood with the pommel. He hit it three times. "Open, damn you!"

The door ignored him.

❧

Christopher was quick to bolt the door behind him. Not that he didn't think Knox could handle an unarmed thief, but he didn't want anyone coming in *or going out*. He'd spent the better part of the spring and summer trying to kill Nysa Dulgath, and this time he was determined to succeed.

I took you in, paid your debts, fed, clothed, and protected you. Now is the time of your reckoning. Your chance to repay my kindness. Fail, and I won't know you. Do you understand?

Christopher understood perfectly. This was his moment for the taking or the losing. As far as make-it-or-break-it moments went, they didn't come any clearer than this.

He was in some sort of grotto beneath the monastery, a small stone chamber dressed up to look important. A shaft of daylight came in at a slant from an overhead opening. The light was muted by a cloudy sky, but still bright in that otherwise dark place. It illuminated a gaudy chest.

That looks promising.

Next to it lay Nysa Dulgath. She was on the floor, hands folded over her breasts, gown smoothed out. Her eyes were closed. She didn't move, didn't breathe. The only other people in the chamber were two young monks and an old man with a ridiculously long white beard, all of whom cowered on the far side of the chest and Nysa's prone body.

No, it doesn't get easier than this.

"You're the abbot here?" he asked the bearded one. He still held his sword but let it rest against his thigh. "Augustine, isn't it?"

The man nodded.

The chest was open and Christopher walked over. No gold.

I guess that was asking a bit much.

Instead, he saw only a bit of plaid cloth. "What's with the rag?"

The abbot didn't answer, but his old eyes watched every move Christopher made.

"I'm lucky to find you. A pair of rogues—the same ones that tried to kill Lady Dulgath and abducted her for ransom—have come here. You're in great danger. They were hired by Sheriff Knox, who had some crazy notion put in his head by the lady's handmaiden that Nysa is a demon. The man is obviously insane, but capable. I figured it out—because I'm smart that way." He smiled.

The abbot and his cohorts didn't smile back. Christopher was certain the two younger monks would start crying soon.

He glanced back at the still-barred door then added in a softer voice, "I'll kill the treasonous sheriff when I leave here, ensuring justice is done."

Christopher moved to Lady Dulgath, causing the monks to retreat.

Such brave guards.

He studied Nysa as she lay on the stone floor. Such smooth skin, lovely cheeks, flowing hair, and that narrow waist. Even pale with death and splattered with dried blood, she was beautiful. Normally he couldn't stare, wouldn't dare ogle the countess, but nothing stopped him now.

Her breasts, normally something he would be eager to inspect, repelled him. He refused to look at the wound, that dark ugly depression near where her hands were folded. Christopher wasn't squeamish, but that hole in her chest was disturbing.

What a waste.

He sighed. "Looks like I raced all this way for nothing. I'm too late. She's already dead."

"No. I'm not." Lady Dulgath's eyes opened slowly, as if they weighed many pounds.

Christopher stepped back, squeezing the handle of his sword.

"Thank you for coming so quickly," Lady Dulgath said. Her voice sounded calm, relaxed, but he noted a strange reediness. She spoke as if from a hollow place, with a breathless quality that—in another time and place—might have been interpreted as seductive. "I was hoping you'd get here soon."

"You—you knew I was coming?" Christopher glanced at Augustine as if the abbot were guilty of something, but Fawkes didn't know what that might be.

"Of course," Lady Dulgath said in her strangely normal, nearly lighthearted tone, the odd, airy flutter still present in her words.

Christopher didn't like that sound, that queer hum like blowing across the mouth of a bottle.

"I invited you," Nysa said.

Behind him, Christopher heard the door jiggle and a thump as someone threw themselves against it.

Good luck with that, Knox. The door is six inches of oak.

"You didn't invite me. You ran here thinking you could get away, trying to find help."

"I told Hadrian where to take me—right in front of you," she said. "I knew you'd hear and come to help."

Christopher laughed. He liked the sound of it, how it filled the little room and pushed back against that windy voice that didn't sound the least bit normal. "You misunderstand, milady. I'm not here to help you; I'm here to kill you."

"I know." Came the words in that same awful voice.

Christopher knew something was wrong, something absolutely unnatural about her. The sound raised the hairs on his arms.

"In case you're wondering why I chose you, it's because you killed Sherwood. I like to think his murder will be seen as justification. I want to believe that my decision is as coolly reached and as pure as that, but I can't deny that I do hate you, Christopher Fawkes. I saw his painting only after it was too late. I hate you for depriving me of the chance to speak to him about it. The gods know you deserve to die. I just wanted you to know that what you did to Sherwood made this easier."

"What are you talking about?"

"I'm so glad you got here while I could still move these fingers and speak through this mouth. I didn't come here for help, Christopher," she said with a terrible, pitying tone. "I came here so there wouldn't be any witnesses. Tell me, Lord Fawkes, do you know what *Miralyith* means? In Fhrey—what you call *elvish*—it means Artist. You killed the wrong one."

Chapter Twenty-Four
A NEED TO KILL

Hadrian was desperate.

Royce was left muttering *That doesn't make sense. It should have worked,* over and over as if reason, combined with repetition, could convince the door to open. He'd shown Hadrian how to use his dagger between the door and its jamb to catch and flip the bolt. The gap was wide enough and Hadrian had felt something rise and fall away. Royce examined the door and confirmed that the bolt had been removed. And yet, the door still refused to open.

Thoughts of Scarlett bleeding to death on a muddy path while crying out *You promised to come back* finally drove Hadrian to recklessness. He threw himself against the door, and nearly blacked out from the pain.

"That wasn't very smart," Royce said when Hadrian slumped to the floor, and wrapped his arms around his body.

"We have to get in…" Hadrian took a gasp of air, just a sip. Inflating his lungs pushed his ribs out and made his body shudder in agony. "Scarlett is dying…"

Royce gave the unrelenting wood a frustrated kick, which the door didn't acknowledge in the slightest; it didn't even rattle against the frame. "It doesn't make sense! It should open. You lifted the bolt. It's gone. That should have work—"

"Stop saying that! Stop arguing with the door and just open it!"

"It. Won't. Let. Me!" Royce kicked the door again. "The brace is gone. You felt it. I heard it."

"Is there another? A second bolt?"

"No, there was only the one, and now it's gone."

"Then what's keeping it closed?"

"Damned if I know!"

"Wait—" Hadrian felt suddenly and mortally stupid. "Does it—oh, by Mar! Does it *pull* open?"

Royce looked at him, and for a fleeting moment Hadrian saw the shadow of shock, almost horror, at the thought. Then it vanished. "No!" he snapped, but he gave the door's handle a pull to be sure.

"Then what's stopping it?"

Royce shook his head. "Braced by something. Something I can't see by looking around the edges."

"Something strong." Hadrian rubbed his shoulder and resumed breathing normally, or as normally as a man with cracked ribs could without wincing. "It didn't give even a little when I hit it. It's like a wall of stone."

Royce slapped his back against the door and slid down. He looked sick, and Hadrian was sure his partner's face mirrored his own. They had failed. Nysa Dulgath and Scarlett Dodge were dead or would be soon.

I shouldn't have left her, Hadrian thought. *I shouldn't have let her die alone in the rain and mud. But if I hadn't, Royce might be dead, too.*

"Too late anyway," Royce said in a bitter tone, looking at his own hands as if they had disappointed him. "Fawkes has finished the job by now. Killed her and the abbot. When you visited, did you go in there?"

Hadrian nodded.

"Any other way in?"

Hadrian gave him a look. "Do you think I would have bounced off the door if there was?"

Royce shrugged. "You were the one who asked if the door opened out, remember?"

"No, there's no other exit. It's a tomb. At least Fawkes won't get away," Hadrian said. "And you'll hear no arguments from me this time. You can use whichever weapon of mine you want, and kill him any way you like. I'll even watch. The bastard didn't just kill Nysa, he—"

The door opened.

Royce, who'd been resting with his back against it, jumped up in alarm. It hadn't been pulled wide, but merely swung inward in response to the slight weight Royce had placed on it.

"What'd you do?" Hadrian asked, stunned.

"Nothing," Royce said, glaring at the tiny gap between the frame and the door.

"Take this." Hadrian got to his feet and held out his short blade.

Royce took it with his left hand, then shoved the door inward with his foot.

The scene inside was mostly the same as Hadrian had witnessed days before. The slanted shaft of sunlight illuminated the chest within the small stone tomb. The differences were Nysa Dulgath, who lay beside the box, her hands folded neatly on her chest, and Lord Fawkes, who stood over her body with a sword in his hand.

The door announced their entrance with a creak of its hinges. Pressing down on the left heel of his shoe, Fawkes spun upon it like a child's top, facing them.

"Do it, Royce," Hadrian said. "This is one job that needs to end with a killing."

"No!" Abbot Augustine came around the chest, shaking both hands to get their attention.

Hadrian held up his own hand, warning the abbot to stop. "We aren't going to hurt you—just His Lordship."

"You don't need to kill him," Augustine said.

"Need?" Hadrian said. Fawkes had plotted against and murdered Lady Dulgath, not to mention beating and selling them to slavers. *Need* had nothing to do with it. Hadrian thought of Ralph and wondered whether Royce was rubbing off on him.

Royce didn't move. He stood holding Hadrian's sword, staring at the lord.

Fawkes tossed his own sword away, letting it clang on the floor.

Surrendering? Hadrian thought. *He has no idea who he's dealing with. Royce doesn't care about such things.*

In the three years they'd worked together, Hadrian had learned that Royce refused to abide people like Fawkes. Pragmatic in most ways, Royce never allowed a man or woman to live who had crossed him. While he would never label it as an excuse, his *reasoning* was that leaving enemies breathing was the sort of careless behavior that came back to haunt and possibly kill. In Royce's line of work, staying his hand was just sloppy.

Hadrian had his own theory. Violence always came from somewhere. Most often its origin was taught, handed down as an heirloom from one generation to the next or a gift presented from close friends. That sort of mean streak became part of a person's character and displayed itself through insults and unwarranted cruelty. The other sort was violence born of necessity. Beat a dog long enough and it bites and will continue to bite anyone and everyone, in an act of perceived self-preservation.

Hadrian had known men who had suffered insults all their lives due to their size, name, appearance, or birthplace. These were the first into battle and the last ones out. They couldn't walk away from even a casual slight and needed to prove themselves to any detractors. These were men who expected the worst of everyone. Royce was a step beyond that. *People* hadn't merely belittled or slighted Royce— *the world* had tried, with strong prejudice, to erase him. Hadrian still didn't know the whole story, but he knew enough to believe Royce might have been a show dog that, through cruelty, had learned to be more than mean—he'd taught himself to survive through the precise application of malice. For this reason, Hadrian found it odd that Royce hesitated.

"Go on," he urged. He held a strong belief that Fawkes didn't deserve even a single additional breath.

Fawkes stared at Royce in a manner that—if the lord had any clue about the thief's history and temperament—would have been brave. Then he let out an almost impatient huff, folded his arms roughly, and shifted his weight first to his left, then his right hip.

Seeing this, Royce lowered the short sword, letting it hang against his thigh.

"Royce?" Hadrian asked, stunned.

He didn't reply. Instead, Royce glanced down at the body of Nysa Dulgath, then over at Fawkes.

"Are you going to kill him or not?" Hadrian asked.

"No—no, I'm not."

"Fine." Hadrian pulled his bastard sword. "Then I will."

"No!" Royce stepped between them.

"What's wrong with you? That bastard killed Lady Dulgath, tried to kill us, and…and Scarlett is probably dead by now. Because of him, there's no way to save her—if there even was a chance to begin with."

Hadrian wanted to believe the tall tales…that the stupid cloth in the box was more than just an old rag; that it really never rained in Dulgath in the daytime. He wanted to believe it all, because then Scarlett—

"Scarlett Dodge is hurt?" Fawkes asked, almost as if he cared.

"Congratulations. You managed to kill one of us," Hadrian said.

"Where is she?" Lord Fawkes asked with a strange urgency.

"Still on the path where you fought us. Has to be dead by now. Probably—"

"Take me to her!"

"Right after I kill you."

"I can help." Fawkes turned to the abbot and said, "Augustine, gather the monks. I'll need to speak to all of you when I return."

"Of course," the abbot said, and bowed to the lord.

Fawkes turned back and stared at Hadrian with intense eyes. "If you care for Scarlett, take me to her."

"Do as he says," Royce told him.

"What?"

"I'm serious. I really think he can help her."

"This is…" Hadrian didn't have an answer. Still, he sheathed his weapon. Opposites Day had stopped being funny a long time ago.

The storm had passed, the rain had stopped, and the clouds were breaking up, revealing a setting sun that stained the sky a bloody red.

Scarlett hadn't moved. They found her curled up and lying on her side in the muddy path. Her beautiful hair was matted into the silt that had built up around her. Dirt smeared her face, and blood was everywhere. Some had already darkened as it dried but around her mouth, still bright red. Her eyes were closed and remained shut even as the horses charged toward her.

She didn't move.

"Scarlett!" Hadrian shouted, jumping from his saddle and wincing with the impact as he rushed over. He fell to the ground alongside her body and slipped an arm under her neck. She didn't react. One of her hands slipped off her lap and fell into a puddle, where it stayed. Hadrian cradled her head in his arm and put his hand to her lips.

"It's too late," he managed to say as his teeth locked together and he glared at Fawkes.

"No, it's not," Lord Fawkes said, climbing down from his horse. "Back, Derby," Fawkes told the animal. The horse moved away, obeying as if she understood.

"She's not breathing!"

"She's still here," Fawkes said. "I can feel her. She's not down the river yet. I can pull her back."

"What river?" he asked, exasperated. "What are you talking about?" But Fawkes had closed his eyes and started humming. "What's he doing?"

Royce shook his head. The thief watched intently while the lord began making new sounds and speaking foreign words. Fawkes moved his fingers as if plucking strings in midair.

"Royce, what's going on?"

"I don't know."

Hadrian brushed the hair from Scarlett's face. Tears were welling on his lower lids, and his lips mashed themselves together as he held the woman tight.

Don't you give up. You hear me? You wait! I'll be right back!

But he hadn't made it in time.

If you save her, she'll save me.

But Nysa was dead.

I didn't do it because of Royce.

The first tear slipped down Hadrian's cheek. He let it fall. His stomach was tight, the muscles pulling on his ribs, but he no longer cared.

"It's all Fawkes's fault. Why didn't you kill him?" Hadrian asked Royce.

"Because..." Royce looked embarrassed. "Because he spun on his heel."

"What?"

"When we came in, Fawkes pivoted on his heel—his *left* heel."

"What does that have to do with anything?"

"He's never moved like that before. *He* didn't—but I remember—"

Scarlett jerked violently in Hadrian's arms. Her mouth flew open and she gasped a loud, gurgling breath. She coughed and bent over, retching blood and vomit. Then, sucking in a breath deeper than any Hadrian had heard before, she coughed again before another breath was drawn. Her fingers clutched at Hadrian and, finding his arm, clamped down and squeezed. Then she pulled him to her, hugged him tight. Her other arm, the hand that had fallen into the puddle, came around his neck.

She blinked several times and looked at Hadrian through clear eyes. "I waited," she managed to whisper, clutching him. "It wasn't easy, but I waited. I waited for you."

Fawkes sat down in the mud, looking tired—more than tired; he looked drained. But he was smiling at Scarlett. Hadrian couldn't make sense of anything. Couldn't explain even to himself why the man's look was so wrong. Such an expression didn't belong on the face of Christopher Fawkes.

What in the name of Maribor is going on?

"We need to get her out of this mud," Royce said. "Abbeys have healers, don't they? Augustine should be able—"

"I'm fine," Scarlett said, pawing at her stomach where her dress was torn and stained. Where the stab wound should have been, the skin was smooth. "Nysa saved me."

"Nysa's dead," Fawkes told her.

Scarlett looked at the lord, surprised to see him. Then she glanced at both Royce and Hadrian before saying, "But…I don't understand. Nysa came to me, she pulled me back."

"That was me," Fawkes told her.

Scarlett stared at him for a long time then finally said, "Like Maddie Oldcorn?"

Fawkes nodded. "Like Maddie Oldcorn."

"Do you know what they're talking about?" Hadrian asked Royce.

"They're talking about squirrels living in bird's nests."

"Oh, of course," Hadrian said. "Thanks for clearing that up."

"I was hoping you'd remember," Fawkes told Royce. "All the words in the world couldn't convince you if you didn't believe. Come, we need to get back or Abbot Augustine will worry."

"Well, we certainly wouldn't want that," Hadrian scoffed.

"Hush," Scarlett told him, "and help me up. She—he—healed me, but it's not like—I mean, I did get a sword shoved through my gut."

Hadrian helped Scarlett to her feet. She wavered slightly, leaning on him. He could still picture Knox shoving that steel into her stomach and was dumbfounded that she could stand at all.

"We have a lot of work still to do tonight," Fawkes told them. "The king will want an explanation."

"I know I'd sure like one," Hadrian said.

"It really won't help. The answer doesn't make any sense." Royce reached out for his horse's reins and stopped. He flexed his right hand, then tore the splint off and flexed the fingers again. He pulled the splint off the finger on his left hand and felt it.

"I hope you don't mind, Hadrian," Fawkes said. "But I'll have to deal with your ribs later. It has been a long day, and it'll be an even longer night."

Chapter Twenty-Five
THE FIFTH THING

With its pillars, polished stone floor, and decorative pennants, the Great Hall was the only part of Castle Dulgath that Royce thought resembled a castle instead of an oversized, run-down house of crumbling stone. The chair helped—the way it sat alone on the dais—supporting the king. Kings made all the difference. This one had his full retinue turned out, along with the castle staff. What had once been the comfortable residence of a country lady had become an extension of the power and might of His Majesty Vincent Pendergast, King of Maranon.

Previously, Royce had only seen the imperfections of the place: the fallen tower, the overgrown ivy, the lack of proper fortifications. He'd completely overlooked its charm. The odd statues carved in the strangest of places alluded to stories no one understood; the encroaching ivy wrapped everything in a warm embrace; all of this lent a sort of enchanted whimsy to the home.

That's it, Royce realized. *It's not a fortress; it's a home.*

The Fifth Thing

Like all kings, Vincent didn't look happy, visibly tired after his long ride the night before, which had resulted in him returning angry and empty-handed. He glared at Lord Fawkes, who acted as the spokesman for the group. Lord Christopher Fawkes stood at the center, and a full step ahead, of the group. Fawkes showed no sign of fatigue; he didn't yawn, slouch, or sag in any way. Instead, he remained straight, even proud, before his liege.

"You expect me to believe this?" the king asked in a tone that showed he clearly didn't.

"I do, Sire," Fawkes replied in a strong, clear voice.

Vincent raised a brow. "*You* saw Sheriff Knox separate from the rest of us and followed him to the monastery?"

"I did, Sire."

Royce and Hadrian had strict orders to stand still and remain silent. Above all else, *they* mustn't talk. The two had been accused of the murder of Lady Dulgath and the attempted murder of the king—the latter being the far more serious charge. That Vincent himself was a witness to the crime made their situation untenable at best. The only reason they weren't already hanging from a rope was because they had turned themselves in and had the backing of such respected men. They had willingly walked in with the venerable Bishop Parnell, Abbot Augustine, and Chamberlain Wells all proclaiming his and Hadrian's innocence. Lord Fawkes had done so as well, but Royce wasn't sure how much value the king placed on his cousin's word.

Prior to sunrise, Fawkes had insisted, with a degree of confidence that appeared insane, that he could clear their names and protect them from harm. If anyone else had promised this, Royce would have ridden north as fast as his horse could carry him. But bones didn't mend themselves in an instant, a woman dead on a muddy path didn't awaken without a scratch, and there was no doubt that the *person* he had known as Lady Dulgath now resided in the body of Christopher Fawkes.

Standing in the Great Hall of Castle Dulgath, Royce flexed his right hand. *Not even stiff.* The finger on his left was also healed beyond the memory that it had ever been injured.

Not surprisingly, Hadrian was on board, especially after the pain from his ribs vanished after Fawkes had some time to rest. He'd also pointed out that Royce wasn't actually guilty of anything for a change—as if that mattered. But perhaps more than anything, Royce agreed to stand before the king's justice out of curiosity. He wanted to see what other miracles Christopher Fawkes could perform.

"And you say you witnessed Chrissy fight and kill the sheriff in defense of Lady Dulgath, who lay dying at your abbey?" the king asked Augustine.

"He was most heroic, Your Majesty," the abbot replied, his hands clasped before him in a perfectly pious posture.

The king raised an eyebrow. "Chrissy, heroic? I can't say I've ever seen that side to him before."

"If I may, Sire." Bishop Parnell stepped in. "You underestimate the man. He has changed over these last few years under the tutelage of the church."

"Yes, I'm sure he has," Vincent grumbled, then began a slow shake of his head as his eyes focused on Royce. "But I saw this one aim an arbalest at me, with my own eyes. Why'd you do it?"

Remembering the rules, Royce remained silent.

"I want an answer, or I'll have your head here and now!"

Royce glanced at Fawkes, who nodded.

"If I wanted you dead," Royce replied, "we wouldn't be having this conversation. I was simply trying to save Lady Dulgath."

The king showed his teeth as his face flushed.

"He's right, Sire," Fawkes intervened. "A single squeeze of that lever and you would be dead. You're looking at a man who could have, but didn't, kill you."

"Lady Dulgath wasn't dead," Royce said. "But Knox had said that he'd finish the job the moment she was taken to the infirmary. He'd pointed his finger my way, and everyone in that courtyard wanted a rope around my neck. You weren't going to listen—no one was—certainly not until after Hadrian and I were dead and the lady along with us. I took the only possible route. Everyone believed I was a killer, so I used that to my advantage to try to save Lady Dulgath. It almost worked."

The king's face softened. He still looked angry, maybe more than before, but he believed the explanation. Royce was a good liar, but telling the truth was even more convincing.

Vincent leaned back in the big chair that had once belonged to Nysa Dulgath and her father before her. He steepled his fingers and shifted his sight to the bishop, who remained in the regalia he'd worn the day before. The bishop represented the most reputable of those gathered. "And it's your testimony that Sheriff Knox was the one who hired Shervin Gerami?"

"I can only report what I saw, Your Majesty, and that was Knox speaking to this Gerami fellow early on the morning of the ceremony. After they spoke, the sheriff handed over a purse. At the time, I thought nothing of it. I figured Knox was hiring him to be a sentry or for some other duty. Of course, when the bald man was found on the wall, beside the arbalest, it became clear to me that Knox was paying the man for a more despicable task."

"And the arbalest? Can anyone shed light on how Knox got that weapon?"

Chamberlain Wells looked to Fawkes, who nodded his permission. "I think I can, Your Majesty. The sheriff came to me with the specific request for a heavy crossbow."

"Did he say why?"

"No, but like the bishop, I had no reason to question his motives. Knox was the high sheriff and in charge of Dulgath's security. If he needed an arbalest, I figured there had to be a good reason."

They had gone over most of this at Brecken Moor the night before. Fawkes had explained his plan to hang the whole affair on Knox, claiming the sheriff had hired Royce and Hadrian as *consultants* while secretly planning to pin the murders on them. When Fawkes had grown suspicious of Knox he had warned the thieves. Then Fawkes and the thieves had worked to thwart the sheriff's plot. Augustine had been an eager supporter of the plan, and Royce thought he knew why.

The abbot had been in the room when Nysa changed nests. He'd seen the whole thing. Augustine might have been privy to the secret for years.

When it was Augustine's time to speak, the abbot embellished his version, painting Fawkes as a swashbuckling champion who fought the evil sheriff in a pitched battle, an epic sword fight that lasted "at least an hour." But then again, maybe that *was* how the abbot imagined it happening. His sort was prone to aggrandizing tales to advance their own agendas.

"One thing still escapes me," the king said. "Why would Sheriff Knox, an immigrant from Warric whom Beadle Dulgath appointed, want to kill Lady Dulgath? What could he possibly gain? Can you tell me that, Chrissy?"

They had gone over the story to make sure each had answers to anything the king might ask. Yet after an entire night of discussion, this question had never been raised.

Why did the sheriff do it?

A certain amount of sloppiness was understandable given the exhaustion Fawkes had exhibited after healing Scarlett Dodge and then Royce. But this was a pretty important point to overlook. Like everyone else gathered before the king, Royce watched Lord Fawkes with great anticipation.

Fawkes hesitated. He inspected his feet for a moment, then glanced warily not at the king, but at Bishop Parnell. Then he straightened, and, looking directly at Vincent, he said, "I believe the Nyphron Church is responsible."

The bishop's eyes nearly fell out, and the chamberlain gasped, clamping a palm over his mouth to stifle it.

"That's a serious charge," the king said, and Royce noted that for the first time the insulting tone was missing.

"And utterly absurd!" Parnell shouted.

"I have no proof, Your Majesty," Fawkes admitted. "And yet I'm sure this is so."

"Your Majesty, I—" Parnell started.

The king silenced the bishop with a hand. He kept his focus on Fawkes and said, "Explain your reasoning."

"My belief is the church is seeking to take control of Maranon. The newly appointed Earl Woodrow Braga of Swanwick is a self-professed Imperialist, replacing Earl Purim—an ardent Monarchist. Manzar has always been a bulwark for the church. And I suppose you could say my own father has had a spiritual awakening, as he, too, has shifted his allegiance, nodding in favor of the Imperialists."

"There is nothing *unseemly* about men of good standing taking a greater interest in their church," Parnell snapped.

"No," Fawkes said. "But there is when the church pressures and threatens nobles if they don't agree to side with them against their king. I spoke to Lady Dulgath several times after arriving here. She explained how her father had received repeated threats from the church. Beadle had remained strong and was able to weather their intimidation, but it seems they were taking a stronger stance with Lady Dulgath. She was told that if she refused to comply with their wishes, she would be replaced. I suspect if Knox had lived, there would have been a convincing argument for him to act as steward. As you so keenly pointed out, he'd already been appointed by Beadle himself and so would have been a likely candidate for the earl's successor."

"Who did she say was the source of those threats?" the king asked, allowing his eyes to flicker toward the bishop, who glared at Fawkes so hard he looked on the verge of exploding.

"She didn't," Fawkes replied without the slightest glance at Parnell. "Lady Dulgath was the very embodiment of discretion, Your Majesty. Nor could she trust me, given that my father is an Imperialist. I tried to explain how I had broken ties with him because I saw my father as a traitor to his king, but she only had my word. As you well know, that means nothing these days."

"I see." The king continued to stare at Fawkes with a fascinated expression, as if he were witnessing a magic trick and trying to figure out what he had overlooked.

"This is all a lie!" the bishop nearly screamed. He was red, and sweat beaded on his face.

In a perfectly calm and sensible tone, Fawkes said, "At best, I'm merely speculating. I've already explained I have no proof. I'm not accusing anyone of anything. His Majesty asked to understand my reasoning, and I've stated it."

The bishop gesticulated with hands that formed fists. His face looked as if he could chew through rocks. The king appeared oblivious as he stared with continued fascination at Fawkes.

"The church took you in after your financial fiasco, did it not?" Vincent asked Fawkes.

"They did."

"And what have you become but an ungrateful cur!" Parnell shouted.

"If it is true, that the church has backed you financially, why do you now stand before me, denouncing them?" Vincent asked Fawkes as if the bishop weren't there.

"I am my own man, Your Majesty. That should have been obvious when I left my father's house. My loyalty is to my king, and it cannot be bought with blood or gold."

"But it didn't prevent you from borrowing money falsely, using my name as collateral."

Fawkes faltered, and Royce thought he might finally have been tripped up, but then he realized this was no more than a dramatic pause. "For that I have no excuse, Your Majesty. It is a transgression that has long weighed on my heart and on my soul. I admit my wrongdoing and wish to make amends, to prove myself through deeds rather than words."

The king chuckled this time. "You do impress me, Christopher. I'm certain most of what I've heard is unadulterated codswallop, but...well done. Perhaps politics is more your talent than horse racing." Vincent crossed his arms and cast his sight across the assembled group. "Given so many witnesses of good standing, it's impossible for me to simply reject your explanation of recent events. That means, of course, I'm indebted to you, Christopher. You are to be rewarded. What would you ask of your king?"

This time Fawkes didn't hesitate. "These men were promised compensation for coming here." He gestured at Royce and Hadrian. "As they were instrumental in saving your life, and at considerable risk, I ask that you grant them the payment they were offered. I would pay them myself, but..." Fawkes pretended to reach for a purse that wasn't there.

"Yes, yes, of course, but what for yourself?" the king asked.

"For me? Nothing, Sire."

"Nothing?"

"I don't believe a man should be rewarded for doing his duty to protect his king."

The king smiled. Not a sneer, not an expression of mockery or amusement, but one of true approval.

He's done it, Royce thought, and couldn't have been more impressed if Fawkes had palmed the crown right off the old man's head.

"You say you want to prove yourself through deeds?" Vincent asked. "Very well. It seems I have a province without a ruler."

"Your Majesty, no!" Bishop Parnell exclaimed.

The king ignored him. "Christopher Fawkes, son of Oddsworth, I hereby appoint you Steward of Dulgath, in which capacity you will serve for three years. Should you, at the end of that time, prove a worthy administrator of these lands, I will bestow on you the title of earl." The king looked over at his scribe, who nodded.

He then faced Royce and Hadrian. "Now, what do I owe the two of you?"

"Fifty gold tenents," Royce said before Hadrian had the chance to open his mouth.

"Fifty?" Bishop Parnell said, shocked.

"It's what *Sheriff Knox* promised us," Royce told the bishop. "Being a clergyman, I wouldn't expect you to know the going rate of a quality assassin consultant."

Parnell bit his lip.

"You'll be paid," the king said, "but I must insist the two of you leave Maranon. I won't abide thieves and assassins in my kingdom, no matter what service they might have provided me."

Royce considered asking if he planned to exile Bishop Parnell as well but then thought better of it. He and Hadrian weren't on their way to the gallows and were being paid twice the agreed amount. Fawkes's advice to keep his mouth shut seemed wise after all.

The Fifth Thing

Hadrian exited the castle, feeling better the moment the sun hit him. Being in the Great Hall with so many robes and crowns had felt like being underwater; pressure was everywhere. Leaving as soon as they were paid was the smart thing to do. They shouldn't give the king time to come to his senses and reconsider, but as the reception broke up, Royce had lingered. Fawkes did as well.

I'll be out in a minute, Royce had told him. *I have a few things to talk to Lord Fawkes about before we go.*

This was fine with Hadrian. He had at least one question of his own to deal with, and, like Royce, he wanted to do so alone.

The courtyard was still a mess of storm-tossed banners and toppled chairs. The Dulgath standard still lay in the courtyard where Knox had pulled it down. The arbalest was gone. Vincent had likely ordered it secured moments after they'd left. Having one of those pointed at you was tantamount to looking through a big open door into the next world, an experience anyone—much less a king—wouldn't want to repeat.

Hadrian walked out the front gate, which was still wide open and lacking a guard.

Nothing changes here.

Hadrian looked up at the perfect sky with its perfect sun and puffball clouds.

Nothing at all.

Scarlett waited down the slope and a few yards off to the side with their horses. She was petting Dancer, stroking her neck and letting her tear up thin grass. As he approached, Scarlett looked up, saw him, tilted her head, and leaned out to peer around the horse. She smiled. "No one chasing you this time."

Hadrian glanced over his shoulder. "Nope."

"And Lord Fawkes?"

"Steward."

Scarlett looked puzzled and a bit disappointed. "Not earl?"

"He will be."

She thought about this and nodded. "Did you get paid?"

"We did indeed."

She smiled; then the expression vanished. "So you'll be leaving, then?"

He stopped beside Dancer, clapping her on the shoulder. The horse took no notice of him as she ate the grass. He looked over the horse's back at Scarlett. "Yes, but I was thinking..."

"A dangerous thing for you, I suspect." She grinned.

"You've been hanging around Royce too much." He pretended to sound hurt.

She dropped the grin. "Tell me, what have you been thinking?"

"You're a northern girl; you don't belong down here. I can't imagine you enjoy entertaining drunks in Wagner's tavern for thrown coins." He softened his tone. "You're smart, too. Good in a tight spot and incredibly brave. Took a sword to the stomach and only cried a little."

She scowled. "Didn't cry—eyes just watered."

"That's what crying is."

"I didn't *blubber*, didn't sob. It just hurt is all."

"I know it hurt, and I didn't mean to..." Hadrian sighed. "How did me complimenting you turn into—look, my point is, I was wondering if you'd like to come with us, back to Medford."

"And do what? Be what? Part of your little thieves' guild? I've already gone that way. Didn't work for me, remember?"

"Might be different this time."

She frowned at him.

"So you're just going to stay with Wagner and dance in his bar?"

THE FIFTH THING

"Actually…" She looked up at the walls of the castle. "Last night Lord Fawkes told me that if the king made him earl—and he was pretty sure he might—he planned on cleaning house. Getting rid of the ones he thought might be disloyal. The first to go would be Chamberlain Wells."

"And?"

"And he said if that happened, the job was mine."

Hadrian blinked. "Really?"

"You don't have to look so shocked."

"Sorry—I just—wow, that's huge."

She shrugged, embarrassed. "I told him I don't know anything about running a castle. Lord Fawkes said anyone could learn, but there were only a rare few he could trust. Have to admit…" Her eyes became glassy, and she reached up to wipe them clear. After a cough to clear her throat, she continued. "It felt good to be recognized like that. To be rewarded for something—for doing something good, you know?"

Hadrian's hopes collapsed, one by one, in rapid succession. A series of optimistic dreams, which had only started to take root hours before, winked out with painful pricks like a dozen nasty needles. A faint pressure squeezed his chest as muscles tightened. He nodded and continued to nod, buying himself time to swallow.

"You should definitely do that." He took another breath. "That's an incredible opportunity."

"It is, isn't it?"

He couldn't help thinking that she wanted him to convince her of something.

"I mean, I'm a daughter of a poor farmer, turned thief, turned failed wool spinner, and I'm going to be the chamberlain of Castle Dulgath. It's insane."

"I think you'll make a wonderful chamberlain."

She stared at him for a long moment as tears welled once more in her eyes. "Thank you for saying that."

"No—no, I mean it. I really do. Bet you look really good in blue, too."

"Aren't you just full of shoot and sugar."

"Maybe—I don't even know what that means."

"Neither do I. It's a local thing." She wiped her eyes again. "Look, Dulgath is missing a sheriff, and as chamberlain I bet I could convince the new steward to give you the job. You did okay as a constable."

"I was a lousy constable."

"Just don't drink the ale."

Hadrian smiled, but the edges of his lips turned downward as he did. "The king—your king—ordered us out of Maranon."

She looked as if he'd slapped her. "But you saved his life!"

Hadrian nodded. "Turns out he's prejudiced against thieves and assassins. Can't really blame him, I suppose."

Scarlett looked away then. Her hands found Dancer's neck again, and she stroked the horse while looking at the ground as if it had moved in an unpleasant and unexpected direction. Hadrian knew the feeling and gave her a moment. He clapped Dancer again. "You're spoiling my horse."

"When are you leaving?" Scarlett asked quietly. "Lady Dulgath's funeral is tomorrow. You're staying for that, aren't you? They're going to carry her up to the monastery to bury her next to her father. All the Dulgaths are up there."

"Actually, I think Royce is going to want to head out in just a few minutes. We've been here a long time, but…"

"But?" The single word lingered. Spoken softly, it sounded more like a cry, desperate and fearful.

The Fifth Thing

Hadrian placed his hand on hers. She grabbed it and squeezed. In that moment, Hadrian hated Dancer as she stood between them. If she weren't there, he would have…but far more than a horse separated him from Scarlett Dodge. Of the three of them, Hadrian realized Dancer was the wisest.

Hadrian gave in, letting go of Scarlett's hand and simply shrugging. Looking at her became too hard, too painful. He lowered his head and focused on Dancer's white socks. He wasn't accustomed to losing battles, and while this wasn't one, he felt the loss just the same. He was helpless, beaten by powers beyond his ability to affect.

Dancer took a few steps to the right.

Hadrian lifted his head and saw red hair, lots of red hair. Arms swung around his neck as Scarlett's body pressed against his. She pulled, rising up on her toes to kiss him. Her lips pressed against his, gentle and soft, but firm—hungry. Fingers slid up his neck, reaching into his hair. He heard a sound, a soft hum. Hadrian couldn't tell which of them made it. Scarlett's lips parted slightly and lingered briefly on his. Then her hands released, the arms drew back, and those lips stole away, taking his breath with them.

Lord Fawkes led Royce to Nysa Dulgath's bedroom, which looked unchanged from the last time he was there.

"Must be strange," Fawkes said.

"What?" Royce asked. At that moment, he could think of half a dozen things fitting the description.

"Coming in here through the door." Fawkes smiled.

"Why are we here?"

"Two reasons." The lord crossed to the table with the shell collection, and opened the drawer. When he turned around he held out a brilliant white dagger. "Hadrian said you lost this."

"Thank you. I wasn't planning on leaving the providence until I found this."

Fawkes raised a brow. "Really? Give it back then. I'll have someone bury it."

"Too late." Royce said as he put the dagger away. "What's the other reason you asked me here?"

"I wanted to show you this," Fawkes said, pulling the cloth-covered painting from behind the headboard of the bed. He set it up on the desk. "Sherwood spent two months painting this portrait of Nysa Dulgath. I wanted you to see it. Frame got a little banged up recently, but I put it back together."

Fawkes threw back the cloth.

Royce stared at the image of a young female elf. Her ears came to points; her eyes, a brilliant blue, were teardrop-shaped. Cheekbones were sharp and high, but the most surprising thing was that the elven girl was entirely bald—that and the fact she didn't look like the elves Royce knew. Something in her face, in those piercing blue eyes—she wasn't ashamed of who she was. This person was proud.

"This is you?" he asked.

"What I looked like before I died. I don't know how Sherwood did it. I don't know how he knew. Perhaps he was more than an artist. Maybe he unknowingly practiced The Art."

Royce wasn't sure what the difference was, but he didn't want to interrupt her.

"Sherwood had the ability to see people. Really see them. He told me that, but I didn't believe. He was killed before I saw this. Before I could tell him he was right."

"Doesn't matter." Royce took a step closer to the image. "He knew."

"Yes." Fawkes nodded. He took a labored breath, then spun on his left heel and moved to the window, leaving Royce with the painting. "Do you...do you find it ugly?"

Royce reached up and touched the dry ridges left behind by the paintbrush. "No."

"I can't help wondering what Sherwood would have painted if he'd done your portrait."

Royce found the thought more than disturbing.

"I'm more human than anything," he said. "You can see that just by looking at me. I honestly don't even know how you knew."

Fawkes turned around and stared at him in surprise. "The same way *you* knew about me. Didn't take you but a second. You came in the door ready to kill Christopher Fawkes but didn't. What stopped you? How did you know?"

He shrugged. "The way you moved, the way you stood, how you talked. I recognized it. I recognized you."

"We are more than the bodies we inhabit," Fawkes said. "They're little more than clothes, and yet we judge so much by them." He laughed bitterly. "I, of all people, should understand this truth, and yet..." He looked at the painting. "I never gave Sherwood a chance. He saw the truth in me, but I refused to see the same in him."

Fawkes took a step toward Royce. "You could stay."

"Your king would object, and that would ruin your chance to be earl."

"I'm not afraid of the king."

Royce nodded. "No, I don't suppose you are. But you also don't want to start a war because you're lonely."

Fawkes scowled at him. "I'm really starting to hate this woman of yours."

"Goodbye, Lord Fawkes," he said, and moved to the door. Before exiting, he stopped. "The weather here—you control it somehow, don't you? That's why it's always sunny and warm, but not too warm."

"What's your point? You don't like fair weather?"

The Death of Dulgath

"Too much of anything isn't good."

"Goodbye, Royce Melborn."

The inhabitants of Brecken Dale lined the streets of the village. Everyone was out: husbands, wives, and children held close to thighs. Each was dressed in their best set of clothes—which for many was their only set. But the collars were straight, the shoes bright, the hair neatly combed. Not a hood or hat could be seen, and all eyes were on Royce, Scarlett, and Hadrian. The crowd had been waiting for them.

Royce's first reaction was concern; his second was suspicion. *Has someone peeked into the ramshackle church this morning?* Given how the townsfolk felt about Pastor Payne, Royce didn't think so. *Only when the stench becomes too unbearable will anyone bother to open that door.* The following funeral will likely be attended by the fewest people needed to carry the body to a shallow, unmarked hole.

Why the villagers were out, each watching them with wide eyes and grins, eluded Royce. Given the numbers, the turnout had to be nearly everyone. One father went to the trouble of hoisting his son to his shoulders so the lad could see well. Even Scarlett looked puzzled.

"By Mar!" she said when they came into view of the village market. The place was full of folk. "It's like a fair day."

Wagner, Clem, Brook, and Gill stood with the others.

"Wag?" Scarlett asked, getting down from her horse. "What's going on?" She tied the animal to the post and joined him.

"They know what you did," Wagner replied. "What all of you did, and tried to do for Lady Dulgath, and what you've done for Lord Fawkes."

THE FIFTH THING

"How?" Royce asked.

"Small town, people talk, and I might have mentioned something." The bartender beamed a grin. Scarlett gave him a weak shove that made them both laugh.

Royce looked out over the gathering, boys and girls stared back at him with awe.

We're celebrities. He shivered and thanked Maribor they were banned by the king.

Hadrian didn't get off his horse. He'd said his goodbyes. He and Scarlett exchanged one last look; then she bowed her head, turned away, and headed for the sheltered ivy of Caldwell House. Hadrian watched her go. The door closed behind her, but he continued to look, even then. After a moment more he turned to Royce and asked, "You ready?"

Royce nodded enthusiastically.

Hadrian urged his horse forward, wading through the bodies that were slow to make a path. Royce followed.

"Thank you for everything you did," said a woman, holding a less-than-content chicken in the crook of one arm. She reached out the other hand to touch Royce's leg. He recoiled and gave his mount a kick, making the dawdlers jump back. Once clear of the crowd, he gave another light kick and his horse broke into a trot, heading for the pass. He kept up the quick pace until clear of the village and the nearby farms. Only then did he let his mount settle back into her relaxed walk.

Hadrian caught up, and they rode side by side. Royce expected he'd talk. For once, they had a lot to discuss. The two hadn't had a private moment in more than a day, and a lot had happened over that time. But although the sky was clear, as it always was in Dulgath, Hadrian didn't say a word. He spent most of the trip looking at his reins and playing with the knot.

Farms faded behind them as the trail began its upward grade. Even hunting shacks disappeared as the left side of the path fell away and the right became a cliff. They were nearing the gap that led out of Dulgath and back into Greater Maranon, to that open world where herds of horses roamed.

They'd reach Mehan sometime after dark and get a room at one of the inns. The next morning, they'd head due north, and if they pushed hard, they'd make Ratibor by nightfall. An easy day would see them in Aquesta, but he'd press Hadrian to keep going. With luck, they would reach Medford in five, maybe even four days.

Royce wanted—needed—to see Gwen's face again. Just knowing they were headed that way made him feel better.

She must be very special. You're turning down a title and an estate that would make you wealthy and respected for the rest of your life.

He'd would never admit it, not to Hadrian, and certainly not to Gwen—didn't even like thinking it to himself—but somehow Gwen had become his *fifth thing.* To survive, Royce had only ever required four things: air, food, water, and sleep. He was less bothered by heat and cold than others and could live in a forest or field if need be. But those other four things were absolutes.

Reluctantly, he had discovered Gwen had become the fifth. He could last longer without her than any of the others, but if too much time past, he felt the effects. *Sick* wasn't the right word; *empty* was closer, but even it didn't fit. *Thin.* He nodded to himself at the thought. That was it. He felt translucent, as if less of him existed when she wasn't there.

I just never noticed how little of me existed before; I was a shadow without a person.

He didn't know when it had happened or how he'd let it happen, but somehow when he was without her he felt less than whole. Gwen had stolen part of him and—*No, she hasn't taken anything. She's given me something I've never had, and now I can't live without it.* The idea was unsettling, and he bristled, frowning at himself under his hood.

Royce began to wish that Hadrian would start talking, some nice pointless blathering about flowers on the roadside or how a cloud looked like a girl he'd once known, except that she parted her hair on the other side of her head.

Then, as if Hadrian could read minds, he said, "Well, look at that."

Royce glanced over, assuming Hadrian would be pointing at a rock and insisting it resembled a turnip. Instead, he found his partner staring back toward the village.

Fearing that the villagers had changed their opinions and were now in some fanatical pursuit, Royce whirled his mount around and then sat, stunned.

From their position high on the ridge, they could once again see the whole valley of Dulgath, the village below, the castle and the ocean beyond. And there, arching over all of it, was a rainbow. Clear as stained glass it stood out beneath a single gray cloud as if painted for them.

"What do you suppose that means?" Hadrian asked.

"It means it's raining down there," Royce said. "But there's sunshine, too."

Afterword

Well, there you have it. I hope you've enjoyed reading *The Death of Dulgath*; I know I certainly had a blast reuniting with the pair. Some may know that my wife has a bit of a crush on Hadrian, and there is nothing better than seeing her just before and during a new Riyria tale. That said, I can always write stories for Robin and be happy leaving it at that. Publishing them is another matter entirely, and as I've mentioned elsewhere, whether there will be additional Riyria books "out and about in the world" will depend largely on the desires of *other people*. If the pair starts to overstay their welcome, I have plenty of ideas I can turn my attention to. If people want further adventures, there is no one more excited about that prospect than me…well except maybe Robin. So, don't be shy; drop me a line at michael.sullivan.dc@gmail.com. I might even have a little free short story for you as a way of saying thanks for taking the time to write.

Before we part, I have a few other things I'd like to bring up. First, I want to let you know about **www.michaelsullivan-author. com/maps.html** where you can find high resolution copies of the maps which will allow you to zoom in and see more detail then I can provide in either the print or e-book versions.

Also, I want to take just a minute to encourage you to leave a review (or simply a rating) at sites like Goodreads or your favorite retailer: Amazon, Audible, or Barnes & Noble. Good, bad or indifferent, all I care about is honesty. I'm not sure readers understand just how important these reviews are. Being able to hear from third-party sources can really help those on the fence decide if the book is right for them. Your comments don't have to be comprehensive, just a few words about what you liked (or didn't like) will help others decide. Even if that means they don't pick up the book, that's fine. I realize that no book is a good fit for everyone, and I'd rather have that reader go on to find a different book they can love, than spend time reading my book that turned out not to be a good fit for their particular tastes.

Speaking of Goodreads, I started up a private and secret group there called, *The Dark Room*. It is a place for lovers of the series to hang out. In *The Dark Room* I can answer questions, talk about things that aren't yet public knowledge, and even offer exclusive extras from time to time. If you want an invitation to join, just email. Please put DARK ROOM INVITE in the subject line so it'll stand out.

Lastly, or maybe second to last, I wanted to mention that if you read *The Death of Dulgath* in print, or listened to it on audio, then I want to make the ebook available to you at no cost. Again, just drop me an email, and let me know what file format you would prefer, and I'll send one over. A copy of your receipt would be highly appreciated, but I'm not going to make a big deal about "proof of purchase." After all, it's not like you won't be able to find a pirated copy of the book.

After finishing a book, there are always little things that cross my mind that I wish I could talk about. Things like why I decided path A versus path B and of course those funny little things I thought of but just couldn't put into the book (mainly because they just didn't fit). Robin and I shared a great laugh about something that would have been especially fun in chapter twenty-four. In any case, we've collected all these little odds and ends, along with some behind the scenes stuff in a free e-book called *The Making of the Death of Dulgath*. It won't be made public on e-book sites because it'll contain massive spoilers. For this reason, I only give it away to people after they've finished reading. And you guessed it—just send me an email to get your copy.

AFTERWORD

Okay, I hear the music playing me off the stage, so I'm going to wrap this up. For those that don't know, I once quit writing for over a decade, and during that time I never thought I would have anyone other than friends and family read my stories. That thought was more than a little depressing. Even when I couldn't stay away any longer, and started writing again, I never intended to publish. It was a dream that I had considered out of my reach. I just mentioned how rewarding it is to see my wife enjoy my books. Imagine getting similar reactions from people I've never met. I'm a storyteller, but telling stories in the echo chamber of my own empty room isn't much fun. Well, it actually is, but sharing the tales, and hearing that people have recommended them to loved ones—well that, as the commercial says, is priceless.

People online often thank me for being so "interactive with my readers." I find this almost laughable. Don't they know that my actions are selfish? That I get just as much (and probably more) out of the exchanges than they do? The Internet has provided us many advances in the ability to communicate with one another, but none is greater than uniting people with common interests. So, in case I've not made it crystal clear by now…I just want to close by saying thanks, and please feel free to drop me a line. Truly, opening my inbox and seeing messages from readers is the best part of my day.

Sneak Peek
AGE OF MYTH

Shortly before starting *The Death of Dulgath*, I finished a five-book series called The First Empire, which I sold to Del Rey (a fantasy imprint of Penguin Random House). The first book, *Age of Myth*, will be released June 7, 2016. Here's a bit about it, as well as the first chapter. I hope you'll take a look, and if you like what you see, please consider pre-ordering a copy. This particular series is set 3,000 years before the time of Riyria and tells the *true story* of how Novron saved mankind and formed the First Empire. Apparently the history you've been told isn't *exactly* the truth.

DISCOVER THE TRUTH IN MYTHS AND THE LIES OF LEGENDS.

Since time immemorial, humans have worshipped the gods they call Fhrey, truly a race apart: invincible in battle, masters of magic, and seemingly immortal. But when a god falls to a human blade, the balance of power between men and those they thought were gods changes forever. Now, only a few stand between humankind and annihilation: Raithe, reluctant to embrace his destiny as the God Killer. Suri, a young seer burdened by signs of impending doom. And Persephone, who must overcome personal tragedy to lead her people. The Age of Myth is over; the time of rebellion has begun.

Chapter One
OF GODS AND MEN

In the days of darkness before the war, men were called Rhune. We lived in rhune-land or Rhulyn as it was once known. We had little to eat and much to fear. What we feared most were the gods across the Bern River where men were not allowed. Today most people believe the war began with the Battle of Grandford, but it actually started on a day in early spring when two men crossed the river. — The Book of Brin

Raithe's first impulse was to pray. Curse, cry, scream, pray—that's what people did in their last minutes of life. But praying struck Raithe as absurd, given his problem was the angry god twenty feet away. Gods weren't known for their tolerance, and this one appeared on the verge of striking them both dead. Neither Raithe nor his father had noticed the god approach. The river made enough noise to mask an army's passage. Raithe would have preferred an army.

Dressed in shimmering clothes, the god sat on a horse and was accompanied by two servants on foot. They were men, but dressed in the same remarkable clothing. All three silent, watching.

"Hey?" Raithe caught his father's attention.

Herkimer was down on one knee, sweating as he opened the deer's stomach with his knife. After Raithe had landed a spear in the stag's side, he and his father spent most of the day chasing it. Herkimer had stripped off his wool leigh mor as well as his shirt before gutting the deer. Not so much because he was hot—the spring days were still chilly—but because opening a deer's belly was a bloody business. "What?" He looked up.

Raithe jerked his head toward the god, and his father's sight tracked to the three figures. The old man's eyes widened. The color left his face, and he licked his lips. His expression did nothing to put Raithe at ease.

I knew this was a bad idea, Raithe thought.

Herkimer had been confident and so reassuring that crossing the forbidden river would solve all their problems. But he'd mentioned his certainty enough times to make Raithe wonder. Now the old man looked as if he'd forgotten how to breathe. Herkimer wiped his knife on the deer's side before slipping it into his belt and getting to his feet.

"Ah…ah…um," Raithe's father began with all the eloquence of a croaking toad. Herkimer looked at the half-gutted deer, then back at the god. "It's…ah…okay."

Such was the sum total of his father's wisdom, his grand defense for their high crime of trespassing on divine land. Raithe didn't know if slaughtering one of their deer was also an offense but assumed it didn't help their situation. Raithe's stomach sank. He had no idea what he'd expected his father to say—but something more than that.

Not surprisingly, the god wasn't appeased, and the three continued to stare with growing looks of irritation.

They were on a tiny point of open meadowland where two large rivers met. A pine forest, thick and rich, grew a short distance up the slope, while down toward the point lay a stony beach. Beneath a snow-gray blanket of sky, the converging rivers made the only sound. Only minutes earlier Raithe had seen the tiny field as a paradise. That was then.

Raithe took a slow breath and reminded himself that he didn't have experience with gods or their expressions. He'd never witnessed a god up close, never seen beech-leaf-shaped ears, eyes blue as the sky, or hair that spilled like molten gold. Such smooth skin and white teeth were beyond reason. This wasn't a being born of the earth, but of air and light. His billowing robes wafted in the breeze and shimmered in the sun, proclaiming an otherworldly glory. The harsh, judgmental glare was exactly the expression Raithe expected from an immortal being.

The horse was an even bigger surprise. Raithe's father had told him about such animals, but until then Raithe hadn't believed. His old man had a habit of embellishing the truth, and for more than twenty years, he'd heard the tales. After a few drinks, he'd tell everyone how he killed five men with a single swing or fought the North Wind to a standstill. The older he got, the bigger the stories. But this four-hooved tall tale was looking back at him with large, glossy eyes, and when the horse shook its head, Raithe wondered if a god's mount understood speech.

"No, really—it's okay," Raithe's father told them again, maybe thinking they hadn't heard his previous genius. "I'm allowed here." He took a step forward and pointed to the medal hanging from a strip of hide amid the dirt and pine needles stuck to the sweat of his chest. Half-naked, sunbaked, with bloodstains up to his elbows, and grinning through a wild beard, his father was the embodiment of a mad barbarian. Raithe wouldn't have believed him either. "See this?" his father went on. The burnished metal clutched by thick, ruddy fingers reflected the midday sun. "I fought for your people against the Gula-Rhune in the High Spear Valley. I did well. A Fhrey commander gave me this, said I had earned a reward."

"Dureyan clan," the taller servant told the god, his tone somewhere between disappointment and disgust.

The servant, a gangly man who lacked a beard but sported a long nose, sharp cheeks, and small clever eyes reminded Raithe of a weasel or a fox, and he wasn't fond of either. Raithe also didn't like the servile manner in which the man stood: stooped, eyes low, and hands clasped in front of him. He wore a rich-looking silver torc around his neck—both servants did. The jewelry must be some mark of station, he guessed, or perhaps a reward.

What kind of men travel with a god?

"That's right. I'm Herkimer, son of Hiemdal, and this is my son Raithe."

"You've broken the law," the servant stated. The nasal tone even sounded like how a weasel might talk.

"No—no, it's not like that. Not at all."

The lines on his father's face deepened, and his lips stretched tighter. He stopped walking forward, but his two fingers held the medal up like a magic talisman, his eyes hopeful. "This proves what I'm saying, that I earned a reward. See, I sort of figured we"—he gestured toward Raithe—"my son and I could live on this little point." He waved at the meadow, which ran down the slope to the confluence of the Bern and Urum rivers. "We don't need much. Hardly anything really. You see, on our side of the river—back in Dureya—the dirt's no good. We can't grow anything, and there's nothing to hunt."

The pleading in his father's voice was something Raithe hadn't heard before and didn't like.

"You're not allowed here." This time it was the other servant, the balding one. Like the tall, weasel-faced fellow, he also lacked a proper beard, as if growing one was a thing that needed to be taught. The lack of hair exposed in fine detail a decidedly sour expression.

"But you don't understand. I *fought* for your people. I *bled* for your people. I *lost three sons* fighting for your kind. And I was promised a reward." He held out the medal again, but the god didn't look at it. He stared past them, focusing on some distant, irrelevant point.

Herkimer let go of the medal. "If this spot is a problem, we'll move. My son actually liked another place west of here. We'd be farther away from you. Would that be better?"

Though he still didn't look at them, the god appeared even more annoyed and finally spoke, "You will obey."

An average voice. Raithe was disappointed. He had expected thunder.

The god then addressed his servants in the divine language. Raithe's father had taught him some of their tongue. He wasn't fluent but knew enough to understand the god didn't want them to have weapons on his side of the river. A moment later, the tall servant relayed the message in Rhunic, "Only Fhrey are permitted to possess weapons west of the Bern. Cast yours in the river."

Herkimer glanced at their gear piled near a stump and in a resigned voice told Raithe, "Get your spear and do as they say."

"And the sword off your back," the tall servant said.

Herkimer looked shocked and glanced over his shoulder as if he'd forgotten the weapon was there. Then he faced the god and spoke directly to him in the Fhrey language, "*This is my family blade. I cannot throw it away.*"

The god sneered, showing teeth.

"It's a sword," the servant insisted.

Herkimer hesitated only a moment. "Okay, okay, fine. We'll go back across the river, right now. C'mon, Raithe."

The god made an unhappy sound.

"After you give up the sword," the servant said.

Herkimer glared. "This copper has been in my family for generations."

"It's a weapon. Toss it down."

Herkimer looked at his son, a sheepish, sidelong glance.

While he may not have been a good father—wasn't as far as Raithe was concerned—he'd instilled one thing in all his sons: pride. Self-respect came from the ability to defend oneself. Such things gave a man dignity. In all of Dureya, in their entire clan, Herkimer was the only man to wield a sword—a *metal* blade. While pathetic in comparison to the god's sword, whose hilt was intricately etched and encrusted with gems, his father's blade was wrought from beaten copper. Its marred, dull sheen was the color of a summer sunset, and legend held that the short-bladed heirloom was mined and fashioned by a genuine Dherg smith. That weapon defined Herkimer, so much so that most enemy clans knew his father as Coppersword—a feared and respected title. His father could never give up that blade.

The rush of the river was cut by the cry of a hawk, soaring above. Birds were known to be the embodiment of omens, and Raithe didn't take the heavenly wail as a positive sign. In its eerie echo, his father faced the god. "I can't give you this sword."

Raithe couldn't help but smile. Herkimer, son of Hiemdal, of Clan Dureya wouldn't bend so far, not even for a god.

The smaller servant took the horse's lead as the god dismounted.

Raithe watched—impossible not to. The way he moved, so graceful, fluid, and poised, was mesmerizing. On the ground, he wasn't tall, shorter than both Raithe and his father, who admittedly were both large men. The god also wasn't as broad or as muscled. Raithe and his father had spent their lives building shoulders and arms by wielding spear and shield. The god, on the other hand, appeared delicate, as if he had lived bedridden and spoonfed. If the Fhrey were a man, Raithe wouldn't have feared him. Given the disparity between them in weight and height, Raithe wouldn't fight him, even if challenged. To engage in such an unfair match would be cruel, and Raithe wasn't cruel. His brothers had gotten his share of that particular trait.

"You don't understand. This sword has been handed down from father to son—"

The god rushed forward punching Herkimer in the stomach. As he bent over from the blow, the god stole the sword from off his back. The copper came free with a dull scrape, and while Herkimer was catching his breath, the god examined the weapon with revulsion. Then, shaking his head, the god turned his back on Herkimer to show his servant the pitiable blade. Instead of joining the god in mocking the weapon, the servant cringed. Raithe saw the future through the weasel man's face, for he was the first to notice Herkimer's reaction.

Raithe's father drew the knife from his belt and lunged.

This time the god didn't disappoint. With astounding speed, he whirled and drove the copper blade into Raithe's father's chest. Herkimer's forward momentum did the work of running the sword deep. The fight ended the moment it began. His father gasped and fell, the sword still in his chest.

Raithe didn't think. If he had paused, even for an instant, he might have reconsidered, but there was more of his father in him than he wanted to believe. The sword being the only weapon within reach, he pulled the copper from his father's body. With all his might, Raithe swung at the god's neck. He fully expected the blade to cut clean through, but the copper sliced only air as the divine being dodged. The god drew his weapon as Raithe swung again. The two swords met. A dull *ping* sounded, and the weight in Raithe's hands vanished along with most of the blade. When he finished his swing, only the hilt of his family's heritage remained—the rest flew through the air and landed in a tuft of young pines.

The god stared at him with a disgusted smirk. "Not worth dying for, was it?"

Then the god raised his blade once more as Raithe shuffled backward.

Too slow! Too slow!

His retreat was futile. Raithe was dead. Years of training and combat told him so. In that instant before understanding became reality, he had the chance to regret his entire life.

I've done nothing, he thought as his muscles tightened for the expected burst of pain.

It never came.

Raithe had lost track of the servants—so had the god. Neither expected, nor saw, the tall, weasel-faced man slam his master in the back of the head with a river rock the size and shape of a round loaf of bread. Raithe only realized it when the god collapsed, and behind him stood the servant holding the rock.

"Run," the servant said. "With any luck, his head will hurt too much to chase us when he awakes."

"What have you done!" the other servant shouted. His eyes were wide while he backed away, pulling the god's horse with him.

"Calm down," the one holding the rock told the other servant.

Raithe looked at his father, lying on his back. Herkimer's eyes were still open, as if watching clouds. Raithe had cursed his father many times over the years. The man had neglected his family, allowed his brothers to beat him, and was away when his mother and sister died. In some ways—many ways—Raithe hated his father, but at that moment, what he saw on the ground was the man who had taught him to fight and not give in. Herkimer had done the best with what he had, and what he had was a life trapped on barren soil because the gods made capricious demands. Raithe's father never stole, cheated, or held his tongue when something needed to be said. He was a hard man, a cold man, but one who had the courage to stand up for himself and what was right. What Raithe saw on the ground at his feet was the last of his dead family.

He felt the broken sword in his hands.

"No!" the servant holding the horse cried out as Raithe drove the remainder of the jagged copper blade through the god's throat.

"He's gone," the tall, weasel-faced servant said, trotting back to the riverbank covered in sweat and shaking his head.

Both servants had run off, one on the horse, the other chasing after. Raithe assumed they had fled, a sensible choice. Now the one who had wielded the rock returned.

"Meryl's gone. He's not the best rider, but he doesn't have to be. The horse knows the way back to Alon Rhist." He paused and stared at Raithe. "What are you doing?"

Raithe was standing over the body of the god. He'd picked up the Fhrey's sword and was holding the tip pressed against the god's throat. "How long does it usually take?"

"How long does what take?"

"For them to get up."

"He's dead. Dead people don't generally *get up*," the servant said.

Concerned about taking his eyes off the god, Raithe ventured only the briefest glance at the servant. He was bent over with hands on knees, struggling to catch his breath. "What are you talking about?"

"What are *you* talking about?"

"I want to know how long we have before he gets up. If it's minutes, I'll wait." Raithe looked over at the servant as an idea came to him. "If I cut off his head, will it take longer?"

The servant rolled his eyes. "He's not getting up! You killed him."

"My Tetlin ass! That's a god—gods don't die. They're immortal."

"Really not so much," the servant said, and to Raithe's shock he kicked the god's body. It barely moved. He kicked it again, and the head rocked to one side, sand sticking to his cheek. "See? Dead. Get it? Not immortal. Not a god, just a Fhrey. They die. There's a difference between long lived and immortal. Immortal means you can't die…even if you want to. Fact is, we're a lot more similar than we'd like to think."

"We're nothing alike. Look at him." Raithe pointed at the fallen Fhrey.

"Oh yes," the servant replied. "He's so different. He has only one head, walks on two feet, and has two hands and ten fingers. You're right—nothing like us at all."

The servant looked down at the body and sighed. "His name was Shegon. An incredibly talented harp player, a cheat at cards, and a *brideeth eyn mer*—which is to say…" The servant paused. "No, there's no other way to say that other than he wasn't well liked. And now he's dead."

Raithe looked over suspiciously.

Is he lying? Trying to put me off guard?

"You're wrong," Raithe said with full conviction. "Have you ever seen a dead Fhrey? I haven't. My father hasn't. No one I've ever known has. And they don't age."

"They do, just very slowly."

Raithe shook his head. "No, they don't. My father said he saw one as a boy—met the same one thirty-five years later and he was exactly the same."

"Of course he was. I just told you they age slowly. Fhrey can live for thousands of years. A bumblebee lives for only a few months. To a bumblebee, you appear immortal."

Raithe wasn't fully convinced, but it would explain the blood. He hadn't expected any. In retrospect, he shouldn't have attacked the Fhrey at all. Stupid is what it was. His father had taught him not to start a fight he couldn't win, and fighting an immortal god fell squarely in that category, but then again it was his father who had started the whole thing.

Sure is a lot of blood.

An ugly pool had formed underneath the god, staining the grass and his glistening robes. His neck still had the gash, a nasty, jagged tear like a second mouth. Raithe had expected it to miraculously heal or maybe simply vanish. When the god rose, he wouldn't have his sword, and Raithe would be prepared. He should easily lay him out again. Raithe was strong—he could best most men in Dureya, which meant he could best most men. Even his father would have thought twice about making him too angry, but this was a god.

Raithe stared down at the Fhrey, whose eyes were open and rolled up. The gash in his throat was wider now. A god—a real god—would never permit kicks from a servant. "Okay, maybe they aren't immortal." He relaxed and took a step back.

"My name is Malcolm," the servant said. "Yours is Raithe?"

"Uh-huh," he said, slipping the god's naked blade into his belt. With one last glare at the god, Raithe lifted his father's body and carried it up the slope.

"Now what are you doing?" Malcolm asked.

"Can't bury him down here. These rivers are bound to flood this plain out."

"*Bury* him? When word gets back to Alon Rhist, the Fhrey will…" He looked sick just thinking about it. "We need to leave."

"Go ahead."

Raithe laid his father on a small hill in the meadow. It wasn't much, but it would have to do. Looking back at the god's ex-servant, he found him staring in disbelief.

Malcolm started to laugh, then stopped, confused. "You don't understand. Glyn is a fast horse—has the stamina of a wolf. Meryl will reach Alon Rhist by nightfall. He'll tell them everything to save himself. They'll send a hunting party to find us. We need to get moving."

"Go on," Raithe said, taking Herkimer's medal—a keepsake to wear. They had so little. Then he closed his father's eyes. He couldn't remember having touched the old man's face before.

"You need to go, too."

"After I bury my father."

"The Rhune is dead."

Raithe cringed at the word. "He was a *man.*"

"Rhune—man—same thing."

"Not to me—and not to him." Raithe returned to the riverbank. The whole of the point where the Urum and Bern rivers converged was littered with thousands of stones similar in size to the one the servant had used to bludgeon the god. The problem wasn't finding them but deciding from the vast number which to pick up.

The servant stood with his hands on hips, glaring with an expression somewhere between astonishment and anger. "It will take hours to cover him. You're wasting time."

Raithe crouched and picked up a rock. The top was baked warm by the sun, the bottom damp, cool, and covered in wet sand. "He deserves a proper burial and would have done the same for me." Raithe found it ironic given his father had rarely shown him any kindness, but it was true. Herkimer would have faced death to see his son properly buried. "Besides, do you have any idea what can happen to the spirit of an unburied body?"

The man stared back, bewildered.

"They return as manes to haunt you for not showing the proper respect. And manes can be vicious." Raithe hoisted another large sand-colored rock and walked them up the slope. "My father could be a real cul when he was alive. I don't need him stalking me for the rest of my life."

"But—"

"But what?" Raithe set the rocks down near his father's shoulders. He'd do the outline first before starting the pile. "He's not your father. I don't expect you to stay."

"That's not the point."

"What *is* the point?"

The servant hesitated, and Raithe took the opportunity to return to the bank and search out more rocks.

"I need your help," the man finally said.

Raithe picked up a large stone and carried it up the bank, clutched against his stomach. "With what?"

"You know how to—well, you know—live—out here." The servant looked at the deer carcass that had gathered a host of flies. "You can hunt, cook, and find shelter, right? You know what berries to eat, which animals you can pet, and which to run away from."

"You don't pet any animals."

"See! Good example of how little I know about this sort of thing. Alone, I'd be dead in a day or two—frozen stiff, buried in a landslide, or gored by some antlered beast."

Raithe set the stone and returned down the slope clapping his hands together to clean off the sand. "Makes sense."

"Of course it makes sense. I'm a sensible fellow. And if you were sensible, we'd go—now."

Raithe lifted another rock. "If you're bent on sticking with me and in such a hurry, you might consider helping."

The man looked at the riverbank filled with rounded stones and sighed. "Do we have to use such big ones?"

"Big ones for the bottom, smaller ones on top."

"Sounds like you've done this before."

"People die often where I come from, and we have a lot of rocks." He wiped his brow with his forearm, pushing back the mat of dark hair. Raithe had rolled the woolen sleeves of his under tunic back. The day wasn't warm, but the work made him sweat. He was thinking of taking his leigh mor and leather off, but decided against it. Burying his father should be a miserable task. A son should feel something at such a time, and if uncomfortable was the best he could manage, Raithe would settle for that.

Malcolm set down a pair of rocks, letting Raithe place them. He paused to rub his hands clean.

"Okay, Malcolm," Raithe said, "you need to pick bigger ones or we'll be here forever."

Malcolm scowled but gathered up two good size stones and carried them under his arms like melons. He walked unsteadily in sandals. Thin, with a simple strap, they were ill suited to the landscape. Raithe's clothes were shoddy—sewn scraps of wool with leather accents, which he'd cured himself—but they were durable.

Raithe searched for and found a small, smooth stone.

"I thought you wanted bigger rocks?" Malcolm asked.

"This isn't for the pile." Raithe opened his father's right hand and exchanged the rock for his father's hunting knife. "He'll need it to get to Rel or Eberdeen if he's worthy—Nifrel if he's not."

"Oh, right."

After outlining the body, Raithe piled the stones from the feet upward. He wished he had an extra blanket to lay over his father. He didn't relish setting rocks on his exposed face. Instead, he cut pine boughs, which did a fine job. In the process, he found the other end of his father's sword laying in the brush. He dropped it in the scabbard and considered leaving the copper with Herkimer, but grave robbers would take it. His father had died for the shattered blade; it deserved to be cared for.

Raithe glanced at the Fhrey once more to be sure. "You're certain he won't get up?"

Malcolm looked over from where he was lifting a rock. "Positive. Shegon *is* dead."

Together they hoisted a dozen more rocks onto the growing pile before Raithe asked, "Why were you with him?"

Malcolm looked over, surprised. He pointed to the torc around his neck as if it explained everything. Raithe was puzzled. Then he noticed the necklace was a complete circle. The ring of metal wasn't a torc, not jewelry at all—it was a collar.

Not a servant—a slave.

The sun was low in the sky when they dropped the last rocks to complete the mound. Malcolm washed in the river while Raithe sang his mourning song. Then he slung his father's broken blade over his shoulder, adjusted the Fhrey's sword in his belt, and gathered up his things and those of his father. They didn't have much: two wooden shields, a bag containing a good hammer stone, a rabbit pelt Raithe planned to make into a pouch as soon as it cured, the last of the cheese, the single blanket they had shared, a stone hand ax, his father's knife, and Raithe's spear.

"Where to?" Malcolm asked. His face and hair were sweat covered, and the man had nothing, not even a sharpened stick to defend himself.

"Here, sling this blanket over your shoulder—tie it tight—and take my spear."

"I don't know how to use a spear."

"It's not complicated. Just point and stick."

Raithe looked around. Going home didn't make sense. That was back east, closer to Alon Rhist. Besides, his family was gone.

The clan would still welcome him, but it was impossible to build a life in Dureya. They could cross the Urum River and push west into Avrlyn, nothing but wilderness out there. They might be able to disappear, but he'd have to get past the other Fhrey strongholds. They had a series of outposts along the western rivers, a series of fortresses like Alon Rhist built to keep men like him out. His father had warned about the fortresses of Merredydd and Seon Hall, but he never said exactly where they were. Raithe didn't like the idea of walking into one. And even if he did get by, what kind of life would he have by himself in the wild. By the look and sound of him, Malcolm wouldn't survive the first year.

"We'll cross back into Rhulyn, but go south." He pointed over the river at the dramatic rising hillside covered with evergreens. "That's the Crescent Forest, runs for miles in all directions. Not the safest place, but it'll provide cover—help hide us." He glanced up at the sky. "Still early in the season, but there should be some food to forage and game to hunt."

"What do you mean by 'not the safest place'?"

"Well, I've not been there myself, but you hear things."

"What sort of things?"

Raithe tightened his belt and the strap holding the copper to his back before offering a shrug. "Oh, you know, tabors, raow, leshies. Stuff like that."

Malcolm continued to stare. "Vicious animals?"

"Oh yeah—those, too, I suppose."

"Those...*too?*"

"Sure, bound to be in a forest that size."

"Oh," Malcolm said, looking apprehensive as his eyes followed a branch floating past them at a quick pace. "How will we get across?"

"You can swim, right?"

Malcolm looked stunned. "That's a thousand feet from bank to bank."

"It has a nice current, too. Depending on how well you swim, we'll likely reach the far side several miles south of here. But that's good. It'll make us harder to track."

"Impossible, I'd imagine," Malcolm said, grimacing, his sight chained to the river.

The ex-slave of the Fhrey looked terrified, and Raithe smiled. He could have shown more empathy, especially given he'd felt the same way when Herkimer had forced him across.

"Ready?" Raithe asked.

Malcolm pursed his lips, and Raithe could see that the skin of his hands was white on the spear. "You realize this water is cold—comes down as snowmelt from Mount Mador."

"Not only that," Raithe added, "but since we're being hunted, we won't be able to make a fire when we get out."

The slender man with a pointed nose and narrow eyes forced a tight smile. "Okay, I was just making sure."

"You sure you're up for this?" Raithe asked as he led the way into the icy water.

"I'll admit it's not my typical day." The sound of his words rose in octaves as he waded into the river.

"What was your typical day like?" Raithe gritted his teeth as the water reached knee depth. The current dragged, forcing him to dig his feet into the riverbed. The water frothed around his legs.

"Mostly, I poured wine."

Raithe chuckled. "Yeah—this will be different."

A moment later, the river pulled them both off their feet.

ACKNOWLEDGMENTS

I t takes a great many people to produce a work of this nature, especially under the deadline pressure I had for this book. I find it's impossible to fully express my appreciation. You'd think I'd be able to, given I write for a living. But heartfelt isn't nearly enough and all other words fail. First, of course, I'd like to thank my wife, Robin. If you were a backer of the Kickstarter or a member of the beta crew, you know just a little about how hard she works. What you didn't see is all the effort she put into the book before it reached anyone else. Her structural, line, and copyedits have made this book better than I could have produced on my own, and we all owe her a debt of gratitude.

Speaking of editing, I also want to thank three amazing copyeditors for their incredible talent: Laura Jorstad, Paul Witcover, and Linda Branam. I've worked with Paul and Laura before (both were editors for *Hollow World*), and Linda joined the team after impressing Robin with her attention to detail and unique perspective during the beta read. I'm not sure anyone but writers fully appreciate just how amazing copyeditors are. Only we see where the book started and know how it differs from the final version. I can assure you their contributions have been monumental.

Which segues nicely into the beta readers! This was our largest beta to date. More than fifty people provided feedback, including rating the chapters and answering survey questions. When all was said and done we had rankings for more than a thousand chapters! Thanks to Robin's hard work, the book was in really good shape when it went out. Still, there was room for improvement, and the beta readers contributed tweaks to a number of key scenes. There isn't enough space to go into full detail, but you can learn more in my

ACKNOWLEDGMENTS

e-book *The Making of the Death of Dulgath*. It's free for anyone who is interested in the behind-the-scenes aspects of this book. Just drop me an email at **michael.sullivan.dc@gmail.com** to get a copy.

Once again, we utilized the amazing artistic talent of Marc Simonetti to create the book's cover. If you aren't familiar with his work, definitely check it out. Not only has he created covers for the French edition of my Riyria books and *Hollow World*, but he has also developed stunning work for Patrick Rothfuss's Kingkiller Chronicles, George R. R. Martin's Song of Ice and Fire, Brandon Sanderson's Mistborn series, and dozens of others. I'm pleased to announce that Del Rey will be using Marc for my new series, The First Empire. The first book, *Age of Myth*, will be released June 7, 2016.

Speaking of Del Rey, I want to thank them on a number of fronts. First, they generously rearranged their editorial schedule so you all could get a sneak peek of *Age of Myth* in this book. When *The Death of Dulgath* went to press, they had just finished structural edit feedback, but even so, they were able to have the first chapter copyedited ahead of the rest of the book. Second, I'd like to thank them for their flexibility, which made it possible to get this book released before rolling out The First Empire series. Again, you can read more about that in *The Making of the Death of Dulgath* e-book.

For those who don't know, we held a Kickstarter to fund a hardcover print run for this book. Original estimates for printing, shipping, warehousing, and paying the talented individuals listed above were around $33,000. Robin and I decided to foot $7,000 for the book's production and asked the Kickstarter community for $26,000 for the hardcover print run. If the project failed, the book would still have been produced, just not in hardcover. Well, to our astonishment, the project funded in less than two days and went on to raise more than $73,000, becoming the third-highest-funded fiction project to date. But that's not all. Afterward, people bought all kinds of cool add-ons (posters, T-shirts, coffee mugs, and such), and even more backers joined the party. When Robin finally locked down the project, it had raised in excess of $90,000 from 1,876 people. How crazy is that? So thank you to each and every one of the Kickstarter backers. We made some history and you've made it possible for me to get the book in a number of formats that I just couldn't have done without you. I'm forever indebted.

Works by Michael J. Sullivan

Novels

The First Empire
Age of Myth (June 2016) • *Age of Swords* • *Age of War*
Age of Legends • *Age of Empire*

The Riyria Revelations
Theft of Swords (The Crown Conspiracy and *Avempartha)*
Rise of Empire (Nyphron Rising and *The Emerald Storm)*
Heir of Novron (Wintertide and *Percepliquis)*

The Riyria Chronicles
The Crown Tower
The Rose and the Thorn
The Death of Dulgath

Standalone Novels
Hollow World

Anthologies
Unfettered: The Jester
Unbound: The Game
Unfettered II: Little Wren and the Big Forest
Blackguards: Professional Integrity
The End: Visions of the Apocalypse: Burning Alexandria
Triumph Over Tragedy: Traditions
The Fantasy Faction Anthology: Autumn Mists
Help Fund My Robot Army: Be Careful What You Wish For